PATEL I

From Partition to Perdition

Charles Savary

Black Lodge LLC

Eternally, for Jamiie

TABLE OF CONTENTS

CHAPTER ONE

F ardeen sat in the hallway, clutching the sides of his head and staring at the floor. He was in the Cardiac Intensive Care Unit of Scripps Memorial Hospital in La Jolla, California, and he'd never felt as displaced, uncomfortable, or afraid. He was so cold that his knees trembled, and his legs spastically bounced up and down—although he didn't know how much of that was just nerves. Then, someone calling his name got his attention.

"Mr. Patel?" asked one of the two doctors who'd walked up unnoticed.

One of them was white, and the other Fardeen believed was Indian. But it wasn't just because of his complexion. Sadly, it was how he looked at Fardeen. The Indian doc wore a white doctor's coat over a silk shirt and tie, woolen trousers, and very expensive-looking shoes.

Like most American kids, Fardeen grew up in blue jeans, tee-shirts, and sneakers. But these days, he dressed like his father and uncle always had—no frills, all business. He wore gray slacks, a white button-down shirt, black loafers, and a black belt. Fardeen could tell the doctor's tie probably cost more than his entire outfit, and when he looked at him, the doctor made him feel keenly aware of that fact.

Condescension. That was the expression on the doctor's face. He was around Fardeen's age, and both men were Indian. But their differences were probably as vast as those between Fardeen and the white doctor.

The doctor was a professional, an academic. Fardeen was also a professional but of an entirely different breed. Fardeen Patel was a "motel man."

"Yes, sir?" Fardeen asked, rising to his feet.

"No, no, please, keep your seat, Mr. Patel. Is Dr. Patel's wife anywhere in the hospital?" the white doctor asked.

Just as Fardeen started to answer, his brother Sanjay's wife, Olivia, came clicking down the hallway blowing on a cup of hot chocolate. Despite how it initially appeared, Olivia was beset with grief. Her eyes swelled from not sleeping, and little remained of her makeover, washed away by tears over the past several hours.

Olivia was the one who found Sanjay struggling to breathe on their pool house's floor the previous afternoon. Sanjay couldn't even stand, but because he was relatively slight in build, Olivia was able to drag him outside, where she began screaming for help.

Thank God Mr. Nelson was in his garden. He peered over the fence, spurting water from the hose he held, and yelled, "I'll call 911!" just as Olivia collapsed on the ground beside Sanjay, wailing and cradling his head in her hands and repeatedly kissing him.

Sanjay Patel, or "Dr. Sunny," as all his patients called him, was a maxillofacial surgeon in La Jolla. He had billboards up and down every major artery in and out of San Diego. And his television spots were just as ubiquitous.

Dr. Sunny was extraordinarily handsome too. He had big pearly white teeth accentuating his dark complexion and long eyelashes. And Dr. Sunny made the women of the greater San Diego area's hearts race whenever they met him in person because his television commercials didn't begin to do his good looks justice.

Dr. Sunny was active in the San Diego community,

sponsoring Little League baseball, soccer, and football teams. He participated in dozens of civic and philanthropic organizations, serving on the board of directors of several. Consequently, he and Olivia made the rounds of San Diego's social elite as though they were born to it. And what a spectacular couple they were.

Olivia's beauty surpassed even Dr. Sunny's. Her skin was lighter than his, and she, too, had large, beautiful eyes, except hers were a striking green shade. Her physique was such that she could have been a centerfold. Her hair was naturally curly and blended a dozen dark shades before graduating to auburn curls with blonde tips. Freakishly beautiful was perhaps the best description of Olivia Joseph-Patel.

In addition to their appearances, another exceptional trait of the unlikely couple was that Sanjay was Indian and Olivia was black. Well, her mother, Blanca, was Mexican-American, and her father was originally from Trinidad and Tobago. But that was enough for every white, highborn, clout-seeking patrician at social functions to rip Olivia away and parade around the room with her in a superb, nauseating signal of virtue.

And while all of San Diego County embraced the two as a fashionably modern couple, Sanjay's choice for a mate was the source of some disquiet with his traditionalist parents, more so with his mother than his father.

Fardeen didn't care, though. He loved his brother's wife. She was a fantastic woman, a terrific mother, and very supportive and protective of his brother. And while Fardeen's personal choice was to marry an Indian woman, he didn't think it was anyone's damned business who Sanjay married—including his parents. But the discussion behind closed doors at their parents' home was a different story, and there was a lot of blame for anything wrong that happened to Sanjay, including his current predicament.

"Are you Mrs. Patel?" the doctor asked Olivia

She'd already stopped blowing on the cup of cocoa. And she

stood in the center of the hallway holding it with trembling hands, staring back at the group of men.

"Yes," Olivia said as her voice broke, "I'm Olivia Patel."

"Mrs. Patel," the doctor began before Olivia interrupted him.

"No!" she blurted. She was abrupt, and it seemed she was already resigned to denial.

Having seen behavior like this throughout his career, Dr. McInteer shifted gears and lowered his tone, saying, "Mrs. Patel, would you like to sit down for a moment, please?"

"No!" Olivia said, more forcefully this time, "You tell me what's wrong with Sunny! You tell me right now!"

Fardeen rose to his feet and started toward her, calmly saying, "Olivia,"

But Olivia would have none of it. She shook her head and thrust an open hand forward, dropping the cup of cocoa on the floor.

"Don't, Dean," she said, "just sit back down!"

But Fardeen carefully continued in her direction, opening his arms into which she collapsed. Fardeen pulled her close, resting her head on his shoulder, and it was as therapeutic for him as it was for her because Fardeen wanted to weep, just as she did.

And within a few hours, he would.

The Indian doctor, Dr. Singh, motioned at an orderly walking toward him and said, "Go get maintenance, or better yet, go get a mop yourself and clean this mess up! And bring Mrs. Patel a towel and a warm blanket, right now!"

"Yes, sir, Dr. Singh!" the short-haired female custodian said as she raced off to follow his orders.

A few minutes later, Dr. Singh, Dr. McInteer, Fardeen, and Olivia entered a nondescript conference room that Fardeen could not have found his way back from if he tried. They were all glum as the doctors walked in behind Fardeen and Olivia. Dr. Singh pulled a chair out for her. Then he gently patted Fardeen on the shoulder as Fardeen edged in front of him toward the seat next to Olivia's. And as minuscule and fleeting as the gesture was, it had enormous meaning for Fardeen. It felt like Dr. Singh, a fellow Indian, was saying to him, "I've got this for you. I'm going to make sure your brother is alright. Don't worry." And while that may not have been Dr. Singh's intention, it sure felt like it to Fardeen at that moment.

The discussion started with Dr. McInteer directly addressing Olivia and managing a slight smile. He used her first name.

"Olivia, I want you to realize that it's my job as a physician to share every possible outcome I can with my patients and their loved ones. And given the field I'm in, that always has the potential to be bad news. But, I'd like you to take heart and realize that there's good news and bad in this situation. There's no death sentence here for Dr. Patel, Olivia. But there are some fairly profound things wrong that we need to address before he's out of the woods. Do you understand what I'm telling you, Olivia?"

Fardeen was grateful as he listened to this man. While he was an incurable optimist, he also liked people to speak openly and frankly with him. And often, that tended not to be the case when dealing with Americans. Just tell me. Just get to the point. And while Dr. McInteer hadn't done that yet, his demeanor suggested it was what he intended to do.

"As Dr. Singh and I reviewed Dr. Patel's bloodwork and ECG, it appeared his heart is under a tremendous strain, Olivia. And I can only surmise it's been that way for some time. And that, Olivia, is our first order of business. We need to remove that strain before we can proceed with what would be our next consensus best step, which might include a heart transplant."

Fardeen nodded as Olivia sat motionless, staring back at Dr. McInteer, shocked by what he said. Fardeen knew what the problem was, but so did Olivia. And they'd both known it for a while.

You see, Sanjay was, for lack of a more delicate term, a junkie.

No, he didn't wander the streets at night, looking for his next hustle building to a score. He didn't hold people at gunpoint or break into their homes to get what he needed to buy smack or cocaine or any other illicit street drug. But Sanjay Patel was nevertheless a straight junkie. And where he found solace was not from a dirty needle at the end of a diabetic's discarded syringe, used dozens of times before. Instead, Sanjay got his fix while sitting in the sanctity of the ivory tower that was his stately home in the hills of La Jolla. And although just as strung out, it wasn't from the type of opiate concocted a few dozen miles south as so many of his fellow junkies' was. His poisons were high-order pharmaceuticals produced by corporations who knew precisely what they unleashed on the American public.

Oxycontin, Hydrocodone, Vicodin, and other drugs certainly had their place in medicine. And prescribed and judiciously administered under a physician's careful watch, they were essential to a person's recovery. However, those who profited the most from such drugs were aware of the earnings potential in other quarters. And that potential had nothing to do with a person in pain recovering from surgery. Or a new mother who'd undergone an episiotomy during childbirth. And one of the last things on their mind was anyone who'd suffered from multi-degree burns. Yes, all those people were deserving and needed that pharmacology. But as a group, they were the least profitable in the long term among the spectrum of its potential users. And both the manner and mechanism by which those companies sought to convey their wares fell nothing short of immoral. Evil even.

Sanjay's fall from grace began simply enough. During his first year of practice as a dentist, the emotional toll of constantly dealing with others' pain left the young man overwhelmed. So, it was easy to reach for the nitrous and take a hit or two before going home to unwind with Olivia at the end of a workday. But that was a short-lived solution. And Sanjay found himself feeling more and more stressed as his career moved forward. Ultimately, he decided that dentistry just wasn't for him.

But where exactly did that leave him?

He had a pregnant wife who'd given up her law practice to stay at home. They were already in way too deep with the house they'd built despite the generous offering Olivia's father, a trial lawyer in New York, gave them for a down payment. It was an almost irrecoverable blunder in Sanjay's mind to have incurred all the debt he did to get where he was. And things seemed so bleak that his snorting silly-gas escalated until he stirred to Olivia one day, nudging him awake from the floor in his office. He'd been late for dinner—two hours late.

But being the woman she was, and it was a humdinger of one, once Olivia gave birth to their baby, Holly, she moved to New York to work alongside her father in his thriving legal practice. Sanjay applied and was accepted into the maxillofacial program at The University of Tennessee in Memphis.

He originally attended UT in Knoxville on a full academic scholarship for his undergraduate studies. Whizzing through his prerequisites in only two years, he attended UT Dental school in Memphis after that. Despite a few indiscretions during his undergraduate years, he was an exemplary student in both places. So it was only logical for that to be the place he applied to get into the viciously competitive field. And his academic record and exquisite surgical skills made him a shoo-in.

The next six years were indeed hard ones. But the subsequent spoils seemed worth it all. Sanjay's surgical practice exploded. He managed everything from wisdom teeth extraction to head and neck surgeries. And before long, he was making the kind of money he and Olivia only daydreamed about when their courtship started back in Knoxville.

Unfortunately, and just as it always seems to, addiction reconvened only a year or so after the good things got underway. But it was much more discreet this time. It was a great deal stealthier. And it was severe.

Sanjay broke his collar bone after falling from the roof of their bigger, better home in La Jolla while installing Christmas lights. The pain was excruciating, so he took comfort in the prescription for Oxycontin that his orthopedic surgeon wrote him. But he found a little too much comfort in it and ended up renewing his prescription several times past its expiration through fellow doctors facing the same sickness of addiction. And Sanjay returned the favor in kind. It was like a network of empowered enablers with prescription pads, exchanging unethical interactions with one another for their gratification. And they flew just enough beneath the DEA's radar not to raise a red flag. Horrendous. All because already wealthy and powerful pharma giants wanted more wealth and power, irrespective of the consequences to people's lives.

Ever wanting to stay out of his brother's business, Fardeen stood back from it all. And in fairness, he didn't understand the magnitude of his brother's addiction. However, as time moved forward, it became increasingly apparent. But by that time, it was too late.

Sanjay's practice tanked. He couldn't keep the good people he had working for him because all his missteps also impacted their careers. It was one thing to work for a junkie. But if you were someone with the earnings potential of, say, a nurse's anesthetist and you got subpoenaed to testify against your employer, reality settled in very fast. So Sanjay wound up surrounded at work by other pill-poppers and co-enablers who were either bridled with addiction or had a loved one that was. That was his downfall, too, as all the usual suspects followed.

The California Franchise Tax Board, the IRS, and the DEA all came calling, each more mercilessly than the former. Olivia could have and should have disowned his ass by Fardeen's estimation.

But she didn't.

She stood by Sanjay through it all. She even went to court, suffering through questions about her background and character. And while unfounded, they were every bit as invasive and caused as much humiliation as if she'd been guilty of something.

Her father put a stop to that in court one day, though. Feeling their attorney was not doing his job adequately, Olivia pleaded with her father to take over Sanjay's case. Her father, David Joseph, knew nothing about criminal defense. He was also concerned about his ability to provide dispassionate counsel because Sanjay was his son-in-law. But he eventually agreed. And he was so damned smart and motivated that he ribboned the prosecution's case against his son-in-law after being awarded a continuance. He left the federal prosecutor stammering and stuttering, and the Deputy U.S. attorney ultimately dropped the government's case against Sanjay altogether.

But that was perhaps the only uptick in Sanjay's life throughout the ordeal. Once it was through, he'd provisionally lost his license and had to enter a rehabilitation program before returning to practice. Miraculously, he made it. But not so miraculously, Sanjay wound up in the same horror-scape as before. And his usage soared to new heights. At the zenith of that ascension was where Olivia found him lying on the floor of their pool house, struggling to breathe and unable to speak. It hurt her so badly that it liked to have killed her. But she could not and would not let go. That's because Olivia Joseph-Patel loved her husband. She took her wedding vows to heart, and she'd stand by him forever and through anything.

So that's where life now found her. She sat across from two of the most eminent cardiologists in California as she listened to their prognosis for Sunny. No. she'd stay with Sanjay forever. She'd do whatever she could to make her husband and her home whole again. That's just who Olivia Joseph-Patel was. She worshipped her husband, and if you tried to convince her to do differently, then, boy, you'd better watch out.

CHAPTER TWO

July 4, 1980

A dam and the Ants, Electric Light Orchestra, Hot Chocolate, The Village People. The names sounded more like themes from a children's book than musicians as Fardeen flipped through the record box. It was blue and white with a twisted, psychedelic swirl in its center. And it held at least thirty "45's" in it.

He couldn't believe it. Thirty records? And they had music on either side? Wow!

"Alright, what next?" Gale, the boy from Bossier City, Louisiana, asked.

Fardeen sat on the floor in number 9 of The Sunkist, his uncle's motel in Biloxi, Mississippi. It seemed like a nice place to him. The rooms were older, but his uncle bragged that none of the roofs leaked. And they all had air conditioners and television sets.

It certainly wasn't what Fardeen had pictured before the family landed in Atlanta the week before. He'd envisioned something more like a Vacation Inn when his father told him he'd be spending the summer in a United States hotel.

Per the postcards his parents showed him, Vacation Inns were enormous properties. They had everything from golf and horseback riding to fishing excursions in the Gulf of Mexico. Fardeen didn't care about going out on a boat, though. He was terrified of the ocean.

"C'mon, man! I can't sit here all day! Patsy's coming back in a little while, and she's gonna get pissed that I'm using her record player! So, what? Who's next?"

Fardeen was intimidated by the bold, American boy who referred to his mother by her first name. He imagined his father would beat him if he called his mother "Savitri." But he didn't want to seem like a nerd. So he chose the most rebellious-seeming name he saw in the little box. It was a band called "Cheap Trick." And as they sang "I Want You to Want Me," thousands of Japanese girls shrieked as the singer pled his case.

It electrified Fardeen.

"Gale!" Fardeen heard a man shout. It startled him so much that he dropped the record box and jumped to his feet. When he looked to his left, what he'd thought was just a lump of bedding before was awake now. And the lump sat up on the bed's edge and stared, red-eyed, in the boys' direction.

Gale looked at Fardeen and rolled his eyes before yelling over his shoulder, "Yeah? What, Cal? What is it?"

This boy might be the bravest kid Fardeen had ever seen.

"What did you just call me?!" the red-eyed lump asked.

Gale grinned at Fardeen.

"Oh. Uh. Sorry, Dad," Gale said, smirking while hiding his expression from the man on the bed.

"You're damned right, boy," the man snarled, "I'm your Daddy whether you like it or not! And you're gonna' respect me, or I'll beat your little ass!"

"Uh, ok, Cal, uh, I mean Dad," Gale said, struggling not to laugh.

Gale was so disrespectful. Even if Fardeen disagreed with how Gale's father spoke to him, it was still his father. And Fardeen couldn't imagine talking to his father that way. He didn't realize Cal was Gale's stepfather, although it probably wouldn't have changed his opinion much.

"Hey!" the man yelled toward Fardeen, "Who the hell are you? Are you here to clean up? Well, we don't need no service, alright, had-gee?"

The man's words were particularly stinging for Fardeen. He knew more about what they meant from his upbringing than the man did. A hadji was an Arabic term for a person who'd made the religious pilgrimage to Mecca.

But Fardeen wasn't Arabic. And he wasn't a Muslim either. The man didn't even know Fardeen's name. Yes, he had a Muslim name, but the man didn't know that. Fardeen struggled his entire life with being named after his maternal grandfather, who *was* Muslim. But that wasn't any of this man's business.

"Nope, wrong again, Dad," Gale said as he stood up and faced the menacing man who nestled an empty vodka jug in his lap.

"See, Fardeen's dad owns this place. He owns all of it. He was just checking in on us and seeing how we were doing, and I asked him in."

"It's not my father. It's my uncle, Sir Gale. My family," Fardeen said before Gale shushed him.

Cal almost dropped the empty half-gallon glass Taaka bottle on the floor as he looked at Fardeen. Fardeen could see the man was scared. But he stayed respectful.

Cal, on the other hand, was worried. He'd already acted like a complete jackass about getting extra towels at the front desk. And the night before, Fardeen's Uncle Sid had to come out to the pool and ask Cal to keep it down. Cal was cussing and yelling, so Sid politely told him to lower his voice. Sid said if he didn't, he'd have to leave. And if he didn't want to leave, he'd have to call the law.

Sid couldn't stand giving a customer an ultimatum. He hated calling the police even more. But he'd seen how things could escalate whenever his American customers drank too much.

"I'm sorry, sir. I didn't mean to wake you," Fardeen said as Gale sliced his hands at his waist, signaling him to shut the hell up.

Cal didn't say another word but moved past the two boys to fetch more vodka from his van, and Gale snickered as Cal hurried past them.

The boys spent the rest of the afternoon listening to records on Gale's mother's portable deck while Cal sat out by the pool, getting drunk. Fardeen's Aunt Sara, or Saraswati, watched the drunk man uneasily as she pushed the maid cart between the office and the rooms.

When the sun started going down, Gale said, "Hey! Let's go see *Friday the 13th*! I heard it was killer!"

Fardeen didn't know what that meant. Friday the 13th? That was an unlucky day where Fardeen came from, so he couldn't imagine getting entertained by anything with that theme. Gale saw he was confused.

"It's a movie, dumbass!" Gale said as Fardeen blushed because he felt so naïve.

"Oh, I know," Fardeen said. He wasn't at all convincing, though. Gale nevertheless cut him some slack and laughed, patting him on his arm.

Within seconds Gale was ready to go. He threw on a tee-shirt and stepped into his flip-flops, confusing Fardeen again. Fardeen had pictured showering, dressing up, and preparing more as though he were going to dinner with his parents. The only time he'd ever been to the cinema was as a small child when he saw *The Snowball Express* at a bijou in Ahmedabad. His father thought American cinema was subversive and a waste of time. But after his mother's insistence, he gave in and took the family to see the wholesome Disney feature. His entire family went that evening, dressed up for the occasion. So Fardeen was confused by Gale's blasé attitude but happy he wouldn't have to change out of his swim trunks.

So a moment later, the boys dashed out of the room toward the front desk. Fardeen had to check with his father to see if it was alright to go to the theater, and he also needed money.

The smell of stale air and chlorine was overwhelming when they walked into the office. Fardeen's father, Devan, stood with his Uncle Sid at the counter, speaking in Gujarati. But they immediately stopped as the boys entered. Both the men carefully eyed Gale. They knew he was that idiot in number 9's son, so they didn't know what to expect from him.

"Papa, can I go to the cinema with Gale?" Fardeen asked.

Fardeen's father looked between him and the American boy several times before opening his mouth to give his son a resounding "No."

However, his Uncle Sid placed his hand on his father's chest and said, "Shhh, shhh, shhh," to quiet him.

Then Sid continued, "Of course, you can! I think that would be fine!"

Sid reached into his pocket and pulled out a roll of bills the size of a softball. He had to peel to the bottom of the roll, because most of it was hundreds and fifties. Finally, he yanked out a crisp twenty-dollar bill and handed it to his nephew.

"Whoa!" Gale said as Fardeen's Uncle Sid laughed.

"And you can go across the street and ride on the bumpy cars and the roller coaster after the picture show," Sid said, smiling.

Sitting on the couch without having drawn any attention up to that point, Fardeen's mother, Savitri, stood up and barked, "Siddharth!"

She didn't like the idea of her brother handing so much money to her only baby boy, and she didn't like him speaking over her husband either. That's just how Siddharth was, though. He was always so pushy, always getting his way. He lorded over his sister for the better part of her life because he was a male and eighteen years her senior. But she couldn't stand for her brother to take over and try to spoil her baby.

She lost her battle before it even started, though. Devan abruptly raised his hand and made a lowering motion, directing his wife to be quiet and sit back down. Savitri was enraged. Ol' Sid knew what he was doing, though. And, as always, he had an ulterior motive.

He wanted to make America seem like the most wonderful place on Earth to his sister's family. He was trying to permanently lure Devan to the United States to operate a Florida property he wanted to buy.

It was a two-story, 45-unit, exterior-corridor Morning Inn that had recently lost its flag and was in receivership. It would only be a matter of time before the bank foreclosed and either auctioned the property or sold it for pennies on the dollar of its value. He'd had designs on it for a while.

He even met with the owner, an elderly American fellow, six months earlier and gave him a low-ball offer on it. But the man balked at the idea. He'd spent a goodly portion of his retirement savings on the property, anticipating the business's operations were a cakewalk. It was in his hometown, so he considered it an ideal investment.

But he soon found out that owning a motel of any size was no small undertaking and a twenty-four-hour-a-day duty accompanied it. And within a year of opening, his property became a drug den, and his primary customers were Pensacola prostitutes and their Johns.

Still, he resisted Sid's offer.

The last words spoken at the informal meeting that day at a Shoney's buffet in Pensacola were from Sid. He told him that he'd get his property either way. But what he proposed would get the man at least a portion of his original investment back.

No dice. The old guy wouldn't budge. And now the sharks smelled blood in the water. Soon it would be a feeding frenzy, and it was just a matter of who got their ducks in a row first as to who would walk away with the deed. Sid intended to be that person, and he'd stop at nothing until he was.

Fardeen proudly took the twenty-dollar bill from his uncle and looked back at Gale, who was shocked. Gale was lucky if he got so much as a couple of bucks out of Cal. You could either halve that amount or double it, depending on how much Cal had to drink.

Fardeen hurried them toward the door before giving his parents a chance to change their minds. But just as he reached for the doorknob, his mother called after him, stopping him in his tracks.

"Fardeen!"

Fardeen's family was from Gujarat, the westernmost state in India. But they all spoke perfect English, albeit with a few quirks. One of them was that they rolled their "r's." So when Savitri said Fardeen's name, that r-rolling made it sound like she called him "Farty."

Gale lost it. Farty? Oh, man! That was just too much! He started cackling and holding his sides because he hurt so from laughing. Irrespective of how funny Gale found her English, Savitri continued.

"You will take your sister to the cinema with you?" she asked in defiance of all the machismo that dominated the conversation up to that point.

Fardeen groaned and looked back toward his mother and baby sister, Anaya, who stared at him with her giant, beautiful brown eyes. He loved and wanted to protect her so much. But he just didn't want her tagging along for the movie. Then Uncle Sid interrupted, speaking rapidly in Gujarati again. Savitri responded by plopping back onto the couch and brushing

Anaya's hair. She glared at Devan, who looked on the whole time while her brother took charge of the situation. It outraged Savitri, and that was a point Devan would discover that night when they went to bed.

Once the boys escaped from the office, Gale asked, "What the hell did he say to her? I mean, she shut up fast!"

Without looking over at Gale, Fardeen continued walking and responded, "He said that it was not appropriate for a little girl to go to an American movie theater without her parents. Then he told her that he was only trying to protect the family's good name and that if she went, it could embarrass her later."

"That ain't true, though. Nobody gives a shit here," Gale said.

"Oh, I know. But Mama doesn't," Fardeen said as they both started laughing.

Before they moved even ten more feet, a white Buick Riviera turned into the motel parking lot on two wheels and screeched to a halt. The lady driving, obviously drunk, rolled down the window, and Gale heard his mother, Patsy, call out from the passenger's side. He was pretty sure she was drunk too.

"Gale! Gale! What're you doing, baby?!" she shouted, holding a clear plastic cup containing a cocktail with a spear of fruit floating in it.

Patsy went to The Hilton Hotel's pool that day. Jean, a friend of hers, and her husband stayed there for the 4th of July. And the accommodations were far better than those at The Sunkist. Its pool was enormous and had a bar in its shallow end. You could swim up, take a seat, drink all afternoon, then have a burger from the short-order grill on duty.

"Hey, Patsy. I'm going to the movie with Farty, here," Gale said.

A burly man with curly silver-gray hair and a matching beard who sat in the Riviera's backseat exploded laughing.

"Farty!" he hollered, weaving back and forth, struggling not to spill his drink.

It was Jean's husband, Buster.

"You don't call me Patsy, son, do you hear me?!" Patsy shouted across Jean, who leaned back in her seat, trying to stay out of the battle.

"Yes, ma'am," Gale said. Then Patsy threw him a curveball.

"Look, you need to take your sister with you! Eight Flags was closed for the holiday, and she had to sit out by the pool with Jean and me all day! She needs to have fun too!"

A little girl in the rear passenger's seat leaned forward and stared back at Gale. It was his sister, Gilly. But Gale didn't want her to go to the movies any more than Fardeen wanted his little sister, Anaya, to go. So he thought fast and came back to his mother.

"Patsy, it's not appropriate for a little girl to go to an American movie theater without her parents! I'm only trying to protect you and Cal's good name because if she goes, it could embarrass y'all later!"

"Huh? What?!" Patsy yelled over the eight-track, blaring Boston's "More Than a Feeling."

"What?!" Gale asked sarcastically, trying to dodge his mother before continuing, "Nope! Sorry, Patsy! Gotta go now!"

Then Gale grabbed Fardeen's wrist and raced with him toward the theater, crossing over McDonnel Avenue, rushing past Angelina's Deli, and only slowing once they were in front of the Water Boggan water slide. By the time he slowed down, he just laughed while Fardeen stared over his shoulder, frantically looking back toward the motel and praying his mother didn't hear any of that.

Even as anxious as he was, Fardeen couldn't help but notice the smell of food coming from the small corner store as they passed it. It made such an impression that he had to ask Gale what that unbelievable aroma was.

"Oh, man, that's their chili dogs! And they're so good, man! You could get us one on the way home, and I'll buy us the Cokes and some Hubba Bubba!" Gale bargained as Fardeen nodded, not knowing what Hubba Bubba was. Fardeen knew what a chili dog was, though. But he'd never had one before because his mother, Savitri, was a strict vegetarian. Moreover, she wanted her children to be strict vegetarians, so any protein other than something like beans or lentils that summer was verboten.

But that smell!

Gale was so cool. He had to be the coolest kid in America, Fardeen thought. When they got to the theater, they couldn't buy tickets to *Friday the 13th* because it was rated R. But Gale bought tickets to *Herbie Goes Bananas* instead. Then he told Fardeen not to say anything and follow his lead.

Once they got to where the usher tore the ticket stubs, the older teenage boy said, "Back again, huh? How many times can somebody watch *The Empire Strikes Back*, dude? Where's your sister?"

"Aw, man, she's at the motel playing with her Strawberry Shortcake dolls or some shit," Gale said, "it's just us men tonight."

"Is that right?" the usher said as he gave Fardeen the once-over.

"Yeah, man. We're just hanging out tonight. Prolly' grab some beers or something later, but we wanted to check out this movie first. It's supposed to be badass." Gale said as he rolled two one-dollar bills around their tickets and handed them to the pimply-faced usher.

The young man smiled, taking the tickets before he tucked them into his Surf Side Cinema vest, and said, "Yeah. That's what I hear too. Concessions are to your right, and we have two-for-one candy tonight because it's the 4th. Enjoy the show, gentlemen."

And just like that, Fardeen and Gale got channeled into the velvet-roped lane of an R-rated movie, all due to Gale's wily finagling. Yep. Gale had to be the coolest kid in all of America, Fardeen thought to himself.

However, halfway through the movie, Fardeen wished the usher hadn't been so lax and permissive. He also wished he'd never accompanied Gale to the cinema and that he'd never have to endure another American movie for as long as he lived. That was because *Friday the 13th* scared the mortal hell out of Fardeen, and he found himself squealing and writhing just like all the teenage girls in the theatre, clutching their boyfriend's arms and covering their faces. At one point, Fardeen even grabbed Gale's arm and hollered because what he watched on the screen was so disturbing. Finally, having enough, Fardeen leaped from his seat and bolted toward the exit. Gale wanted to get up and follow after him, but it was just too funny. So he sat chuckling and trying to catch his breath for the remainder of the movie.

"Why? Why do Americans find that entertaining?" Fardeen asked on the quiet walk back between intervals of laughter from Gale.

Finally gaining enough composure to speak, Gale said, "Come on, Farty. Don't be like that, man. It's just a movie, alright? It ain't like you were watching a documentary or some shit, man."

Fardeen had enough. He stopped and put his hand on Gale's shoulder, who walked ahead of him. When Gale turned, Fardeen said, "My name is not 'Farty,' Gale. My name is Fardeen. And I would appreciate it if you would stop calling me that."

After thinking a second, and because of the look on Fardeen's face, Gale could tell he'd gone too far. Hell, Gale wasn't a cool kid at all. And he already got picked on enough to know how it felt. He didn't want to be one of those guys that treated people that way.

So he backed off and said, "I'm sorry, Fardeen. I didn't mean anything by it, alright? It's just how kids in the USA talk to each other, ok? I didn't want to hurt your feelings or anything, man."

Gale's words meant the world to Fardeen. He smiled back at Gale and said, "It's ok, Gale. I know you're a pretty nice guy."

Then the two boys threw their arms over each other's shoulders and plodded toward Angelina's for one of those big chili dogs.

Once Fardeen took his first taste, he discovered chili dogs were even more delicious than he imagined. The boys stood at the counter and scarfed them down, passing a bottle of Coke and a bag of Fritos between one another after each bite. It was the most decadent and enjoyable experience of Fardeen's life to that point.

Angelina's served the bright red wieners on a soft white bun, bathed in chili. Their chili was a deep, rich shade of brown, and they topped them with onions and yellow mustard. Although it was way saltier than Fardeen was used to, he gnawed on that dog as though it were his last meal. The piquantness of the chili, the tartness of the mustard, and the crunch of the Fritos, followed by a sweet swig of Coca-Cola. They all came together perfectly.

"Dude!" Gale said, "Slow down, man! What? Don't your parents feed you?"

"I'm sorry!" Fardeen said excitedly. He continued with mustard on the tip of his nose, "I've never had anything like this before! It's just so delicious!"

Fardeen finished his chili dog in less than thirty seconds and stood as he stared anxiously at Gale, who ate his more slowly. Fardeen looked like a beagle, staring up at his master, waiting for the go-ahead to eat something.

When Gale got to his last bite, he set it back in the little paper boat Angelina's served it in and handed it to Fardeen.

"Dude. My God. Just take it, man," he said as Fardeen ripped it from his hands and swallowed the last bite, whole.

Afterward, just as promised, Gale ponied up for a pack of spearmint Hubba Bubba. That's when Fardeen realized it was bubble gum. He'd had bubble gum before at home in Gujarat. A friend of his father's brought it back from America sometimes along with a box of Dum-Dums suckers whenever he came to visit and drink coffee with his father on Friday afternoons.

But when Gale handed Fardeen the small, soft cube of bubblegum, it was nothing like the "Super Bubble" he'd had in the past. That stuff was rock hard, and you had to chew it for several minutes before you could even begin to think about blowing a bubble. Hubba Bubba not only came in different flavors. But it was soft from the get-go and ten times as sweet as Super Bubble.

Gale then demonstrated another feature of Hubba Bubba, its strongest selling point in 1980s America.

"Check this, dude," Gale said as he began blowing a bubble. He blew and blew until a grapefruit-sized bubble obscured most of his face.

Fardeen was aghast. Bubble gum was delicious and fun to chew. But he also knew it to be sticky, and if you got it on your face, sometimes it would linger in little patches for days before you could wash it off. He remembered his mother, Savitri, trying to get it off his face with lighter fluid. That's why she forbade him from chewing it. Nevertheless, Gale kept blowing until the bubble popped and covered his face with the minty green gum. Fardeen shuddered. But he was astounded when Gale peeled the entire mass from his face without a trace left on it. Then he popped it back in his mouth, started chewing again, and smiled at Fardeen.

"Wow!" Fardeen said in amazement.

When Gale realized he had a captive audience, he continued. He reached into the brown paper bag he'd set on the counter while they ate and pulled out a small black envelope with purple writing that said "Pop Rocks."

"Hold out your hand," he said, smiling.

"Why?" Fardeen asked, unsure what might happen next or what Gale would do.

"Just do it, man!" Gale insisted.

Fardeen held his hand out, and Gale flipped it over, ripped the envelope open with his teeth, and poured a palm-full of tiny purple crystals from it into Fardeen's hand.

"What is this?" Fardeen asked, looking down at his palm.

"It's candy, you stupid nerd!" Gale said, laughing, "Put it in your mouth!"

The movie was a bust for Fardeen. It left him a little leery of Gale's cavalier attitude about things and how they might impact him versus how an ordinary American kid might react. Yet, a part of him trusted Gale.

Even though the movie scared the daylights out of him, he had to admit that it was still fun. Besides that, he didn't want to look like a "chicken" like Gale called him earlier when he wouldn't go into the pool's deep end. So Fardeen gulped, opened his mouth, then carefully poured the crystals into it.

Within moments, his eyes widened as he stared at Gale, who nodded back at him. The crystals disintegrated as they released a robust grape flavor in Fardeen's mouth. They were so sweet. Then, true to their name, they began to "pop." And that's when Gale got excited as he looked at the expression on his friend's face.

"It's the sizzle that makes you giggle!" Gale said, laughing.

It continued crackling in Fardeen's mouth until he feared something bad might happen. So he reached for the Coke in Gale's hand and started to take a big chug of it. But Gale yanked it back and said, "No! No way, dude! You can't drink Coke with Pop Rocks!"

"But why?" Fardeen asked, inadvertently swallowing the candy and bubble gum with a purple-stained tongue.

"Man, some kid in California or Idaho or somewhere did that shit. And his stomach exploded! He died!" Gale warned.

Fardeen winced as he thought about what might have happened. Then he pictured Sid waking his parents up and bringing them across the street to the deli where he might otherwise lie dead on the floor were it not for his friend.

America was fun. But Fardeen didn't know if he could ever learn to navigate all it offered without something bad happening to him or someone to guide him.

They were merely a child's musings. Yet, they were so prophetic.

After spending thirty minutes in Angelina's, the boys braved crossing Highway 90 to get to the amusement park across the street and ride the "bumpy cars," as suggested by Fardeen's Uncle Sid. They did a lot more than that, though, all on his uncle's dime. They rode the Tilt-A-Whirl, The Octopus, and The Wild Mouse roller coaster. After taunting and daring each other, they even rode The Bullet. Its stature as a thrill ride came not only from its violent, neck-jerking motions but also from the fact it was rusted and appeared it could come apart at any moment.

Fardeen had never experienced anything before like he did that night. He underwent sensory overload from the chili dogs to the movie to the amusement park and the Pop Rocks. And by the time the night ended, he was sure of one thing, principal among others.

He wanted to live in America more than he ever wanted anything. And he'd do whatever to make it back here once the summer was over. He loved this place. And he wanted to stay here forever.

CHAPTER THREE

"Ahhhhhh!" Savitri squealed, running from the door of number 1 at the newly-christened Seagull Motel, which used to be a Morning Inn.

Fardeen dropped his suitcase and raced toward his mother, followed closely by his father, Devan, and older sister, Sridevi. When they reached her, his mother stood pointing toward the room, urgently bouncing at the knees. Its door was half-opened, and she'd ducked her head in to look at the room out of curiosity.

Devan yanked Fardeen behind himself and carefully approached the room. As he did, Fardeen saw something that stunned and horrified him. Devan reached under the tails of his shirt, pulled out a snub-nosed black revolver, and continued toward the room. Savitri screamed again, which mirrored every emotion Fardeen felt at that moment.

A gun? To wit, his father had never fired or even held a gun before. But he'd spent the summer with his brother-in-law, and Devan witnessed so many things in the wee morning hours as he sat in the office with Sid drinking coffee. Thankfully, it always happened long after Savitri and the children were in bed. But those brief yet desperate exchanges were lessons for the young Indian man.

Among the less harrowing events were domestic disputes, teenaged prostitutes with knives, and drunken airmen. But it moved on to assaults, brawls, and even an armed robbery attempt by an old veteran from the local VA hospital.

The World War II vet was too drunk to stand upright as he slurred his demand for Sid to open the cash drawer. He was also a regular patron of The Sunkist, who wouldn't remember anything the next day. Devan sat on the couch watching as Sid pulled out a pistol and held the old vet at gunpoint. Devan was sure Sid would kill him. Instead, Sid slowly walked over and carefully disarmed the man. Then the poor vet collapsed as Sid caught him and ushered him back to the room he'd been unable to make rent for that morning.

That ultimately benign yet frightening incident taught Devan a lesson: America was dangerous. Despite all the television programs where everyone was happy and seemed to resolve whatever problem or tragedy they faced after a thirty-minute synopsis, none of that programming told the real story.

Even after that, Devan was hesitant to accept his brother-in-law's offering of a firearm, but the more he contemplated how things might have unfolded were Sid not armed on several such occasions, his reluctance disappeared.

Devan inched toward the room, with his right hand holding the pistol, trembling as though he'd drop it. Fardeen couldn't imagine who was in that room that terrified his mother so badly. As his older sister, Sridevi, hugged his little sister, Anaya, to her chest, she felt the same way. Who or what was beyond that doorway, eliciting such terror from their mother? Savitri was a humble and respectful woman. Yet, she was prone to let loose if she believed anyone posed a threat to her husband or children. She wasn't afraid of much in those instances.

The whole clan, save Savitri, relaxed when they saw Devan stand erect and roll his eyes after peering inside the room. They felt even better when he stopped trembling and turned toward them, lowering the pistol to his side and shaking his head. But then he got mad all of a sudden.

"A rat?!" Devan screamed at Savitri as his relieved expression gave way to an angry one.

"A rat?! I've seen bigger rats than this at your mother's house, and you scream and upset the children?!"

Devan's pitch was loud now. And he spoke in Gujarati, which everyone vowed not to do in public once they arrived in Tomahawk. But Devan was so upset that his temper vetoed that rule, and now he stood, screaming as loudly as Fardeen could remember as he waved the gun around.

An even greater piece of misfortune was that that's all the Tomahawk police officer saw or heard as he rolled into the parking lot, spitting a combination of sunflower seeds and Skoal into a foam 7-Eleven cup. All he saw was a damned foreigner at that damned motel, waving a damned gun around and hollering like a damned savage.

The officer quickly skidded to a halt, opened the door to his squad car, and pulled out his pistol. Taking a knee behind the door, he raised his gun, pointed it through the window, and yelled, "Drop it! Drop it right now!! Put your hands in the air and get on the ground!! Get on the ground!!"

A startled and terrified Devan did as instructed. Almost. He laid down on his back with his arms out to his sides.

"Rollover, you son-of-a-bitch!" the officer shouted, "Roll over and put your hands behind your head, funny man!"

Fardeen moved in the direction of his father. But his movement was stopped by the loudest, most terrifying sound he'd ever heard as the officer fired his gun into the air and yelled, "Don't move! Don't you move again, or I'll blow your ass away!"

Terrified, Fardeen froze and held his arms out as he stared at his now-weeping mother and sisters huddled together next to their old Buick Le Sabre, whose rear end nearly touched the ground because of its failing shocks and the trunk so full of their belongings.

It took almost two hours, three more police cars, and fifteen off-duty Tomahawk policemen to sort out that Devan was the new "owner" of The Morning Inn. But it was The Seagull Motel now, a name Devan devised while looking out over the Mississippi Sound from the balcony of The Sunkist Motel in Biloxi. The officers were acutely pissed off, too, drawn away from their Thanksgiving dinner and a gripping Detroit-Chicago NFL game that looked like it would go into overtime. It couldn't have been a worse inauguration for Devan and his family into the American hospitality industry.

But it wasn't over yet. After things calmed and the law left, the Patels followed the interim caretaker to the manager's apartment. She'd watched the whole thing unfold but hadn't bothered to intervene or try and explain who the Patels were.

As the middle-aged woman, who wreaked of cigarette smoke and bleach, creaked the apartment door open, everyone in the family's hearts sank. It was a 20' by 15' efficiency apartment that someone refashioned from a guest room. Beyond it was another room, partitioned into two separate bedrooms. And whoever occupied this place before was untidy, to put it gently.

"Mr. Patel? Mr. Patel?" the woman asked as Devan walked to the center of the room and looked around. He'd not grown re-accustomed to that surname yet. So it took him a moment to realize she was talking to him.

But he was also distracted standing in the middle of the nastiest, most disgusting living quarters he'd ever seen. Open cans of Van Camp's pork and beans littered the floor along with cans of Armour Star potted meat, Evan Williams bottles, and blue shop towels, heavily stained with axle grease. The room would have smelled like gasoline were it not for the unbearable odor of the uncleaned litter box in the corner.

"Mr. Patel?" the woman said more emphatically as Devan turned around to face her.

She wasn't sure if he spoke English, so she was glad when he acknowledged her after she called his name. Her name was

Elvira Marks, and the management company told Sid they hired her "just to keep the wheels on the damned thing" until after the auction and Sid could put his new manager in place.

Elvira secretly hoped they'd either retain her or maybe even sell the motel to her instead. She had over $10,000 stuffed away from the proceeds of a settlement she engineered by slipping in a McDonald's. And she was willing to put all that down and split the take with the bank 50/50 until she paid the debt off.

However, what poor, stupid, uninformed Elvira didn't realize was that Siddharth Shakur offered $325,000 for the flea-bag motel, sitting just off Interstate 10 in the race-by town of Tomahawk, Florida. The market value of the property was more like $500,000.

Unlike his overzealous Gujarati contemporaries in the business, Sid held steady and went conservative on investing in properties within 100 miles of New Orleans due to the sudden craze over The World's Fair coming in 1984. That was the popular thing to do, with everyone envisioning they'd have to turn people away, no matter how many rooms they could afford to build or buy. Instead, Sid bought several undervalued properties that were not much different from The Morning Inn. His purchases were scattered along the interstate from Mississippi into Louisiana, but they all had a common trait. They were either bank-owned or on the verge of being so. Sid liked getting them at auction, but the competition became so robust in recent years that he usually approached the bank with an offer he knew would best that of his competitors.

Tired of waiting for Devan's response, Elvira said, "Sorry about the apartment. But the last people in here lived like animals."

That was a deception, as Devan would discover when he watched the woman load up her Volkswagen van with the last box of her things—including her cat—thirty minutes later. It was *her* apartment, and this was how *she* lived.

Devan's orientation after that was minimal. The resentful widow spoke rapidly, telling him where things were, like the laundry room and the Coke machine. Then she sped past the instructions on check-out time, which rooms were down (fourteen of them in total), and the general lay of the land. She also purposefully left out how many occupied rooms there were, who was in them, and that part about the boiler.

It was on the verge of blowing. That little gem was something Devan would discover a few weeks later when a drenched motel guest banged on the office door at 2 AM, fit-to-be-tied and wanting a refund. The boiler's main lines exploded and sent water rushing into the rooms immediately adjacent to the boiler room. And the guest's clothes—apparently the only ones he had—were folded up on the floor in the bathroom for some reason. So he either had to put them on or go to the front office in his underwear. He opted for the former and cussed the entire time he put them on before storming to the office.

It seemed the only thing Elvira got right was the bank's instructions for her to have the commode in the bathroom plumbed with a bidet spray nozzle. It was a hose, customarily used by people from the Indian subcontinent in lieu of toilet paper. Devan was positive that had Elvira not, Savitri would have jumped back in the car and driven back to Biloxi, taking Fardeen and the girls with her. Using toilet paper was simply out of the question and was a filthy practice that neither she nor anyone else in the family observed.

It was such a horrible day and an even worse indoctrination into the family's new business and home. There were no welcoming American faces or that fabled Southern hospitality upon their arrival. It was quite the contrary. They all felt afraid, unwelcomed, and unwanted.

So a few minutes later, when Sid pulled up in a convertible Mercedes with the top down and his blonde, American girlfriend in the passenger's seat, Devan didn't know whether to hug him or punch him in the face. Sid's wife, Saraswati, was a childhood friend of Savitri's. And it showed incredibly poor taste, albeit some daring, for Sid to show up with one of his American concubines—particularly at a time like this. Savitri would've raised hell had she not been so glad to see her older brother.

But all of Devan's anger disappeared once Sid came in the office, counted the register, and read Elvira the riot act, cursing her because the till was $50 short and there wasn't a registration card to be found. He straightened her ass out real good.

Then Sid did something that shocked even his sister. He offered to stay for a few more days and put her and the kids up in a Vacation Inn his friend owned in Pensacola while he helped Devan acclimate.

It was a very welcomed and generous offering on his part. Savitri refused, insisting she'd stay with Devan, as did Fardeen. But her eldest, Sridevi, was all over it. Sridevi said she'd take Anaya with her, and they'd stay in Pensacola until things settled down more.

"And how will you get there?" Devan asked his defiant teenage daughter, who glared back at him with eyes ablaze and who looked just like her mother when she got mad. And, at the moment, Sridevi was mad as hell, so she was practically her mother's twin.

Speaking of whom, Savitri interrupted and said, "I will take them."

"Oh, no. Oh, no, no, no, no, no," Devan said, shaking his head and looking down, "you drive in the middle of the road, and you can't see at night! Impossible! You don't even have a license in Gujarat, and you've seen how the police act here! Out of the question!"

But just before World War III could ensue, Sid offered for Candy, his buxom, blonde girlfriend, to take the kids in her car. It was only a two-seater, but Anaya could sit on Sridevi's lap.

So with that settled, Candy pulled around and helped load up the trunk before driving off toward Pensacola with Sridevi and Anaya in tow.

And that left Fardeen, his parents, and his Uncle Sid sitting quietly and deciding how to move forward in this terrible, horrid, new place. Fardeen never felt so challenged or alone as he watched his sisters ride away. At times, he may have argued with Sridevi, particularly about her treatment of Anaya. Yet Fardeen still looked up to and counted on the support of his older sister.

But he felt encouraged when Sid got behind the desk, counted the drawer again, and raised the till back to $200. Sid acted like a boss because that's what he was and had been for some time. He walked the grounds with Fardeen and his father, bravely knocking on doors and telling everyone they'd have to register with the front desk again the following morning. He was amazed at how professional and simultaneously forceful his uncle was with the guests, some of which were downright frightening to Fardeen. But that's how Sid behaved the whole time over the next week, as he stayed much longer than initially planned. He didn't act the way his father described in discussions between his parents that Fardeen overheard at night. He seemed a lot more reasonable, but he sure-as-hell knew more about what he was doing than Devan did.

Savitri smelled as strongly of bleach every day as Elvira had on their arrival. She spent the first several mornings cleaning the apartment while Sid—but mostly Fardeen and Devan—cleaned the rooms. Then she moved on to the office, scouring the floor on her hands and knees, stopping only briefly to hail the men back when someone came in to rent a room or ask a question.

Cleaning rooms was a demeaning experience for Devan. While he wasn't a wealthy man back home, he was still highly educated, had a successful shoe store, and the family lived much better than most of his children's friends' families did.

But to clean up after some of the least educated, filthiest people he'd ever seen rapidly took its toll on Devan's pride. And he didn't take a shine to guests hollering after him for extra soap or ashtrays, both of which still bore the Morning Inn logo. Unfortunately, that circumstance led to even more trouble after Sid returned to Biloxi, inadvertently leaving his brother-in-law to deal with the matter.

The first day after Sid left, Devan walked into the office after Savitri called him on the Radio Shack walkie-talkies Sid brought. When Devan entered, he saw the well-dressed, young black man he'd seen check into number 17 standing at the counter. Devan was so concerned there might have been a problem with his room.

The day before, the man came out of the room in fresh clothes a half-hour after he checked in and drove away. So Devan found it curious when he went into the room the next morning and found some of the man's belongings still in it, including a shoebox containing the door hanger, two ashtrays, several packs of matches, four foam cups, and three bars of soap. The man didn't look like someone who might loot a motel room as he was well-dressed and drove a fancy two-door Oldsmobile. To Devan, he looked like Venus Flytrap, the disc jockey from the television program "WKRP" he enjoyed watching back at The Sunkist.

It was just as well, though, because Devan didn't have the energy to confront the man as he'd had his fill of confrontations for the time being. Still, he wondered why the man stood there in the office as though he had some business to attend to with Devan.

But he did.

"Mr. Patel?" the handsome young man said as he held out his hand to shake Devan's.

"Yes, I'm Patel," Devan said while shaking hands and nervously probing the man's expression for any indication of why he was there.

"My name is Kevin Green, Mr. Patel, and I'm with the corporate headquarters for Morning Inn," the man said, just as Devan noticed the shoebox from the man's room resting on the counter.

"I'm afraid we may have a problem here, Mr. Patel," he continued, shifting from being courteous to taking a dour look on his face.

"Sir? How so?" Devan asked, unable to conceive of what the problem was. Devan cleaned that room himself, then checked and even double-checked it, following the protocols of his seasoned brother-in-law.

"You'll always miss something," Sid told Devan, *"at least until you get used to what to look for. But you must learn because I know my sister. She's not going to clean rooms for very long. And the first time she finds a used rubber in the bed or has to clean up a person's sick, her housekeeping days are through,"* he continued through a chortle. *"Then, unless you want to clean them yourself or have Sridevi do it, and I know you won't do that, you'll have to hire a housekeeper, probably two or three, though. And let me just tell you, Devan. Around here, that is the laziest group of people you've ever seen. They will surely miss things. And it's up to you to notice them."*

But as Devan stared between the shoebox and the young businessman, he was positive he'd checked everything. He even checked off the items on the "Sunkist Motel Executive Housekeeper Checklist," Sid brought from Biloxi with the walkie-talkies.

Picking up the box, the man began his discourse.

"I found these Morning Inn branded items in my room, Mr. Patel. They violate Morning Inn's franchise agreement, to which your sales contract was subject. That also means we're entitled to enforce the $75,000 liquidated damages clause against either the former owner or you as the new owner," the man said without emotion as he stared back at Devan.

Devan felt his heart pounding and looked over at Savitri, who he could tell was equally shaken. He started to protest, but he stopped himself. Although he wondered what happened to them when he agreed to move to Tomahawk, Florida, Devan had great instincts. So he managed to stay silent long enough to let the man speak again.

"Listen," Kevin said, "I don't want to do that. And Morning Inn certainly doesn't want to do that. But could you do me a favor, Mr. Patel?"

Devan then felt the rush of adrenaline from his initial scare, and his scalp tingled, and he fell off his game and abruptly said, "Yes, sir! What would you like me to do?"

Kevin Green's ploy was very effective, just like it usually was. He opened by putting the fear of God in someone, softening them up. But truth be known, the Morning Inn company's founder was a decent, hard-working man who'd endured many of the tribulations Devan now did. While he'd passed away a few years earlier, The Morning Inn founder, Cecil Mourning, left a corporate culture empathetic to its franchisees and anyone else in the industry. Kevin Green was an exemplary emissary for that culture too. However, they had to maintain order. They couldn't allow their name to be disparaged or have someone think they were staying in a Morning Inn rather than The Seagull Motel. So they eventually paid visits when a franchisee lost their flag, just to ensure proper de-branding.

"I need you to remove anything at all like this on the property," Kevin said, holding up an ashtray, "and that means bar soap, matches, signage, anything. And you can reach me at this number but only on Fridays," he said, holding out a business card for Devan. "I'm also going to mail you a walkthrough checklist to make sure you comply, and it's the same one I use on visits like this one. Ok, Mr. Patel? I'll be back in a few weeks, Mr. Patel, and I trust you will do this for me. Am I right?"

"Yes sir, yes sir," Devan said anxiously as the man reached

out, shook hands with him again, bid Savitri a good day, then walked out and drove away.

It could have been any number of things. It may have even started with the giant rat in number 1 the week before. Or it could have been getting hollered at and threatened by the police with gunfire. The apartment's condition was to blame for some of it, as were the grueling hours Savitri spent washing, scrubbing, and wiping until her hands were raw from chemicals. But now, having been terrified by the threat of financial ruin was perhaps the icing on the cake. And whether it was any one of those things or the combination of them all, Savitri broke down and began to cry. She bawled unapologetically, holding her face in her hands, refusing to look back at Devan or see anything else. She wanted it all to disappear.

That's how Fardeen saw his mother when he came into the office for more Windex. It's also an image he'd remember. And it changed him forever.

CHAPTER FOUR

Wednesday, December 31, 1980

F ardeen was giddy as the Greyhound pulled into Biloxi's bus station. And his excitement grew when he stepped off the bus and saw his Uncle Sid and Aunt Sara waiting for him in the parking lot. He hadn't been back to Biloxi since moving to Tomahawk, and he was anxious to see if things there were just as splendidly hospitable as he remembered. Biloxi didn't disappoint either, right from the get-go.

As Fardeen reached Saraswati, his Uncle Siddharth bear-hugged him. Fardeen was never so happy to see his aunt and uncle as he inhaled Sid's aftershave and heard him say, "It's so good to see you, nephew!"

After Sid put him down, a short man wearing an apron walked up, holding a brown paper bag with grease sweating through its bottom.

"Two gyros, one vegetable, one steak, two cheeseburgers, and two fries?" the older man asked as he handed Sid the bulging greasy brown bag of food.

Sid gave the man a ten-dollar bill, and it startled him, "No, no, sir. You already paid us inside."

But Sid insisted, taking the ten-dollar bill back and stuffing it in the man's front shirt pocket, saying, "I know, Poppa Alex! But this is for you!"

It was apparent then that Sid had already dined at the bus stop under who knew what circumstances. Poppa Alex, who brought the food out, seemed puzzled as if he didn't recognize Sid, which he didn't. But he took the ten bucks out of his shirt, held it up, and said, "I appreciate this, sir! I do!" before tucking it back in his front pocket, grasping Sid's hand a moment with both of his, then walking back inside the station to his lunch counter.

Their exchange was surprising to Fardeen. His Uncle Sid was notoriously cheap, according to his parents, anyway. Fardeen never found him that way, although his father told him the only time Sid came out of pocket for something he didn't have to was when he was showing off.

Whatever was in that bag started making Fardeen salivate. The scent of onions was the strongest, then beef, glorious beef. Savitri forbade beef at home. However, Fardeen secretly developed a taste for it at The Sunkist in Biloxi over the summer. It was so much richer and more flavorful than goat meat or chicken, which were all that Savitri allowed his father to eat, and that was only seldomly. A marginally observant Hindu, Devan was allowed to eat those once she gave up on him being a vegetarian. But considering the bouquet of aromas coming from every direction around The Sunkist, the temptation was more than Fardeen could withstand.

There was Angelina's next door, the char-grilled smell of Burger King a few blocks away, and the steaks people cooked, seemingly every night, sitting around the pool drinking beer. So Fardeen snuck burgers, hot dogs, chili, pickled sausage, or just anything else he was able to devour within a few seconds without getting caught. No one else in his immediate family ate beef, though.

But Sid did. Fardeen's Uncle Sid did several things that few might approve of back in Gujarat. Like Fardeen's mother, Sid was Hindu because their Muslim father converted shortly after moving to Gujarat. In reality, though, Sid wasn't anything.

Technically, he was agnostic. But if there'd ever been a Temple of Siddharth Shakur, that's where he would've worshipped.

That didn't bother Fardeen, though. Neither did Sid's cars, money, girlfriends, nor anything else about the man.

Sid pushed the greasy bag into Fardeen's chest and urged him toward a cotillion-white El Dorado with a stainless top, which sat humming, remarkably quiet a few feet away. Then he opened the door and pushed the passenger's side seat forward, allowing Fardeen's Aunt Sara to climb into the back. Afterward, he waved Fardeen into the front seat, patting him on the back as he entered, holding the bag of food in his lap. Unfazed by the seating demotion, Saraswati put on a set of earmuffs from the large purse she carried before Sid climbed in and pulled onto Highway 90.

At first, it wasn't clear why his Aunt Sara did that. But it made more sense once Sid reached the highway and turned toward The Sunkist. Sid reached down and turned on the digitally displayed radio to the local rock station. He turned it up all the way, too. Within moments, Fardeen and Sid devolved into whatever realm of imagination The Rolling Stones singing "Start Me Up" took them. At the same time, Saraswati wore her earmuffs as she flipped through The Daily Herald's pages, looking for sales on fabric, thimbles, and thread.

The Mississippi Sound raced past on the driver's side of the car, as did the historic homes of Biloxi on the passengers' as Mick Jagger sang in the background, almost as if narrating. Sid swayed a little bit in the driver's side, mouthing the lyrics, while Fardeen looked to the right side of the car, watching Biloxi's beautiful ancient homes fly by. He couldn't imagine living in one of them, but he wanted to. He very much wanted to.

Sid spoke up after a mile or so, hollering over the music.

"It's all untouched! No one is here yet! It's all pristine, nephew! They put all their money into New Orleans! Even Armand!"

The "they" Sid referred to were his fellow Gujarati moteliers and hoteliers, while the man to whom Sid referred was Armand Popat, who was quite a character. Armand's mother was French, and his father was from Gujarat. Although only in his twenties, Armand was a multi-millionaire. It was all due to his business dealings, mainly in the hospitality industry. As a result, he was both respected and hated by his fellow Gujarati business associates.

That was the extent of Fardeen's familiarity with Armand Popat. He knew who he was and that he got started the same way his father did now. He'd even heard his mother mention that she was somehow related to Armand, but that was about it. He'd never met the guy. Never laid eyes on him. However, Armand's influence and experiences were ultimately and fatefully intertwined and on a trajectory with Fardeen's. Neither of them knew it yet, though.

Fardeen found the Sunkist Motel just as he'd left it as Sid turned and parked alongside the front office, going in and relieving his front desk person. Well, for the most part, it was the same. The office was buzzing with people checking in, the parking lot was full, and the cars raced passed on Highway 90, just a few feet away as they always had. But a few things were missing compared with the days Fardeen spent there over the summer.

There was the glaring absence of other boys his age. The swimming pool area was dormant, and there weren't kids playing lawn games on the sparse grassy areas around the pool or the field behind the cottages. That much wasn't at all the way he remembered.

What's more, as Fardeen looked across the street at the amusement park and arcade that normally overflowed at this hour of a summer day, he saw very little activity. It was open —it wasn't shut down or anything. It just wasn't the same. Families didn't stand in line to board the half-dozen or so rides the park featured. Fathers weren't hunched over in bumper cars with their youngest one between their legs while the older kids rammed into them in other ones. Young mothers didn't stream across the highway, holding the hands of a bunch of children on either side of themselves.

As Fardeen took in all these things, within moments, he reflected on what an eventful and inspiring summer he spent there only months before. But now, it seemed to slip farther into the past the longer he looked on.

He thought of Gale, the boy from Louisiana with whom he'd spent most of his days the week after he first arrived. And as cool and as worldly as Gale was, he was only the first of about ten or so other kids Fardeen got to know, some of which were even wilder than Gale.

Many of The Sunkist's guests were the families of officers and NCOs from the local Keesler Air Force Base. They were usually longer-term renters, waiting for homes on base or in parts of the world Fardeen never heard of. Just as diverse as their origins and destinations were, so were their personalities and stories. But Fardeen sat and listened to all of them. He was fascinated by the degree to which a person's experiences could vary, one to the next, within the same nation. Yet, they still came together as Americans.

There were hundreds of vastly different cultures across The United States of America. And some of them found their way, if only for a time, amicably sitting poolside at The Sunkist. People proudly shared their cultures too. Fardeen watched people from Illinois eat boiled crayfish or "crawfish" for the first time while, the following night, serving up trays of Chicagoan hot dogs on poppy-seeded buns to their newfound friends. He saw black people from Georgia break bread with white Iowans across a concrete picnic table with versions of their fried chicken spread across it. And either group graciously argued how much better the other family's offering was. He watched dozens of interactions like those that summer, and they energized him each time. Truly, The United States of America was a place like none other in the world's history, where cultures melded, and people actually realized their dreams of life, liberty, and the pursuit of happiness. It was inarguable. He witnessed it firsthand, albeit from a naïve boy's romanticized vantage.

Yet, whenever all those people left The Sunkist, while bittersweet, it left Fardeen feeling earthbound. The familiarity they fostered with one another only made Fardeen feel more like an outsider.

His Uncle Sid was never out there by the pool either, sharing stories. Siddharth wasn't ever impolite. But he kept his distance, and that confused Fardeen. It was "the hospitality" industry, after all. Shouldn't Uncle Sid and Aunt Sara be out by the pool, joining in all the fun, telling stories of Gujarat, even if they didn't have a hot dog or a hamburger?

But poor Fardeen wasn't well-versed in reality just yet. He'd not seen any of the things Uncle Sid had. Those things were, at times, gruesome, repulsive, disgusting things, capable of disheartening even the most optimistic soul. They were the worst things anyone could imagine about the human race. In the coming years, Fardeen would experience many of them, though. And it would break his heart.

Above the office, the manager's apartment where Sid stayed most nights was small but far more accommodating than Fardeen's home at The Seagull in Tomahawk. Sid's apartment was where Fardeen slept on the floor over the summer while his parents and sisters stayed in one of the cottages.

The centerpiece of the living area was a giant Zenith television housed in a console. It had a remote control, which baffled Fardeen, and it was perpetually on, whether or not anyone watched. The furniture was all American, as were the paintings and decorations. There was not so much as a remnant of Gujarati culture anywhere, and Saraswati couldn't stand it for that and other reasons.

Most of the time, she stayed in their home in an upscale subdivision across the Biloxi Bay with their younger children, a son, Wali, and a daughter, Sinu. That left Sid to lead the life of a bachelor, which he exploited every chance he got. The apartment was a testament to his lifestyle too. The bedroom had a California king-sized waterbed and a second, smaller television, which rested on a bureau in front of a wall covered with mirrors. The bathroom just off the bedroom was 1950s-chic with ceiling-to-floor pink tile and matching fixtures. The only other room was the kitchen which was almost the same size as the living area to which it opened. It had a refrigerator in it that served water from the front. Fardeen thought that was like something from *Star Trek* or *Space 1999*. A door in the center of the living area opened to an L-shaped balcony facing the pool area on one side and the amusement park and the Mississippi Sound on the other.

The Sunkist was dead center of an area in Biloxi called "The Strip." People called it that because it was home to several small motels, nightclubs, and lounges that, in years past, played host to illegal gambling, prostitution, and other unsavory enterprises. However, following an all-out purge in the 1960s, more family-centric businesses developed on The Strip. Silly Golf, the waterslide, bowling, and a cinema were among those, and they were all things that Fardeen enjoyed during his summer in Biloxi. Eventually, a few national hotel brands descended on the area. Armada Inn built a hotel less than a mile away from The Sunkist. And Christensen built a gigantic complex a few blocks away from that. It all seemed like it would be catastrophic for the small motel owner. However, it had the opposite effect. Biloxi became a destination of sorts rather than a second thought. So the demand for affordable rooms skyrocketed.

However, an undercurrent of depravity and lawlessness lingered on The Strip. Many of the nightclubs shut down, and the law entirely expunged gambling just like they promised they would. But old habits die hard, so while the whore-mongering and gambling went away, strip clubs and the narcotics industry popped up to replace them. Biloxi always had ties to the underworld, but the 1970s rang in a whole new epoch in that history. The old motel owners went with the flow, and while they didn't directly participate in the unlawful behavior, they assuredly profited from it.

However, Fardeen's Uncle Sid was different because he had no connections with the old establishment, and he was Indian. Consequently, he had to run a much tighter ship than his American colleagues in the same business. He realized that if he wound up with a bunch of whores and junkies in-house like so many of the other motels did, the city would be on his ass so fast that it would make his head spin.

That was a lesson Sid recently learned the hard way.

When a city councilman's niece OD'd in one of Sid's rooms, it made the paper's front page. It was unfortunate, too, because it didn't even happen on his watch. He was on a rare vacation with his wife and children when an eighteen-year-old kid he hired part-time to watch the front desk rented a room to the underaged girl. The kid was supposedly even complicit in providing her with the heroin. While that all got detailed in the article, it didn't mention that the kid was American. It just said that a teen overdosed in an immigrant-owned motel on the beach, and while it didn't implicate Siddharth, it nevertheless made the suggestion.

The outrage was cataclysmic. Churches and civic groups banded together, organizing protests and rallying their congregations. Sid received a Notice of Public Nuisance from the city, threatening to shut him down and force him to forfeit his property. The local news station was waiting for Sid when he pulled up to his motel, as were dozens of picketers holding signs. That was the day he returned from vacation. But it was also the first time he learned of the incident, and it was just a fine "How-do-you-do?" after spending five days in Florida at Disneyworld with his wife, her mother, and two screaming toddlers. The city padlocked the front door to the office because the kid watching the place was in police custody and had abandoned it.

Then, in one last excruciating and insulting gesture, they arrested Siddharth a week afterward.

On that Saturday morning, two Biloxi officers waited for him at the foot of the stairs leading to the manager's apartment. They didn't have their guns drawn, and they weren't at all militant about the matter. Nevertheless, they cuffed the Gujarati motelier, placed him in the back of a police car, and took him to jail.

Were it not for the intervention of a Biloxi businessman, a man named Kim Fontenot, Sid might have stayed in jail until his arraignment almost a week later. Sid hadn't any idea what to do, and Saraswati sure didn't. But Kim did. He owned Silly Golf, and he bailed Sid out of jail and drove him home after introducing himself. During that drive, Kim tried to explain everything Sid faced and why. However, unbeknownst to Kim, it was like a kitten driving around with a Bengal tiger, giving it advice on surviving in the wild.

"Man, these people over here, I just don't know, man," Kim started.

"They all up in the church, and that's where 'dey power comes from," Kim said as he turned onto Highway 90 in the nearly identical Eldorado Sid owned at the time.

"But Imma give you my cousin's numbah. He's a lawyer in New Awleens, and he don't play around with folks, a'ight? He's made fa'dis shit here, and he'll do ya'right," Kim continued.

Sid, who'd sat alongside drunkards and dodged projectile

"vomiteers" in the holding tank and then sat in a cell with three other men, didn't know what to make of this man's compassion. Was he a plant? Was he someone trying to get Sid's property for himself?

Then, the young man, originally from New Orleans, almost as though he'd read Sid's mind, said, "Look, we all in this together on The Strip, man. I don't need a buncha' Bible thumpers mauradin' around the street while I'm handin' out putters and balls, a'ight? They just tryin' to blame you because you ain't from here, But they scarin' my business away, and they know it, too. They gon' back off. Just let 'em go fah now, man."

Sid remained quiet for the rest of the drive home, only nodding at Kim's small talk and descriptions of the things going by on Pass Road and then across the causeway toward Sid's home. When they pulled up in Sid's driveway, Sid extended his hand toward the handsome, very young man and said,

"I will not forget this, Mr. Fontenot. I will not ever forget it. I will pay you for my bond tomorrow, and I will hire your cousin. And if I can ever do anything for you, please come to see me. sir."

Sid's words were so captivatingly genuine that they surprised the young man. Kim thought he'd been clear that he helped Sid as much for himself and his business as anything else. Nevertheless, Kim was appreciative, smiling and shaking hands with the weary Indian man he could tell was exhausted and afraid.

"Hey, man, my name is Kim, a'ight? It's Kim. And it's like I told ya', we all in this together down there on that Strip, man. Just call my cousin like I said. He'll set you right, man."

And, boy, was Kim ever telling the truth about his cousin.

Sid placed the long-distance call to Lawrence Fourcade, Esquire, the following morning. But he could hardly understand the man's English, and the guy seemed almost disinterested to the point it worried Sid. Sid would've even sworn that the man was talking to others about unrelated matters in between intermittent reassurances of, "Yeah, yeah, ok, I got it."

However, on Tuesday morning, Sid became a believer when the local newspaper printed a retraction. It cited the circumstances surrounding the overdose and the involvement of those truly guilty in the matter, according to arrest records. But the piece de resistance was when Sid read the op-ed in which the editor of The Daily Herald mentioned Siddharth by name and personally apologized for the paper's thoughtlessness.

The challenges narcotics present to society are considerable. We overstepped our bounds in our haste to inform our readers of law enforcement's efforts to curtail their influence. As a result, we may have inadvertently and injuriously presented inaccurate information about one of our subscribers and fellow Citizens. We apologize to Mr. Siddharth Shakur and his family. We also want to assure people that Biloxi is and has always been a forward-thinking community that opens its arms to all cultures and walks of life, as does the Daily Herald.

Perhaps the funniest thing about the editorial was that a Colgate English graduate and second-year Tulane law student wrote it. And Camille Aucoin scribed the words as, a few feet away, Lawrence Fourcade reeled in a shark off the coast of Grand Isle, which he clubbed to death then nonchalantly threw back into the Gulf. Danny Sproles, the Herald's editor, regurgitated the missive Camille wrote verbatim in the paper's Tuesday morning edition.

After that, almost no one bothered Siddharth Shakur. The police became more custodial as they should have been in the first place. Sid stopped receiving hateful letters from the Chamber of Commerce about false advertising because of his bait-and-switch $8 room sign. And letters from local churches that threatened to disrupt his business came to a halt. Hell, the churches even replaced those letters with several invitations for Sid and his family to join them in worship on Sundays.

But one person didn't share the paper's apologetic and permissive stance like the Biloxi Police Department and everyone else seemed to. That was the Harrison County Sheriff, Alvin Smith.

One morning about a week after the paper's retraction and apology, Sheriff Smith showed up at The Sunkist with two deputies in an unmarked black Chevrolet. Siddharth didn't know what to make of it at first. So he stood up from his chair behind the counter and watched as the men approached and entered the office.

"Good morning, gentleman," Sid said nervously, "how can I help you? Is there a problem?"

Then Siddharth gulped as one of the deputies turned and locked the door to the office after the three men were inside.

But Alvin didn't say anything. He just stared up and down at Sid as he breathed loudly through his nose. It was apparent he was incensed about something. Then, finally, he spoke.

"You may think you're fooling everyone, but you ain't foolin' me. I know all about your ass, and you ain't foolin' me. I know everything about you and how you got here. Biloxi might not give a damn about what kind of shit washes up on its beach. But it damn sure affects the rest of Harrison County, and that's my domain, boy, all of it. You got that? And I'm gonna run your ass back to Pakistan or wherever in the hell you're from."

Sid stood quietly, thinking it was his best option to let the man speak, forgoing the opportunity to correct the backwoods lawman's mischaracterization of his origins. Even if he were in the right, Sid knew he couldn't win with a man like the sheriff.

Alvin turned after a few more seconds, and one of the deputies unlocked and opened the door for him. Then they filed out of the office and tore out of the parking lot.

After they left, Sid picked up the phone and called Kim Fontenot.

"Aww, man, that's just the way he is," Kim told Sid, *"Al's 'aight, he's just tryin' to be a tough guy, man. Don't worry 'baht him."*

Sid stood at the front window of The Sunkist, and he could see Kim, standing in the booth of Silly Golf, passing out putters as he held the phone between his ear and shoulder, talking back to him. Kim had on a fluorescent orange visor and a white golf shirt and labored as he spoke. After he got the group of snowbirds taken care of, he looked up and stared in the direction of the Sunkist. Seeing Sid, he waved his arm over his head, then gave him a thumbs up.

"Are you sure?" Sid asked through the phone's receiver, which he'd stretched across the office to stand in the window.

"Yeah, man! Don't worry 'baht it, Sid. I'm tellin' ya, that's just Al's way. Ignore it, a'ight? Listen, I gotta run, man," he said.

As Sid continued staring across the highway, he saw a van pull up in the Silly Golf parking lot, and several kids got out and started moving toward the booth where Kim stood.

"Say no more, my friend. And thank you. I see you are prospering, and I'm happy for you," Sid said.

Sid was surprised when he heard Kim start laughing through the phone. Then Kim said, as he laughed, *"Yeah, man! Live long and prospah!"*

But it all served as a warning to Siddharth Shakur: keep your place, Indian. Because we're watching.

At least, that's the way Sid interpreted it.

CHAPTER FIVE

After the last bite of his cheeseburger, Fardeen burped as he sat on The Sunkist's balcony, watching all the cars pass by on the highway.

"Young man!" Saraswati griped at him.

While there was no blood relation, his Aunt Sara was more like a second mother to Fardeen and his sisters than an aunt.

"Excuse me, Mami," Fardeen apologized.

She was only doing what his mother would've wanted by correcting his table manners. The two women were lifelong friends, and Fardeen knew that she ever had his best interest at heart. Still, it perturbed Sid.

"Go inside! Do you want to keep him a child his whole life? Go! Go, Saraswati! The men are talking!"

Saraswati did what Sid told her to, but she defiantly flicked water into Sid's face from the pitcher she carried as she walked past him, back into the apartment she so hated. She was always a pushover for Siddharth, getting trampled on throughout their marriage. But Fardeen was her best friend, Savitri's son. And she knew her friend would not appreciate Siddharth turning Fardeen into a vulgarian like her husband was. So she was simply looking out for him as she knew Savitri would want her to.

Fardeen's visit to Biloxi wasn't just a vacation, although that's how it felt to him. His uncle reminded him that he was there to learn about property maintenance. Specifically, he was there to learn about air conditioners, electrical work, and plumbing. Those were the three pillars of daily operations in small hotel and motel ownership across the entire industry.

They also presented the most significant opportunity for savings to owners. Calling a repairman was financially devastating, as so many Indian owners learned the hard way over the years. So the opportunity-cost savings beyond that was being able to do the work yourself. Otherwise, Sid told Fardeen, you had to hire maintenance personnel. And the pool from which you had to choose consisted of people that may or may not even have the requisite skillset. You didn't know until you hired them, no matter what their references told you. The occupation was also a magnet for drunks, junkies, felons hiding from the law, and those just too incompetent to pursue a specific craft anywhere else. Sid said you were at their mercy if you hired someone like that. It wasn't exactly a group you wanted to be beholden to. They'd leave in a heartbeat. And they'd do it at the most inconvenient time, relishing every moment as they went. Then they'd move on to their next transient station in life, probably another motel.

Sid preached to Fardeen for a long time until he could tell the boy was running out of gas. He realized Fardeen was a little overwhelmed by it all. So he told him to get some sleep as they'd be getting up early the next day. There were already several maintenance orders at the front desk, and he was missing room nights by not having them tended to. Those would be the rooms they'd start with, first thing. Then they'd come back to other rooms as people checked out.

"Up, up, up!" Saraswati snapped, yanking the cover from Fardeen as he lay on the living room floor in the manager's apartment at The Sunkist. While abrupt and a tad shrill, it was the same way Fardeen's mother woke him each day, so he was used to it. He even had to remind himself he wasn't at home in Tomahawk as he rose and stared around, disoriented for a moment.

"Your Uncle is waiting for you by the pool. Go have breakfast with him," Saraswati continued as she rolled up his bedding and gestured toward the door.

Unlike his father, Fardeen's uncle emulated Americans at every turn. He attempted to speak like them, listened to the same music they did, and even dressed like them, depending on what he was doing at the time. When he was behind the front desk, Siddharth dressed conservatively in slacks and a plain, collared shirt. Then, he wore satin shirts unbuttoned halfway down his chest if heading out on the town, which he accessorized with various jewelry pieces on his fingers and around his neck. Sid wore blue jeans, tennis shoes, and an Izod shirt when relaxing by the pool or walking around the property on casual days.

So Fardeen barely recognized the man sitting at the concrete picnic table wearing a khaki tradesman's shirt with a name patch that read "Sid," brown work pants, and black work boots. Fardeen chuckled a little because Sid looked so peculiar to him. But when he saw the response it prompted in his uncle's expression, he quickly stifled himself and acted as though he was just glad to see him.

"Good morning, Uncle Sid," he said as he plopped down across the table from Siddharth.

"Good morning," Sid said, staring back at his nephew to ensure he wasn't making fun of him.

As he watched Fardeen eat his breakfast, Sid rattled off everything he had planned for the day. They had to clean the window units in the rooms because they were all clogged from cigarette smoke—some of them to the point they didn't blow cold air at all. Next, they would hang a new door in number 7 because a drunk guest punched it off its hinges. That should take them way past lunch. Then they'd end the day inspecting the rooms like he'd showed them how to do in Tomahawk.

They would go behind Saraswati and Nancy, a housekeeper he recently hired that he was trying to train, using that same checklist Fardeen was intimately familiar with now.

Siddharth couldn't help beaming with pride as he watched his young nephew eat breakfast. Sid thought Fardeen favored his and Savitri's mother, Virika, the boy's grandmother, and that he was such a good-looking boy.

"You'll be a good businessman one day, Fardeen. You'll own a motel like this, and everyone is going to like you," Sid said as he stared at Fardeen.

Fardeen pretended not to hear him because the last thing he wanted at that point in his life was to run a motel. But that would change. So he gulped down his tea, picked up his plate, and headed back toward the apartment like his uncle's words never registered with him.

"No, no, no! Leave that here, Fardeen. We've got work to do," Sid said as he rose from the table, "Saraswati will get that."

Fardeen turned back and did as his uncle told him. Then he followed Sid to the back of the property where the utility building was. During his entire summer stay, he'd never gone into that building. So when Sid unlocked and swung open the barn-style doors, Fardeen was amazed. The inside of the building, about 2,000 square feet, looked like a showroom floor for tools and equipment. Caged lighting hung from the ceiling, which shone down on wall-to-wall, polished concrete floors. Shelving extended along each of those walls and held tools, supplies, towels, gas cans, air conditioners, cleaning supplies, chlorine, chemicals, and things Fardeen didn't even know what were.

A once-again prideful Siddharth stood next to his nephew and said, "Devan would probably envy something like this, wouldn't he?"

Fardeen stepped into the building and quietly said, "He

might, Uncle. But you'd have to tell him what all of these things are first."

Siddharth burst out laughing and grabbed an unexpecting Fardeen, hugging him from behind, "Yes! Yes! I imagine I would, Fardeen!"

Despite all his uncle's crowing about "having the tools you need" and "making things so much easier," Fardeen felt as though he would collapse before making it across the property to the apartment's stairs that night. He spent the whole day racing behind his uncle, following orders and pushing a metal mechanic's cart that didn't roll so well over the uneven asphalt of The Sunkist's parking lot. He loaded air conditioners, took them to a concrete slab Sid devised specifically for servicing them, and he cleaned every air conditioner on the property that day. His fingertips were raw from getting sliced in a dozen places on their evaporator coils, his back ached from hoisting the units onto the cart, and his spirit ailed from the dressing down his uncle gave him all day. By evening, he was in another world as he rolled past the pool, pushing the cart sans air conditioner, when his uncle called out to him from where he sat by the pool.

"Fardeen! Where are you going with the cart?"

As Fardeen looked up, he didn't know where he was going or what he was doing. Fardeen was delirious. He worked through lunch, attempting to impress his uncle, and was exhausted by that time.

"Siddharth!" Fardeen heard his Aunt Sara shout from somewhere on the property, although he wasn't sure where.

Then, as he opened his mouth to respond to his Uncle Sid, he felt a familiar, cool hand touch his forehead and push his hair back before pulling his head down. It was his Aunt Sara, and she transformed into a tigress within a moment of his head resting on her shoulder.

Siddharth never got so good as Saraswati gave him that evening. She exploded, shouting across the property at her impudent, uncompassionate husband, holding Fardeen's head with one hand and pointing and waving at Sid with the other during her tirade. She guided Fardeen to the office while Sid talked to an Air Force sergeant about weekly rates. A moment later, in a supreme show of defiance, Saraswati charged from the office with the keys to Siddharth's El Dorado in hand, pushed Fardeen into the backseat, forced her mother, Bairavi, and her two children into the front, and shot out of the parking lot, slamming on the brakes several times. She was taking the child home, she hollered, home to Tomahawk and Savitri where he would be safe and free from Siddharth's abuse.

Saraswati didn't make it a mile down Highway 90, though. Part of the reason was that Bairavi repeatedly struggled to close the door over her sari that dragged along the ground from the passenger's side. Then the two children wedged between Bairavi and the dashboard cried and screamed. But the most damning thing was that Saraswati Shakur pulled onto Highway 90 at 5 miles per hour and never accelerated three miles per hour above that.

Cars swerved, horns blew, fists shook, and people hollered. That convinced Bairavi that her daughter just drove her onto a thoroughfare toward American hell as she became inconsolable, hugging the children to her breast and wailing.

That's just how the Biloxi motorcycle patrolmen found them all, too, when he pulled Saraswati over. Bairavi was panicked, as were the children. Saraswati was livid. And there was a teenage boy in the back seat who seemed oblivious to the world. The officer presumed they were "rushing" him to the hospital because the boy seemed so out of sorts.

Thanks to the kindly sergeant that gave him a ride in his pickup, Siddharth arrived moments afterward, pulling up slowly, several car lengths back at Sid's suggestion. He'd dealt with police before and knew he'd better proceed cautiously. But he'd also developed an unlikely relationship with the Biloxi Police Department because despite what the rest of the community thought, Sid was one of the most compliant motel owners with the most transparent operations up and down The Strip. He called the police just frequently enough to keep his property wholesome while not badgering them. It turned out to be a relationship of mutual respect and understanding.

Thank goodness for that, too. Because it only took everyone a few minutes to sort things out. The officer graciously ignored the multiple driving infractions, including Sid's expired tag and Saraswati's driving without a license. The officer would have otherwise seemed compassionate toward Siddharth to the casual observer. However, there was something more at play, and only Sid and he knew what that was.

Yes, part of the officer's leniency was due to Sid's publicly operating above board in his business. He also didn't want to fool with arresting a distraught woman in front of her mother and children, all of whom frantically cried as the messy scene unfolded. But an even more compelling issue than those was that the officer, Tommy Ballesteros, was homosexual. He was a decorated police officer, a Vietnam veteran, and a married father of two little girls, but patrolmen Ballesteros also had a boyfriend in New Orleans. And whenever the boyfriend visited, they stayed at The Sunkist Motel with Sid's explicit assurance that they did so in solitude and with the utmost discretion.

Sid was not the type of man to blackmail anyone or turn the screws on them—at least not the wrong ones. He'd never have suggested that the officer was in danger of having his indiscretions revealed. This situation was more of an implied request and a tacit nod of the cap from the officer. Each time something like this happened, Kim Fontenot's words came racing back to Siddharth because they were so hauntingly prophetic. *Look, we all in this together on that strip, man.*

Indeed.

ॐ

All Fardeen wanted to do once he climbed the stairs to the apartment a half-hour later was collapse onto the floor. He didn't even want any of the delicacies he usually enjoyed in Biloxi. But he knew it wouldn't be that simple. He could see that in Siddharth's eyes as his uncle climbed from the sergeant's truck and stared at Saraswati as she unloaded her mother and the children. She was in for it, and there was no getting around it. Fardeen felt so guilty. If he'd just been a little stronger, a better man, then they wouldn't be to this point.

But still, another part of Fardeen blamed Saraswati, just like he blamed his mother when she became unruly with his father. Fardeen's mother, Savitri, was an aberration of traditional Gujarati culture. While she was as decent a woman as any man could want, she also had an indignant stripe that caused her to rebel, particularly against her older brother, Siddharth. She'd been that way ever since she was a little girl. And, over the years, and much to Sid's dismay, his wife slowly became a minion of his sister Savitri's. It wasn't often, and it was never for selfish reasons, but his wife could ignite just as readily as his disobedient sister under the right circumstances.

Tonight, however, Sid was at his limit. Saraswati not only raised her voice to him, but she did it publicly. Then she embarrassed him in front of Biloxi's Police Department. So it was no surprise when Sid slammed the door and charged into the apartment behind the whole disjointed party. He moved so urgently that Fardeen felt he'd better thrust himself between his aunt and uncle.

As his uncle leaned into him, Fardeen could feel the heat coming off of Sid's body and his heart beating in his chest. Then when Saraswati started chattering back, Fardeen became enraged, turning his back on his uncle, still barring him with his arms.

"Be quiet, Mami! Be quiet!!" he hollered, finding the courage to jump into the fray.

"Yes! Yes!! Be quiet!" Bairavi screamed at her daughter. She sat on the couch, holding onto her grandchildren that struggled to get to their momma and protect her.

The night ended with the entire family, including the little ones and Fardeen, hugging each other in the center of the apartment on West Beach Boulevard, every one of them except Sid in tears. It was a watershed moment that needed to happen, though. There'd been such tension from so many different sources that came together all at once. Siddharth, despite outward appearances, was constantly stressed with the balancing act he had to perform among the business, the city, his home life, and his newest love interest, whichever one that might be. Saraswati's anguish fed Off all of Sid's woes, but, in addition, she had to deal with raising their children while taking care of her aging mother. Then there was Fardeen. And Fardeen was overwrought with all the new responsibilities he'd take on after his uncle's tutelage. Fardeen didn't want to disappoint anyone if he could help it. So, perhaps, his burden was the greatest of all.

That night, Fardeen cemented in his mind what became a lifelong obligation to perform a duty to his family. It was a duty to which he'd always rise and never shirk. And that was to shoulder the load like a man and do whatever life required of him to make sure his family was safe.

It would prove to be such a tall order.

CHAPTER SIX

April 17, 1981, Tomahawk, Florida

By the time Fardeen returned to Tomahawk, four months after leaving, his outlook had changed. He viewed the entire world differently, particularly where it intersected with the motel business. He wound up loving it.

He practically ran The Sunkist before he left, tending to every aspect of its daily operations. He helped with the housekeeping, maintained the pool, mowed the grass, and ran the front desk like an ace. He'd also learned to repair dripping faucets, running toilets, and temperamental window air-conditioning units. He could turn a wrench or spackle a hole in the wall better than any maintenance man who shifted from property to property on The Strip, leaving their employer high-and-dry each time. He got to know all the police officers, many of whom were discreet patrons of The Sunkist along with their lady friends. The other regulars all knew him too. Strippers and ladies of the evening, whose patronage Sid limited to a select few, gave him the nickname "Dean," which Fardeen loved. It was so American, like Dean Martin or James Dean. It was also a welcomed surrogate for his real name, which he'd struggled with his entire life.

Fardeen had pictured returning to Biloxi as a chance to goof off like he did the previous summer. But it turned into so much more for the boy. People loved and respected him at The Sunkist, and he'd taken on responsibilities far beyond those of an average kid his age. His Uncle Sid was all too happy to let him, too, as was his Aunt Sara. Fardeen freed Sid up to be home and go out on the town more. So everyone was happy in Biloxi for a time and just as sad to see Fardeen leave.

Devan and Savitri initially intended him to go to Biloxi for just a few weeks. But when they discovered he wasn't allowed to enroll in school without better documentation of his academic background, they allowed him to stay longer. A month turned into two, then three, until it was almost time for another summer season. So it was high time that Fardeen returned to Tomahawk and helped his family. Besides that, Savitri desperately missed her little boy and lay awake each night, wondering what he was doing. She knew her brother wouldn't let anyone harm one hair on the boy's head. But she wanted and needed Fardeen home.

The first thing Fardeen noticed as his sister pulled onto The Seagull property was trash everywhere—at least by his newly-established standard. He saw McDonald's bags and waxed paper cups on the grass, and cigarette butts peppered the asphalt. Suddenly, it was as though his Uncle Sid rode shotgun with him, evaluating the property, hollering into his ear, pointing and holding him accountable for everything wrong.

Fardeen was so disgusted that he didn't even wait for Sridevi to stop before he jumped out of the car and started picking up trash. He hollered back for his older sister to bring him a can from the office while he began picking up all the refuse that looked as though it had accumulated the whole time he was gone. He felt like everyone should've known better than to let the property get this way. So he got a little huffy when his mother came outside to greet him.

Savitri took the sides of his face and kissed Fardeen on the forehead before hugging him close. He was glad to see his mother. And her embrace felt like a panacea for all his ills. But only for a moment. When his sense of duty took over, he gently pushed Savitri away.

"How could we let the property get this way, Mama? What's wrong with you?"

Then, Savitri, who'd endured things with so much more gravity than those he dealt with in Mississippi, became unglued. She slapped the hell out of Fardeen. And when he raised his head back defiantly, she slapped it in the other direction. But Fardeen bit his lower lip and raised his head through tears, indignantly staring back at his mother, breaking her heart when he did. He didn't want to disrespect his mother any more than she wanted to strike him. But he thought he was a man now. And he had to be rebellious, disrespectful, or whatever the business required a man to be.

Watching the whole exchange from a distance, Sridevi raced up carrying a wastepaper basket with a look on her face as though she wanted to tell her younger brother something. She had a lot of things to tell him. But they weren't things she dared mention in front of her mother. Sridevi had three hours to say whatever was on her mind, but she hadn't said a word to Fardeen because she hadn't known how to. She handed him the can and stood back to see what might happen. But all Fardeen did was take it and return to picking up trash.

Sridevi pulled her mother backward as Savitri resisted and continued staring at her baby boy, whom she was now sure that her brother had poisoned. But Sridevi took her mother back to the office while Fardeen continued policing the grounds.

There were some developments over the past few months that Fardeen wasn't aware of because he'd been in Biloxi. The first of those was as tragic as it was unlikely. His father, Devan, started drinking alcohol which he'd never done in Fardeen's life. And he didn't just have a drink or two to take the edge off, although that's how it started. Devan rapidly graduated to drinking all night, sitting behind the front desk as he accommodated the occasional overnight customer before

Savitri relieved him in the mornings. The habit came to Devan fast and snowballed before Savitri realized there was a problem.

It began several months back when a few workmen, regulars at The Seagull, invited Devan for a cold beer in the parking lot. At first, he repeatedly turned down their offer to their loud, tipsy protests.

"Aw, come on, Mr. Patel! Just a coupla' beers! We won't tell the Missus!"

Mr. Patel.

Devan liked that address. It made him feel important for the first time since moving to the U.S. permanently. The men were great customers too. Their company kept The Seagull going during the lean winter months. So Devan appreciated them and their business, too, as they'd sometimes rent up to ten rooms a night.

They were Pennsylvanians whose company contracted with the City of Tomahawk and several other regional municipalities to construct storm drains. They'd previously stayed in Pensacola, but they got priced out of their rooms by the seasonal tourist business over the summer. After that, they moved to another motel a few miles away. But that property catered to an unsavory clientele and was in a horrible, unincorporated area to boot. Their tenure there ended when they came out one morning to find their trucks looted and their machinery vandalized for no other reason than the idiot perpetrators couldn't steal it.

Their outraged foreman, Chip Calvin, pulled into an empty Seagull parking lot one Sunday evening. He came into the office, removed his cap, and addressed Savitri respectfully, asking to speak to the manager. Looking on from the couch a few feet away, Devan was instantly impressed by the young foreman. He rose and walked over, introducing himself as the owner. Chip presented his case, telling Devan the most important thing to him was his men's safety, the safety of their equipment, and the continued assurance that they wouldn't get kicked out because of rate hikes during busier times.

After talking at length with Chip, Devan called Siddharth in Biloxi, explaining the circumstances. Once Sid stopped cussing him out because of the reversed charges for the call, he still didn't give the answer Devan wanted to hear.

"Just tell them you will do whatever they want. We can always increase their rates once they're in-house and they've moved their equipment there. But don't guarantee rates, no matter what you do!"

Devan felt like Chip could tell everything being said by his expressions as his brother-in-law barked through the phone. But after hanging up, Devan rebelled, going his own way, and he provided Chip the guaranteed rates he wanted. He'd stand by that guarantee too.

The following Saturday morning, a group of trucks pulled onto the property, hauling heavy machinery as handsome young American men in flashy white shirts and blue jeans darted around, shouting directives as their trailers backed into the parking lot. It felt like such a coup to Devan. He'd negotiated this business, and it was based entirely on his efforts.

They were also excellent and courteous guests. They brought life to the formerly dead property, moving in and out of the office to get change for the Coke machine while stopping to talk to Devan and Savitri when they did. Sometimes they'd keep Savitri company by playing backgammon with each other in the office or just standing at the counter talking to her. They were all so young and came to view her as a mother because they were so far from home, just as she was.

She sometimes threw their laundry in with the linens, folding it neatly out of the dryer and putting it in their rooms before they returned in the evenings. They even passed a hat around at work one day to collect money to buy a birthday present for Anaya, Devan and Savitri's youngest. They got her a Betty Crocker Easy-Bake Oven from the K-Mart in Pensacola and a birthday cake from J's Bakery. And it was quite the scene when they all stood in the office, a bunch of roughneck Pennsylvania boys singing "Happy Birthday" to the little Indian girl as she blushed, hiding behind her mother's sari.

After that, Devan couldn't help but honor their daily request for his company in the parking lot. He found himself hunched over the bed of Chip's pickup every night, sucking down beers and laughing at the stories they all told, although he didn't understand most of them. Still, it made him feel included. At first, he faked drinking the beer because the taste was so bad to him. But he eventually started swallowing it because they'd notice him nursing the same can for a couple of hours without grabbing another one. Devan couldn't stand the idea of losing face in front of his newfound friends, so he got to where he gulped beer down as fast as the rest of them.

They took to calling him and Savitri "Mr. P" and "Mrs. P" and did things like sweeping up their cigarette butts from the parking lot and bringing their dirty sheets and pillowcases to the office at Chip's insistence. That cut housekeeping time nearly in half.

Yes, they were pretty good guys. And both Savitri and Devan cared a great deal for all of them.

So when Michael Santucci pulled into the parking lot before noon one day, weeping and driving Chip's prized possession, his 1976 F-150, Devan raced from the office to see what was wrong.

Michael, or "Mikey," as everyone called him, could hardly speak because he cried so hard. He sat, repeatedly shaking his head before he began banging it on the steering wheel, honking the horn each time.

Devan reached into the driver's side window, turned the truck off, pulled the keys out, and put them in his pocket. Then he opened the door, gathered the young man into his arms, and guided him toward the office, signaling Sridevi and Savitri to help him console the boy.

Once they got the nineteen-year-old tradesman to the couch in The Seagull's office, he had such a gruesome tale to tell.

Chip Calvin was dead.

A couple of hours earlier, as he guided a culvert into a roadside ditch from above, the straps holding it broke, and the two-ton piece of concrete crushed Chip. But it wasn't as easy as all that. Chip was alive for a good while, at first flexing and releasing the fingers of his protruding hand as a signal to that effect. And all the men gathered around hollering at Chip, telling him to hold on and that they'd get him out, even though they knew he couldn't hear them. Mikey dove into the muddy bog where the culvert fell and took hold of Chip's hand, gently squeezing it and stroking his forearm.

But the boys were on a county road in the middle of nowhere, and by the time Jared Kowalczyk got back with the dozer, which may or may not have even made a difference, Chip's hand signals had ceased. They all looked on as his flexion slowed, then stopped altogether in the grasp of Mikey's hand.

Chip was probably better off considering the condition they found him once they got the culvert off of him. But it hurt like hell to see Chip that way and to realize that he was gone.

It was the worst thing Devan, a tender-hearted soul, had ever experienced. And it hardened him. He couldn't imagine his friend, Chip, lying beneath that concrete pipe for so long, unable to breathe with his face crushed in a way Mikey described to be so horrible. It tore Devan apart. It was just too much. He'd broken bread with this man who had honored his wife and children. Chip was so young, so good-looking, and kind. Worse still was that he was a family man. He kept a Polaroid of his wife by his bed and one of his little boys who looked just like him.

In the days following, things only got worse. Polar

Construction, the outfit from Bethlehem, Pennsylvania, that hired all the men, pulled out of Florida. The crew shut down, picked up, and hauled everything out of Tomahawk to move to Louisiana, presumably never returning. The implications, both emotionally and financially, were devastating for the Patels.

Devan and Savitri stood in the parking lot as the young men loaded their trucks and trailers before heading West. All the boys formed a line to say goodbye to the Patels before they went, many of them crying as they hugged Savitri, Sridevi, and Anaya, before shaking hands with Devan.

A few days after that, Arkland Polar, the company's president, also a very young man, came and settled his father's company's bill with The Seagull. As he spoke with Devan and Savitri at the counter, he said he was concerned about getting sued by the Calvin family. Neither Devan nor Savitri knew what he was talking about as he rambled, so Arkland was confused at the end of his rant when Devan said, "That's good. I hope Sir Chip's wife is taken care of."

Once the boys from Polar were gone, Devan and Savitri's lives returned to a lonesome existence. They missed all those boys buzzing around the office, bickering over backgammon stakes to the verge of fisticuffs before Savitri intervened and settled them down. It was sad to remember them throwing a football in the parking lot, and they both longed for the Saturdays when the crews split up into teams and played sandlot football next to the motel. They even recruited Devan a couple of times as a "receiver." They always told him to go long, never intending to throw the ball to him. That was a mercifully good thing.

For the first time, the Patels felt the sting that accompanied small motel ownership due to the human factor. It was difficult to provide shelter for other people on an ongoing basis without becoming attached to them, particularly as young as the boys from Polar were.

Yet it was the inevitable nature of the business they'd chosen.

Then to have one of those people die while in their care, even if it had nothing to do with them, was overwhelming to the young Indian couple. But they couldn't help being as sorrowful as they were, and they would miss Chip forever, particularly Devan.

After Polar left, Devan descended into a funk of resentment and self-pity, questioning every decision he'd made that brought him to Tomahawk and the misery he felt as a result. As a pathetic tribute, Devan carried a lawn chair each evening to the parking space where he used to stand around Chip's truck with the other men, laughing and cutting up, and he drank beer after beer until he had to relieve Savitri at the desk. He missed their companionship and how they made him feel as much as he did Chip. The financial destitution their leaving brought was just an excruciating bonus.

All these things were nothing Fardeen could have known when he returned to Tomahawk. He left as a hesitant and sheepish boy but returned from Biloxi as a man, or so he believed. And he'd expected everyone to greet him that way instead of the sad, distant way everyone acted. His father didn't even bother coming out to greet him as his mother did. Sridevi scarcely spoke to him on the way home apart from asking him if he needed her to pull into the rest stop at Alabama and then again at Florida.

Of course, he'd find out about everything that had happened within a few days of returning. And by that time, Devan's drinking, fortunately, corrected itself. Devan couldn't allow his boy to see him the way he was, so he kept his distance for the first several days after Fardeen came home.

But there was another bit of news that Fardeen wasn't aware of yet. It was something that already shocked the rest of the Tomahawk Patels, none of whom were sure how to react. And that was that Fardeen was going to be a big brother. Savitri was unexpectedly pregnant. So it was time, Devan felt, to get his house in order and make things right again, and the baby was a clarification of that fact. He didn't want to allow his stress and grief to overtake him. He was Gujarati and a Patel. And he was raised better than that.

Fardeen was surprised when they gave him the news over dinner that week. He hugged his parents and told them how happy he was. And he said he hoped he would have a little brother. He heard Sridevi's faint harrumph over his shoulder when he said that to his parents. Yet, he was so happy from the news that he turned and hugged both Sridevi and his little sister, Anaya.

It was a happy day for the Patel family.

CHAPTER SEVEN

Tuesday, August 11, 1980

Between the summer he spent in Biloxi, and when the family permanently settled in Tomahawk, Devan accompanied Siddharth to Atlanta for a hotel and motel owners' convention. Sid was, of course, a braggart for the duration. He flashed money and talked loudly in the hotel lounge, insisting that Devan join him and his cronies for one toast or another.

But that wasn't like Devan at all. Nor was Devan interested in the scores of strippers and escorts that flocked to the lounge after hours. They all looked painted and cheap to him, and it made him ill to watch them cozy up to almost every man sitting at the bar. Devan wanted to be with his wife. And he counted the hours until they'd be together again.

As much as he wanted to fit in with everyone at the conference, Devan felt out of place for several reasons. But he was also concerned about his family's history. So, just as he'd done for the past decade, he decided to forgo the name "Patel." Instead, he identified himself as Devan "Kothari," his mother's maiden name. Given the Patel name's prominence in Gujarat, he realized there'd be a slew of them at the convention. If he'd said he was a Patel, he knew the subject would invariably come up about who his parents were. Where were they from in Gujarat? Do you know this Patel or that Patel?

He feared he'd face the same obstacles in America as in Ahmedabad once they figured out precisely which Patel family he came from. And he didn't need all that baggage. He wanted to start afresh.

Devan entered the motel business because Siddharth lured him into it. Siddharth was an erstwhile thug from Ahmedabad who'd come to America and done very well for himself. As the global economy hurtled toward recession, Devan became intrigued by his brother-in-law's purported success. His shoe sales leveled off. Then when they trended downward, he knew he had to do something.

He wanted more for his children, particularly his only son. He wanted Fardeen to be a professional man in The United States, like a doctor or a banker. And he was content to toil in the hospitality industry to provide such opportunities for him. He'd never have accompanied Sid to Atlanta if he weren't serious about coming to America permanently.

Devan wasn't merely bored at the conference. He was also disgusted. His brother-in-law's affiliations repulsed him. The men were loud and crude, and they talked over one another. But perhaps the most detestable thing about them was that they all appeared to look to Siddharth for his approval each time they spoke of business or even told a joke. They were a bunch of lackeys, and to Devan, being beholden or subservient to Siddharth told him everything he needed to know about the kind of men they were.

To hear Siddharth tell it, many of the men were wealthy Americans, but Devan couldn't imagine that based on their behavior. Sid was never particular about whom he kept time with in the past, and this outing appeared to be no different. The men he cavorted with were loud and stormed the elevators en masse as they pushed past ordinary tourists and hotel patrons, some of them being women and the elderly. They lingered in the lounge from when it opened right after lunch until it closed. And they shouted at the wait-staff when they didn't find things to their liking. They were exceedingly profane and abrasive, and instead of walking to the nearest trash bin, they threw their cups, cigarette butts, and whatever refuse they held at the time onto the ground. They were an awful lot and didn't seem to care how they behaved or whom they offended as they went.

Some of the men who got drunk enough in the lounge that night began speaking in Urdu, which puzzled Devan. Urdu was the native language of Pakistan, and it was also native to Jammu and Kashmir. It seemed like such an odd sampling of men. Siddharth was originally from Srinagar, the summer capital of Jammu and Kashmir, but he spent much of his rearing in Ahmedabad. And Devan had only ever known him to speak Gujarati, although his accent was peculiar. But he spouted off in Urdu as though he was one of them as the night carried on.

The prospect of being indebted to Siddharth for the rest of his life nauseated Devan. Siddharth wasn't ever anything but a hooligan, and so far as Devan could tell, not much had changed.

But, as all loving parents do, Devan was willing to endure whatever was necessary so that he could provide for his family, at least as well as he had in Ahmedabad. But he hoped his children might have better opportunities than in India. He was locked in now. He'd sold his shoe store and his parent's villa in Ahmedabad. Savitri and the kids stayed in London with her Uncle Vajra and his family, waiting to rejoin him. So he'd better make the best of it, whatever "it" was to be.

Devan wandered out of the lounge when none of the other men were looking and sat down in the sprawling lobby whose ceiling extended fifty feet overhead toward skylights. The seating was a molded plastic round with a planter in the center, and it held a variety of tropicals, succulents, and flowers. It was unimaginably beautiful to the young, impressionable Gujarati, just like the rest of the hotel's décor and accommodations were,

Devan sat, thinking about his son. Fardeen would've loved the trip as he was a zealot for anything American, and this hotel was a shimmering example of all its excesses and extravagance. Fardeen was overjoyed when he learned the family might move to The United States. Every day, he'd ask his parents if they'd reached a decision or gotten any more news from his Uncle Siddharth. Devan hated to admit it, but Fardeen resembled the imbecile sitting a dozen yards away in the bar. Fardeen even moved like Siddharth, raising his hands and gesturing wildly at times. It was strangely endearing to him. But he prayed their similarities ended there.

As Devan grappled with his station in life and all that faced him, an older man moseyed up, leaning on a cane before plopping down in the space next to him. He sat so close that Devan thought of asking the man to inch over a bit. But then he thought better of it. So he just sat, staring back at his idiot brother-in-law through the French doors leading into the lounge as Siddharth raised his glass and made his sixth or seventh toast. Devan lost count by this time.

The man interrupted his concentration when he spoke to Devan.

"What is your name, sir?" the old white-haired man asked in English with a British accent, "Where are you from?"

He caught Devan off-guard.

"Me? Are you speaking to me, sir?"

The man laughed and said, "Yes. Yes, son. I'm talking to you."

Devan stared at the man, wondering if he might be some sort of a spy sent by Siddharth to test him. That would've been so typical of his brother-in-law. Or maybe the man was snooping of his own accord, trying to discover more about Siddharth's business. Siddharth instructed Devan not to visit with anyone unless he was present—especially if they were Gujarati.

As he studied the man who either didn't or couldn't stare back at him directly because he had a cataract in his left eye, Devan believed he was harmless, so he answered. But he dangled a pointed suggestion at the end of his response.

"My name is Kothari, sir. Devan Kothari. And I'm from Gujarat. Just like you, I guess."

"How'd you guess?" the man asked in Gujarati before they both laughed for several moments.

When their laughter died, the man said, "Kothari," very slowly. "hmm. So, tell me. Are you one of Siddharth's people?"

Devan paused before he answered. Siddharth's people? Siddharth, the idiot? Siddharth, the individualist? Siddharth, the egomaniac? How was it that Siddharth even had "people" at all?

Then reality sank in, and he had to answer the man honestly. Yes, if he was going to bring his family to the United States, he was indeed one of Siddharth's people. But that characterization was more offensive than if the man had walked up and pissed in his face.

"Yes, sir. I work for Siddharth," Devan said coolly.

The man nodded several times, looked away, and then motioned to a waitress who moved across the lobby with a tray of different cocktails from the restaurant destined for the lounge because it was running low on booze. Then, taking two flared pint glasses from the server, he presented one to Devan as he slid a twenty-dollar bill onto her tray.

"Oh, Mr. Patel! Thank you, sir! That's so generous!" the young lady said before disappearing into the lounge.

"Sir, sir," Devan begged. "I don't drink, sir."

The old guy turned up the oversized Manhattan as though he were drinking water, sucked down the entire cocktail, exhaled, and looked at Devan.

"Oh, you will, though. Of course, you will," the old man said.

Devan lowered the glass to his lap in defiance of the man. Who in the hell did he think he was? Devan didn't give a damn if he was Gujarati or not. How dare he make presumptions about his character, let alone in the proximity of Siddharth, who Devan began to despise more and more?

"And your name, sir?" Devan asked.

The man belched before continuing, which put Devan off even more. Devan had thought he might be a Londoner based on his accent. But clearly, he was uncivilized.

"I'm Rudra. Rudra Patel," he said as he held out his hand and shook Devan's.

"You're the one with The Albatross, aren't you? The property you named after a bird?" the old man said, snickering and rudely pointing toward Devan with a crooked finger.

Devan set his glass down and shot up from his seat in a white-hot flash of rage and said, "It will be The Seagull, you old bastard! My property is The Seagull! Why don't you get up off your ass and go back to whatever farm you came from, field hand?"

Devan didn't know why he reacted that way so rapidly. Maybe it was all the pressure he was under, combined with being so uncomfortable at the conference and missing his family. Devan was about to apologize for his outburst before the man began speaking again.

Rudra chuckled and struggled to stand before falling back into his seat, continuing to laugh. Then he leaned onto his cane and looked back at Devan.

"Oh," he coughed, "you're Ajai's boy, aren't you? I knew it! And if I were you, I suppose I'd feel the same way!"

Devan was stunned. How did this old crusty rat know his father's name? Moreover, how did he know who Devan was? And just what was the man's suggestion about his father supposed to mean? Then he figured the man was just what he suspected at the outset. Either he was another crony of Siddharth's, or a nosy old bird, trying to poke his beak into someone else's business.

Devan reached into his pocket, peeled a few one-dollar bills away from the roll, and threw them at the man's feet. He wasn't about to get humiliated by some low-life from Bombay State buying his drink.

He turned around and stormed off toward the elevators as the man quietly laughed.

Devan couldn't sleep that night because he shared a room with Siddharth, whose snoring was otherworldly. But he also couldn't stop thinking about the man in the lobby earlier that evening. He hated to consider it, but he knew well why the man said what he did about him and his father.

It was because Devan, in a rare expression of anger, behaved just like Ajai, even though he was nothing like him. Still, the way the man spoke to him suggested he knew that Devan was in the midst of hard times and had fallen from grace. And it infuriated and embarrassed him. He concluded the man must've been Siddharth's ally. How else could he have known so much about his family and motel?

Devan's father, Ajai Patel, was a successful tobacco farmer from Kheda, Gujarat, with a legendary temper. Unlike his slight, intellectual son, Ajai was a large man, six-foot-five, with a hulking frame, and he was also apt to go off when he felt like someone wasn't listening to him or when things moved beyond his control. He served as a Gujarati farmers' trade association president and exploded during meetings when the chatter got too loud as he spoke. That happened at every session too.

People were afraid of Ajai Patel. When his booming voice echoed across the meeting room, every man there stopped talking.

But the most profound and tragic instance of Ajai's temper was when he got into a fight with one of his workers.

Because of its expansive borders with other nations and an absence of a formal immigration policy, India was a haven for minority groups who fled to it for sundry reasons. Of all Southeast Asian nations, India hosted more of such groups than any other. Nationalists seeking asylum from religious and ethnic persecution and those coming for economic reasons were the most significant component of that Indian demographic. Some crossed the border daily and performed farm work and other menial tasks, while others came to India to remain there permanently.

Even though Gujarat didn't share a border with any regional nations like Pakistan, East Pakistan, Bhutan, or Nepal, it still had its share of migrants, primarily incentivized by better wages.

Ajai didn't pay much attention to the reasons for those that made it as far as Gujarat. Instead, he viewed them all as indigent, low-cost sources of labor. And compared to the treatment they received in other places—including their home countries—Ajai's was relatively good. He built places for them to live on his plantation, paid them what he considered a fair wage, and never asked many questions about why they were there or from where they came. He honestly didn't care.

But when he caught one of the workers asleep on a tractor one day. Ajai lost control.

He insulted him in the most humiliating manner until the man had no choice but to engage Ajai. Any man would have done the same thing in the face of Ajai's words because they were so harsh and demeaning. But during the ensuing struggle, Ajai beat the migrant to death, repeatedly smashing his head into the tractor's engine until he was unrecognizable as being human. Ajai had brained him. The man's wife and children raced across a tobacco field, screaming from a distance. But by the time they got there, blood gushed from several wounds in what used to be the man's head, and he lay lifeless in the grass.

That's how the *Gujarat Samachar* described the altercation.

And Ajai got arrested after the AP wire picked up the article. The headline read, "CRAZED TOBACCO PLANTATION OWNER BRUTALLY KILLS DEFENSELESS REFUGEE!"

On assignment in Ahmedabad, a British journalist penned the story, which was none-too-friendly to Ajai or the tobacco industry. He used the incident to segue into the plight of refugee minority groups, using Ajai's indiscretion as a jumping-off point. The story circulated in every major newspaper in the civilized world, and the resulting outcry was ruinous for Ajai's family.

First, Lorillard Tobacco Company canceled its supply contract with the hapless farmer. Then Phillip Morris International and, finally, British American Tobacco followed suit. While India accounted for less than 10% of each company's tobacco imports, and Ajai's farm produced a measly portion of that, the financial implications of his actions were potentially devastating for the corporations. So they immediately severed ties with Ajai Patel.

Had it not been for an idealistic young Saudi that ironically wanted to distance himself from the evils of the oil industry by moving into tobacco, Ajai would've been out on the street. Consequently, after many negotiations, the Saudi paid Ajai a fraction of his tobacco plantation's valuation from just a year earlier. And sadly, Ajai was happy to get it.

As Devan moved into the breakfast area of the dining hall designated for members of what would become the Asian Property Owners' Association or APOA, followed by Rudra Patel and a huge white man, he felt uncomfortable. The men seemed to keep time with every move he made and everything he did that morning.

He'd run into Rudra and the man on the elevator first thing. And though he told himself he was just paranoid, Devan couldn't help but feel like Rudra engineered their crossing paths rather than it being happenstance. He pictured him on one of those walkie-talkies like Sid used, getting signaled once he left his room.

Rudra had a *Wall Street Journal* folded under his arm, and he was already smiling when the elevator doors opened. He bellowed, "Kothari! Good morning!" as Devan stepped on board.

Despite Rudra Patel's constant attempts at striking up a conversation on the elevator ride down, Devan spoke very little, and he quickly stepped out and walked to the front desk when it reached the first floor. At Siddharth's insistence, Devan agreed to pay for their room nights, and since this was the last day of the conference, Devan wanted to settle his bill immediately. He couldn't wait to get on the plane and leave Atlanta that night.

But just as the girl behind the front desk placed his portfolio on the counter, a wrinkled hand dropped a gold American Express card on top of it. Then another one grabbed Devan's hand, which held his wallet. It was Rudra Patel.

"Please, Miss Washington, charge Mr. Kothari's and his companion's expenses to my card."

"Absolutely, Mr. Patel," the pretty young black girl said, smiling.

When Devan started to protest, Rudra interrupted him.

"Ah. Please, Mr. Kothari. It is a business deduction for me. And I know how expensive this trip must be for you," he said politely.

"And knowing Siddharth as I do, he's having you pay for it all, isn't he?"

"But," Devan started.

"Ah. Please, please, Mr. Kothari. Please allow me to do this. My sole request is that you inform Siddharth that I did it, but only after you are back in Alabama," Rudra said.

That puzzled Devan. It made him reconsider what he'd thought about Rudra before. Devan couldn't imagine why, but the man acted as though he wanted to stick it to Siddharth. It made Devan feel like the man sought to restore some of Devan's dignity while simultaneously demoting Siddharth and his ego. Whatever the case, Devan knew it would infuriate Siddharth, and privately, that made Devan very happy. Rudra chuckled as he saw Devan's expression, and then Devan felt like the old man could read his mind.

"Mississippi," Devan said.

"Sir?" Rudra asked.

"I'm going back to Mississippi with Siddharth. I have no business in Alabama. And my property will be in Florida."

"Oh, yes, of course," Rudra said, before laughing and saying, "but the Americans have an expression. Six of one, half a dozen of the other!"

Then Rudra started laughing again until he coughed uncontrollably. When Devan was sure he wouldn't cough up a lung, he politely nodded and walked toward the dining area.

Sid, who'd slept like a baby, beat Devan downstairs that morning, and Devan was eager to reconnect with him. Devan got up as early as Siddharth, but Sid still made it out the door first because he liked to take the stairs. Siddharth was terrified of elevators. But he pretended he thought stairs were healthier than gliding up and down in an elevator like a lazy American.

Rudra and the man with him stayed back while he signed his credit card receipt. But then they started following Devan again, catching up to him as he entered the breakfast line. As much as Devan appreciated Rudra's generosity, he was beginning to annoy him. Why was this man so focused on him? What did he want?

Losing patience halfway down the buffet, Devan twisted around and addressed the giant redneck standing behind him.

He prayed he wouldn't beat the hell out of him, but he'd had enough.

"I'm thinking of having pineapple with my eggs? How does that sit with you, Popeye?!"

Just as soon as the words left his mouth, Devan regretted them. Popeye? Really? But that was the only image he could gather in his brain. And as the giant man looked back at Rudra in confusion, another suggestion came to Devan. Hulk. The Hulk. That's what he should've called the man. Not Popeye. Damnit.

As Devan entered the dining area, he only saw black hair, pastel shirts, and gray or khaki slacks. And it made him feel so uneasy, based on his previous experiences at venues like this. According to Siddharth, the Americans were insufferable liars and usually had underlying motives for everything they did. But in Devan's limited experience, Americans were affable and courteous if you caught them in a group setting. And they didn't seem to want anything from one another.

But if you got a bunch of Indian moteliers and hoteliers gathered in the same place, it was one giant gripe session, and you'd better batten down the hatches. They had more complaints than anyone and demanded restitution on the spot. That was especially true for the crews his brother-in-law ran with at these meetings. His associates were the loudest, most aggressive, and unyielding kinds of men. Despite what Siddharth told him about them, Devan wondered how many of them even owned properties. He envisioned them merely being Siddharth's or someone else's puppets, and it troubled him to consider that he was just before being among that number.

Devan attended four such meetings over the previous eighteen months—three of them before his family permanently left Gujarat, then this being the fourth. At each meeting, it seemed like the Indian presence grew more prominent. Because this was exclusively a group of "Asian" property owners, there was nothing *but* attendees from the subcontinent. And most of them were Gujaratis. But Siddharth seemed to keep his distance from that segment of them.

"Brother!" Devan heard over the din of the crowd.

After looking around, he caught sight of Sid motioning him toward the seat next to him at a table full of men, who already seemed to bicker with each other. Just as he moved that way, though, Devan felt a hand touch his shoulder, and he turned around to see Rudra Patel smiling at him, holding a plate full of sliced pineapple, orange slices, and strawberries.

"I'd be honored if you'd sit with me at my table, Mr. Kothari," Rudra said, "I'm not here with any other hotel men, and I don't know as many gentlemen here as your brother-in-law does. But I'd welcome your company."

Devan looked back toward Sid, whose expression slowly changed as he lowered his arm. He went from smiling and waving to looking very concerned. By the time he rested his hand on the table, he had looked angry. That was all Devan needed to see.

"And I'd be honored to join you, Mr. Patel," Devan said to Rudra, who glowed at his response.

The big goon took ahold of Rudra's arm and walked toward an almost empty table in the center of the room. The only person seated there was also the only woman in the room. She was a beautiful older lady but still several years younger than Rudra. Devan felt like she must've been Rudra's wife.

"This is my wife, Pooja," Rudra said as the large man pulled his chair out for him and rested his plate on the table.

The woman rose and said, "It's nice to meet you, Mr. Kothari."

Again. What was with these people? Devan felt like he must've been the topic of conversation the night before in Rudra's room, but he couldn't figure out why. That is until Rudra started talking to him again. With his first words, Devan realized he'd heard him right the night before, and this man knew who he was precisely

"I knew Ajai," Rudra said, just as Devan put a piece of papaya in his mouth. He stopped chewing and looked across the table at Rudra, who laughed.

"We are friends!" he said, "We are good friends! Well, we used to be good friends, Mr. Kothari."

Once Rudra confirmed he knew Ajai, Devan realized he'd only toyed with him thus far. If he knew Ajai and that Devan was his son, he knew Devan's real surname was also Patel. And apart from Siddharth and his cronies, so were most others' attending the conference.

Devan's father, Ajai, died several years before. It was a painful remembrance for Devan. Because when Ajai died, he and Devan had been estranged somewhat. All the disgrace and upheaval his family experienced because of Ajai's temper, Devan had placed squarely on his father's shoulders. It challenged everything about his upbringing. Who he was. What his purpose in life was. It was all overwhelming to a nineteen-year-old Devan Patel when it occurred. Consequently, due to the public shame of losing nearly everything, Devan changed his name from Patel to Kothari, his mother's maiden name. He wanted no association with his father any longer.

"He was very successful! A very good businessman! He was very prosperous, and he made a lot of money!" Rudra continued.

Devan never cared about materialism. And he thought many of his fellow Gujaratis misinterpreted what The Vedas or Hindu scriptures described as prosperity. Devan interpreted prosperity as a willful exchange of one's energy for money. But Devan believed that one should, in turn, use that money for the greater good and the benefit of many.

Yet he felt that somehow that ideology became perverted along the way within American culture. Instead of reinvesting in their people, many American Gujaratis opted to buy expensive cars and opulent homes. Gujarati men preferred big, roomy American cars, like Lincolns and Cadillacs, with giant leather seats and frigid air streaming from several directions into the cabins of their land barges.

Once they reached a certain level of success, their wives refused to have anything less than a Mercedes-Benz, scoffing at the very idea of driving a Volvo or an Audi. Then, their children —particularly the boys—drove Porsches and BMWs. And it seemed the more successful their families became, the more the young men's predilections bent toward Lamborghinis, Ferraris, and Maseratis.

It was so curious to Americans within the communities where the Indians settled. They watched the sons of the lowly Indian family that moved into town a few years before who owned that little motel by the Interstate as they pulled alongside them at the pump and gassed up their exotic, European sports cars. The American men often had subscriptions to Motor Trend. So they knew that car sitting at the pump next to them was worth more than their house.

What they didn't know, though, was that the poor little Indian family had fourteen other properties just like the one they owned in their town, most of which they paid for in cash, just as they did everything else.

Devan's life experience, albeit in India up to this point, wasn't much different, and at times he felt hypocritical about it because of how his parents brought him up. They had a lovely plantation home in Kheda and villas in Ahmedabad and Surat. But even those didn't rival the vulgar displays of wealth he'd seen on his American outings thus far.

One Gujarati lived on an island that had its own lighthouse. He also owned the biggest boat Devan had ever seen. Another one had a helicopter pad in the backyard of his palatial Sandy Springs home. He used it, he told Siddharth and Devan in the bar, to go to his "many properties in Georgia."

Devan looked down. He realized this man knew a lot more than he let on. But he wasn't about to act spoiled and leave the table to join Siddharth yet. So rather than acknowledge everything Rudra said, Devan decided to act aloof.

"Please, Mr. Patel. My name is Devan. Call me Devan, sir," he replied.

"And you call me Rudy, alright? My name is Rudra Patel, but please call me Rudy," Rudra said.

"Yes, sir," Devan replied.

Everyone returned to eating after that, saying little. Devan didn't know what to say next because he grew tired of hashing out and reliving his father's crime to people over the years. It was another reason he was in America now. Every defense he offered in the past always seemed ludicrous and hollow anyway.

There was no escaping the truth once you boiled it down to its rudiments. His father, a wealthy plantation owner, beat a lowly man to death within a hundred yards of the man's family. The man's children and wife watched as the husband and father breathed his last breath. And as a result, Devan's family lost everything. No matter how you wanted to frame it after that, it was just noise. The truth was the truth, and in this instance, it was horrific. It was embarrassing, it was shameful, and it was painful.

After a prolonged silence, Rudy was the one who finally spoke up. It was as though he knew what ailed Devan. Devan felt like the man might understand everything, especially if he knew his father, as he claimed.

"Devan, I'd like to apologize for my behavior yesterday. It was untoward and rude. But I meant nothing by it. I only wanted you to realize that I knew who you were. I wanted you to know that we are the same. But we didn't get that far, did we?" Rudy asked.

After thinking a moment, Devan responded.

"No, sir. We didn't. And I'd like to apologize as well. I was disrespectful, so please accept my apologies, Rudy," Devan said.

"Oh, nonsense," Rudy said, "you weren't any more impolite than anyone would've been with some old man getting into their business. I'd say you were quite mannerly under the circumstances. Sometimes I forget myself, Devan. And Pooja isn't always there to shut me up, so I have Mr. Herndon accompany me in most places. It's just in case I let my mouth overload my backside!"

Rudy laughed and gestured toward the brute sitting next to him, who scarfed down country ham, sausage patties, and biscuits as fast as he could raise them to his face. He wiped his mouth and hand in his napkin and presented it to Devan, saying, "Jimmy Herndon, Mr. Ko-thar-uh. Pleased to meet you."

Devan shook Jimmy's hand, then stared across the room at Siddharth's table. Everyone seated there was loud relative to the tables around them. They shouted at one another, pointing at times, then laughing at others, but they all seemed ingrained in whatever discussion took place among them. That is, everyone except one person. Siddharth looked back at Devan with the same expression he did earlier. It was apparent that something bothered him about Rudra Patel. Being the ever-curious soul he was, Devan wanted to find out what that was. So as Siddharth raised his glass of orange juice to his mouth, still staring back at him, Devan continued his discussion with Rudy.

"You said you knew my father, Rudy. How did you know him?" he asked as he chewed on his papaya.

"Oh. Well. That's a very long, interesting story, Devan," Rudy said, "Your father and I moved in many of the same circles back then."

Devan was quiet a second before saying, "I see."

He wasn't listening to Rudra because he was so distracted by Siddharth. Rudra could've told him he won the Nobel Prize for Chemistry, and Devan would've given him the same response.

But when Rudra went on, Devan became more attentive.

"Devan, what happened to your father and your family was his fault. But his biggest mistake was showing compassion to those Muslim infiltrators. He gave them work when they wandered around aimlessly in Ahmedabad before. He gave them a place to live on your family's plantation. He paid for their children's medical care and treated them as his equals. And that, Devan, was his undoing. I imagine you even grew close to some of them, didn't you? You're kind like your father," Rudy said.

Devan looked back toward Siddharth's table. He saw Siddharth still staring at him, and he never stopped looking back as he pulled a pack of cigarettes from his front pocket and lit one. He watched Devan the whole time.

"No," Devan said, "I wasn't close to any of them. But perhaps I should've been, Rudy. Maybe if I'd treated them more like fellow men, and maybe if my father had been more egalitarian, things might not have happened the way they did."

Devan could feel himself growing emotional and was just before getting up from the table and walking away before Rudy spoke again.

"Balderdash!" Rudy said, "That's absurd! I assure you, Devan, your father did more for those people than their parents did for them wherever they came from! He did more for them a thousand times over! He was attacked! And he defended himself, just as any man would have!"

Devan just couldn't catch a break today. He didn't want to talk about his father anymore. He didn't want to talk about Kheda or Ahmedabad, or Gujarat. All he wanted to do was go home. But Rudy continued.

"Devan. I'm sorry. I'm sorry for what happened to your family too. Ajai was acquitted. And the infiltrator's wife got a huge payoff from the tobacco giants so she could raise her mongrels better than they ever would have lived if they hadn't worked for

Ajai Patel! Ow!"

It was apparent that Pooja kicked Rudy under the table. Devan started laughing, followed by Rudy and his big bodyguard, who'd probably watched Pooja kick Rudy dozens of times in the past.

Devan looked back at Siddharth's table again, and his expression had grown from angry to unadulterated rage while watching them laugh. So, Devan stayed steady at the wheel. But he cheerfully redirected the discussion.

"You speak English with a British accent, Rudy," Devan said, "you speak so well. You speak beautifully. It seems native to you."

Devan knew that successful Gujarati men of Rudy's stature couldn't wait to talk about themselves. He probably had a very successful property in America, if not two or three. So he sat back and waited for Rudy to respond. And Rudy obliged.

"Oh! Oh! That's another long story! My first job was with the British High Commission, and," Rudy began.

But his words disappeared into the background noise as Devan cut his eyes over to Siddharth's table again, just as Rudy's gazed upward toward the skylights and his ego took over.

If Siddharth's eyes had shot sunlight, they would've burned a hole in the side of Devan's head. And if they'd reflected his rage, it would've sizzled straight out of the other side of it.

CHAPTER EIGHT

T he rest of the morning progressed just as Devan envisioned once he went to the hotel's conference center—again with Rudy.

All the speakers were young white men representing the various companies that serviced the hospitality industry. American Foods, Beverly Laundry & Linen, Universal Cable, and Fremont Air Conditioning had representatives. And every last one of them metaphorically got the shit beaten out of them on stage. Indian motel owners shouted out individual problems they experienced, demanding satisfaction. It was chaos. None of the representatives were older than twenty-four, so they cowered, balked, and one even became belligerent, hollering in his Georgia accent, "Well, if you'd just let me finish a Goddamned sentence!"

He was the only one who earned any respect as the crowd laughed, rose to their feet, applauded, and allowed him to continue.

But Devan was nauseated the entire time as Rudy and everyone else laughed. Devan was an intellectual and preferred reading rather than being lectured to. He was excited about being in America because it was home to so many great authors, such as Faulkner, Welty, Steinbeck, and his favorite, Hemingway. He'd much rather have been touring Rowan Oak or slogging his feet through the same wet sands Hemingway once did in Key West. His conception of America, albeit romantic, had nothing to do with dissecting the hospitality industry's innards.

He always had a book in his hand and liked to write in his journal. In it, he documented everything that happened to him each day. People he'd met. Places he'd gone to for the first time. He spent at least an hour a day logging these things. Except he didn't do that during this trip. He'd tried, but on the first night in Atlanta, just as he finished the first paragraph, a nosy Siddharth startled him as he looked over his shoulder.

"Why are you writing my name in a book?" Siddharth asked, causing Devan to fumble with his pen several times before resting it on the room's corner table.

"It's nothing," he told Sid, "nothing. I'm just writing in my journal about everything that happened today."

"Then you won't mind if I read it, will you?" Siddharth asked daringly.

"You can't read my journal, Siddharth! These are my private thoughts! I write about everyone I know in here!" Devan said.

"Why? Why do you do this?" Siddharth asked.

"Why? I don't know why. I suppose I do it to have recollections of my life, and I find it very useful. It helps me remember things. And it calms me. I can't explain it any better if you don't understand that," Devan said.

"Well, I don't understand it," his brother-in-law snapped, "but I can tell you that you'd better not write down anything I do while we're here in Atlanta. Your wife could tell Saraswati. And if she does that, it could break her heart. And Vitri would do it too. You and I both know she would."

"Ugh," Devan groaned, "I don't let Savitri read it. I don't let anyone read it, Siddharth."

Siddharth laughed as he turned back toward the room-service menu on his bed. He continued with his back to Devan.

"My poor brother-in-law. You have so much to learn about women. So, so much," he said, putting on his reading glasses, sitting down, and scanning the menu.

It was supremely insulting to Devan. He was so angry he didn't want to speak because he felt like he'd insult Sid. But he couldn't fight the urge.

"Really? Well. I suppose I don't want to learn about the type of women you consort with apart from Saraswati! And that's just fine with me, Siddharth!"

As much resentment and hostility as he had, Devan was still frightened of Siddharth. Sid was a tough guy on the streets of Ahmedabad. And just like they did Devan's father, everyone feared Siddharth. Rumors circulated that Siddharth had even killed a man with a knife when he was fifteen. So when he looked up from the menu at him, Devan was terrified. He thought for sure that Siddharth would get up and beat him. But he was surprised when, after a moment, he just laughed at him.

"Yes! Yes! That's right! Nor should you want to learn about women like those! Because if you did, I'd kick your ass. And I'd tell my sister about it!" Siddharth howled just before he returned his attention to the menu.

As the last morning session ended, most of which Devan tuned out because it was so dull, he and Rudy rose from their chairs in the conference center. Siddharth quickly stood up a few rows ahead and turned to look at his brother-in-law again. His disciples, mostly very young men, bathed in Polo cologne, glanced toward Siddharth to see what he'd do next.

After Devan turned back to go to the room, a very handsome young man walked to the row where Siddharth sat. He had on sunglasses, and he had a blonde-haired bimbo on one arm and a Thai version of the same on the other. Siddharth's clan erupted once the man joined everyone, and they all yelled, "Armand!"

The handsome young man shook hands with Siddharth, who smiled and took hold of the back of his head, patting him on the chest with his closed fist.

Devan didn't see any of that, though, because he got distracted by Rudy grasping his shoulder again.

"Listen," Rudy said, "unless you want to sit here until five o'clock listening to an insurance salesman from Stone Mountain Mutual, I'd like to invite you to lunch with Pooja and me. I have a place not far from here that my son operates. He's a chef. And Devan, the only reason he's a chef is because of your father."

That was intriguing. Devan couldn't imagine how his father might have had anything to do with a chef's career path in America. So, if nothing else, he wanted to hear more about that. But he also couldn't help picturing how angry it would make Sid if he disappeared for the afternoon session.

"I'd love to accompany you and Pooja, Rudy," he said.

"Excellent!" Rudy hissed as Jimmy Herndon took Rudy's arm and guided him down the aisle, motioning for Devan to follow.

All Devan's preconceived notions about who Rudy was, evaporated when Devan exited the hotel with his party, and a limousine rolled up to greet them. Jimmy Herndon pulled the door to the limousine open, allowing Rudy and Pooja to enter first. Then he patted Devan on the back, letting him sink into the plush leather seat next to Pooja. Afterward, Jimmy got in the front passenger seat.

Devan did his best to appear calm, but he felt like Rudy could tell how astonished and impressed he was.

"Brioche de Peches!" Rudy called out to the driver with a perfect French accent.

They hadn't gotten any farther than the interstate onramp before Rudy started talking business.

"Maybe next year, I'll host this conference at my property downtown. I have a Michelin-starred restaurant in my hotel.

They served Jolly Giant carrots and peas at this place and had the gall to call it *undhiyu* on the provisional menu. Disgraceful!" he barked as Pooja patted his knee to calm him.

The limousine raced along the highway, making Devan feel like a captive behind enemy lines. He didn't know this man or his wife. He knew nothing about them. And even as insufferable as Siddharth was, he was still familiar. Devan felt a little bit like a traitor.

"It's your next exit! Then turn left at the stoplight!" Rudy confirmed to the limo driver before beginning his story.

He leaned over and looked at Devan, smiling. And despite how friendly and welcoming that smile seemed to him, Devan couldn't help but feel like something belied it. Something much more calculating and possibly sinister. But he was wrong again.

"As I told you at breakfast, Devan, your father and I were close friends. And we communicated with one another even after I came to America. He's the one that paid for me to come here."

Nothing sounded extraordinary to Devan yet. His father had a penchant for helping people that were close to him. It was quite a point of contention with his mother, Manorma, because things never seemed to work out the way Ajai intended. She always insisted people took advantage of Ajai—until he had enough and told her to be quiet.

But when Rudra spoke again, he didn't sound rude or uncouth. He spoke in the King's English. And he used words Devan later had to look up in the dictionary. Devan knew his father was a giving man. So Rudy's honeyed words weren't a surprise. However, they didn't sway the contempt Devan had for his father. Ajai bought the man a ticket to America? So what?

"I was an angry young man, Devan. And many times, my choleric reaction overshadowed my intentions. So even when my protests were justified, others lost sight of that fact. No one respects an indignant man as they do a penitent one. And because of my temper, I lost my livelihood. I could not help myself, though, Devan. I always spoke and acted, sometimes before I thought clearly. I vented my anger rather than controlling it. I behaved that way for years until I learned to utilize my outrage for the greater good. But I still combat my anger, just as your father did his. And from what I can gather, you do as well."

Perhaps, Devan thought, this man was wiser than he'd assumed. He expressed the same misgivings Devan had about his own temper and seemed very insightful. Devan considered the words of Mahatma Gandhi, whom his father couldn't stand, on his personal struggles with anger.

How I find it possible to control it would be a useless question, for it is a habit that everyone must cultivate and must succeed in forming by constant practice.

After reflecting a moment, Devan returned his attention to Rudy as he went on.

"Because of my rage, I suddenly had no way to take care of my family anymore. Well, at least not in our accustomed fashion," Rudy continued.

"Your father hired me for a time on his plantation, but the work was something I couldn't do very well. I've been sickly my whole life, Devan. That's why I have this infernal cane!" Rudy said, laughing, pulling the brass-handled stick from his side and shaking it.

Rudra wasn't joking. He'd been sick his entire life because he contracted poliomyelitis as a little boy. A young British doctor told his parents there wasn't much he could do for the child and that Rudra wouldn't live into his teens. But somehow, the hard-headed Gujarati pulled through and made it this far.

Rudy continued his story when he stopped laughing.

"And don't think those savages I oversaw didn't take the advantage! I never knew when one of them slept or was working!

Did they care? No! Of course, they didn't! And your father's business in my quadrant suffered, as a result, Devan. Production fell, and Ajai didn't meet his quotas set by the tobacco companies. It was such a disgraceful thing for me. Your father knew I loved and would protect him to my dying breath. But business is business, and I realized this, Devan."

Rudy was visibly angry before taking a deep breath and calming himself. It was as though Devan witnessed him putting everything into practice he'd just espoused. And, on a level, it made Devan respect the man.

"One day, your father approached me in the kothara as the field hands began unloading their hauls. I can't forget the look on his face that day, no matter how hard I try, Devan. He looked so upset, and the image still haunts me. It looked like someone twisted his heart in their hands," Rudy said.

Devan began feeling worse by the moment. He felt terrible about mocking Rudy in the lobby the night before. He felt especially guilty about telling him to go back to whatever farm he came from. However, he remained silent, just like he always did in situations like these, and he let Rudy speak.

"Your father, Devan. Your father was so compassionate. He refused to fire me for a long time, which was what I deserved. I deserved everything I experienced at that point. My loud, vulgar mouth and temper brought me to that juncture, so it was only rightful that I accepted the dictates of my fortune, even if it meant dealing with those insufferable, lazy field hands."

Despite his harsh words, Rudy spoke in a thoughtful and measured tone. He talked like a man atoning for his misdeeds rather than asserting blame on others for them. And it impressed Devan.

"Your father told me things had not worked out like he thought they might. It was a day I'd anticipated for some time, even as I dreaded it. But then he surprised me. Just like Ajai always did, he'd already thought several moves ahead. Rather than cutting me loose, he told me he had devised a plan. He said he wanted to pay for me to come here, Devan. He told me India was no place for a man like I was in my condition, and he was right. He was so kind and empathetic," Rudy said.

As harrowing as Rudy's tale was, Devan felt it was an injustice to allow his father to, yet again, be canonized by someone who benefited directly from his selective empathy. And he wasn't about to let that happen again.

"Well, he was compassionate sometimes, Rudy. But sometimes, he had a very conservative mindset. And he was hateful and unforgiving as often as kind," Devan said.

Rudy's silence was as loud as if he screamed at the top of his lungs. Then Rudy's eyes looked like they'd boil right out of his head. But just as he did before, Rudy appeared to govern his emotions, scaling them back before speaking. However, Devan didn't exercise the same degree of control. Sensing he was on unstable ground, he screwed up his courage and began relating everything about the dark side of Ajai Patel that he loathed.

"He denounced my wife, Rudy. He refused to acknowledge our marriage, and we didn't speak for years afterward," Devan said.

"It wasn't until my son was born that he had a change of heart. He didn't accept my oldest daughter, but he yielded once my son, Fardeen, came along. And I can only presume it was because he was a boy. So tell me something, Rudy. Does that mean my love for my children should've hinged on my father's whim? Does it mean I should've loved one less because she was a girl? Or if I named them something for which he didn't approve?"

Rudy sat back and chuckled. It eased the tension for a second. But then he continued, which ramped it right back up to the level it was before.

"I can't say that I hold him at fault for that, Devan. That's with all due respect to your wife, but I understand why Ajai felt that way. I wouldn't stand for my son marrying a Muslim either," he said.

After attempting to control his anger as Rudy had, Devan gave in to his temper. And he raised his tone and went on the offensive.

"Savitri is not Muslim, Rudy! They would've imprisoned me or worse had she been! You know this! They would've beaten me in the streets of Ahmedabad! As if it were any of their damned business, to begin with!!"

Rudy looked surprised at first. But then he explained things as he knew them to be.

"I know about this situation somewhat. Ajai related it to me in his correspondence. And he may not have openly acknowledged your marriage, but he was proud when your daughter was born. He told me this," Rudy said, shocking the hell out of Devan.

"But tell me something, if your wife is not Muslim," he continued, " why did you give your son a Muslim name? I believe you, Devan. But I'm nevertheless curious. Isn't her mother from Srinagar? Ajai said her father was a Pashtun, a militant at that. Is that not true?"

Devan was stunned. Now the man knew his son's name? He groaned, shook his head, and exhaled. Then he started talking again as if explaining something for the thousandth time.

"My wife is Hindu," Devan continued indignantly, "as is her family. And they paid a much greater price to be Hindu than anyone you knew in Gujarat, sir. I named my son after her father because he came into the world just as her father, Fardeen Shakur, left it. It was an emotional time for everyone. It was emotional for everyone except my father, of course. Fardeen Shakur traveled across India in the middle of the night, fending off Muslims, Sikhs, and Hindus alike. They might have raped

Savitri's mother and killed her family. But my father didn't so much as pay for a midwife or come and visit us. He stayed in Kheda, and I can only assume it was as he sat and smoked his pipe as my wife struggled in labor."

Then Devan fell back into his seat and remained quiet. He felt that perhaps he shouldn't have said anything. But Rudy hurt his feelings with his presumptions about his wife and her family. Her mother, Virika, although outspoken for a Hindu woman, was the most devout Hindu and the strongest woman he'd ever known—including his mother, Manorma. And sitting silently and letting the old man denigrate Savitri's family was more than Devan could stomach. But now he'd spoken his piece, which was enough for him.

Rudy sensed the discussion had headed off the rails, so he tried to make light of the situation with humor.

"Oh, but those people from the North," Rudy said, smiling playfully.

Devan didn't seem amused, so Rudy moved on from there.

"So you're telling me that Siddharth Shakur is Hindu? Is that what you're saying?" Rudy asked as though challenging Devan.

Devan lowered his head and rubbed his temples before looking up and holding his hands out to his sides.

"No! I'm not saying that at all! I don't know what in the hell Siddharth is, Rudy! If I had to say he was anything, I'd say he was nothing! Siddharth worships Siddharth, and that's all I've ever known him to do! And I've looked on as he did it in every reflection he caught of himself. A mirror, a window, or anything else he passed!"

Rudy surprised Devan with how hard he laughed at his words.

"Hahahaha! But you're right, aren't you? You're right! Oh, the man is such a jackass! But he's a good businessman, Devan. He's a very good businessman and a savvy motelier, although not perhaps as savvy as he believes he is!"

After Rudy settled down, Devan spoke again.

"I don't care about such things, Rudy. I never have," Devan said calmly.

"I believe in prosperity, Rudy. But I also hold my ambition in check, unlike Siddharth. He would sell his organs if he got enough for them. He's an uneducated toad. But he presented an opportunity to leave Gujarat, so I accepted it. And I don't want my children exposed to my father's disgrace more than they've already been. But I'll be damned to hell if I apologize for it every day for the rest of my life!"

And with that, the limo grew silent. Rudy wasn't upset with Devan, but he didn't want to provoke him further, so he sat silently before speaking up again after a minute or so. But this time, it was his turn to talk. It was his time to educate Devan on matters from the past. He needed to relate everything that brought them to where they sat now in a limousine racing down the interstate toward his son's restaurant.

"I couldn't make it here, Devan. Even though I worked much harder than most, it was always a hopeless job. I worked in a hamburger restaurant in Sausalito, California, for a few weeks until I couldn't stand it any longer. It was my job to skin and slice potatoes early in the mornings. And in my ignorance, I didn't know what they prepared and sold as food. Can you imagine how I felt when I discovered that?" Rudy said with a troubled expression.

"From there, I moved to Sears Roebuck and Company in Oakland, where I worked as a stockboy. That didn't last long either because of my health. The younger men moved twice as fast as I did, but it was because I walked with a cane. Nevertheless, it was too much for a middle-aged immigrant with a limey accent!" Rudy continued.

This time, it seemed to Devan like Rudy attempted to make

excuses for something. He came across as an apologist for his apparent wealth rather than bragging about it as Siddharth would. He let the old man talk, though. He let him say whatever he wanted to.

"Then finally, I started selling encyclopedias from door to door. One of your father's associates was an executive with Encyclopedia Britannica and got me the job. The entire time, your father and I corresponded through letters. He sent me a check with each letter, telling me to persevere and that things would change. Even though I was glad to receive it, I looked forward to his correspondence as much as the money. Your father was a very bright, eloquent, and genuine person. He was inspirational. He was like an older brother to me."

As the limo slowed to a halt, directly across from a Dunkin Donuts, Rudy couldn't resist commenting.

"You see?" he declared, "Look at the parking lot!"

Something Devan would never have noticed, but Rudy did immediately, was the Morning Inn directly behind the Dunkin Donuts. Its parking lot was full, as was Dunkin Donuts'. And Rudy pressed his face to the glass and stared for the duration of the limousine's long turn onto the thoroughfare

"Breakfast!" Rudy shouted once he leaned back in his seat, "It's breakfast the Americans want!"

"It's so logical!" he said, "And it just slipped my mind! Bhavin was right! That dirty, brilliant son-of-a-bitch!"

Devan laughed, but he was still intrigued by Rudy's business acumen. He also hoped Rudy would continue with his story, which he did.

"Oh, where was I? Yes, the encyclopedias. That job required a lot of travel, which was a blessing. It was difficult for me because I couldn't walk well. But I didn't have to pay rent anymore, and I got to stay in motels all over the eastern United States. That was my territory. It was a welcome change from paying for a basement apartment and keeping my food in an icebox that only partially cooled," Rudy said, snickering.

"As I filled out my weekly expense report in my motel room one night, I realized how much money Encyclopedia Britannica made from my efforts. The most glaring figure on that report was my motel charges. They were over $50 per week. That was far more than my commission, Devan! That motel had twenty-two rooms, and I figured that even if it were full only half the time, that was still over $500 a week! I just couldn't believe it! That was so much money back then, Devan. Especially to a poor Gujarati immigrant like I was!"

Rudy's recollection elevated his spirits as he spoke.

"So, I vowed that night to save enough money and buy a motel one day. I'd do whatever it took to break into that business even if I had to starve myself—which I wound up doing half the time. I'd have a motel one day."

But then Rudy's mood abruptly darkened. He stopped talking, and Pooja reached over and touched his cheek, herself tearing up a bit.

After everyone sat a few moments without speaking, the limousine moved into a quiet neighborhood. Ancient oak trees canopied the road winding through its center, and the car rolled into the parking lot of Brioche de Peches at 11:37 AM. Devan couldn't have been happier when the car stopped because he was so hungry. He sure hoped Rudy's son could cook. He hoped even more that it wasn't Indian food because, just like Fardeen, he'd developed a taste for American cuisine. All the bad stuff. Hot dogs, hamburgers, French fries cooked in beef tallow. He loved it all.

The restaurant was in a building that appeared to have been a filling station at one time. But in the place of its gas pumps, there were giant half-barrels filled with a border of marigolds whose centerpieces were large, staked tomato plants stretching into the sunlight. And the arriving party was greeted by a young man, slapping his hands together and dusting flour off himself.

"Raj!" Pooja shouted as she wiggled over Rudy to get out of the car. Then she raced over and hugged the young man, who smiled and raised her from the ground.

Raj Patel, Rudra's son, was Gujarati. But he was also totally Americanized, and you'd never have even guessed he wasn't American from birth. To Devan, he symbolized everything about American youth culture, especially those things he didn't understand. He wore blue jeans and a white tee-shirt with the words *Oingo Boingo* on the front, partially obscured by an apron, and he had a small gold hoop in his left ear.

Raj Patel, in a word, terrified Devan. He imagined pulling up one day to The Seagull and Fardeen greeting him like this. He felt like Rudy might share some of his feelings because he growled as he let Jimmy Herndon help him from the limo.

"Raj!" Rudy said, hugging his son before pushing back a moment. He flicked Raj's left earlobe with his middle and index fingers, saying, "What's this? What is this?"

Raj laughed at his father and said, "Don't worry, Papa. It's just something my boyfriend picked up for me for my birthday."

Rudy stopped laughing and quickly thrust Raj backward, holding him at arm's length. But then Raj burst out laughing.

"I'm kidding! I'm just kidding, Papa!"

Pooja stood close by, and she couldn't take her eyes off Raj. It was as though he hypnotized her.

Rudy and Pooja's marriage was unconventional, just as Devan was about to find out over lunch. Pooja, it turned out, was Raj's Mami or aunt. She married Rudy after her sister, Hanika, died giving birth to Raj. It was a marriage of convenience more than anything, all because Rudy couldn't stand the thought of raising a child alone. But he could never fall for another woman as he had for Hanika.

"Could I see the journal?" Jimmy Herndon asked Rudy, startling Devan a moment.

Jimmy referred to the Wall Street Journal, which he usually pored over in the bathroom in the afternoon after Rudy read it from front to back, and he looked for any notations Rudy made in it. Rudy laughed and pointed toward the limousine.

"Of course! I left it in the car."

And with that, Raj, Pooja, Devan, then Rudy entered the restaurant, one behind another.

"I've got a beautiful table outside for you, Mami," Raj said, smiling and looking back at Pooja.

Pooja, in tears, touched Raj's face and said, "Doesn't he look just like Hanika, Rudra? He's so beautiful, just like she was!"

Rudy frowned and said, "Indeed he does," as he urged the party through the restaurant.

It perplexed Devan how the patrons and staff looked at them as they walked toward the rear door. Predominantly white and affluent married couples sat and enjoyed lunch with their children. Men in suits looked up from intense exchanges. And even young couples on lunch dates made eye contact with Rudy and, inadvertently, Devan when they walked past them all.

"Rudy!" one of the businessmen hollered, "I got that info on that Dynamax IPO whenever you want to look at it with me!"

Two clowning men, obviously fellow stockbrokers who coveted managing Rudy's portfolio, leaned toward the man's table with their hands cupped at their ears. When the ambitious young broker noticed them, one of them said, "Oh, I'm sorry. I thought you were EF Hutton, Mr. Kennesaw! My apologies!"

Then the men at both tables laughed and returned to their discussions.

Wow. Devan just couldn't imagine anything like this. Whenever he pictured stockbrokers, he thought about the arrogant ones that may as well have cracked a whip across his back whenever they came into his shoe store. They were rude and condescending. They weren't like the handsome, jovial Southerners that held such apparent regard for Rudy. Despite Devan being the only game in Ahmedabad that offered Johnston and Murphy Oxfords, the wealthy businessmen were categorically unimpressed and distant apart from barking orders. Sure, most of his inventory consisted of Adidas, Pony, and Nike knock-offs, which he sold hand-over-fist to kids. But he'd fought hard to carry the genuine J&M footwear line shortly after opening his humble store years earlier, which he hoped would cater to the Ahmedabad elite.

A sweet scent rushed into Devan's nose as they exited the building through the back door. It smelled like vanilla swirled into a fruit of some kind. He found the next aroma equally appealing but foreign and sharply contrasting to the fruit. It was the country ham that Brioche de Peches offered during their all-day breakfast. Raj served it with Belgian waffles, among other dishes, with a peach syrup he devised himself.

That syrup put him on the radar of culinary critics all over Atlanta.

They just loved Raj. They loved everything about him. The son of an immigrant who braved the waters of Atlanta's finicky and unforgiving culinary critics and carved out such a niche for himself? Forget about it. They adored Raj Patel and lapped up every menu offering he had, recounting the virtues of each more emphatically than the last one they tried.

But that syrup.

Raj stewed thirty pounds of whole Georgia peaches every night until they disintegrated into a tender, fruity matrix, to which he added a ten-pound bag of sugar. After diluting it with spring water, he allowed it to simmer for another hour over the lowest flame setting of the stove. Then, as a brilliant final addition, he stirred in cinnamon, crushed vanilla bean, and a dash of nutmeg, using a long skinny paddle he made out of a broom handle and a dustbin to mix everything. Afterward, he filtered it into jugs and transferred those vessels to the cooler to keep in inventory for two weeks until it was ready to be reheated and used as needed.

Everybody begged for the recipe and even argued with him to get it, but Raj never gave it up. He refused.

Raj's signature dish, the restaurant's namesake, was a bottom layer of brioche, then a slice of country ham, fried until crisp at its edges. He nestled a fried egg, over easy, on top of that. Then he placed fresh Georgia peaches over it along with a dousing of his peach syrup and crowned it with another grilled piece of egg-washed brioche, a tad more syrup, and a sprinkling of pine nuts across the top. He pressed it all down for fifteen seconds in a ripping hot pan, then dropped it on a plate, chopped it in two, and served it after only an 87-cent investment. He charged $8.75 for his master creation, which chefs from all over the country poorly imitated.

Sample headers from the *Atlanta Journal Constitution's* food section:

"PEACHES AND PIGGIES AND POULTRY! OH MY!"

"FORGET GEORGIA! BRIOCHE DE PECHES IS WHAT'S ON MY MIND!"

Raj Patel was a sensation, but things were just getting started for the young Gujarati-American chef. He wound up with restaurants in Los Angeles, Chicago, San Francisco, and New York City. In another twenty years, he'd have a thirty-minute show on a major food network channel devoted to his many culinary fusions. He was just another of the many success stories of Gujaratis in America. But his success was also marked by celebrity, and he became quite the heartthrob dressed in his brilliant white chef togs and the colorful bandanas Pooja made for him, which he wore in place of a toque.

After personally ferrying three plates of Brioche de Peches' eponymous dish to the table, Raj asked, "Will Sir Herndon be joining you today?"

Rudy looked at his Rolex, then laughed and said, "I think Mr. Herndon is indisposed for at least another hour! Check back with us, though, boy!"

The dish hijacked Devan's senses as soon as the plate touched the table, and he took his first bite.

For starters, it was beautiful. Raj served it on a fine white china salad plate, and the bun glistened in the sunlight as it sat atop the mound of fruit, country ham, and a runny fried egg, all glazed with that magnificent syrup with both of the latter oozing out of the sandwich's sides. It crunched from the pine nuts, which lent the dish an incredible texture and earthiness. Devan chewed the first mouthful in which he managed to capture every element of the delicacy. That single bite resoundingly answered Devan's question about that heavenly aroma when they walked past the open kitchen onto the patio earlier. But when all those flavors blended on his tongue, they forced Devan to moan involuntarily and drop his fork onto his plate. This one was destined for a journal entry when he returned to Biloxi that night.

Once he opened his eyes after lilting back down from the ether, they met with Raj Patel's, who stared back at him as he smiled brilliantly and nodded.

"I think it's better than Hardees' country ham biscuit offering, sir. Don't you?"

Devan wiped his mouth, stood up, and shook the talented young chef's hand.

"I don't know who Hardee is, sir. But he should go back to the fields, the office, the grocer's, or wherever he used to work!" Devan said in as flattering but sincere a manner as he could.

Devan's words meant so much to Raj, just as they would

to any chef. He grasped Devan's hand in both of his, touched his shoulder a moment, then leaned over and kissed the top of Pooja's head.

"I love you, Mami!" he said before he turned around and went back into the restaurant, winking at Rudy on the way.

"Ugh! It's a good thing the boy can cook," Rudy blustered as Raj walked away, "because he can't foot a column of numbers or scare up enough ambition to plunge a toilet!"

Rudy's laughter got interrupted by another kick to his shin.

"Ow!" he barked, looking over at Pooja, who sat glaring at him as Devan laughed.

CHAPTER NINE

A fter they finished eating, taking the next half-hour so that Devan could savor every bite, it was time to talk business. Rudy looked at Pooja, and she rose from the table and walked back toward the restaurant.

She turned around and said, "I'm going to visit with Raj and see if he has more of the vanilla ice cream he gave us last week."

Rudy nodded briefly, then she turned and walked toward the kitchen.

Devan realized this was it. It was the reason for Rudy's inexplicable fixation on him. It was clear he wanted to talk to Devan about something. Although Devan couldn't imagine what that might be. And the conversation began simply, although somewhat abstractly.

"I love America," Rudy said before falling silent again as he stared across the table at Devan.

Ok, Devan thought to himself. Sure. Devan loved America too. Perhaps not as much as Fardeen did. But what was his point? Rudy continued.

"I came here as an older man, and I had nothing. I had a young pregnant wife back home, though. And I was ambitious. So I'm the perfect example of what a smart man can achieve in America, no matter how old or from where they come. Devan, I own twenty-five properties very similar to yours. Most of them have brands, but some of them do not. And let me tell you, motels like yours are the spun gold of our industry. You can name your property what you want to. You can rent to whomever you want and make just as much damned money as you want. There are benefits to having a brand, so don't misinterpret what I say. But I must confess, I miss the days when I wasn't required to strip my rooms and start over every three years. New furniture. New lighting. It's madness. Utter madness."

Despite the limousine and the gratuitous recognition people paid Rudy, he wasn't saying anything Devan already hadn't heard from Siddharth. Still, he stayed quiet and let Rudy speak.

"But," Rudy said, "I also own seven of the largest luxury hotels in the Southeastern United States. I have two such properties here in Atlanta, one in Dallas, Houston, and another in Memphis. And I also have one in Miami and another in New Orleans," Rudy said, as though he thought Devan should've caught on by that time.

"I know," Devan said calmly. But he was lying and what Rudy told him was shocking.

"I suppose the point I'm trying to make to you, Devan, is that none of that happened by accident," Rudy said as he continued to stare at him.

"You see," Rudy continued, "as much as I love the United States, it was at first difficult for a man like me to find a place in it because my ancestry—our ancestry—didn't come over on a European ship that landed on the East Coast."

Devan looked down at his plate and the remaining pine nuts floating in the syrup. And he wished Pooja would rejoin them with that ice cream she mentioned. Maybe she could interpret things for Rudy because he was losing Devan fast. But she never came.

"It took many men to declare America's independence from Great Britain, Devan, over two hundred years ago. It took resolve, bravery, but more than anything else, it took a unified front,"

Rudy said with his eyes appearing as though they pled for Devan's understanding.

But Devan's expression remained vacant as he looked back at Rudy. He *wanted* to understand what he meant. And he *wanted*, at the very least, to offer him a dissenting opinion. But he didn't know what Rudy implied with all he just said to him. It began feeling like he was talking to Siddharth.

Rudy delved deeper.

"What are your thoughts on the Irish?" Rudy asked.

This guy was all over the board now, and Devan began feeling the same way he had when he regretted not joining Siddharth for breakfast. But, once again, he thought before he spoke.

"I. What? Are you referring to Irish Americans? Or do you mean people from Ireland, Rudy?" he asked.

Rudy laughed as he looked at Devan.

"I mean any Irishman you've ever known or heard of, Devan. That's what I mean. What do you think of them?" he said.

Devan paused for several seconds and said, "I haven't given any thought to the matter, Rudy. And forgive me, but I guess I don't understand."

Rudy smiled a second before pushing back from the table and speaking again.

"I see," he said, "well, allow me to share what one of them said a long time ago. His name was Sir Edmund Burke. Are you familiar with him?"

Devan felt challenged. He believed Rudy was testing him, trying to see how learned he was. Devan answered Rudy, but he spoke in Gujarati for the first time since meeting him.

"Rudra, I am Hindu. I am a father and a husband. But I am also Indian. Of course, I know who Sir Edmund Burke was."

Rudra seemed delighted at Devan's response. He smiled as

though Devan had met some benchmark or leaped some hurdle before going on.

"Well then, may I remind you of something he once said?"

"By all means," Devan responded, motioning for Rudy to continue.

"He said, *'Those who don't know history are destined to repeat it.'* And no truer words were ever spoken by Sir Burke."

Rudy caught a glint of understanding in Devan's eyes, so he continued.

"You see, our people are not so different from Americans, and I've embraced their ancestry as my ancestry, just like all Americans do, if for nothing else than posterity's sake. Americans had an idea. And they fought to defend it, and every day I live, my vantage of American culture rewards me. Look at my boy, Devan. Just look at him. Do you think they'd accept him on any level if he were an American hot-dog vendor on the streets of Ahmedabad or Jaipur? Do you? I guarantee you they wouldn't!" Rudy said, becoming angry.

"Savages," he finished, sounding exactly like an Englishmen as he said it.

The men were interrupted.

"Papa?" Raj asked after walking up unnoticed and breaking the tension at the table.

"Oh, yes, of course," Rudy said, taking the triplicate credit card receipt on the little black tray. Rudy tucked his American Express beneath it.

Rudra owned Brioche de Peches, but he never threw his weight around or showed up wanting anything for free. He thought that might set a bad example and leave Raj's employees feeling like they deserved some accommodation or allowance simply because they worked there. He wanted Raj to experience the rigors of operating a business, including control over food cost, spoilage, and theft. The restaurant business, Rudra knew, was one of the hardest to earn a profit from. The margins were narrow, the labor cost was insufferable, far beyond what you paid the ingrates you hired, and there was ample opportunity for theft. So Rudra accounted for every dime that flowed into or from the business. And that included anything he ate or drank.

He protected his boy. He nurtured and positioned him to run the business one day with the same expertise he'd acquired over the years.

"Everything was wonderful," Rudy said, "I could do it all over again!"

He'd purposefully not introduced Devan earlier, leaving them both confused. So he made their introductions.

"Devan, this is my son, Raj. Raj, this is Ajai Patel's son, Devan. We're visiting with one another, talking about old times," Rudy said.

Raj instantly jerked his head toward Devan and said, "Mr. Patel, please forgive me. I wish Papa had told me who you were. And I'd like to tell you that I couldn't be here if it weren't for your father. I'm so grateful to him and my family each day."

Devan didn't understand all the fuss. He nodded at Raj and shook his hand before Rudy curtailed the discussion.

"Yes, that's fine. I'm sure he appreciates you too. Now, off with you," Rudy said as Raj continued staring at Devan for a second before returning to the restaurant.

Once he was out of sight, Rudra continued.

"You see," Rudy said, "I honor American ancestry just as I do my Indian ancestry, Devan. A name can be such a powerful thing in this country. It confers so much about a person, even more so in some cases than in India," Rudy said solemnly.

"In which way?" Devan asked, "Because I can't imagine that being the case here."

Rudra looked back at him, evaluating his expression. He knew this was an uphill battle. He only hoped Devan would hear him and might understand him.

"I suppose I wish you'd learned these lessons before coming to America. But I realize that since Siddharth brought you here, you only learned them to the extent of his understanding. And you might even have learned more from him than you should have," Rudra said.

"Lessons? What lessons are you talking about, Rudy?" Devan asked as he sat back in his chair and crossed his arms.

Devan was an intellectual. He wasn't an imbecile, and the idea this man posited insulted him. Did he believe Devan was incapable of making his own decisions or that his brother-in-law controlled everything he did or thought? The idea offended him.

Rudy shook his head and looked down. It hadn't started well. And he wasn't sure he could help Devan as he'd intended. Siddharth might've already discussed things he wanted to discuss with him. Perhaps Siddharth also reached him in a way he couldn't because of his age. Maybe it was too late for Devan, and he was already ruined by the promise of unimaginable good fortune, even if it came at a horrible cost.

So he played his hand and went for broke.

"I wasn't just friends with your father, Devan. We were cousins, and that makes us cousins too. We're both descended from a long line of successful merchants and landowners, Patidars. And there was no greater testament to our heritage than Ajai."

Devan was shocked. But he was also a little leery because his father never mentioned a "Rudra" Patel to him. Then again, he knew so little about his father's family because most of them were dead by the time he was born. And Rudy wouldn't be the first man named Patel that attempted to ingratiate themselves by their association with his father.

"I understand your frustration, Devan. I do. It was a horrible thing that happened to your family. But you should listen. You should listen when an old Gujju like me, as your generation calls us, tries to tell you something."

Devan wanted to say something back to this man, now claiming to have his best interest at heart and that he was also a relative. But he had nothing meaningful to counter Rudy. So he gulped and tried to explain himself as best he could, given the magnitude of what he'd just told Devan.

"Of course, Rudy. Of course, I apologize if I seem distracted. I'm listening. Rest assured, I'm listening, but I'm also a bit shocked," Devan said.

Rudy looked sideways at Devan and said, in Gujarati, "So you don't believe me? You don't believe what I'm telling you?"

Devan stared back at Rudy, realizing he should play along if he wanted to hear more. He didn't know if this old guy was crazy or what. But Rudy sure seemed to know a lot about his father and his family. So, he shook his head.

"No, sir. I believe you. It's just my first time hearing about this. I hope that doesn't offend you, but my father never mentioned you before. Please. Please, sir, go on," Devan said.

Rudy continued to look at Devan, ensuring he had his attention and that he was receptive to everything he was about to tell him about his father. Ironically, Devan intimidated a man like Rudy Patel. Rudy knew Devan was a learned man and that he could decimate him in any intellectual debate should it arise. So he approached Devan from another angle.

"When we were boys in Gujarat, your father and I used to hunt frogs," Rudy continued, "We carried cloth sacks from the plantation your grandfather owned, the ones the field hands used to harvest tobacco. And for no particular reason, we chased and captured frogs! Do you know what would've happened to us these days? Do you realize how restrictive Gujarat has become with such things in the past few years?"

"I do, Rudy," Devan said, "restrictive with some things, yet so permissive with others. A Brahmin can beat a Dalit to death if he dares eat his meal within a few feet of him. But if a boy chases a frog in a field, he can ruin himself. He can go to prison and let half of his life pass by him."

Devan's passive-aggressive intent was to elicit outrage or at least some defense to his comment. What bothered him, though, was that Rudy slightly smiled at what he said. He was sure of it. The man smiled.

So he was dumbfounded when Rudy spoke again and said what he did.

"You speak the truth, Devan," Rudy said, gesturing toward him, "everything you say is true. But this was a different time, and almost a different place than Gujarat is now. I don't remember how old we were, but your father and I disregarded all the rules!"

Rudy began laughing again.

"We tore through the fields of my uncle's tobacco plantation with our mischief! And we were a couple of young Gujaratis that didn't much care what people thought!" he continued.

Then, once he caught his breath, Rudy went on.

"You don't understand how things were back then, Devan. They were so different. But, in fairness, we didn't understand either! We scoffed at convention! We balked at our ancestors and everything sacred! We were so young and so alive! So irreverent and foolish!" Rudy said.

Following another bout of laughter, Rudy continued. But this time, he shocked Devan again, rocking the foundations of what little respect he still had for his father.

"And we drank!" Rudy shouted.

"Pardon me?" Devan asked, unsure of what Rudy meant.

"We drank!" Rudy said.

"You drank? You drank what?" Devan insisted.

"We drank wine!!" Rudy shouted.

"Wine? What do you mean wine? My father never drank alcohol his entire life, Rudy," Devan said, fueling Rudy's laughter.

"Oh! Oh, boy! That's just what you think! Ajai Patel drank! And he drank plenty!" Rudy cackled.

"He didn't only drink! But he provided every young Gujarati with enough alcohol to keep them liquored up for weeks at a time!"

After thinking again for a moment, Devan believed this old man was full of shit, a liar. He wasn't any better than the people Siddharth usually introduced him to. Devan wanted to get up and race back to the hotel—on foot if he had to. But he couldn't because he didn't know the way. He had to ride back to the hotel in that car that looked like something from a funeral procession. And that's how he felt, too. He felt doomed, in a sense. Just what had he gotten himself into by coming to America? And why had he gone to lunch with a crazy man? Were even the Gujaratis in this country liars as Siddharth had warned him?

Rudy calmed down and began talking again, sensing how Devan must've felt.

"Oh, don't worry, Devan. Your father was every bit the man you estimate he was. But he was a great deal more. He wasn't afraid of anything! He was a huge man with big rippling muscles from working in the fields! And he didn't tarry with rules or boundaries! He was a real man!" Rudy said, slapping his bicep.

"He made his wine from bananas and papayas or whatever else he had on hand—we thought he was a magician! He filled barrels with fruit. Then he mashed it down, poured giant bags of sugar over them, and covered it with water. Then he sprinkled

Englishman's bread yeast across the top of it. We all stood by, amazed, asking, 'Ajai? How can this give us wine? When will this be ready to drink?' But he always told us to be quiet! He told us to go home and return a few weeks later! Then when we came back, we all sat in the kothara and drank until we couldn't see straight! Such glorious times! So wonderful! They weren't like they are here with the Saturday Night Live Fever discos and the cocaine powder!"

Unless he just wanted to break his heart, which seemed unlikely, this man didn't have any reason to lie to Devan. So Devan had no choice but to accept what he told him as the truth. It was just another strike against his immoral father in Devan's mind. And it hurt. As a Hindu, it hurt so terribly to consider his father wasn't all he'd held himself out to be, even beyond the things Devan already loathed.

As Rudy watched Devan, he realized his tale had the opposite effect of what he wanted. Instead of laughing along with him, Devan folded his arms and looked around the patio. So, Rudy slowly toned his laughter down and sighed.

"Devan, I didn't intend to hurt your feelings or disparage your father. I only wanted to tell you a funny story about him, one you'd never heard. It seems the only memories about him you cling to are the ones that make him out to be a monster, but he wasn't. He was a good man, a powerful one. But he was once a mischievous child, growing up confused as we all were," he said.

Devan still refused to make eye contact with him. So Rudy approached Devan from yet another angle. If he couldn't earn his respect by revealing they were cousins and was so resigned to the idea that Ajai was inhuman, then maybe he could reach Devan another way. As old and passive as he'd become, the old Gujarati marsh crocodile still had cunning. And what better way to ally yourself with someone than to point toward a common enemy?

"Do you know how the Englishmen referred to us? And I

mean all Indians, not just the Gujaratis but all Indians. They called us Hindustanis, and India was Hindustan. Do you know why I believe they did that, Devan? I think they did it as part of their construct to keep us in line. They took advantage of our morality, which was something they used to oppress us. Rather than observing the tenets of our culture, they weaponized them. It was about control for them, Devan. They treated us as children to better control us while they pillaged our natural resources. And it was all for the furtherance of The Crown. Then they perverted our castes and pitted us against one another. It took me a long time to accept this as the truth."

Devan briefly cut his eyes toward Rudy as though he were somewhat surprised at his words

Then Rudra pulled the stops out.

"Let me tell you another story, something that happened years later," he said.

Devan glanced back at Rudy with a worried look. What next? Would he find out his father was a dope fiend? Or perhaps he was an international terrorist. But before his dread, mingling with his imagination, took hold, Rudy started talking again.

"You were a little boy during this time."

Devan exhaled. Instead of his initial fear about what Rudy might say, it started sounding like one of the many lectures his mother, Manorma, gave him as a troubled teenager. Nevertheless, he sat and listened.

"It was 1952," Rudy said.

Instantly, Devan snapped to attention. 1952 was a year he'd never forget. And despite wanting to hear what Rudy said, his mind drifted backward instead of listening to Rudy's tale.

In 1952, Devan witnessed a boy get beaten to death mercilessly. And he'd never forgotten it, nor would he. Ever.

The child was a simpleton. He was a Dalit, or an untouchable, as they called them back then. And his parents weren't much further beyond the spectrum than he was. His name was Rupam, but everyone on the streets of Ahmedabad jokingly called him "Rupee," after the Indian currency. They'd throw him coins or give him fruit as they mostly pitied the poor creature.

One afternoon, Rupee, who the British High Commission hired to sweep the streets in front of the British Consulate, moved toward a café next door, sweeping up dust in the direction of some men sitting at a table. It infuriated them. Then, they went berserk when Rupee sat down and began eating his lunch a few feet away. How dare a Dalit eat in front of them?

One of the men rose, walked over, and forced him to the ground with his foot. Then they all beat Rupee. They kicked him in the head, punched him, and relentlessly pounded on him as he screamed and held his arms up in submission. He didn't know what he'd done to anger the Brahmins. Nevertheless, he apologized and tried to give the men his lunch, offering it up while never looking at them. But that only seemed to provoke them more.

The men didn't just thrash Rupee, though. They beat him to death.

A few yards away, a boy straddled his new bicycle, shocked at what he saw. That boy was Devan Patel. And he screamed at the men to stop as Rupee languished in pain.

Across the street, a man walked out of the consulate and moved into the fray. Then he dropped to his knees and raised the boy's head from the ground, fending off the angry men with a stick. But he was too late. Rupee was gone. Devan walked over, still sitting on his bicycle as he hadn't learned to ride it. And he stared in horror as Rupee gasped a few times before dying.

The mob dispersed. But after a few minutes, it was replaced by several skittish-acting Englishmen from the consulate who hovered over Rupee and the man. Instead of helping, though, they began jeering and cursing at the man, telling him to mind his own business. One of the men reached down, grabbed the stick, and struck him with it. But when he went to hit him a second time, the man stood up, yanked it back, and snapped it over his knee. The Brits recoiled and raced back into the consulate, shouting back at the man and pointing at him over their shoulders. Devan couldn't understand them because he didn't speak English at that age. But it was clear the man and his heroics angered them.

The man shook his head and kicked the ground, toppling a moment before catching himself. He was upset by whatever they'd just yelled at him. Devan didn't know it, but they told him he was fired and not to come back, or they'd have him thrown in jail.

When the man looked up and noticed Devan, he stunned him when he called him by name.

"Devan? What are you doing down here? Is your father in Ahmedabad or Kheda today?"

"Kheda, sir," Devan answered.

"Where is your mother? Where is Manorma? Is she with him, or is she here?" he demanded,

"She's here, sir," Devan said as he began to cry. He was only six years old and didn't understand anything going on. But he watched that man walk out of the important building, which meant he was an important man like his father. And all important men knew each other.

Devan looked down at Rupee, whose eyes and mouth were locked open. His face was frozen in terror, and blood oozed onto the ground around his head. Devan gagged. Then he heaved and vomited down the front of his shirt.

The man carefully took a knee and pulled a handkerchief from his suit pocket. He rubbed the sick from Devan's mouth and pushed his hair back from his face.

When he finished, he said, "Now go! Go home, Devan! You've got no business riding around on your bicycle downtown!"

"Yes, sir," Devan said as he started bawling.

"And stop crying! Only little girls cry! You're a man! And you're disgracing your father!" the man snapped.

Devan turned his bicycle around and shuffled toward his parents' villa, going as fast as possible without pedaling. He knew he was in trouble. He was in big trouble. The important man surely would tell his father he'd seen him that day. And Devan wasn't supposed to go as far away as he did on his new bicycle. But Manorma was asleep. So he'd plodded along, block after block, until he was far beyond the boundary Manorma set for him.

As Devan replayed the events of that day in his mind, his heart pounded. And almost thirty years later now, he was again on the verge of tears as he sat on the patio of Brioche de Peches. It was such a life-altering experience and left an enduring impression on him.

But his anxiety wasn't just wrought by his recollection. It was also because the man sitting across from him, Rudra Patel, recounted it vividly and with the same clarity and detail as his mind did. That's because Rudra Patel was the man that attempted to intervene on Rupee's behalf that day before scolding Devan and urging him to go home.

CHAPTER TEN

"Are you joking, sir?" Devan asked, struggling not to cry like he was six years old again, "Who put you up to this? Did Siddharth tell you about this day? Did he go into one of my journals like some thief or ghoul, digging up my past?"

Before Devan even finished speaking, Rudy began shaking his head.

"I don't know what that man did regarding your journals, Devan. But I assure you what I'm telling you is from my experience," Rudy said.

"If Siddharth told me this," he continued, "I certainly wouldn't relate it to you now as I would've taken his words as lies. Siddharth is an evil, intemperate man, Devan. He is confused, spiritually. He has no place here in America among hardworking Gujaratis. But he sits in that rat trap in Mississippi as though he reigns over us all. I cannot abide Siddharth Shakur or anything for which he stands. And men like him could prove to be our undoing here. He takes his cues from other evil men and learns unspeakable business practices from them even now."

It was just so much information to absorb at once. And it overwhelmed Devan. He just wanted to go home. He wanted to lie down with Savitri in their cottage at The Sunkist, put Anaya between them, and fall asleep while his little girl fumbled with his ear, just as they'd done all summer.

But Savitri and the children were in London. And they wouldn't come back to America until he made a final decision.

He'd spend the night in that same cottage, fussing with the stove that was older than he was and eating oatmeal for dinner once he got it working, while Siddharth went out on The Strip, cavorting, drinking, and partying.

Devan was all alone. And he'd continue to be alone, even after he flew back to Biloxi. And it was the worst, most solemn feeling he'd ever experienced. He wanted to die.

"I don't want to upset you, cousin," Rudy said, "and I didn't intend to cast myself as a hero to you. I want nothing from you. I don't need anything from you. But I feel it's incumbent upon me to stage all that waits for you in Florida. I know your father would appreciate it just as I appreciated his help. This business is not for everyone, Devan. Siddharth is heartless. And he might leave you by the wayside if you fall out of his favor by doing something he disapproves of. And I don't want to leave you in the wilds of this country as I found myself. It's a hundred times worse than when I first came here."

Devan sat in contemplation a moment. But he started trusting Rudy again, particularly in light of his words about his brother-in-law. He realized Siddharth was just as he described.

Siddharth was evil. And he'd risen to prominence in an unimaginably short time. It was inexplicable to Devan. How could so many respect, fear, or resent Siddharth, who operated such small properties relative to Rudy's? Yet everyone seemed to know him at all the meetings—even those Devan knew to be respectable Gujaratis.

"I realize everything I'm telling you may be overpowering, Devan. But I'm telling it all to you for a reason," Rudy said.

"And just what, praytell, is that reason, Rudy?" Devan asked.

Rudy smiled a second, then laughed.

"You commented on my English, but I have to tell you, Devan, you sound as foppish and condescending as all those Englishmen I worked for at the British High Commission," Rudy chuckled.

Devan didn't laugh. He just sat and waited for Rudy to make his point.

"I'm telling you this because you needn't hide behind Manorma's name anymore. You are a Patel. You're not a Kothari. And I knew and respected Manorma's father, Ben. He was a good man. But you have nothing to be ashamed of here or anywhere else. I know you're a brilliant man, Devan. Your father used to brag about you in his letters. He talked about how you stayed with your studies, sometimes hours into the night," Rudy said.

That surprised Devan. Indeed, he stayed up at night reading, studying, and trying to make himself a better and more prosperous person. But his father never gave any indication he understood that. Quite to the contrary, he often beat on Devan's door at night when he noticed his light was still on as he read or scribbled in his journal. And he told him to go to bed instead of asking why he was up or what he was doing.

Rudy went on.

"No, there's no caste system here in America. At least, none described. But there is a pecking order, Devan. And the thought of Ajai's son falling into a league with someone like Siddharth leaves me awake at night. I don't believe it's right, and I don't believe it's how things should be. You are a Patel, Devan, as are your son and daughters. Your circumstances left you alone in the world to make the decision you did about your name, and perhaps it served its purpose for a time. But make no mistake. You are a Patel. And I assure you that you want to embrace your surname here in America. You want to steer clear of all the pitfalls and contradictions to what you perceived this place to be. If I've done nothing else in my life, I've made sure that name, our name, means something, as have thousands of other men like me. But, perhaps it came at a much greater price to me than it did them."

After his speech, Rudra became somber, just as he had earlier in the car. He looked down at the table and patted his forehead with his palm. When he noticed a female server whisking past the table, he stopped her.

"Miss? Excuse me, miss?" he said as a handsome young black man raced behind her and nervously stared at Rudy.

"Yes, sir. What can I do for you?" the young lady asked.

"Could you bring me a Jameson Old Fashioned, with extra ice, please, ma'am?" Rudy asked.

The server said, "Oh, I'm sorry, sir. The bar is only open from six until ten. It won't be open for another few hours."

The young man interrupted and said, "Of course, Mr. Patel! Right away! Kimberly just started today, and I'm still showing her the ropes! But she'll get that right out to you, sir!"

"Thank you, sir," Rudy said, brightening for a moment.

Again, Devan was astounded by the respect these Americans gave Rudy. It was irreconcilable with how he'd observed them treat Indians in the past. They treated Rudy like a member of the Brahmin caste in India.

The men sat silently as Rudy waited for his cocktail. Within moments, the girl rushed up with two lowballs, placing one in front of Devan. He could tell how strong it was because of the aroma it let off.

"I'm so sorry, Mr. Patel!" the server said as the shift leader stood behind her, watching everything she did, "I didn't know! I mean, I just didn't realize! It's my first day, Mr. Patel! Please forgive me!"

About that time, Raj walked up and asked, "So, what's the problem? What's going on?"

"I apologize, Mr. Roger!" the girl insisted, "I promise I didn't know Mr. Patel was your father!"

Rudy laughed, interrupting the unfolding drama, and said, "There's nothing to be sorry for, young lady. And nothing is going on, boy! Now get your ass back in that kitchen! Don't make me get up! Don't embarrass me in front of your cousin! It's been a long time since I took this cane to your ass, but it's still not beneath me!"

Raj looked at his employees a second, then when Rolando, the shift lead, gave him a surreptitious nod, Raj laughed, patted Rudy's shoulder, and turned back toward the kitchen.

Rudy's reaction impressed Devan. He was amazed by his compassion and his congenial humor. The situation may have played out so differently in Gujarat with a man of Rudy's stature. It also served as a valuable lesson for Devan about dealing with Americans moving forward for the rest of his career. Like Gujaratis, they splayed into a hierarchy delineated by their station in life. It was similar to the way they split into different castes in India. America had its Dalits and its Brahmins and all castes between them. But they all deserved respect in Devan's mind.

After the tense exchange and out of pure curiosity, Devan thought about taking a swig of the cocktail in front of him. But he refrained. Then Rudy reached over and swiped it, placing it in front of himself and laughing as he rudely pointed that crooked old, weathered finger at him again.

"Now, Devan, remember. You don't drink!" he laughed.

After everything returned to normal, Rudy continued his history lesson.

"I suppose you realize that Pooja isn't my wife, Devan. Of course, she is my wife, but not in the traditional Hindu sense," he said.

Devan's curiosity peaked as he wondered about the peculiar relationship between Rudy and the pretty, older Gujarati woman who'd patiently spent the entire day among boorish, overbearing men, especially Rudy. As she sat at the table in the middle of the room at breakfast, the sari she wore looked like the plumage of a beautiful exotic bird to Devan. And the bindi in the center of her forehead brought back memories of how Savitri carried herself as a teenage bride. She'd long-since abandoned that tradition, but at his insistence, she came to America adorned in the same way until Siddharth put a stop to it.

"You can't come over here looking like that!" he growled as soon as they walked into the Sunkist office with their bags, *"You look like something on a bag of rice in the grocery! Take it off! Take it off right now!"*

As Savitri darted into the bathroom in shame, Devan realized the family's pilgrimage to America wouldn't be near what he'd anticipated or hoped it would be. Siddharth was still the same bullying thug he'd always been. But he was in charge now. And he seemed more confident and arrogant than ever, emboldened by his familiarity with American customs. The most troubling thing was that he appeared to be aware of his advantage over Devan. Unlike in the past, they couldn't just get up from his mother-in-law Virika's table and go home. No, they were thousands of miles away from that option. They had to take whatever Siddharth did or said, and they had to do it humbly.

"I wondered about that," Devan said, watching as Rudy finished the first cocktail before plunging into the second one, crunching ice in his mouth.

"Pooja was my sister-in-law, Devan. But I married her so she could come here to care for Raj. She is my wife by law, but she's the sister of my real wife, Hanika," Rudy said.

Rudy became somber again. He sat quietly for a long time, as did Devan. After a while, Rudy abruptly started talking again.

"Years ago, Devan, I spent half a day in a high school gymnasium in Beaufort, South Carolina. I tried to sell encyclopedias for which the state paid most of the cost. But none of the parents were interested. They were either very wealthy or dirt poor. It was just like Bombay State. The wealthy already had encyclopedias, and the poor didn't know what they were. I was so tired. I'd traveled across the entire state, from Greenville to Charleston. And I only had $16 to show for it. But I sat, patiently following all the rules in my handbook from Britannica. And I cursed myself the whole time. How could I have been so foolish to come to America? What business did a Gujarati such as I was, have trying to sell books to people who couldn't even read? Back home, important men consulted me leading up to Partition, and I was one of the only non-Anglo-Indians that continued to work for them afterward. But I went from that to sitting across the table from people that couldn't form complete sentences as they spoke. It was humbling and disgraceful, Devan. But I kept my eye on the prize. I had a bus ticket to Raleigh for the following morning. And I was so excited, partly because I was moving into a stronger market but also because I couldn't wait to go to the Western Union office and get the money your father sent me. Paying me with a check became impractical as I traveled so much. So it wasn't nearly as uplifting as when your father wrote to me and folded a check between the pages of his letters. I'd sit for hours, reading and rereading his recollections of all that happened in Bombay State. He related all the things I missed about being home. Our friends. Our family. It was, at once, heartening and disheartening. I so missed Bombay State. I so missed India."

Devan realized this story didn't have a happy ending. Yet he couldn't peel his eyes from the man that suddenly and strangely looked just like his father.

"As I walked away from the Western Union office, I counted my money, putting each bill into envelopes devoted to different things. I had enough money for food, laundry, savings, and a dollar or so for entertainment," Rudy said as he enumerated each category on his fingers.

"And between that and the money Britannica paid me, I was in good shape for the next two weeks. It was the most wonderful feeling in the world, Devan. You can't possibly imagine," Rudy said.

He was right. Devan couldn't. Devan had never been in such a dilemma, so he sat and continued to listen.

"But then, as I moved back toward the bus, I heard someone calling my name. I couldn't hear her at first because of my elation and because she called me 'Paddle.' But the more times she called out my name, it began to register with me. So I stopped and turned. And the last thing I remembered seeing for years afterward was a young lady motioning for me to return to the office. I realized something was wrong, Devan. I just knew it. Something was terribly wrong."

Devan felt as though he knew how this was about to end, but he absurdly held on with hope.

"There was a telegram that came with the transfer. And it came across the wire after I got the money Ajai sent," Rudy said.

Devan sat wide-eyed as though he were listening to some ancient tale from ago. But he was incapable of speaking. Indeed this was a tough old bird. Rudra Patel was the real article. He was the type of man Devan wanted to be. And Devan owed him so much more respect than he did Siddharth.

"I stood at the counter, watching a fish swim around in a bowl next to a jar of pig flesh in tubes, floating in a red brine. The woman read the telegram back to herself, word for word, and I watched her mouth the entire time, more intently than I'd ever watched anything. Then she handed me the telegram."

Devan already knew the outcome, partly because of Rudy's demeanor but also because Hanika wasn't there and Rudy was married to her sister now.

"That telegram changed my life forever, Devan. Your father sent it to me, so it was a mixed blessing. I suppose it could have come more callously than it did, and I'm thankful he's the one that told me. But it read the same, nevertheless. It said that my wife, Hanika, was dead. She died giving birth to Raj."

Devan sat as his eyes welled with tears, just as Rudy's did. He put himself in Rudy's shoes and wondered how he might react to the news that Savitri was gone. Not just that, but the notion of receiving that news, oceans away from where she was at the time, was a crippling, unimaginable thought. It made Devan want to sign on with Siddharth if only to bring her and the children to him immediately.

Then, just as quickly as he'd become so gloomy, Rudy rebounded and found a silver lining.

"But it also told me that I had a son. Your father said he was a big baby, eight pounds and eleven ounces. And he also told me he looked like my Hanika, which he does. And so I wept as much for that blessing as I did because I'd lost her. I made quite the spectacle of myself in that bus station parking lot, Devan."

Devan thought it was ludicrous to be concerned about not seeming manly at such a time. It astounded him as Rudy continued talking.

"Two elderly women from the South approached the old blubbering foreigner, and had they not taken either of my arms, I would've fallen onto my face. One of them held my cane as they put my arms over their shoulders before a big Southern man with a crew cut came over and helped me onto the bus. I'll never forget their compassion. It changed the way I viewed southern Americans. And I felt guilty for everything I thought before."

Rudy fell into another span of silence, staring off into space.

Devan ultimately broke that silence and said, "What did you do, Rudy?"

"What did I do?" Rudy said, as though Devan had asked him an absurd question, "What did I do? I got back on the bus. And I did what I had to do. I went back to work. I couldn't live off of your father's generosity forever, Devan. And I had a son, a wonderful, beautiful son to take care of. So I went back to work."

Devan was baffled. He sat in disbelief, looking at a man he'd been wary of within the past twenty-four hours, then liked, despised, and now liked again. He more than liked Rudy, though. He revered him. He thought he might be the bravest, strongest man he'd ever met. All his self-pity over the past several years made him feel ashamed.

It was such a profound sight in Brioche de Peches that afternoon. Two men at very different junctures in life sat together. One was on the verge of leaving the world as another sat on the cusp of life's remainder, trying to determine his place in it. One was reflective, and the other hopeful for the future. But both were Gujaratis and had the same ancient blood coursing through their veins. They were both Patels.

Rudy wasn't through yet, though.

"The love a man has for his son transcends everything, Devan, including the grave. So, when I learned you'd be here this week, I was compelled to meet you. And people can laugh at an old fool like me, but I know Ajai called to me to come here and meet with you. Something troubles him, and I believe I know what that is. He longs to make peace with you and see that you and his grandchildren are safe."

It was one of the things about Hinduism that Devan dismissed as mysticism. His father was dead, and he didn't communicate with anyone. He appreciated Rudy's concern, just as he was happy to discover he had a relative in the United States other than Siddharth—a powerful one. He prepared to resist any more glorious recollections of his father that attempted to paint him as anything more than he was. But he was comforted by what Rudy went on to say.

"Devan, I'm going to give you my business card. I know you won't use it because you're as hard-headed as your father. But, please, don't find yourself alone in America as I did. Don't relearn the lessons I already learned for you. Don't repeat history. And keep your bearing, young cousin. Stay focused on what's most important to you, and that should be your family. You can learn much from Siddharth, and you should. But I'd advise that you take everything he says with a grain of salt. He's not like us, Devan. That owes nothing to whatever his religion is, though. Siddharth is evil. His kind of evil glows in the shadows of The Vedas, the Q'ran, and the King James Bible. And it's an unapologetic manner of evil."

What Rudy said was disappointing to Devan. He didn't merely want his business card. He wanted Rudy's guidance, his wisdom. He was amazed he had a family member he'd never known. And it seemed he wasn't merely well-versed but an expert in the field Devan had chosen. Rudra Patel was a powerbroker, a Brahmin within the American caste system. Devan had so much to learn from Rudy. And he didn't want to miss the chance.

The closest thing to someone like Rudy he knew of was the distant cousin of Savitri's, Armand, who was in the motel business. But, supposedly, he was a young man, much younger than Rudy or Devan. And Devan couldn't picture himself learning from such a person, no matter how successful they were.

So it suddenly seemed such an injustice that he only now met Rudy Patel. Everything about him was right, whereas every instinct he had about Siddharth begged him to pack it all in and go home to Gujarat. It was so fatefully cruel that Rudy presented himself now.

Devan drew all those feelings back, thinking about Rudy and everything he'd gone through. It was so much worse than anything he'd endured. And he did it all for the love of his family. Still, he thought he'd give it a shot.

"Why can't I work for you, cousin? Why can't you teach me all these things I need to know?" Devan asked.

Devan was taken with Rudy Patel by this time and appreciative for his reaching out to him. But he could tell by Rudy's expression that it just wasn't meant to be.

"Ah," Rudy said, "if I were only five years younger, I'd gladly take you under my wing. But I'm not a young man anymore, Devan. I'm not even an old one. I'm a very old man and a sick one at that! It's time for me to sit back and reflect on what my life has meant rather than what it holds moving forward."

Devan looked down at the table, and Rudy could sense his disappointment.

"I've received an offer for all of my properties, Devan. And the offer is considerable. It's nothing I can disregard, and it will benefit Raj and his family for the rest of their lives. The offer came from a group of investors called a Real Estate Investment Trust. But you should take heart in this and learn from it moving forward. They offered me twenty-six million dollars for my properties, Devan. It's more money than I could ever spend," Rudy said with a stone face.

Devan looked up from the table with his eyes wide open. Had he just heard Rudy correctly? Twenty-six million dollars? For motels? No, just as Rudy said before, it was nothing Devan could comprehend.

"So, you see, the die is cast for me, Devan," Rudy continued, "but that doesn't mean I'm not here to answer your questions and help you in any way I can."

Devan still couldn't get past the dollar figure Rudy spat out. His father received less than one-tenth of that for an enormous tobacco plantation in Kheda. So how could this man, who his father helped get started in business, earn such a payday?

But Rudy continued, knowing just how unimaginable that amount of money might be to Devan.

"It's not as easy as all that, Devan. There are stipulations with any offer. And one of them is having a management company in place upon the transfer. Things aren't like they used to be. Most branded properties already require a management company or some other emissary between the property owner and operations. I know the current requirement of the Christensen franchise is a net worth of $3 million. And they're unyielding in this requirement, just as they are with their very restrictive covenants. It's an all-out mess, Devan! But you see, I won't deal with these things any longer if I sell. I'll move to Sarasota with Pooja, and we'll sit in our condominium and have dinner as the sun sets. And I'll wait for that confused boy to give me grandchildren, which I'm sure he eventually will."

It all sounded so beautiful to Devan. Like a fairy tale. He couldn't imagine being in the financial position Rudra was. To sit with Savitri, drinking coffee and staring out at the Gulf of Mexico was unimaginable to him. But the thought of doing that with that many millions in the bank was unthinkable.

Realizing his good fortune eclipsed everything he said to Devan after that, Rudy extended a laurel branch.

"I can't help you as you want me to, Devan. I can't use you on one of my properties because they're all under contract. And I lose more and more control over them by the day. Most of my hotels have young attorneys and executives with this Real Estate Investment Trust staying in them, ensuring compliance with their ridiculous requirements. You'd have nothing to learn from how they do business, at least not what you need to learn."

Devan's admiration and intrigue transformed into envy as Rudy spoke.

"But I can invite you and your family to experience Diwali with their American relatives. I presume being in America hasn't influenced your appreciation of your ancestry enough to preclude that."

Devan remained silent, still mesmerized by the amounts of money Rudy described. But a part of his brain captured that last suggestion. So he piped up and said, "Yes! Yes! Of course! We'd love to celebrate Diwali with you, cousin!"

Rudy laughed as he set his business card on the table and

slid it toward Devan. Just as he did, Pooja returned to the table. The waitress from earlier followed, carrying a tray with three ramekins of hand-churned vanilla ice cream and three cups of steaming black coffee.

Pooja sat down and complained about her experience dealing with people from the kitchen. Raj came to the table, flipped a chair around backward, and sat down. Then a white girl with brunette hair and a glowing smile walked onto the patio and joined them, setting her backpack on the ground. It was Raj's girlfriend, Elisa. She was a Yankee from Ohio, an accounting major at Georgia Tech. She'd eventually give birth to a son and a daughter. The boy would helm a family LLC that created generational wealth using his grandfather's substantial estate, while the daughter would achieve acclaim as an author of poetry.

And within moments, the table transformed from being a couple of disheartened, emotional Gujaratis to a table full of American family members, each with different bearings but all converging on the same place, at the same time.

Sadly, it was the last time Devan saw his cousin, Rudra Patel, alive. Rudy died a month afterward due to complications from his lifelong ailment. And that left Devan wondering what might have been if they'd only crossed paths earlier in life. Nevertheless, he forged ahead and executed things to the best of his ability. He yielded to that idiot Siddharth's instructions and did what he told him to do along the way.

And he also did as his cousin instructed him, evaluating everything Siddharth told him. But the most important thing he did was change his name. He changed it back to Patel. And that's how his name and those of his family appeared on their applications for Social Security cards once they became United States Citizens. Savitri, Sridevi, Fardeen, and Anaya were all Americans. But they were also Patels.

CHAPTER ELEVEN

T he Indian caste system is a complex social stratification, with its origins dating back over three millennia—a thousand years before the birth of Christ. While it has lingering implications for Indian society, its regimentation is far less inflexible than it once was.

Beginning in the mid-1800s, the British, first through the British East India Company, followed by the British "Raj" or direct rule after The Indian Rebellion, attempted to account for India's massive population through a national census. Their intent, however, was not the furtherance of the Indian people rather, they did so primarily to assess taxes on landowners in one of the world's largest nations. They utilized the ancient caste system, perverting it to facilitate their ambitions. They sought to establish order and promulgate laws, hoping to create a society more reflective of Western values and culture, one they could rule more handily. The system evolved into a stringent segregation of India's different peoples and cultures using its ancient, pre-existent castes.

That was the enduring legacy of the British Empire. They wielded the caste system as they would have any other weapon and did it with such avarice. Before the British arrived, Indians paid less mind to their caste system's hierarchy. And they freely moved among different castes. But once the Englishmen came, people who once intermingled, intermarried, and lived peaceably became separated according to caste. It wasn't much different from American segregation, which was an ancillary manifestation of the passage of the Thirteenth Amendment to the US Constitution that abolished slavery or any other form of peonage.

But in 1950, following India's independence from the British, discrimination based on caste was made illegal. Moreover, allowances or reservations for the lower castes and tribes of India were made, which established quotas for governmental roles ordinarily reserved for the upper castes.

The intercaste distinctions of Hinduism originate from Brahma, the Hindu God of Creation. While Westerners generally view Hindus as polytheistic, it's a mischaracterization. Hindus are *henotheistic*, which means they worship a single God while acknowledging, or at the least, not denying the existence of other gods. However, the prevailing view of Hindus is that those other gods are iterations of Brahma rather than distinct deities.

The four principal castes or varnas of the Hindu system are the Brahmins, Kshatriyas, Vaishyas, and Shudras. They are symbolic of Brahma's physiology: his head, arms, legs, and feet. And each caste is distinguished by its relative function. However, those broad categories branch into a dizzying number of other castes based on everything from religion (dharma) to profession (karma). That furcation swells the number of castes into the tens of thousands.

The Brahmin caste came from Brahma's head. Consequently, their caste consists of those of higher thinking and spirituality. They are the most venerated and prestigious caste, comprised of clergy, educators, and intellectuals. And historically, their charge is as the keepers and disseminators of sacred and vital knowledge, while their influence resonates among the other castes.

The Kshatriyas are representative of Brahma's arms. Accordingly, they are the ruling and governing caste. Just as one's arms articulate the mind's dictates, they are the effectors of Brahma's will. And their name connotes authority or "kshatra" according to the ancient Vedic texts, which are the canonical equivalent of the Christian, Hebrew, and Muslim scriptures. They are the keepers of Hindu moral law. They are also the elite warriors, and they, along with Brahmins, are considered the upper castes.

The Vashiyas, the representation of Brahma's thighs, are historically farmers, merchants, and tradesmen. But as time progressed, they became increasingly involved with the financial community and money lending. And they ceded things like mercantilism and agrarianism to other groups.

The final caste is the Shudras, who come from Brahma's feet. They are the laborers and those charged with menial tasks. The distinction between their caste and another group, which falls outside the caste system altogether, was often blurred.

The latter group is the Dalits, also referred to in times past as "untouchables."

September 4, 1928, Srinagar, Princely State of Jammu and Kashmir, Bharat (India)

Virika didn't have much of a chance from birth. Nor did her younger sister, Daksha. They were the two youngest of twelve siblings whose father, Ishan, furrowed drainage for Srinagar's sewerage. He and his wife, Ela, were Dalits. They were untouchables. And their lives were equally challenging growing up. They'd wed when they were very young, after which Ela immediately became pregnant, and she stayed that way for the next twenty years.

Life was difficult for the little girls beyond their relegation outside of the caste system as Dalits. Both their parents died from cholera when the girls were eight and six years old, leaving them, along with those siblings who still lived at home—four boys—to fend for themselves.

Most of the older boys left home when they were very young. And they wound up as grifters and thieves, while the other boys were well on their way to doing the same except for one, Vajra. He was the closest age to the girls and was good-hearted. But due to a lack of guidance, Vajra was unambitious and struggled to survive, just like the rest of the family had. After Ishan died, Ela died shortly after, and Ishan's mother, Turvi, took the remaining four boys into her home. She eventually took the girls too. But only after they panhandled for several weeks, sleeping in alleyways and foraging trash for melon rinds, orange peels, or whatever else they could find to survive.

But without exception, even in their lowest, most desperate moments, the older little girl, Virika, insisted she and her sister recite the only mantra she knew, which she overheard her brothers recite each day. It was called the Savitri Mantra and was a ceremonial prayer to the goddess Savitr. Ordinarily reserved for the upper castes, her parents required the boys to perform it each morning.

Virika also parsed a third of whatever the girls scrounged to eat as an offering. She placed it in a large basket they found that she'd adorned with a mulberry branch a compassionate street vendor gave her as he took pity on the dirty little girls that walked the streets, holding hands with one another. They likely could have been rescued on several occasions. Yet whenever someone approached them, usually a man, Virika grabbed her little sister's hand, and they ran away.

The hardships Virika endured gave her greater resolve to pray and meditate, confident that Savitr heard them and that their grandmother would come for them one day. And once she did, it vulcanized Virika's convictions, leaving her a thankful and devout Hindu for the rest of her life.

Something else her destitution did was cultivate an element of her character that made her an eternally headstrong woman. She conveyed that to her female descendants. They were all strong-willed and resilient women. And they were tenaciously Hindu, all originating from the example Virika set. They were tigresses in a world that perpetually tried to subjugate them both in India and abroad because they were female. That was Virika's legacy to her daughters, granddaughters, and beyond, and it was formidable.

Turvi's guilt for abandoning the girls overwhelmed her. And it came to a head one day at the market. She overheard men talking about two luckless, feral little girls who refused to accept help and recoiled when anyone tried to ask them a question. It broke Turvi's heart.

So, she set about to find her granddaughters, asking others if and where they'd seen them. Eventually, a young boy pointed her toward an alleyway where he'd discovered them a week earlier as he chased a cat he wanted to capture and keep as a pet.

Sure enough, when Turvi went to the alley, Virika and Daksha lay beneath some dismantled crates, clinging to one another in their sleep. Their faces were dirty, and the bottoms of their feet blackened from walking Srinagar's streets barefooted.

"Nani!" Virika squealed as Turvi shook her awake. Virika stared up at her face, behind which the sun shone brilliantly. Turvi appeared like a deity, and Virika leaped into her arms, amazed but thankful she'd found them.

Turvi walked down the streets in shame, looking down as she held Virika's hand with her right and Daksha's with her left. She imagined that every eye was on her and that all the men on the streets whispered what a disgraceful existence hers must be to abandon children, two little girls, especially.

Nevertheless, she made it home just as the boys returned from work. While happy to see their younger sisters, the boys privately wondered what it meant for the family and how Turvi could sustain them. It was something Turvi had also pondered the entire march homeward. They barely had enough pineapples, tamatars, beans, and rice to exist, and they often went to their grueling jobs on empty, growling stomachs.

Consequently, Turvi's compassion proved short-lived, albeit through no fault of her own. Turvi became overwhelmed, trying to feed all six children. She often had to ration their food, allowing the boys to eat first. After all, they continued their father's work, bringing the only income to the household. The girls couldn't earn anything beyond being whores, and they weren't even old enough to do that. She couldn't allow them to starve, yet they were such an extraordinary burden to her and her ability to keep the boys fed.

Turvi considered herself a principled woman, but she decided she must do something to protect the boys. She had to get rid of Virika and Daksha. It wasn't an uncommon dilemma for orphans of the era and those who stepped forward to raise them. There were channels and avenues, if you will, to remedy the crisis. But those remedies seemed inordinately cruel to Turvi.

However, she had no choice. She could keep the children together and allow everyone to starve. Or she could send the girls into the world to be cared for by others better suited to the task.

So, one morning as the children slept, Turvi called on a man, Manraj, to assist her with her predicament. Her dead husband mentioned Manraj once in the past in an unflattering light. Manraj was Punjabi but purportedly had affiliations all over Bharat. And after speaking with him, all the rumors and the things her husband said about him proved true.

"I can certainly find a place for your little ones, Turvi. And I'm going to charge you nothing for doing so in consideration of my friendship with your husband. Where are the girls? Do you have them with you now in Srinagar? How old are they? Do they have any diseases? What are their teeth like?"

Manraj's words ripped Turvi apart as they punctuated what she was about to do. But she thought about her grandsons and how they favored her son and husband so much. Then, she considered how their mother, who looked just like the little girls, couldn't keep her legs closed long enough to consider the consequences of not doing so. So she found the resolve to answer Manraj.

"Yes, sir. They're here with me, sir. And no, sir. They have no diseases, sir," she said, staring down.

After their exchange, she bargained to present Virika and Daksha to Manraj in the market the following morning. She didn't look up for fear of being disgraced or beaten by the young, flashy Punjabi Sikh.

"I appreciate your kindness, sir. But may I ask, isn't it customary that someone pays for young girls such as these? I don't know the traditions regarding such things, sir, so I apologize if I insult you. I'd just as soon leave with them forever than affront you with my ignorance," Turvi said.

Manraj then knew he wasn't dealing with an imbecile. This old bitch knew exactly what she did and said. So he swallowed, stopped biting into his apple, and walked toward Turvi, who was sure he'd strike her. But he didn't.

"Well," Manraj began as he scratched the side of his nose with his thumb, "under ordinary circumstances, the girls would be older, of childbearing age. Then, I might earn a premium if they were infants. The Englishmen pay top dollar for babies. I'm afraid, Turvi, that your granddaughters fall between two different markets for me. So where does that leave us?"

Still not looking up, Turvi managed the courage to speak while looking over at a table of pineapples.

"I have no understanding of these things, Sir Cheema. So, I only ask for your compassion, and I plead with you to do what you feel is best and wisest, sir," she said as she rocked back and forth involuntarily because she was so afraid.

So at 9:30 AM the following morning, Turvi sold her granddaughters, Virika and Daksha, into slavery for the rest of their lives. And she did it for the US equivalent of $27. But, tragically, their enslavement sent them to opposite ends of Bharat.

Virika was to remain in Srinagar. Then Manraj sold Daksha to a prosperous merchant from Bombay State named Popat.

The sisters clung to one another as Manraj tried to pull them apart while Turvi raced away in tears. After separating them, Manraj forced Virika and Daksha in opposite directions. But the little girls continued to scream and managed to grasp their hands with one another a final time as several merchants rushed forward and helped separate them again. When they finally did, the entire market was in an uproar, leaving Manraj staring over either of his shoulders in fear. Along with so many other transactions he frequently conducted, this one was illegal. And he stood to lose everything if someone realized what was happening and got upset enough to report him.

All the ugliness and horror of what took place dissipated after it resounded across the market as loudly as the little girls' crying and desperate pleas did moments earlier. Then Virika left with her new masters, the Shakurs, a Muslim family from Srinagar, and Daksha left with Manraj. Only Daksha was bound for Ahmedabad in Bombay State, where she'd eventually marry Adesh Popat, the eldest son of the prominent Gujarati family to which Manraj sold her.

Life for both of the little girls continued on disparate paths. After Daksha married Adesh Popat, it found her living with little by way of want. However, she experienced beatings from her insanely jealous and controlling husband for the rest of his life.

Her sister's life was decidedly different. Virika also married within the family of her captors. But, mercifully, her Muslim husband, Fardeen, wasn't nearly as assertive or demanding as Daksha's. Fardeen's reluctance and timidity frequently placed him at odds with the girl he'd taken as a wife once she reached the age of twelve. She neither respected nor understood that in a man. She viewed it as a weakness and was resentful of him at first. Their adversarial but mutually adoring relationship continued for decades until they both died within a year of each other.

"I'll not do that," Virika once declared through a crumpled face as the Shakur family insisted that she pray to Allah while she ate dinner with them. Marking just how rebellious she was, the recitation of thanks occurs privately rather than communally during an Islamic meal. She needed only to thank God before taking a bite of food, and she could've easily "faked" it, but she refused even to do that. And despite Fardeen's protests in front of his family, the little girl remained adamant.

Yet he loved her, and her resilience captivated him all the more. She was so hard-headed and unyielding for a woman. She opted to sit on the floor in the next room by herself, eating the dinner she prepared, rather than joining the Shakurs at the family table. Then the family was stunned when Fardeen rose, lifted his plate, and sat with his young wife in the next room where she used to sit alone before they were married.

When the couple's first child was born, the turmoil continued. The family insisted the boy be named Mahir after Fardeen's father. But Virika refused. She demanded that her son have a Hindu given name. After hours of bickering, as Virika struggled through a long and excruciating labor, they reached an agreement. And the first child of Fardeen and Virika Shakur was named "Siddharth."

The baby entered the world breached, but once they yanked him from the womb, he came out screaming and clawing like nothing the midwives had ever seen. It was as though he insisted on hurling himself into life, on being alive with or without their help. He was incorrigible, demanding, and aggressive, but he miraculously calmed after they rested him on his mother's chest.

"Siddharth," Virika, the exhausted teenage mother, cried to

the baby, whose eyes were wide open, as black as midnight, and seemed to focus on whomever he looked at instead of staring into space as ordinary babies' did. He also gnawed at her fingers, demanding that his mother immediately begin nursing him.

"You'll be so much! You'll change the world, and so many people will respect you!" the sapped, proud young mother wept as she raised Siddharth to her breast, and he began to suckle.

CHAPTER TWELVE

October 24, 1947, Srinagar, the Princely State of Jammu and Kashmir

1947 found the entire nation in a state of chaos. After 200 years, the British were on the cusp of leaving Bharat forever. It was the culmination of long efforts by anti-colonialists like Mohandas Gandhi, Motilal Nehru, Bal Gangadhar Tilak, C.R. Das, and other freedom fighters. India's independence was hastened by the decimation of the British economy during World War II. Around the same time, they withdrew from other colonial holdings like Burma (modern-day Myanmar), Ceylon (now Sri Lanka), Jordan, Palestine, and Egypt. They simply couldn't devote the resources to maintain India, which they once referred to as the Jewel in The Crown of The British Empire. They also lost control over the elites or zamindars, who were land owners and wealthy merchants to whom they bestowed royal titles under the British Raj system. They were the ones who collected taxes in their provinces and enforced the will of the British. They were concentrated in the northern part of the nation, while the British selected specific people to be land owners who were required to remit their taxes directly in the southerly states. Once control was lost, it left the British incapable of ruling either directly or indirectly. The Indian Navy mutinied, and fearing the same would happen with the other Indian branches of service, the British were forced to leave. No other region in the nation experienced the resulting cathartic upheaval more than the princely state of Jammu and Kashmir.

The British withdrawal immediately preceded Partition,

through which two independent nations formed: India and Pakistan. Yet the way things happened left so much to be desired —particularly in the Northwest region of the new Indian nation, bordering newly-formed Pakistan. It became a crucible for the ensuing social unrest among different ethnic groups, which somehow found a way to live in harmony up to that point. Those groups were Hindus, Sikhs, and Muslims. And there was a definitive line drawn between the former two and the latter.

The atrocities on both sides of the confrontation were horrific and included pilfering, murder, mass rape, and forcible impregnation, all intended to humiliate and demoralize the opposition.

In August of 1947, Muslim Saifs attacked and boarded a train from Waziribad bound for Jammu. Using axes, knives, and swords, they murdered every non-Muslim passenger on board, sparing no one. The Nizamabad Lohars killed them and seized their belongings.

It seemed the train's engineers were complicit in the massacre. Because they inexplicably stopped the train between Waziribad and Jammu at, presumably, a predetermined location. And then the unimaginable happened. After the killings, the train continued to Jammu, pulling into the station loaded with its slaughtered cargo of passengers.

However, the British press didn't pick up the story. There was never any mention of the atrocity or its implications for the continuing discord in the fledgling nations.

While it was a patent abuse of the government's control over the press, it also left the region's people, particularly those in Jammu and Kashmir, blinded. Most of them didn't know the chaos and impending violence they faced until it was too late.

It wasn't all one-sided, though. The Hindus fought back, killing over 100,000 Muslims in Jammu and Kashmir during the subsequent months.

The entire region was a bloodbath. And it was all attributable to the capricious, poorly executed, and ill-timed British withdrawal from the subcontinent.

It was certainly no place for an interfaith married couple like Siddharth Shakur and his young wife, Virika. So they were left with a monumental decision. They weren't safe remaining in Jammu and Kashmir. That was a point made abundantly clear by Virika's older brother, Vajra.

Vajra kept close contact with his sister, Virika, after his grandmother, Turvi, sold her into bondage. He also forged a relationship with his nephew, Siddharth, throughout the boy's early life. He felt his responsibility was to instill Hinduism in his nephew, albeit through such confusing and mixed messages for the child. Vajra, at once, hated and embraced Hinduism. While he faithfully prayed each day, he also cursed Brahmin tenets. They were doctrines that left him relegated to a humble life of servitude and subservience.

Tragically, he instilled his sentiments in the boy who grew up irreverent, bombastic, and confused.

Siddharth's father, Fardeen, was Muslim. But confidentially, Fardeen felt that most religions were abominations of what Allah intended. So he was also somewhat of a dissenter, accepting those moral aspects of his faith that he thought served humanity and rebuffing those he found objectionable. However, he always remained steadfastly faithful and observant of Allah.

Fardeen couldn't stand Vajra. He resented everything about him, from his defiant swagger to his outspoken nature. Fardeen was a quiet, contemplative man, whereas Vajra was loud and braggadocious. But what Fardeen detested most about his brother-in-law was his wife's adoration for him. And she imparted her cherishing to her son, Siddharth. That was nearly more than Fardeen could stand.

So Fardeen was disgusted when Vajra showed up at the Shakur's household one evening, just around dinnertime, as he always seemed to time his visits. Moreover, he came with a present for Fardeen's son. When Fardeen answered the door, he saw Vajra standing, holding a raggedy football with busted stitches under his arm. Exacerbating Fardeen's disgust was that Vajra wore what looked like a makeshift uniform.

He wore a black forage cap like the British police wore, along with a khaki shirt and pants, all of which appeared Vajra picked up secondhand. Every article of clothing was too big for the puny Dalit, and he fidgeted with the rope holding his pants up. It was clear to Fardeen that Vajra attempted to look like he was in the Rashtriya Swayamsevak Sangh, or "RSS."

The RSS, an ultra-right-wing Hindu paramilitary group, was organized among young, brave revolution-minded men to instill honor and develop a sense of Hindu unity. Its formation was a hallmark of the social unrest in the nation leading up to Partition. The organization hoped to create a Hindu culture that might one day supplant the British Raj or monarchal rule over India. They also sought to compel the Maharaja to sign the instrument of accession, thereby making Jammu and Kashmir a part of India.

When Muslim sympathizers began an uprising in Poonch and the Maharaja lost control of nearly all the western districts, he had no choice. He requested military support from India, which they agreed to. However, that support was contingent upon Jammu and Kashmir relinquishing their independence and joining the Indian nation. So the Maharaja conceded and signed the instrument.

Looking him up and down, Fardeen knew right away his Dalit brother-in-law was not an RSS member. He couldn't be. Beyond his Dalitism, he had no semblance of a military bearing or any other trait the RSS might find compelling enough to enlist the slob. Fardeen would've laughed at Vajra had he not made him so angry. Still, he couldn't help but get a jab in.

"It's somewhat late for postage, isn't it?" Fardeen said

through an impudent smile.

But Vajra just ignored the swipe. Then he addressed Fardeen with a complete absence of formality or reverence.

"Is my sister here?" Vajra asked.

Fardeen never got the chance to tell Vajra to go to hell or to get off his stoop because Virika interrupted him, followed closely by Siddharth charging into Vajra's chest and hugging the man. It was a peculiar sight because Siddharth, while only twelve, was a big imposing figure who appeared to be several years older. He looked like a man. Whereas Vajra was gimpy, frail-looking, and much shorter than Siddharth.

"Vajra!!" Virika shouted as she pushed past Fardeen and hugged her brother alongside Siddharth.

Fardeen sneered, turned away, and went to the table for dinner, joining his parents and two younger sisters. He presumed his brother-in-law wouldn't be far behind him.

He was right.

In the middle of dinner, right after he spooned another serving of mustard fish onto his plate, Vajra spoke. And what he said left everyone at the table uneasy.

"You should leave. You're not safe here," Vajra said while chewing with his Dalit mouth open, staring directly across the table at Fardeen.

Everyone sat silently for a moment before Fardeen spoke up.

"What? What do you mean we're not safe?" he asked.

He believed he knew what Vajra referred to, but it was such inappropriate timing.

Muslims were swiftly becoming an endangered species in Jammu and Kashmir. There was talk that Maharaja Hari Singh exercised his newly found autonomy from the British Empire to ensure that the only people remaining in Jammu and Kashmir were either Hindus, Jains, or Sikhs. While he didn't openly endorse them, the Maharaja tacitly utilized the RSS to realize his aspirations. And he allowed them to take actions he could not politically afford to take himself. The only legitimate measures available to him would be those sanctioned by the Indian government. But those would come at a cost.

Nevertheless, it enraged Fardeen to have such a message delivered to him by a ditch digger. Something else that distracted him was the badge Vajra wore on his chest. It was tin and looked like he made it the day before in some shop, using the most rudimentary tools. Yet Vajra wore it as though it conveyed some meaning or authority. It bore the letters "RSS."

"I mean you should leave," Vajra said, smacking, "you should leave Srinagar and never return. And if you don't? You'll die."

Fardeen had enough. He shot up from the table and rounded it to meet Vajra face-to-face. But just before he could get his hands around Vajra's throat, Fardeen's father, Mahir, slammed his hand on the table, rattling the dishes and making everyone cower. Mahir's wife, Serina, hung her head, fearing what her husband might do next.

"Sit down, Fardeen!" he shouted.

Mahir was a peaceful man. But if provoked, he became as violent and fearsome as the greatest savage among his tribesmen.

"Take your hands off of him and take your seat, boy!" he yelled at his son.

Fardeen looked between his father and Vajra and began to ball his hand into a fist. His father acted like an old fool, he thought to himself. He had no idea what a Dalit liar was capable of, especially under such circumstances. But just as he drew back to pummel Vajra, his father interrupted him again.

"I said to take your seat!"

Fardeen released Vajra, allowing him to slump back into his

chair.

Vajra never blinked nor put up any opposition to Fardeen. He had the same indolent expression on his face the entire time. But that was because Vajra was accustomed to taking a beating. And had Fardeen been allowed to carry on, the Dalit would've been none the worse for wear. Because that's what Vajra's life was all about. It was about taking a beating. So as Fardeen stared back at Vajra, it infuriated him even more. Vajra just seemed so inelastic and impervious to anything.

"What do you mean," Mahir continued, "that we'll die if we don't leave Srinagar?"

Vajra returned to eating, smacking, and being as brazen as he'd been since arriving and said, "The RSS is planning a purge of all Muslims in Jammu and Kashmir. And this comes from the high command."

"The high command?!" Fardeen shouted, rising to his feet again, "You talk like you're in league with someone, you fool! But you're not! You sound like an ass! You sound like a moron! And what is this badge you wear, you ridiculous toad??"

"Fardeen!" Mahir hollered, "I'll not ask you again, son! Take your seat and stay quiet!"

Virika began crying and clutched Siddharth's hand.

Siddharth spoke, saying, "Papa, sit down and listen!"

That turned Fardeen into a madman. He looked at his son as Virika clung to him, and he said, "Boy! I will beat you to death! Don't ever talk to me like this again! Do you understand?!"

"You'll keep your hands off of him under my roof, boy!" Mahir said, "Now sit back down and don't open your mouth again!"

That evening, the paternal ties that bind fathers to sons were strenuously pulled in both directions. But Mahir's was the final word. So Fardeen sat back down and listened to whatever the Dalit had to say. It was a fortunate thing he did, too.

"There's a contingent of Pashtun raiders," Vajra began, "and they're coming for the airport. They intend to attack and loot all planes as they land. Then, they'll move on to the railway once they take hold of Srinagar. They're going to block all trade into Kashmir."

Now Mahir was mad. He wasn't necessarily mad at Vajra but more so at the message he delivered. Mahir paid attention to all going on across the country, even though based upon secondhand and sometimes thirdhand hearsay. While it sickened him to no end to hear about the treatment of Muslims by Hindu and Sikh tribes, he'd realized the actions would not be unilateral for very long. And if what Vajra described was true, it had begun.

He faced a much more significant problem, though. And that was because of his son's involvement with a Hindu. His family was in danger because they were Muslim. But also because Virika was Hindu. And the fact that his Muslim son married and fathered a child with a Hindu added a potentially more incendiary element to their circumstances.

They had no quarter.

The family kept a low profile even before the widespread unrest that came with Partition in August. But it was only a matter of time before his predicament became known. All that required was a simpleton like the one sitting at his table to make that happen—even if it wasn't his intention.

Strangely, he'd grown to love his daughter-in-law, who birthed his first grandchild. She gave him a boy, a big strapping boy in Siddharth. Siddharth was strong in every sense. Though only twelve, he'd achieved notoriety as a tough guy among the kids on the street. They mostly detested him, but they also respected him. He refused to sit in a classroom for very long and always wound up in a fight when he did. But Mahir was still very proud of Siddharth, and he believed he'd be a great man one day.

However, if what Virika's brother said was true, and he had

a woeful, disheartening suspicion that it was, the family, all of them, were in great peril. The potential danger could come from either side, although the outcome would likely be the same: genocidal violence.

Ruthlessness and barbarism seemed to give way to kindness and understanding in that age. It confounded Mahir how the different groups of people living in harmony for centuries were suddenly at odds because of a legal document. Moreover, the depths to which all these young men prepared to sink were abysmal.

People that were once neighbors became adversaries. There was no allowance for leniency or a moment's consideration for the past. It didn't matter if men played together as little boys or broke bread with one another's families. The dictates and aspirations of both sides seemed absolute. So there was certainly no hope for any regard paid from either side to a Muslim man married to a Hindu woman.

No, the outlook couldn't have been bleaker as Mahir sat and listened to Vajra's warnings.

Mahir continued questioning him, ignoring Vajra's boast about any "high command," an apparent lie.

"This seems to be sensitive information you're relating, Vajra. I trust that you heard it as you said, but how, may I ask, could your superiors obtain such knowledge?" he asked Vajra in a non-confrontational tone. "How could they know what the Pashtuns plan?"

His diplomacy worked. Within moments, Vajra began giving details of how the intelligence fell into the hands of the RSS. Had anyone in the stalwart organization known he'd done so, it would have cost Vajra his life, as would the tin badge and absurd costume he made for himself. Vajra was no more a member of the RSS than the British House of Lords. However, times were desperate. So the RSS enlisted people in whatever capacity they could to keep the flow of information streaming upward. It would take more than their solo efforts to stave off Pakistani influence in Jammu and Kashmir, political or otherwise. Vajra and his badge were a manifestation of that desperation.

Vajra answered Mahir.

"A Swayamsevak infiltrated the Pakistan army. He dressed as a Muslim and learned about their plans. He risked his life to bring this information back, and the Maharaja and India owe him a great debt for his service," Vajra said.

Despite his brashness and apparent lack of education, Mahir found Vajra compelling. But he also terrified Mahir. Nevertheless, he addressed Vajra in a final attempt to gauge if his perception of things was accurate. He knew they were, but he needed to hear what someone else thought might happen. He wanted to hear someone else say it.

"But, we're Muslim, Vajra. We're not Hindu. Virika is Hindu, but she's only a servant. I don't even know if anyone outside this household knows she's married to my son," he reasoned.

Immediately, Vajra began shaking his head, causing Mahir's heart to race as he fell into the darkest of contemplations.

"Do you think that matters?" Vajra began.

"Do you believe if they gain control over Srinagar, they'll say, 'Oh, alright. She's Hindu and has a son, but she's just a servant.' Is that what you think? And whoever goes from door to door, based on their inquiries, no matter Hindu or Muslim, do you think they'll just move along and wish you well? No. I think you're dishonest with yourself, sir. I'm telling you now. You need to leave. You need to take my sister and my nephew and leave."

"And go where?!" Fardeen shouted, unable to hold his tongue anymore, "Where would you have us go?! West Punjab? Into the tiger's mouth? Or how about Bengal? Uttar Pradesh? Do you think we won't face the same threats there but by different hands? I think it's *you* that's fooling yourself, ditch digger! We're safest staying right here! Here, among people that we know!

People that we trust!"

"Fardeen, that's enough," Mahir said somberly with remarkable patience and a heart heavier than it'd been since his father passed. He was utterly despaired.

Mahir raised all his children in Srinagar. He lived a humble existence, but it was a fulfilling one. They had a garden where they grew everything from tamatars to radishes and beans. His wife, Serina, and their daughters went to the market weekly, shopping and trading among Hindus, Sikhs, and other Muslims. His friends often came over for coffee in the afternoon, which Virika prepared. She made it in a manner that was more delicious than anything they could buy in a café, preparing it one cup at a time. As unruly and overbearing as he was, Siddharth made several friends in the neighborhood. Often, Mahir had his coffee on the stoop out front as he watched the boys play football or cricket using shoddy, improvised equipment. Siddharth always excelled, calling out commands to all the other boys. He looked like a coach, a fully grown man instead of a child. It made Mahir proud in front of his friends as they sat, drank coffee, and watched.

And as things stood, only a month ago, he could still board the train and occasionally visit his mother and sisters, taking Siddharth with him.

But it seemed like all of that was about to end. Civility was dying right before Mahir, and he was powerless to do anything about it. So his focus shifted from preserving his way of life to simply surviving and protecting his family as long as he could. In his mind, it was unfitting for a sixty-seven-year-old man to be in this situation. SO, he was forced to sit and listen to whatever a Hindu Dalit's instructions were to remedy it all.

"You could go to Bombay State, to Gujarat," Vajra said as he belched and reached for his water glass.

"Pardon me?" Fardeen interrupted.

Gujarat? Why on Earth would he suggest Gujarat? Unfortunately, Fardeen believed he knew the answer but was still astounded by the Dalit's gall and thoughtlessness.

"I said Gujarat. You could go to Gujarat. It's where my sister Daksha lives, and she flourishes there. She works for a businessman named Popat," Vajra said, matter-of-factly.

Fardeen slapped his hand to his forehead. He was afraid this might happen the entire time. Yes, there were murmurings that Daksha moved to Gujarat after enslavement and that she did well. He'd also heard that she married into a family that found her work beyond tunneling ditches and sifting through sewerage. But it seemed implausible, so he never mentioned it to Virika. He didn't want to upset or give her false hope for something he couldn't clarify. Still, he braced himself for the oncoming and inevitable onslaught of questions from his naïve, sheltered wife.

"What?" Virika asked, rising from the table, "Daksha is in Gujarat? And she does well?"

The disbelief in Virika's voice was matched only by her sudden disdain for her current situation, which was precisely what Fardeen feared and why he'd never divulged anything to her.

Then Vajra spoke again, lowering the boom and confirming that all he'd just said was true.

"She does. She's a laundry matron for this Popat family. And they treat her very well according to her letters," Vajra continued.

"Letters?" Virika asked as her fiery spirit seemed to ignite simultaneously with her heart breaking.

"Yes," Vajra said, "she corresponds with me from time to time. I sometimes don't receive her correspondence because she always sends it to the home where we grew up. But from what I understand, when Eshal reads them to me, she does quite well.

She tends to the family's laundry, then she's done for a day. Her letters sometimes make me wish Nani sold me instead of her! I can do laundry! I do my laundry every month!"

Then Vajra began laughing and looking around the room, although no one found his words as funny as he did. So he stared back at his plate before tearing back into the delicious fish they served him.

Fardeen realized what was about to happen. His wife, a pathetic orphan who clung to any remembrance or affiliation she'd ever had with her parents and older brothers, would insist that they leave Srinagar just as her brother did. But her insistence came with additional demands in light of all Vajra had just said. It didn't change that her words cut through Fardeen, challenging his authority and leaving him speechless for a moment.

"I want to go to Bombay State, to Gujarat! I want to go tonight!" Virika insisted, cupping Siddharth's face to her side as she stared at Fardeen indignantly.

"What?" Fardeen asked, though he knew good and damn well what she'd said.

"I want to go to Gujarat!" she repeated as Siddharth reached forward and forked another mouthful of fish into his face while his mother stroked his head.

"And what do you hope to gain by going to Gujarat, woman?!" Fardeen shouted, "Do you think they'll welcome you with outstretched arms and give you a job and a place to live?! Do you think they'll protect you from this insurgency sweeping the nation?!"

Yet another time, Virika didn't understand the important words her beautiful man used. But she remained adamant, saying,

"I don't know! I don't know what they'll do! But if Daksha found prosperity there, then I shall, too! I'll go there! And

Ganesha will guide me!" she said, glaring back at Fardeen.

Ordinarily, a Muslim man would've beaten her to the ground if not to death. Had he chosen to do so, a typical Pashtun like Mahir wouldn't have done anything to stop him. But Fardeen wasn't that type of man, even as desperate as the situation was. Jammu and Kashmir was changing, perhaps for the better or maybe, the worse. All Fardeen thought about was that his wife was on the side of picking up their belongings and turning tail immediately. And it didn't sit well with him.

He managed to lower his tone and speak with the same noble conviction his father did, realizing that his temper served no purpose under the circumstances.

"We will not go to Gujarat," he said, "or anywhere else. We'll remain here, just as I said."

No one responded to the young, handsome man's deliberative words. They all just sat silently for a moment before he continued.

"Srinagar is my home. I know nothing about Bombay State. Or anywhere else in India. And I will be damned if I leave behind a life of prosperity to go to a faraway place, all because a ditch digger who probably hasn't eaten for days sits down at my family's table and tries to scare us! No. It's out of the question. We shall not go to Gujarat, Virika. You may get your sister's address and correspond with her if you want to rekindle your lowly status as a Dalit. But we're not leaving."

Mahir was near tears as he sat and watched his son take charge. He was so proud. But another part of him, that which sought to protect and preserve his family, gnawed away at his conscience. He had decades of experience beyond Fardeen's, so he knew things were not always as black and white nor cut and dried as they might initially appear—especially to a young man. But he let his son take a stand.

It only took moments for Vajra to respond in kind. He

stopped eating, stood up, and began his retort. Wiping his mouth with his napkin and then throwing it on the table, he started.

"Why do you think I'm here?" he asked, "Do you think it's because I have anything to profit? The things I've told you have already begun. The Lashkar [CS1]is moving toward Srinagar as we speak. They may be here in days, hours even. And what should concern you is what their intention is. Women are being kidnapped and raped. They kill their fathers and husbands without mercy.

I gave Siddharth a football tonight. But I wanted to give him a cricket bat because I know that's his favorite game. However, I need the bat I intended for him, Fardeen. I need the bat because after I leave tonight, I'll use it with my brothers to clear the snow and ice from Srinagar's runway for Indian soldiers coming from Dehli to land at the airport. And they're coming for a reason. If the Pashtuns get close enough to the airport, they will be stunned when the Indian Army greets them. So, why do you say these things? Why do you doubt me? Would you like to come with me tonight to the runway to confirm this? We could use another man. But if you don't want to, then listen to what I'm telling you!"

That's when the last scintilla of doubt and hope simultaneously left Fardeen's and Mahir's minds. This Dalit spoke the truth. Jammu and Kashmir was on the verge of becoming a different place. Whether it remained independent or became a part of either Pakistan or India was in the air. There was a manifold of influences competing with one another for its destiny.

But no matter what, the outcome would likely be tragic for the Shakurs.

CHAPTER THIRTEEN

"Hush!" Fardeen hissed at Siddharth as the covered truck he, his son, and Virika sat in the back of slowed to a halt.

The morning after Vajra's visit, Fardeen called on a childhood friend, Bansi, whose father owned a produce distributorship in Srinagar. Their business flourished, and they shipped vegetables and wares all over Northwest India. They owed Fardeen and Mahir several weeks' wages from summer, but Fardeen said he'd forgive them if they could help him. After a contentious meeting between Fardeen and Bansi at the business just outside Srinagar, the men struck a bargain. Bansi would get the Shakurs as far south as Jammu City. But after that, they were on their own.

Because of his brother-in-law's ominous warning, Fardeen intended to make it to Bombay State—or at least the hell out of Kashmir. His father, Mahir, insisted upon it, partly because it lessened the already unimaginable burden of keeping his family safe. But more than that, Mahir felt his grandson's best chance at survival was if they left Srinagar. And Siddharth was who mattered to Mahir the most.

The previous evening was the last Mahir and Fardeen spent together. And they embraced after dinner, the only two people at the table who knew what the following day would bring. Or, at least, they thought they did.

"Rapeseed," Bansi answered the RSS member's question about what he transported.

Bansi knew the man. His name was Veer, and he'd known him all his life.

"So, if I investigate, I won't find poppy straw or anything like that?" the insistent young man asked. He dressed in a uniform similar to Vajra's costume from the night before, although this man looked more professional and commanding.

Bansi gulped, cursing himself for having agreed to this ill-conceived plan as he stared at Veer, who glared right back at him. To hell with the pittance he owed. It wasn't his or his family's fight. And he hoped Maharaja Singh would meet his goals and rid Jammu and Kashmir of Muslims for all time. That consideration tempted him to give Fardeen and his family up before he thought better of it. Bansi was in too deep now. He was just as guilty as they were.

"Absolutely not," Bansi said as he leaned back in his seat, smiling.

Then, Veer, the Swayamsavek, started laughing, "Well, it's a good thing! That way, we don't have to pull off in the field and smoke together!" he said as he brandished a pipe, then reached over and patted Bansi's forearm that rested on the cab door.

Fardeen desperately motioned for Virika and Siddharth to lie flat in the truck's cargo hold. Then he pled with them to be quiet as he hoisted several sacks of tamatars, rapeseed, and beans over them. After that, he positioned himself at the rear curtain and trained his ear to hear whatever he could. He had a knife from his mother's kitchen in his hand and planned to deliver its edge to whoever flung that curtain open. He sat with tears rolling down his face as he gritted his teeth and breathed heavily. He prepared himself to do what he swore he'd never do: take another man's life.

Narain, the other Swayamsevak with Veer, paced around the truck as his partner chatted with his friend. Narain had no friends, though. He had no siblings, and he had no wife. The RSS was his only purpose in life, and his association with it meant everything to him, even if it didn't mean anything to his feckless colleague.

Narain would've sworn he heard a rustling in the cargo hold as he and Veer approached the vehicle from behind a few moments earlier when they flagged the truck to the side of the road.

But maybe it was just his imagination.

Then, when he started walking toward the truck's cab, he heard something again. It was unmistakable this time. He heard someone sneeze.

Narain raised his Lee-Enfield rifle to his shoulder and turned back toward the truck's rear. It was just as he thought all along. Why was a truck racing down the road in the middle of the night, headed south? Hari Singh forbade travel on this route. So, who would take it upon themselves to do so, disregarding the Maharaja's decree?

"Veer!!" Narain shouted as he started toward the back of the truck, holding up his rifle.

Narain could hear that idiot laughing before Veer finally responded, "Yes! Ok! Give me a second!"

That's when Narain realized he was on his own. It was up to him to drum out whatever insurrectionist or hooligan hid in the truck's cargo area.

He slid the bolt-action of his rifle and moved forward. Whoever was in there would pay for it with their life. He'd make sure of that. So he continued on the dirt road that wound through a poppy field, with his rifle raised.

When he reached the tailgate, he nudged its curtain open with his rifle and peered inside.

At first, he couldn't see anything. Then, as he looked more intently, he saw two sets of eyes, inches above the cargo hold floor, staring back at him. But as he squinted to confirm that, he felt a burning sensation in his neck. He looked to his right and saw a man twisting a knife before the man pulled it backward and thrust it into his throat.

Blood spurted from Narain's neck as he dropped his rifle and grasped his throat with both hands. He staggered toward the truck's driver's side and watched as Veer noticed him. Veer broke from his conversation with Bansi and immediately brought his rifle to bear.

"Narain!" Veer shouted, watching his fellow Swayamsevak fall to his knees with the whites of his eyes shining in the moonlight.

Fardeen knew he only had seconds to act. So he jumped from the truck and raced around toward the driver's side, colliding with Veer, who stumbled backward while Fardeen fell to the ground on his back. Veer got his bearings first and instantly fired two shots, one striking Fardeen in the head. Veer then moved toward Fardeen with his rifle raised.

But before he reached him, someone plowed into his side, throwing him off balance. He looked down and saw, of all things, a little girl. She held him around his waist before she reared up, clawed at his head, and screeched. He thrust her backward, then butted the girl in the center of her face with his rifle, bursting her lips and sending her bouncing onto her backside.

"Little bitch!" he shouted as he trained his rifle to blow her head off.

But just as he squeezed the trigger, he too felt the sting of Serina Shakur's exquisitely honed boning knife. Except his injury was to his back. And his shot fortuitously whizzed just above Virika's head. Veer dropped his rifle and struggled to grab the blade lodged perfectly in the center of his back, just beyond his grasp.

"No!" he heard his friend Bansi scream as he raced toward the commotion.

Twisting around, Veer met eyes with another child, a boy. And its eyes were as black as the sky behind him as he stared back at Veer. It was the boy that had stabbed him.

Upon reaching the boy, Bansi backhanded him and shouted, "What are you doing, you animal?! What is wrong with you?!"

Veer heard Bansi continue to scold the boy, but Bansi's shouting slowly began fading as it gave way to the thumping in his ears. Veer also felt the wind escape his body with every desperate gasp he made. The knife punctured his left lung, so he couldn't hold his breath no matter how desperately he tried. He started to feel himself going under but couldn't help but look back at the boy again. In his delirium, Veer thought that surely the child was an evil spirit.

He rolled onto his side, unable to lay back for fear of pushing the knife deeper inside himself. He was still delirious when he watched Bansi kneel to the ground and pick up his rifle.

What was he doing? Then Veer realized his good friend must be trying to save him from the evil spirit.

But, now completely blind and on the verge of seizing, he heard Bansi clumsily arm the rifle and say, "Forgive me, brother. I'm sorry."

Afterward, a single shot rang out across the fields on the rural pass between Srinagar and Awantipora.

Bansi had no choice but to do what he did. It didn't matter what his intentions were. An RSS contingent caught him transporting fugitives as the princely state of Jammu and Kashmir collapsed onto itself. He would've faced dire consequences if he'd stayed quiet and done nothing. The more Bansi thought about it as he stood on the road with smoke from the gunshot still wafting around him, he realized the boy probably saved his life.

"Grab his legs!" Bansi shouted at the boy, staring down the road in either direction.

Then he joined Siddharth, helping him haul Veer's body ten yards deep into the thigh-high crop of poppies. Afterward, they went to the other Swayamsevak's body and did the same thing as Virika lay across Fardeen and wept hysterically. Bansi took hold of the rifle's barrel with both hands, swinging in a circle, then hurled it into the field on the opposite side of the road.

As he gasped, Bansi looked around nervously to see if the two RSS members had a vehicle anywhere. Seeing nothing, he marched toward the girl laid out across her husband, wailing.

Bansi was astounded by how calm the boy behaved through it all. He looked over at Siddharth, who stared back at him, expressionless as if awaiting further orders. It didn't seem to matter that his father lay dead in the center of the road.

Then, when they reached Fardeen and Virika, the boy's cold machinations continued.

"Mama! Mama!" the boy demanded, "Get up, Mama! We have to get off the road! We have to leave here!"

The boy's stoicism and insistence astonished Bansi because he'd struggled with what to say to the young, grieving girl who approached madness. It was as though the boy answered a call, following some cosmic cue or divine ordinance, that it was time for him to be the man.

But they were all shocked when Fardeen began moaning, sending Virika onto a whole new plane of hysteria.

"Fardeen! Fardeen!" she screamed as she launched herself onto his chest, grabbing both his cheeks and pushing his hair back on his head.

"Woman," Fardeen groaned, "get off my chest."

Fardeen Shakur was alive.

The shot to his head merely grazed him, knocking him unconscious. It was a miracle.

Bansi had no clue what to do next as he stood, bewildered,

staring down at Fardeen and Virika, who passionately kissed every inch of her husband's face. As his rational thinking returned, he thought it might've been better if Fardeen were dead. He could drag him into the field alongside the Swayamsaveks, then return to Srinagar without the boy and his mother. He could kill them and leave them to rot with the others. Given the country's current state, they wouldn't find the bodies for weeks.

That didn't matter, though, because Siddharth spoke up, usurped control, and provided an alternate plan.

"We need to continue south, to Jammu City," the twelve-year-old boy said, whose voice was as deep and coarse as a man's.

"Someone will look for these men. Their mothers, their wives. Someone. You must take us further south like you promised," Siddharth demanded.

Bansi stared at the boy a moment, incredulous that he gave suggestions as though they were orders and behaved as though anyone not heeding them was a fool. But what the boy suggested was exactly what they wound up doing. Bansi and Siddharth loaded Fardeen into the cargo area, and then Siddharth joined Bansi in the cab for the rest of the way.

They hadn't made it an hour down the road before Siddharth said, "I think I should drive."

Yet again confounded, Bansi looked over at the boy and said, "What? What did you say?"

After a moment, Siddharth said, "I think I should drive. You seem tired and nervous. You seem scared, so I want to drive."

"Let me tell you something, boy!" Bansi started before they both noticed headlights coming toward them from the south.

They were a good distance away but were moving fast. It was far too early for someone to be on the road unless they had official business to tend to. Bansi put both hands on the wheel and began driving as though he were in the city. Then, as the other vehicle got closer, he halted.

"What are you doing?!" Siddharth shouted.

As the other vehicle approached, shining light onto the road in front of them, it slowed, almost coming to a stop. It was another truck. Then, its horn abruptly sounded, and they watched as it accelerated past, and someone waved when it went by.

Bansi sat with his eyes closed and panted as he pondered his next move. That was just some fool out driving at night. But the now four fugitives had a half day's travel left. So it was likely they'd meet someone else on the road. And who would it be next time?

"You see?" Siddharth said, "You're afraid! You should never have stopped, and you should never have thrown that gun into the field! Now let me drive!"

Bansi had about enough of this brat, but then, as he looked over at Siddharth, he noticed something. The boy sat with the blade from earlier, even though Bansi had no recollection of him pulling it from Veer's corpse—none whatsoever.

But the facts remained. He sat in the middle of nowhere, next to a bigger and stronger man than he was, although the man was actually only a boy. And the boy had a bloody knife clenched in his hand.

So he said, "Very well."

Then he opened the door and walked around to the passenger's side as Siddharth slid over and took the wheel. Siddharth drove the entire last leg of the trip, stopping only once to check on his Mama and Papa while Bansi filled the truck from one of the tanks in the cargo hold.

Bansi didn't even go to the market, which was why he'd traveled to Jammu City in the first place. Instead, he went back toward

Srinagar, stopping to refuel a few times and another to hoist his entire shipment over a bridge into the Jhelum River. He fabricated a harrowing story about being robbed at knife-point as the bandits loaded his cargo into the bed of a truck before racing away. Cunningly, he said the heist took place somewhere around Awantipora, which he believed might explain the two Swayamsevak's corpses they'd ultimately discover in the vicinity a few weeks later.

Siddharth, Virika, and Fardeen wandered around Jammu for hours, not knowing how to move further south. But once again, Siddharth came to the rescue. As Virika and Fardeen sat in a shady spot in front of a seamstress' shop, Siddharth panhandled on the street. Fardeen thought it was disgraceful, but he was too exhausted to protest, so he sat back and kept an eye on his son while Siddharth pled for alms, putting them into a sack he took from the truck. It wasn't his first time at panhandling, although Fardeen wasn't aware of that.

Siddharth's Uncle Vajra taught him the unsavory craft, telling the impressionable young man, "If people have more, they should give to the people that don't. I don't have anything. Do you?"

His uncle's reasoning made perfect sense to Siddharth, even though he wanted for nothing and grew to be huge, eating several meals a day that his grandmother, Serina, prepared. Sometimes, he ate those meals during breaks between begging on Srinagar's streets, where he'd join Vajra and his friends. Serina thought he was in school the whole time. Instead, Siddharth smoked, drank, and wagered his alms playing Pachisi, often walking away twice as prosperous as his sad tales from begging made him on the street.

By sundown, the Jammu streets started clearing. The pitiful trio sat hunched on the ground next to one another and talked about what to do next. It was too late to find anything to eat, but Siddharth stood up and told his parents he had enough money for them to eat all week, and he could get more the next day.

Fardeen got angry, although he was incapable of expressing it as vehemently as he usually would. So he said, "Siddharth, come. Come sit down, son."

Siddharth obeyed his father and knelt in front of his parents.

"Don't you see, son?" Fardeen began, "Don't you see what a fool I've been? I took an infidel's advice, and now I'm on the streets of a faraway place while my son begs for me. Can't you see that, son? Does that not make sense? I've shamed Allah, son, and I've disgraced my family."

Siddharth rose and stared back at his father in contempt as Virika sat and held her breath. Fardeen was distant from the boy his entire life, while Virika was not. So she knew what Siddharth was capable of and how his mind worked.

Fardeen continued.

"We'll take what Allah provided to us in your sack. And we'll make our way back to Srinagar in the morning. This entire journey was nothing but folly. But now we have to find a place to rest, and it certainly won't be on the street. Allah has seen to that through his mercy. So give me the sack, son. Give me what Allah provided to us."

Siddharth stood motionless, staring back at his parents. He made no gesture to hand the sack over to his father, nor did he give credence to anything Fardeen just said. It seemed he had other plans for his bounty.

Then, after a moment, Siddharth spoke. And the words he said broke his father's heart.

"Allah?" Siddharth asked as he stared at his mother, seeking her support, but she stared down, refusing to make eye contact with her imperious child.

"I know nothing of this 'Allah,' Papa. Does he live in Srinagar? Does he live here in Jammu City? Tell me, Papa, because I'd like to meet this man. I never saw him today while I stood in the sunlight and you sat in the shade. Was he here when the man shot you with the gun and beat my mother? Is he the one that protected you when you couldn't stand up? Is he the one that drove that truck here while you laid down in the back of it, and that coward wet his pants? He sounds so brave, Papa. So brave. It seems like he protects you at every turn. So, I'd like to thank him, Papa. I'd like to thank him for all he's done. But I also have a message for him, Papa. I want to tell him something."

Raising the sack of money he begged for all day, Siddharth twisted it in a circle and wrapped the cinch around his wrist.

"Please tell Sir Allah he can have my money when the moon crashes into the Earth. He can have it when the seas boil and the ocean washes over all of Bharat. He can also have it on the day you become a man. But that's not today, is it Papa? It's not today."

Siddharth's words were an abomination, one which left Fardeen speechless. Before he even finished them, Fardeen thought about how remiss he'd been as a father. He also realized that he'd never truly known his son. He'd left the boy's rearing to a Hindu while working in the fields all over Jammu and Kashmir and doing various odd jobs in Srinagar. He worked from early in the morning until the sun went down, and he was never home, so he relied on Mahir and Serina to raise and indoctrinate the boy into Islam. But it seemed that his parents failed him miserably.

Because what stood in front of him now was nothing but pure evil, a minion of Iblis, the Islamic being of all things unholy. Siddharth was a manifestation of every sin Fardeen ever committed, the most egregious of those being his taking a Hindu wife.

Yet, Fardeen still loved Siddharth. He couldn't help himself. He loved him so much that instead of Siddharth's words prompting him to rise and possibly kill him for his blasphemy, they made him reflect. Perhaps Siddharth was right. Maybe he was the fool, and Siddharth was the wise one. What had Allah ever done for him? He shuddered to contemplate the answer to that and the stirrings of doubt that began to well within him.

But just as his introspection peaked, he heard an old man's voice shout, "You need to clear out of here right now! This is not a sidewalk for Dalit grifters! This is my daughter's shop! And you'd be wise to leave here! My son-in-law is a Swyamsevak! I'm sure he'd find it interesting that Dalits hang around his wife's business! I can't imagine what he and his friends might do, so go! Shoo! Off with you!"

Virika and Fardeen followed the man's orders as Fardeen raised on all fours, and Virika started helping him up. Fardeen could barely stand from both his wound and heat prostration. His legs wobbled as Virika tried to steady her husband and help him away from the unhospitable stoop. But their son interrupted their exodus as he addressed the old man.

"Sir, sir?" Siddharth said, "We are not Dalits, sir. We came from West Punjab."

The old man asked, "Pardon me? What did you say?"

Then Siddharth Shakur descended into the performance of a lifetime. Lying was second nature to him. But just like the other talents Vajra cultivated, Siddharth took them to the next level.

"Sir, please. We are from West Punjab. We meant to travel to East Punjab, where my sister lived, but they killed her. They killed my sister, sir. And they killed my cousins, too. They killed all of them, except for the little ones they took back to Pakistan."

Millions of people flocked across the Indian border in either direction during Partition. Muslims moved toward Pakistan, while Hindus came back across the border to India. It was, perhaps, the most turbulent period in the history of the ancient nation. So Siddharth's posturing made perfect sense to the old man, whose son-in-law was in Srinagar at the time, overseeing one of the greatest migrations in modern history.

Siddharth's lip started quivering, and his eyes teared as though he had told the truth.

"Please, sir. If you could allow my family to sleep here, we'd be most grateful. This is my other sister, Virika, and her husband, Etash. We are so tired, sir. We haven't slept or eaten in days. We are trying to make it to Bombay State, where my Mami lives. She's waiting for us, but we ran out of money, sir."

Then Siddharth broke into tears, burying his face in his hands as he shook his head from side to side, peaking through his fingers with one eye. By the time Siddharth finished, Fardeen no longer thought his son was evil—he was sure of it.

Nevertheless, Siddharth's histrionics wound up with the family shielded from the elements that night and having a wonderful meal, while Siddharth fabricated story after story about what brought them to Jammu City, each fashioning him as the hero.

The following day, the family that seemed star-crossed over the past forty-eight hours left Jammu City aboard a bus, bound for Ahmedabad, toward the return address scribbled on the envelope Virika cradled to her chest ever since they left Srinagar. Fardeen was still dizzy, but so was his son. However, Siddharth was lightheaded for different reasons. Fardeen tended to a gunshot wound to his head while Siddharth nursed a wad of cash the family that showed such compassion to the Shakurs gave him.

Once they arrived in Ahmedabad and knocked on the Popat's door, two boys answered it together. They kept nudging each other with their hips, battling to be the one who greeted whoever had knocked. They were Chandu and Madhu Popat. After a few moments, a beautiful woman walked up behind the boys. Her silky black tresses flowed down the center of her chest. Her complexion was radiant. And she smelled like a garden of jasmine and roses. The exquisite blue sari she wore was sewn from the finest fabrics in Gujarat, and she wore very expensive jewelry. She had a faint smile that soon gave way to an expression of concern and confusion as she looked back at her bedraggled visitors.

Fardeen was certain they were about to face the same greeting they'd initially received in Jammu City. But this was not some seamstress' crotchety old father that would bark at them and chase them off. This was a wealthy woman, indeed the lady of the home. She'd have them arrested and thrown in jail.

However, he was amazed when the woman broke down in tears and opened her arms, just as his wife did the same, and the two women embraced. The beautiful woman was assuredly wealthy and was the lady of the house. But she was also Virika's sister, Daksha.

CHAPTER FOURTEEN

Wednesday, July 1, 1981, Tomahawk, Florida

F ardeen was bored to death sitting in Tomahawk, checking people in about once every two hours. He could only imagine everything happening in Biloxi at The Sunkist. He envisioned the pool surrounded by people cooking hot dogs and hamburgers, drinking beer, and listening to music. He thought about what the amusement park must look like across the street with all the rides going full speed and lines of people waiting to board them. He could almost smell the food cooking at Angelina's next door and see the dense traffic on Highway 90. He also wondered if any of the dozen or so friends he'd made ever came back over the summer this year. He considered faking a reason to call his uncle about something, just on the outside chance one of them might be there. But he quickly dismissed that idea, realizing how his father might react to a long-distance call.

His mother's duties got scaled back as her pregnancy progressed, which she was over three months into now. Sridevi and Anaya completely took over her housekeeping chores, while Fardeen handled the front desk most of the day, except overnight, which Devan still oversaw. But his mother kept the office immaculate and continued cooking meals and taking care of everyone.

It was a quiet existence for Fardeen and his family in Tomahawk, which sharply contrasted with life in Biloxi. He missed it, too. As slow as things got during the fall and winter months, according to Siddharth, they were still ten times livelier than what went on in Tomahawk. In Biloxi, Fardeen liked checking all the people in at The Sunkist and visiting with them when they'd come into the office for change or a twenty-five-cent cup of coffee and a Morton honeybun, thawed to room temperature, that his Uncle Siddharth sold behind the front desk. They always wanted to talk for a few minutes and appeared just as glad to have someone to converse with as Fardeen was.

None of the guests in Tomahawk seemed much interested in socializing, though. Instead, they bordered on being rude most of the time. He couldn't count the times people asked him if he spoke English. Then there was their complete absence of manners, never saying "please" or "thank you." Nearly everyone in Biloxi was courteous. Sure, you had your occasional rude or problem guest. But that was true just about anywhere or in any business, Siddharth told him. Still, the people who stayed at The Seagull seemed bent on being discourteous for some reason.

As Fardeen daydreamed out of the office's front glass, two Tomahawk police officers pulled into the parking lot, riding in the same squad car. That was another thing. The police were so impolite in Tomahawk. In Biloxi, they stopped by frequently, checking in on the front desk and ensuring everything was alright. But in Tomahawk, they just glared and rolled on through, not even responding if he waved at them. Fardeen couldn't stand them.

Devan wasn't too fond of them either after his family's experience with them on their first day at The Seagull. But he also didn't like how they seemed fixated on whomever they had in-house. So far as he knew, they'd never rented a room to a criminal before. However, that didn't stop the Tomahawk police from treating everyone like they were crooks. Often they'd sit back just off the road and pull people over who were on their way to work or back out of town. They searched their cars, frisked them, and sometimes, according to his guests, they'd even shake them down for money.

"Your left tail light is out. But seeing as you're on your way out of town and the magistrate is closed, I can collect the fine from you now. If you don't, she'll put a bench warrant out for your arrest, boy."

Yep. Devan hated them, too.

Fardeen looked away from the squad car as it wheeled past, not wanting to make eye contact with them. He returned his attention to a project he'd worked on during his downtime at the front desk. He wanted to renumber all the rooms to a three-digit numbering convention. His father didn't like the idea, while Fardeen believed it might give the property a more hotel-like stature.

But just as he returned to working on his hand-drawn map, the bells above the office door jingled. When Fardeen looked up, a pleasant-looking man walked in with a girl around Fardeen's age, maybe younger.

The man was clean-cut with short, grayish hair and wore a light blue shirt, blue jeans, and work boots. He looked like a typical tradesman but a little classier. The girl was skinny, fair-skinned, and had long, blonde, almost white hair. She had freckles covering most of her arms and the visible part of her legs extending down from her seersucker short pants.

"Hello there!" the man said as he approached the front desk with the girl following closely behind.

Well, this was a pleasant departure. Someone entered the office and greeted Fardeen instead of the usual, *"How much for a king single?"*

"I'm working in Pensacola for the next few weeks, and my daughter and I need a room," the man said.

The girl looked pretty to Fardeen, but more than that, she seemed transfixed on him, smiling just as warmly as her father did. They behaved more like the kind of people who might patronize The Sunkist than The Seagull, and their demeanor raised Fardeen's spirits as he smiled back at the girl and answered her father.

"Uh, yes, sir. How long will you be staying, sir?" Fardeen asked, staring at the girl.

"Oh, gosh, young man, three weeks? Maybe a month? We might even be moving here to Toma-la-hawk," the kind man said.

Fardeen's mood elevated more when the girl winked at him. He couldn't stop looking at her. But then he noticed the lights come on in the squad car outside. The man whirled around to see what distracted Fardeen so abruptly. When he saw the police car pull up behind his pickup, his expression changed, and he turned back to Fardeen and said, "Hold on, just a second, son."

Then he went outside, leaving the girl at the front desk. Fardeen heard the man say, "Well, hello, officers!" just as the office door shut behind him. At about the same time, Sridevi walked in from the laundry room with a stack of linens and set them on the counter. She smiled and greeted the girl, but she grimaced and hurried toward the stairs leading up to the apartment when she saw the man talking to the police outside.

Fardeen hardly noticed Sridevi at all, though. He couldn't peel his eyes from the pretty young blonde who finally spoke, extending her hand and saying, "Hi, my name's Michelle. What's yours?"

Fardeen nervously held his hand out and said, "Hi, I'm Dean."

"It's nice to meet you, Dean," the young lady said as she shook his hand.

Then Fardeen realized his hand had begun to sweat, so he jerked it back quickly and apologized.

"Oh, I'm sorry. I was working in one of the rooms earlier, and my hands are kind of sweaty. Here. Let me get you a towel!" he said, grabbing a washcloth from the stack of laundry Sridevi left on the counter. He was so embarrassed as he handed it to the girl.

He could see the girl's father over her shoulder. He stood in the parking lot, chatting up a storm, being very animated, and pointing in different directions. Just then, Devan walked down the steps, followed by Savitri, Sridevi, and Anaya. He heard his father groan as he moved past him, followed by his mother calling her husband's name.

"Devan, don't!" Savitri said urgently, following Devan toward the door.

Just as Devan reached the door, the man outside turned back toward the office before waving to the officers. They waved back to the man and slowly pulled out of the parking lot. The Patel family had a collective sigh of relief as the smiling man walked into the office again.

"Oh, hi there!" he said, even cheerier than before, "My name's Thomas Cole! Pleased to meet you!"

He thrust his hand forward, briskly shaking Devan's as he entered the office.

"Was there a problem, sir?" Devan asked as he watched the policemen pull out and drive off.

"Problem?" the man chirped, "Oh, no! No problem at all! I haven't gotten my Florida tag yet, and my Kentucky tag is expired. I was just explaining that to the officers. Nice fellows!"

Devan and Savitri looked at one another, relieved but concerned about whatever was said outside. Meanwhile, Fardeen was still captivated by the pretty girl who'd never stopped looking at him as she smiled.

It turned out that Thomas was a carpenter hired by a wealthy Pensacola man to renovate a pool cabana. He said he couldn't find work and was about to leave town when he saw the ad in the paper. He responded to the ad and was supposed to meet the man later wherever he wound up getting a room. But the dang rooms in Pensacola, he said, went for at least thirty bucks a night before tax, so he widened his search out from there. He didn't want to keep the man waiting, and he told Devan that he'd sure appreciate getting an early check-in if the motel had a room available.

"Of course, sir," Devan said.

Devan was still a bit concerned. But The Seagull needed the business, and he was always glad to get a long-term renter. It was just one less room he had to rent in a day. Besides, the man was so polite and kind. Devan wanted to help him in any way he could.

After getting an imprint of the man's card and fetching him towels and soap, Devan directed Sridevi to show him and his daughter to their room. But when Devan handed Thomas his card back, Thomas Cole suggested something more.

"Sir, do you have any rooms that are out of commission? You know, rooms that might be damaged or need repairs? If you do, maybe we could work something out."

Devan immediately warmed to the idea, thinking about the fourteen rooms he still had down since arriving in Tomahawk. If this man's appearance and behavior were any indications of his carpentry skills, Devan would gladly give room nights in trade.

"Yes, sir, I do, sir," Devan said, "and I might be interested if you believe you can repair them."

Instantly, Fardeen bristled at the idea. He could fix virtually anything wrong in those rooms. His father just hadn't given him enough time to address them. He constantly had him working behind the front desk, pulling rooms, or doing laundry. But then, Fardeen realized that if Mr. Cole stayed, that meant Michelle stayed too. So he adjusted his attitude.

"Terrific!" Thomas said as he smiled and shook Devan's hand again, "But I'll pay for nights, of course, until I get a chance to see what all you have going on in those rooms. And if it's something I can't handle, you can just keep my card on file. Just charge me as

I go! I'm sorry, I didn't catch your name, sir."

Devan said, "My name is Patel,"

Devan's worries about Tomahawk and putting his family in the position he had lingered with him. But Thomas Cole was suddenly a bright spot on the horizon. Then it grew even brighter when Thomas stopped at the door, wrapped his arm around his little girl, and spoke to the Patels again.

"You know, Mr. Patel, I have to tell you something," Thomas said as he unbuttoned the top button of his shirt and pulled up a necklace.

He choked up a little as he looked down and held up what looked like a small silver coin or amulet dangling on it.

"This is St. Christopher, Mr. Patel," Thomas said as his eyes glossed with tears, "he is the patron saint of travelers. My momma gave me this last year before she died, Mr. Patel, and it was a month after I lost my wife, Michelle's mother. I'd hit some hard times and moved around from place to place, and I just couldn't seem to make anything work. But before she died, momma told me what was about to happen. She told me I'd find myself in the wilderness but to always keep this medallion with me and that St. Christopher would deliver me into the hands of caring people. You and your family are those people, Mr. Patel. And God has a purpose for you, just like he does for Michelle and me. May God bless you, Mr. Patel."

Michelle wrapped her arms around her father's neck and started crying as he tousled her hair and kissed her head. Then a teary-eyed Sridevi followed the father and daughter out of the office to show them to their room.

Devan didn't want to turn around because he knew what he'd see and what it might mean. But ultimately, he gave in and turned to see his wife, Savitri, bawling into a washcloth as she slowly nodded her head up and down.

"This is a sign, Papa!" she wept, pointing her finger upward,

"This is a sign! And you'd be wise to treat it that way, Devan Patel!"

Devan exhaled and slowly walked toward his emotionally distraught and quite pregnant wife, hugging her and stroking her hair. Little Anaya cried, too, rushing into her mother's side as Devan reached down and cupped the back of her head.

While moved by Mr. Cole's words, Fardeen couldn't shake the image of the beautiful, blonde-haired, freckled girl he'd fallen for within a matter of minutes after she walked into the office. He couldn't wait to check on the girl and her father once things settled down and Devan relieved him from the front desk.

Unfortunately, that took a lot longer than he anticipated. He'd ordinarily welcome people lined up to rent a room. But they'd suddenly sprung up from nowhere. And after a few hours, as his thumbs tired and his patience waned, he got sick of people trying to check into The Seagull. He didn't even care if it cost them business. All he wanted to do was check on the Coles—particularly Michelle. He couldn't wait to finish his shift so he could go and visit them, but he had to come up with some ruse for doing so.

His luck changed when he looked up and saw Michelle walk into the office wearing Holly Hobby pajamas with her hair pulled back neatly in a bun. Fardeen shot up from the rickety office chair he sat in most of the day and greeted his new love interest.

"Hi! I mean, hello! What can I do for you, Miss Cole?" he blurted, wiping his face with his forearm.

"Hi, Mr. Dean," Michelle said softly, and Fardeen would've sworn she was even prettier than the last time he saw her. Yeah, Fardeen had it bad. And her calling him 'mister'? That was the clincher. Done deal. Game over.

"We didn't have an ice bucket in our room, Mr. Dean. Could I get one from you, please?" she asked.

Fardeen was speechless for a moment as he stared at his heartthrob. He hadn't realized it, but she'd had makeup on before. But now, her face, complexion, and all those beautiful freckles were clearly displayed. She tucked her right knee gently into her left one. And she tugged at the bottom of her pajamas so she wouldn't expose too much of herself to Fardeen.

Then Fardeen snapped out of his trance, realizing what she'd just asked him. There wasn't an ice bucket in their room because The Seagull didn't have an ice machine. Terrified of losing face, Fardeen shot back an all-out lie to Michelle after he looked around the office for a moment, struggling to find any possible way he might appease her.

"Uh, I'm sorry, Michelle! Our ice machine is on the fritz!"

Fardeen hoped he'd gotten that right. *On the fritz?* What did that even mean??

"Oh," Michelle said, shifting between her right and left knees, driving Fardeen wild as she did, "Okay then, Mr. Dean."

Michelle turned around and started back out the door, shattering Fardeen's heart a little more with each step. His mind raced, trying to come up with some way to stop her. He would do just anything, anything, to make her stop. Finally, he shouted something to try and keep her from leaving him.

"I can get you some ice from 7-11, though!"

It even *sounded* absurd as the words left his mouth. Who was he kidding? 7-11 was almost a mile away, and his father wouldn't relieve him for another two hours. Not to mention that there was no way Devan would let him walk that far at night to fetch a bag of ice, even if it was for a valued customer.

Fardeen was relieved when Michelle giggled and said, "Oh no, Mr. Dean! It's not that important! But you're so sweet!"

Michelle moved back out of the door, dangling his heartstrings along her way. Then, after the door closed, Fardeen fell back into the office chair, rubbing his temples with his right hand. But the roller coaster ride wasn't over just yet.

A moment later, Michelle opened the door again and asked, "Dean? Would you mind walking with me to the 7-11 tomorrow to get some ice and other stuff? Daddy loves Watermelon Stix and Ruffles, and if I have someone to go with me, he won't have to go to the store, so I know he'll let me."

"Yes!" Fardeen gushed before she'd even had a chance to finish speaking.

That made the little girl laugh as she said, "Thank you!" before walking out of the office for good.

Fardeen couldn't make himself fall asleep that night. All he could think about was his future as a motel owner and his life with Michelle. Between his knowledge about business and her father's carpentry skills, they could make The Seagull the best motel in the panhandle of Florida. They could have children together and build a beautiful house next door to the motel. He'd allow his parents to live at The Seagull. And he'd build a house for Sridevi and Anaya too. Sridevi was too mean to get a man, so she wouldn't mind taking care of Anaya until she went off to college. This was it. It was the perfect plan, just like his Uncle Sid always told him would come together.

CHAPTER FIFTEEN

"Up, up, up!" Savitri snapped, yanking the cover from Fardeen as he lay on the living room floor in the manager's apartment at The Seagull.

It didn't take him long to remember yesterday's events, though, so he shot up like a rocket and embraced his mother. He caught Savitri off guard, but she was so happy to have such a loving greeting from her baby boy that morning. She hugged her son and kissed him on the cheek before he charged from the room and into the shower. Things were going to be alright now. Savitri could just feel it.

The good fortune continued when Fardeen got to the office, ready to face a day of pulling bedding and galivanting around the property like a man—especially if he could do it in front of Michelle.

When he got downstairs, Fardeen saw a Lincoln Continental parked out front, and he saw his father standing across the desk from three very important-looking men. They were all older, probably fifty or so, and they wore expensive-looking clothing and had smiles on their faces.

"Mr. Patel, Mr. Cole told us what you agreed to do for him, sir. And we'd like you to know that he has the full backing of Horizon Christian Ministries, and we're prepared to fill this motel every night if you can help us out some with the rates," the distinguished-looking gentleman said, leaning over the counter.

"Excuse me, sir?" Devan asked.

"Mr. Patel," the man continued, "we have an outreach program for people just like Thomas and Michelle. People who are in crisis and have no place to go. Our ministry is about to build a beautiful hostile and school in Pace to service these needs, and that's how we came to know Thomas. The Lord brought him to us when Thomas responded to our want ad for construction workers. I'm sure he told you about it."

"Well, um," Devan started, "he mentioned something about building a cabana for a wealthy gentleman in town."

The man quickly turned and looked toward the other two as if getting their take on what was just said. Then all three of them laughed.

He turned back around, still giggling, and said, "Mr. Patel, Thomas was just being prideful. He hasn't worked in some time, has no money, and that probably stings him a little bit, don't you imagine?"

"Well, Mr. uh," Devan said, probing for his name.

"Carmichael. My name is Chester Carmichael, and this is Mr. Prescott Stuart and Dr. Harvey Beecher."

The other two men nodded and held their hands out to shake Devan's as he continued speaking.

"Mr. Carmichael, Mr. Cole gave me a credit card, and I already took an imprint of it."

Devan wanted to ensure he got paid immediately in case these men's good-heartedness went by the wayside.

Again Carmichael looked at the other two gentlemen before turning around with a worried look and saying, "Did the card have his name on it?"

"Yes, sir. It's standard procedure in my family's properties to verify a cardholder's identity before accepting it as payment," Devan replied, rattling off Sid's directives from memory.

The man looked relieved. Devan guessed he was glad Mr. Cole

hadn't given him a stolen card.

"Mr. Patel, I'm afraid you've been bamboozled. I'm certain that the credit card company will refuse payment when you submit the receipt. And I'd like to apologize for that on Thomas's behalf. I'm sure he would have corrected the matter before he tried to leave. But, look, let me do this."

Mr. Carmichael pulled out a long billfold, took out three one-hundred-dollar bills, and rested them on the counter.

"That should take him through the next two weeks, shouldn't it?" he asked Devan, whose eyes lit up, and his pulse rose a bit at the sight of that much cash.

Still a little leery, Devan took the money in hand and eyed it for a moment, which Mr. Carmichael found funny, so he laughed.

"It's not counterfeit, Mr. Patel. I assure you. Look, here's my card."

He handed Devan a business card with his name and contact information beneath the words *Horizon Christian Ministries*. The address was local, as was the phone number. This guy was legitimate. And it was all Devan could do to keep from reaching over the counter and hug him. Full every night? Had he heard him right?

He began nervously negotiating with the man who told him he needed several rooms immediately. Mr. Carmichael went on to say that he'd be incrementally adding rooms over the coming weeks but that by August, he'd fill The Seagull to capacity. Then Mr. Carmichael pulled out a credit card Devan had never seen before. It was a Carte Blanche.

"Uh, sir," Devan managed, "I cannot accept this card. I do not have the authority to accept this card. I don't know what it is."

Devan sobered a little, feeling like he knew it had all been too good to be true. Then, without a word, Mr. Carmichael produced an American Express Gold. Devan's mood swung upward again.

He'd seen that card before. He knew what it was as well as what it meant. It confirmed that the man standing there trying to rent rooms was a wealthy man. Maybe God was on his side today, just as Thomas Cole said, Devan thought.

Devan was agog. His mouth hung open, and he fumbled around the front desk to find a piece of paper and pencil.

"Uh, sir, uh, let me see," Devan muttered, scrambling to find something to write with.

Fardeen raced into the room and took a pen from the plastic King Kong coffee mug next to the adding machine. He presented it to his father and smiled back at the men.

"Uh, ok, uh, name?" Devan asked stupidly.

Devan was clearly out of his element here. So, Fardeen took the pen back and said, "Papa, I will get these gentlemen's information. Momma needs your help upstairs."

Devan looked incredulously at his boy for a moment. But as he did, he could see his brother-in-law, Sid, staring right back at him, so he did what his boy suggested and moved toward the stairs.

The other men snickered as Devan walked away, which he heard clearly. But Fardeen quelled that by interrupting them, "Name you'd like to register the rooms in, sir?" positioning his pen to get the rest of their information.

By the time Fardeen finished, he'd booked fifteen rooms at twenty-five dollars a night for thirty days, which was unheard of on the Interstate. Even more impressive was that Devan previously edged closer toward twenty dollars at the outset of negotiations. But Fardeen reoriented that, telling the men his father hadn't looked at the registration log for the coming months. He said that Florida Power had already claimed at least twenty rooms for three weeks during hurricane season. They'd have to get a better price to release the rooms.

"Just book it," Mr. Carmichael said, placing his hand onto

Fardeen's, glaring at him.

As Fardeen stared back, there was something so cold about the man's words and expression. It made him shudder a moment, pausing before he continued. But once he finished, Fardeen earned over $11,000 for The Seagull within just a few moments. Fardeen was ecstatic, the important Americans were happy, and it was all over. Fardeen was the hero of the day. He pranced back up the stairs like a peacock, telling his mother about what all he'd just pulled off.

Savitri fell apart, just as she was prone to do these days, and she grabbed her boy's face and repeatedly kissed him. Devan, however, sat on the couch in the manager's apartment and scowled at his son.

"Ah, yes. The legacy of Siddharth continues!" Devan proclaimed before Savitri met him halfway across the floor, hollering and wagging her finger at him.

Fardeen wasn't about to engage in this same battle he'd listened to for so many months now. However, he was usually on the other side of it, defending Devan from his mother's insults. Not today, though. Never today. Fardeen was proud and deserved all the accolades his mother gave him.

Besides that, Fardeen had a date. He had a date with Michelle, and it was a date with destiny. He was just before making that date too.

"I absolutely love Charm's Blow Pops!" Michelle said as she grabbed a handful of them and dropped them into the Big Gulp cup she used as a grocery basket on the candy aisle of the 7-11.

"Me too!" Fardeen said, holding his cup out for her to fill it.

The walk down the rural highway that led to the 7-11 had been awkward. Fardeen struggled for something to say while Michelle prattled on about nothing. The only moment of excitement was when a Tomahawk police car briefly chirped its siren and slowed next to the couple as they strolled along. Fardeen thought they'd stop and harass him, so he prepared himself to be humiliated in front of what he was beginning to feel was the love of his life. But he was shocked when the squad car suddenly tore away from them toward the Interstate.

Ever since Michelle and her father arrived and his father helped them, it was like someone looked out for him and his family. He was even less religious than his father. But it just seemed that a higher power looked over them once the Coles came to stay at The Seagull.

"Oh!" Michelle squealed as she reached the end cap of the aisle that she and Fardeen walked down, "Big Daddy Sausages! My favorite!"

The waifish girl yanked one of the sausages from the display, tearing it open while staring back at Fardeen. He looked around, certain that cop car would pull back up and haul him to jail for shoplifting. But then his attention fell toward Michelle as she flicked her tongue on the end of the sausage and batted her eyes while staring back at him.

That's when Fardeen realized how innocent Michelle was. She had no idea how using her mouth that way made a man feel. So he ripped the sausage from the child's hand and crammed it into his Big Gulp cup. How could Mr. Cole not raise his daughter better? His father would've beaten Sridevi to death if she did anything so crass or whorish!

Fardeen hauled Michelle toward the check-out counter, slamming their Big Gulp cups on it, asking the clerk, "How much?!" in the same manner he found so objectionable when working at The Seagull. He had to get out of there with her. He had to get out immediately, get her back to the motel and forget about her forever.

"Did I do something wrong, Dean?" Michelle asked as they trudged through the ditch in front of the 7-11 on the way back to The Seagull. Then she began to cry.

Fardeen swiveled around and saw the most pitiful creature he'd ever seen. Her lower lip trembled, and the pain in her eyes overwhelmed him. So he calmed down, walked up to Michelle, and hugged her. Michelle wilted in his arms before grasping the back of his head and kissing his ear.

"I'm so sorry, Dean," she whispered. "I'm so sorry. I didn't mean to do anything wrong," she cried.

"It's ok, Michelle. You didn't do anything wrong," Fardeen said as he pushed away from her, brushed the hair from her eyes, and stared back into them. She looked so beautiful to him at that moment. Maybe things would be okay. Perhaps he could teach her how to behave more like a lady. And she'd have to before he'd even consider becoming involved with her. She was just so innocent and in need of his support and direction. He put his hand on her cheek and caressed it before moving back toward The Seagull.

It was 6 o'clock by the time they got back. And just as Mr. Carmichael promised, the parking lot of The Seagull was nearly full. If this was the parking Horizon Christian Ministries needed for just fifteen rooms, Fardeen thought they would need to pave some more on the adjacent lot.

"I'm going to go take Daddy his goodies, Dean," Michelle said, seemingly unsurprised by all the traffic in the parking lot and the people milling about.

"Ok," Fardeen said, "would you like to have dinner with my family tonight?"

Instantly, Fardeen realized his mouth had gotten way ahead of his brain. He didn't want Michelle to see their horrible apartment or eat the food he was sure she'd find revolting. She was probably used to eating hamburgers every night or steak or meatloaf. He couldn't imagine she'd find rice, vegetables, and fruit palatable. He was panicked until she spoke again.

"Oh, Dean! That's so sweet! I'd love to! But Daddy and some other people here are having a prayer group tonight, and we're meeting in our room," Michelle said with an apologetic look.

Fardeen found it curious, however, that she hadn't offered for him to come along. But then he thought, even as young as she was, she probably realized that he wasn't Christian. So he pushed back from his offering as fast as he'd made it.

"Oh, ok. I understand," Fardeen said.

Then, making up for everything, Michelle leaned forward and kissed Fardeen's cheek, and he thought he might faint. Her lips were so delicate and touched a spot on his face, just between his cheek and right ear. He could smell her perfume as she pulled away, smiling before she winked at him and headed into the parking lot toward her room. Fardeen was in hormonal overload as he watched Michelle walk away. She looked back once with that beautiful smile and waved at him over her shoulder with her free hand.

Fardeen was in love. He was hopelessly in love.

But then Fardeen turned toward the office and saw his mother and sister, Sridevi, staring at him, and he realized they'd watched the whole encounter. The look on his mother's face told him she'd indeed watched someone, an American girl, kiss her little boy. Savitri was livid.

Fardeen looked down, afraid to make eye contact with his mother, and started toward the office. He stared at his feet as he plodded forward, not daring to look up for fear he might have to look Savitri in the face. Just as he reached the office door, he felt his mother's unmistakable pinch and tug at his ear. But it was so much more urgent than usual.

"What is this?" she barked at him in Gujarati.

That's when he knew he was in real trouble. Mercifully, his

big sister came to his rescue, also speaking in Gujarati, saying, "Mother, please! Leave him alone!"

Savitri wasn't having it, though. She yanked Fardeen in front of herself, then pulled his face up by his chin and snapped at him like a barracuda. But Fardeen pulled away from her and went into the office. Sridevi stopped her mother from following him and redirected her to the car because they had the weekly shopping to do. Fardeen was sure the issue wasn't resolved yet, though.

Devan was behind the desk with Anaya when Fardeen walked in. She was seated in his lap as he read to her from a giant book with Sesame Street characters on the front of it. He peered up from his bifocals and said, "Ah! The hotelier has returned!"

Even though it was a jab at Fardeen, he knew his father was only kidding. It was Devan's way of calling attention to their set-to the day before without making him relive it. Devan was a kind man and couldn't stand confrontation. So it was easiest for him to make light of a situation through humor and move on from there. But Fardeen was still compelled to explain things to his father, whom he respected more than anyone.

"I'm sorry, Papa," he said, "I didn't mean to overstep my bounds with those men. It's just that Uncle Sid,"

And at that point, Devan didn't want to hear anything else for fear he'd lapse into resentment and envy.

"Enough! Enough, son. It's alright. I should have just been happy my son was so smart that he could close a business deal the way he did. These people will bring us a lot of money, Fardeen. They're already here, and there's more of them coming."

Fardeen looked back at all the activity in the parking lot he'd chosen to ignore to get past his mother. It looked like a zoo, too. In addition to all the cars taking up the parking spaces, probably twenty or thirty people were moving around, mostly teenagers. That and all the money it signified was probably the best explanation for Devan's forgiving attitude and happy mood.

As Fardeen watched everyone from the window, his father walked behind him and placed his arm around Fardeen.

"You made us a lot more money from this than I would have, Fardeen. And I'm so proud of you, son. You were born to this business, just like your uncle. I'm very thankful for that too."

His father's words soothed Fardeen. They took away all the guilt he'd felt about commandeering the transaction in front of those important men. They also clarified Fardeen's resolve to have the most successful motel on the I-10 corridor. He hugged his father and patted his younger sister, Anaya, on the head, who'd slipped up behind them. Fardeen was so happy now.

CHAPTER SIXTEEN

November 9, 2020, Sripps Memorial Hospital, La Jolla, California

Fardeen woke up and winced when he saw the crinkly, seersucker fabric of the candy striper's pinafore standing in front of him. The beautiful young blonde pushed a cart full of chips, snacks, and candy. She spoke in a low, whispered voice, but Fardeen's reaction scared her.

"Oh, sir! I'm so sorry! Did I wake you?!" she asked.

Lending to the irony was that the first thing Fardeen caught sight of on her cart was a cupful of Charm's Blow Pops. He gasped.

"Sir?! Are you ok, sir?!" the girl continued, reaching out and touching him on the shoulder.

Fardeen slapped her hand away and rose to his feet, fully prepared to annihilate her as he clenched his fists at his sides. He'd kill her this time! He'd kill her! He'd pulp her head on the floor and kick her repeatedly, then fall to his knees and strangle her until she stopped breathing! And then he'd kill Thomas Cole the same way!

"Dean! What's wrong?" he heard his sister-in-law, Olivia, plead as she grabbed his shirt and tugged him backward, snapping him out of it.

That's when he realized he'd nodded off. It's also when he realized he'd relived, yet another time, the horrors of his interaction with Thomas, Michelle, and Horizon Christian Ministries. As always, he was relieved he'd only dreamt about it and wasn't living it any longer.

But he'd only awakened from one nightmare into another one. Because his baby brother, Sanjay, lay a few yards away, catatonic and, perhaps, not long for this world. Fardeen breathed heavily for a moment, then apologized to the girl.

"I'm so sorry, young lady. I'm so sorry. You just startled me," Fardeen said after exhaling and falling back into his seat. Had his sister-in-law not been there, it was no telling what he might have done.

"Dean?" Olivia asked him, "What's wrong? What did she do?"

Then the landscape abruptly changed as he sat next to Olivia, interlocking her hand in his.

"Get your damned hands off of me!" Fardeen heard a woman's voice yell as he stood up in the corridor outside the CICU.

Fardeen felt he didn't even need to look up because he knew the woman. He looked up anyway and saw his baby sister, Anaya, walking backward from around the corner, pushing hospital employees away.

She fought off security and orderlies as she moosed her way into the Cardiac Intensive Care Unit, breaking the rule for the maximum number of people in the visitors' waiting area. As Fardeen watched his embattled sister move into the hallway, walking toward him while looking over her shoulder at her aggressors, he was so proud.

Anaya was simply beautiful. She wore a black low-cut dress, expensive shoes, and a silver Rolex dangled from her wrist. Her gorgeous black hair with a modern streak of blonde fashioned into it flowed backward because of how fast she moved. The look on her face was 100 percent Patel, and she eerily favored Fardeen's mother in stature.

Anaya was a straight firecracker. Her temper surpassed her mother's, and her beauty transcended that of any other woman in her family. Anaya was super-educated and stunningly gorgeous, and she was also one of the most feared litigators in the Southeastern United States. But more compelling than anything else right now: Anaya Patel was pissed off.

"Where's my brother?!" she hollered down the hallway as she met eyes with Fardeen.

But her outrage deteriorated with each step she took until she was a bundle of tears by the time she got to Fardeen and fell into his arms, weeping. She knew the drill. It had always been this way with Sanjay.

Ever since he was a little boy, Sanjay tried his parents' patience and broke the hearts of everyone in the family at some point or another.

When Sanjay was three years old, he crammed a screwdriver into an electrical socket at The Seagull. His heart stopped, and had Fardeen not taken CPR during PE at Tomahawk High, Sanjay would probably already be dead.

Sanjay thought it would be funny to stage his death when he was only six. So he had his friends, staying at his family's property at the time for his birthday, go tell his exhausted father, seated behind the front desk, that someone ran over him in the parking lot. When Devan reached his baby boy, laid out on his back, Sanjay looked up and said, "Gotcha!"

Devan beat the hell out of Sanjay until Savitri pulled him off him. Then she beat him, too, and sent all the boys staying on the property home.

Then, when he was thirteen years old, he and some older local boys who were friends from school thought it would be fun to leap off the I-10 bridge into Escambia Bay. That didn't end well either. Sanjay clipped his foot on the rail as he jumped from the bridge, and he tumbled end-over-end for sixty feet until he splatted on the water's surface and sank like a stone. It only knocked the wind out of him. But he wound up a few hundred yards or so down the river before being able to climb to the shore. Disoriented and lost, he wandered through the woods for a couple of hours before he wound up walking onto someone's property. However, they had already organized search parties by that time, and the Escambia County flotilla scoured the water for the mischievous young man's corpse, positive he was dead. Devan beat the shit out of him after that too. But discipline never seemed to resonate with Sanjay.

So Anaya was accustomed to grieving over her little brother, even though it had always been in vain. But something told her things were different this time. When she got the call from Fardeen, saying he'd booked her a flight and that she needed to fly to San Diego immediately, she knew things were serious. Then, when she pushed back from Fardeen, his eyes confirmed it for her, and she fell back into his chest, crying.

"Why?" she cried, "Why does he do this to us, brother? I love him so much! Why?"

"It's ok, Turtle. He'll be alright. Everything will be fine," Fardeen said, although he didn't believe a word he spoke.

Olivia joined the heartbroken siblings, reaching her arms around them and crying.

"I'm so sorry, Annie!" she said, "It's my fault! It's all my fault!"

Anaya reached out to her sister-in-law and hugged her for the first time. Then she cried, saying, "No! No! It's not your fault, Olivia! It's that selfish bastard's fault that's lying in there on his ass while we all stand out here crying for him!"

"Turtle," Fardeen said before his spunky little sister pushed him away and gave Olivia a full embrace, and the two women cried together in the hallway.

As he stood alone, Fardeen wished his wife, Krisha, had made the trip with him. She was the only one truly able to comfort him.

Krisha grew up in Houston, and Fardeen got introduced to her during Diwali several years before. Arranged marriages among Indians were a thing of the past, particularly those that lived in America. But theirs may as well have been arranged because Savitri was so emphatic that they'd make such a wonderful couple. Savitri couldn't stand any of the girls Fardeen brought home. One of them was obviously a whore, and then the others were idiots altogether.

Krisha was assuredly chaste, albeit Americanized. She'd been a football cheerleader and a point guard on the ladies' team for the Dulles High Vikings when Savitri introduced them years before. The feisty girl was a walking contradiction. She was gorgeous and darker than any woman in Fardeen's family. Yet she spoke and carried herself like the girls from the movie "Heathers," even as she wore traditional Gujarati dress and groaned at the offerings in the Diwali buffet line on the last day of the celebration. She had a quick mouth and a chip on her shoulder, just like Fardeen's Mama.

"Do you want to get out of here and take me to Wendy's when this bullshit is over? I'm dying for a Triple and a Frosty," she asked Fardeen.

Fardeen was the only one there dressed like an American, wearing a University of Florida sweatshirt, jeans, and Air Jordans. Krisha stirred emotions Fardeen hadn't felt since he was a kid.

"Yes! I love Wendy's!" was all he could manage, though, as he stood in the buffet line with a plateful of eggplant and chutney.

The two went on to Wendy's, and they fell in love with one another in the parking lot, eating as Fardeen blathered about the motel business. Krisha studied every expression and evaluated every word her impromptu suitor spoke.

The day after she graduated from high school, Fardeen took

a knee on her parent's driveway and pled with her to be his wife while Siddharth waited in the passenger's side of his Cadillac. During his spring break, Fardeen had driven Siddharth to scout a property in Sugar Land, Texas. Fardeen had no sooner slipped the ring on Krisha's finger and kissed her hand before Siddharth laid on the horn.

"Come on, boy! We have business in Texas!" he yelled over the rap music blaring from the Cadillac as Krisha's parents stood in disgusted amazement a few feet behind the couple.

Krisha followed Fardeen to The University of Florida, although she had several scholarship offers from Vanderbilt, Tulane, Duke, and Baylor, which would have kept her close to home.

Fardeen loved her passionately. And he so wished she was with him just then.

CHAPTER SEVENTEEN

September 17, 1981, Tomahawk, Florida

By September, The Seagull continued to be as busy as Mr. Carmichael said it would be. Devan and Fardeen frequently had to turn pull-up business away because they were so full, and Devan partially regretted it each time. As remote as the property was, he didn't want to have gained notoriety for always being full once these people left. He certainly didn't regret the business, though, and he always enjoyed it when Mr. Carmichael showed up on Fridays to sign his credit card receipt for an additional week of rooms.

Another bright spot was that Thomas Cole made good on his promise to help Devan with the rooms. He was a master carpenter and replaced the drywall in several rooms, bringing them back into inventory which Horizon Christian Ministries quickly lapped up with their demand. Thomas also replaced the linoleum floors in the office with tile and installed new windows in four rooms. Because he was decent, Devan felt he might be taking advantage of Thomas, so he offered to pay for his services. He figured he was already getting paid by Horizon for the rooms and that it wasn't fair for him to avail himself of Thomas' generosity.

But each time he tried to pay him, Thomas refused. He opened his arms the last time Devan offered and hugged him, which Devan found particularly uncomfortable.

"Brother," Thomas said, "I'm just doing God's work. And with every wall I repair, every tile I set, and every door I hang, I'm building my palace in heaven, not in Florida."

Sridevi, who'd accompanied Devan to Thomas Cole's room that day with fresh towels, started snickering on the way back to the office before Devan laid into her.

"Hush!" he snapped, "You could learn from a man like that!"

"I suppose I could if I wanted to start a tile business in my next life," she said under her breath before Devan whipped around.

"What? What did you say, girl?!"

She just smiled, leaned up, and kissed her Papa on the head, though.

"Nothing, Papa," she said, smirking, which forced Devan to smile back. Light-hearted moments with Sridevi were so rare. He didn't want to spoil it.

As the father and daughter walked to the office together, Devan mumbled, "Besides, I picture you hanging doors more than I do you laying tile."

He continued walking, but Sridevi stopped and said, "What? What did you say?"

Devan started laughing as he turned to his daughter, stretched his arm out, and pulled her close for the rest of the way to the office.

Devan allowed himself to accept his good fortune rather than second-guess it as he walked and thought about what all this business meant to her and his other children.

But he knew this wasn't forever, and he'd hoped The Seagull would build its reputation on clean rooms and safety rather than being a place that was impossible to book a room. Not just that, but these people cost a lot of money to accommodate. There were six, sometimes seven people, staying in one room, and it didn't even matter if it was a single or a double. Naturally, that drove the amount of linen used through the roof. The Seagull's towels and sheets came from Biloxi and Mobile because the companies servicing Pensacola Beach were too expensive. So there was always a lag between their orders and receipt of their sheets, pillowcases, and towels.

"What are you doing over there, Devan," Sid asked weekly over the phone, *"selling towels out of the back door?"*

Devan always dreaded that call and got to the point he made Savitri answer the phone just so she'd have to deal with her brother's needling instead of him.

Michelle usually came to the office in the early evenings to spend time with Fardeen. And it was the brightest part of his day. Their flirtations were innocent enough, mainly because Fardeen was afraid of being alone with her. She'd stand at the counter, talk to him, and even run errands on the property so he wouldn't have to get up. She also accompanied him whenever he fixed air conditioners or changed lightbulbs. Fardeen liked when she came with him because the people staying at The Seagull treated him differently when she was with him.

As the Seagull's occupancy swelled to capacity, Devan's and Fardeen's shifts began bleeding into one another. But it wasn't due to checking people in at the front desk. The enormous demands of having so many people in-house were overwhelming, and there were only so many hours in a day. They were always short of quarters in the drawer, so Devan had to go to the bank several times a week.

The 7-11 used to handle their shortfalls in change. But it got to where they had to turn them away for the same reasons. And that was because of all the increased traffic in the store. The Horizon crew, almost exclusively teenagers, lived off of chilidogs, microwave burritos, Slurpees, Doritos, jerky, giant pickles, Snickers bars, and Sweet Tarts. They walked up and down the highway between the 7-11 and The Seagull, seemingly all day and night. They lined up at the convenience store's Asteroids machine, which drove up the demand for quarters even more than the Coke machine at The Seagull did. And that old thing burned up inside a couple of weeks after Horizon's people arrived.

"My God, Mr. P! What the hell are y'all doing out here?" Ricki, the service tech from Coke laughed one Tuesday afternoon, wearing his pin-striped shirt with a Coca-Cola patch on the front.

"I serviced this machine Sunday, and it's already empty? And the compressor done give out!" he continued through a chortle.

Then he held up the sackcloth bag filled with quarters and jingled it,

Devan disregarded his question and said, "Please, Sir Ricki. That looks to be at least one hundred dollars in quarters. Please, come to the office. Let me buy that change from you."

Ricki laughed and said, "Sure, Mr. P. You got it, man. It's that much less I have to carry!"

Horizon accomplished something else for Devan. The people in town started waving at him as he drove up and down the highway. They'd never seen so many people at that motel, and even though they had to stand in line to pay for their gas, they were delighted. A bunch of youngsters buying up the shelves in 7-11 was a sign that things were picking up in little Tomahawk, so they took notice, just as the city officials did. Suddenly, a steady, consistent stream of money came into their coffers that wasn't there before. If it kept up, they'd be able to complete that renovation of the Tomahawk High Indians football stadium and several other projects around town.

Fardeen regretted trading shifts with his father that week, but he had to. Devan was worn-out. Fardeen couldn't stand working nights and would be glad when his father recuperated. Nights were always the worst. And it seemed they were even worse the more people they had in-house. Sometimes Fardeen longed for the days before Horizon Christian Ministries set down in Tomahawk despite their money. Except, that is, for Michelle being there and how she made him feel. She made everything better, and he couldn't imagine being at The Seagull without her.

He hadn't been on his shift an hour that evening before it all started. Around eleven o'clock, a boy entered the office holding a dollar bill out, presumably to get change. But he didn't even ask for it. He just dropped the bill on the counter and stared at Fardeen. This guy looked like a real piece of work too. He had the right side of his head completely shaved, and the remainder of his long, dirty blonde hair hung over the left side of his face. He wore a white Van Halen concert shirt with black sleeves and had his right ear pierced.

Annoyed, Fardeen sat quietly, trying to force the boy to ask for change. Then, realizing Fardeen was put off by his failure to say anything, the kid just stood there staring. Fardeen wasn't giving in, no matter what. Neither was the kid, though.

After a good fifteen seconds passed, another boy walked into the office, He had on wildly colored short pants that looked like they were made out of tent material or something, and he wore a sleeveless white tee. From the get-go, Fardeen could tell there was something different about him. He was very prim and had a perpetual smile on his face. He walked up behind boy number one and stood, patiently waiting in line for service. But Fardeen and boy number one were locked in a standoff.

Finally, boy number one spoke up, sneering at Fardeen.

"Is something wrong with you?"

Fardeen debated whether to respond before saying, "No, there's nothing wrong with me. Is there something wrong with you?"

"Do you see that fucking dollar, A-rab?" the boy asked, poking his finger onto the bill.

As he'd learned about himself the past few months, Fardeen

wasn't exactly a wordsmith under anxious situations. So the best he could come back with, which he was sorry for before he finished speaking, was,

"Yes. Do you see that fucking dollar?"

That was the first time Fardeen had uttered a curse word in his entire life. He felt so uncomfortable doing it too.

Then the second boy spoke up, saying, "What's your problem, Matthew?"

He was no longer smiling as he walked to Matthew's side, staring at him while Matthew continued glaring at Fardeen. It was as though the second boy knew Fardeen crossed a line and that he was protecting Fardeen. Then the second boy surprised Fardeen by grabbing the dollar bill from the counter and slapping it onto Matthew's chest.

"Go!" he snapped at Matthew. But Matthew didn't budge. He just kept staring at Fardeen.

Fardeen couldn't imagine what he'd done to make Matthew so mad. Then he decided he hadn't done a damned thing. His thoughts turned toward the pistol his uncle gave him that he'd hidden in the file cabinet a few feet away and how he might get to it if things escalated. But then Matthew ripped the dollar bill from the second boy's hand, flipped Fardeen off, and hurried out of the office.

After he left, the second boy turned around, smiling again, and said, "Wowsers!" placing his hand in the center of his chest.

"That was a close one!"

While in Biloxi, Fardeen came across males that acted like this boy did, although infrequently. And excepting a circumstance or two, they were ordinarily nice, albeit he didn't understand them.

The boy thrust his hand out, palm downward like a woman, and said, "I'm James!"

Fardeen sure hoped James didn't expect him to kiss his hand. So he grabbed James's fingertips and shook them instead.

"Hi, James."

"You're Dean!" the boy squealed, making two fists under his chin.

"Yes, I am," Fardeen said, wondering how in the hell the boy knew his name.

Then James began clapping his hands next to his left cheek like he'd just guessed the Showcase Showdown on The Price is Right.,

"Oh, I knew it! I just knew it!" he said, "And you can call me Jamie! My Dad used to try to call me Jimmy, but can you just imagine? Moi? A Jimmy? Oh, I don't think so, honey child! I don't think so! Nooo thank you, ma'am!"

Jamie was so animated and energetic as he spoke that Fardeen couldn't help but smile at him and laugh a little bit.

"How did you," Fardeen began before the young man interrupted him.

"Oh, Michelle told me about you! She told eeeverybody about you!" Jamie said, rolling his eyes upward as he pointed at Fardeen.

"Michelle was right about you too, Mr. Dean! You have Egyptian eyes! Are you from Egypt? I've never been to Egypt! Well, Jamie's never been anywhere, you know what I'm saying? Well, except, of course, a truck stop here and there, do you know what I'm saying??" he said, cackling.

That's when Fardeen recognized another trait the boy exhibited that he'd been warned about in Biloxi by his Uncle Sid. Jamie was on something and was as high as a kite. Looking closer, Fardeen saw that his pupils were the size of dimes, a tell-tale sign that Sid trained him to look for. But just as Fardeen started to ask him to go away, Jamie got his attention.

"You know, Michelle really likes you, Mr. Dean," Jamie said, bouncing his eyebrows up and down. That was all Fardeen needed to hear. Nothing else mattered to him after that.

"Really?" Fardeen asked before catching himself, clearing his throat, and lowering his pitch.

"Oh, really?" he asked.

"Ohhh, absolutely, Mr. Dean," Jamie said, shaking his head from side to side, "she's head over heels!"

Then Fardeen began to wonder how well Jamie knew Michelle. He assumed they were in the same prayer group or whatever, but just how familiar with him was Michelle? It was apparently well enough that she confided in him. That troubled Fardeen, but it also explained a lot about her behavior. If Mr. Cole let her hang around boys like this one, it was no wonder she acted the way she did in 7-11. What Michelle needed, Fardeen thought to himself, was a mother.

"Welp!" Jamie said, "I have to go! Duty calls, you know what I'm saying?"

After he said that, Jamie raced toward the door before turning around and saying, "Oops! Hello? Earth to Jamie! I need some change too, Mr. Dean!"

Fardeen quickly opened the cash drawer and had four quarters in Jamie's hand before asking for his dollar. He was so anxious to get him out of the office that he'd forgotten to ask for it.

"Thank you, kind sir!" Jamie said before repeating the exact motion he had a moment earlier.

He raced to the door, then turned back, put his hand on his waist, and said, "Uhhh, hello? Calling all cars! I forgot to give you my dollar!"

He gave Fardeen his dollar, and Fardeen was relieved and thankful for his honesty because his father would have hit the ceiling if the drawer were short, even a penny in the morning. Devan wasn't worried about theft but rather Fardeen's responsible handling of the register. He tore into Savitri one time so hard that she didn't speak to him for days, and Fardeen certainly didn't want to relive that.

Fardeen was so tired. It was the part of the night he hated. He would've otherwise enjoyed the solitude, but being near the Interstate, he realized how dangerous it was should he nod off or stop paying attention for even one second. His uncle's words lingered in his head.

"Oh, you will get robbed in Tomahawk, nephew. Believe it. At some point, they will rob you. That's why you should do everything you can to prevent it from happening, and then you need to be prepared when it does so that it doesn't happen again."

Then Siddharth placed a nickel-plated .32 caliber pistol in Fardeen's hand as he stared into his eyes.

"You shoot them in the chest, Fardeen. You shoot them in the chest until they're on the ground, which should only take two or three rounds. Then you shoot them in the head with whatever is left, nephew. That will send a message to the rest of them. 'Do not trifle with The Seagull' is the message you'll send, nephew. I only hope your father isn't fool enough to let it happen while my sister is behind the front desk. Because they will kill her, they will kill Savitri or even worse before they do."

It was chilling advice, but it stuck with Fardeen. He imagined Sid had the same discussion with his father before giving him the pistol Devan pulled out that first day at The Seagull. As he contemplated what Sid told him, Fardeen wheeled over to the file cabinet in his office chair, opened its bottom drawer, and pulled out the pistol from beneath the Pensacola phone book.

Sid hadn't just given him the gun, though. He taught him how to shoot it, too. He had him over for lunch one Monday while Nancy, the housekeeper, watched the front desk at The Sunkist.

Siddharth's neighborhood was in an unincorporated part of Biloxi. The three lots he owned backed up to an inlet from Back Bay. And for all practical purposes, they were out in the country. So he allowed Fardeen to shoot eggs off the top of milk jugs.

"You're a crack shot, nephew!" his Uncle Sid told him when Fardeen blew the eggs off three milk jugs before missing the last one, puncturing the milk jug and sending it hurtling backward. They repeated the exercise several times before going back inside for lunch. Then Nancy drove Fardeen back to The Seagull in Mr. Sid's car.

Fardeen stirred awake as the sirens wailed and the brilliant blue lights flew past the office. Something was happening on the property!

He jumped up from the desk and rushed toward the door. Remembering another of his uncle's caveats, he stopped and locked the office before hurrying toward the police cars.

He thought about how absurd everything his father expected of him was as he ran. He was just a child. Most American boys spent their summers playing baseball or camping or at the beach, so far as he could tell from watching television. But no matter how they spent their time, he was sure it wasn't washing and folding sheets, scrubbing vomit out of carpet, or unclogging toilets filled with putrid shit that made him want to throw up himself.

When Fardeen reached the back of the parking lot, he saw spotlights from the police cars that shone on two boys wrestling on the ground while thirty or so people stood around hollering. Thirty people? Where in the hell had all these people come from? Yet, there they were.

As one of the boys rolled over and positioned himself over

the other one, Fardeen recognized him as Jamie, the boy from earlier. But there wasn't anything effeminate about Jamie now as Fardeen watched. His face was locked in a snarl, and he was repeatedly pounding his fists into the side of the other boy's head.

"FREEZE!!" he heard a policeman yell from the PA of one of the squad cars.

It was as though Jamie hadn't heard it, though, as he continued to pound away at the other boy.

Then, for the third time in his life, but certainly not the last, Fardeen heard the unmistakable crackle of gunfire. One of the officers had fired his gun into the air, sending everyone dodging behind cars or running away. Following that was the sound of two shotguns arming.

As though versed in some protocol, Jamie thrust his arms in the air, staring back at the officers and shielding his eyes with his forearm from the blinding lights coming from the police cars. Then, the shrill instruction from the officers continued.

"PUT YOUR HANDS BEHIND YOUR HEAD, ASSHOLE!"

Jamie rolled off his victim, and that's when Fardeen realized the other boy in the altercation was Matthew, the one wearing the Van Halen shirt in the office earlier.

Fardeen watched as the officers cuffed Jamie and hurled him into one of the squad cars. Looking back, he saw that Jamie had beaten the shit out of Matthew. Matthew's nose bled, and his right eye already began to swell. Fardeen felt guilty because he realized the fight was probably because of his earlier exchange with Matthew.

But just as he started panicking, he felt a delicate caress on his wrist before it slid into his hand and intertwined with his fingers. When he turned, he saw Michelle staring at him. It was the most pleasant sensation. Then, when she smiled at him and touched his cheek, that other sensation became a distant second place.

About that time, a portly woman with multi-colored curlers in her hair wearing a robe pushed past Fardeen and began shouting.

"What're you doing with my baby?!" she shouted at the policemen, pointing at her son.

"Ma'am, stand back. Your son is under arrest," an officer snapped back at the woman.

"Arrest?!" the woman shouted, "What in the hell do you mean under arrest?!"

The officer whipped around, pulled his cuffs out, and held them up with his right hand. Then he shouted, "I said he's under arrest! What don't you understand about that, you fat assed, ugly bitch?!"

Fardeen felt like he watched one of the obscene R-rated movies on Home Box Office he'd seen while in Biloxi. It didn't feel like reality to him. Nothing remotely like this ever happened while he worked on his uncle's property. As much as he hated to, he realized he'd better get to his father before he made it downstairs. Fardeen was sure that the gunshot woke his parents up, and he felt he'd better explain things before they came into the parking lot and saw all the police cars.

But when he turned around, he saw that it was too late. Devan stood a few feet behind, staring back at him. He could see the blue lights flickering in his father's wide open, very awake eyes, and his expression horrified Fardeen. He looked to his right and realized he was still holding hands with Michelle, so he instantly ripped his hand away, but again, too late. He could only imagine what his father thought. Here he stood, holding hands with an American girl in the parking lot set to a backdrop of people fighting and shouting as police officers fired guns and arrested people. At least, that's how he believed his father would view it.

But Devan remained silent as he watched everything. Then he raised his hand and motioned for Fardeen to come to him. His father took a lot of grief from his mother and uncle for not being more assertive and proactive. But something you could say about Devan was that he was a very cautious and contemplative man. He didn't dive headlong into anything. And he always deliberated before he acted or even spoke. His cool demeanor and thoughtfulness were on clear display, and it scared Fardeen more than the cops, the belligerent kid, or anything else happening at the moment.

"Fardeen, what is happening?" Devan asked his son.

"I don't know," Fardeen said, "I think two men were fighting in the parking lot, and someone must have called the police."

Fardeen instantly thought about how that must have sounded to his father and how it all probably appeared. *Someone* called the police? Why or how would *someone* have known to call the police when he didn't? Did this happen as he stood in the parking lot holding hands with an American girl?

Fardeen could read all of that in his father's expression. Then, with perhaps the worst timing and poorest judgment, Michelle sashayed up and retook Fardeen's hand. But Fardeen ripped it back and flung his arm in the air, moving several feet away. She seemed so hurt as she looked back at him and said, "Dean?"

Fardeen didn't know what to say, but Devan did.

"Young lady," he said sternly, "you should go back to Sir Thomas' room. You have no business being in the parking lot at this hour, nor any business at all with my son."

That was a pretty clear statement and directive from someone even Michelle could recognize as an angry parent. But surprisingly, she seemed unfazed by Devan's words. Michelle looked back at Devan like they were the only two people standing there. Then, without saying anything, she turned around and walked back toward her room. Fardeen would feel bad about it in the morning. But right now, all he wanted to do was assuage his father's disappointment and have the chance to explain things—at least as best as he could.

Ordinarily, a motel owner would try to get more information from the police about what caused them to come to their property to arrest people. But Devan wisely knew he had nothing to gain and everything to lose by engaging the police just then. So he put his hand on Fardeen's shoulder and directed him toward the office before falling in behind him. He knew he'd be talking to the police soon enough. And just as he and Fardeen entered the office, two more police cars sped onto the property.

"Go to bed, son," Devan said as they made it inside.

"But, Papa, please let me explain," Fardeen begged.

"No, there'll be time to explain tomorrow. I slept several hours today, so I'll finish this shift. Go upstairs and go to bed. And please try not to wake your mother. I'll speak to the officers when they're finished."

"But, Papa, I was the one that was here when things got started! I need to tell the police what happened so they know it didn't have anything to do with us! I don't want them to arrest you too!" Fardeen demanded.

Realizing Fardeen may have a point, Devan said, "Very well. But don't say anything unless they speak directly to you. Let me answer their questions until I don't have an answer for them. Alright?"

"Yes, Papa," Fardeen said, still embarrassed and ashamed he'd let something happen during his watch that was bad enough to wake up his father.

Devan looked awful. He had dark circles under his bloodshot eyes. And the only thing Fardeen was sure he'd eaten over the past twenty-four hours was a bag of hot fries and some Dolly Madison powdered doughnuts from 7-11. He'd bought them for

Devan when he found him slumped over at the front desk asleep that afternoon. So he wasn't about to abandon his father amid all the turmoil he felt primarily responsible for causing. He'd wait with Devan and talk to the police, relating everything that happened before the fight started. And he'd try to put in a good word for Jamie, too.

But the police never even stopped by the office before leaving, not one of them. They just raced away with Jamie in the back of one squad car and his mother in another because she didn't know how to keep her mouth shut. Fardeen was relieved, but Devan was concerned. While Fardeen viewed not talking to the police as a fortunate thing, Devan believed their distancing indicated something deeper, potentially dangerous. He didn't know what it was, but it was just what his instincts told him. And Devan Patel's instincts batted a thousand that night.

After the police cleared out and it became apparent they had no interest in getting the Patel's take on things, Devan said, "Okay, son. Go on to bed now. I'm sure they'll follow up with us in the morning. You can speak to them then."

Fardeen reluctantly nodded at his Papa and then hurried up the stairs, leaving Devan alone in the office.

A few moments later, as Devan sat down at the front desk, a police car turned into the property and sped up in front of the office. A policeman got out, opened the office door, leaned in, and tossed the room key he'd confiscated from Jamie onto the counter. But the only thing he said as the key slid across the counter and fell onto the desk behind it was, "Strike two."

Devan didn't realize it, but the officer referenced the tabs the Tomahawk Police Department kept on The Seagull. It was the second time they answered a call to the property after something egregious happened, which, to them, spelled trouble. The first occurred after the Patels were there for only minutes on the first day. Dozens of officers responded to Devan's having an unregistered firearm for which he didn't have a license to carry. Technically, he'd broken no laws because Florida was an open carry state, and once they established his identity, they left without further ado. However, they did confiscate his pistol, which he could reclaim only after completing a firearm safety course, obtaining a hunting license, and then showing evidence of having purchased a bond.

They were way out of line. But just as they suspected, Devan didn't know any better. If he'd only mentioned the matter to his brother-in-law, Sid would have been outraged and likely sued the hell out of the Tomahawk Police Department. But even if Devan had known better, he would probably have done what they asked anyway. He'd rather do that than stir up anything with Sid.

But now, after all of this happened, the police's behavior was very suspect to Devan. He'd sensed that something was off all along. He felt like people watched his every move. His hunch was right, and he realized that based on the officer's warning.

After sitting at the desk for a while, Devan sighed and opened the bottom desk drawer. He dug through the extra miniature bars of soap they kept as a backup if their deliveries were late. At the bottom of the drawer was a half-pint of Aristocrat vodka someone left in one of the rooms. Devan took the bottle out of the drawer, wheeled around, and grabbed a foam coffee cup and the two-liter bottle of 7-UP he kept on the bureau behind him. Then he opened the bottle and filled the cup almost full of vodka before dousing the rest with 7-UP.

As he swirled the cup and raised it to his nose to smell it, he considered all that had happened earlier. He was so anxious about everything. He was worried about the police, his son's safety, and the likelihood he might have to kick the Horizon folks off the property if anything else happened. That would prove to be financially devastating if he did.

But then a final few thoughts came to him. And those were about his wife, whom he'd sworn to that he'd never drink again. He also thought about Sridevi and how she had such disdain for the business. She'd watched him rapidly deteriorate when he started drinking. As strong-willed and indignant as she could be, her response to his drinking was ten times worse. Instead of flying off the handles and admonishing him the way Savitri did, all she ever did when she could tell he'd been drinking was cry. Well, that and she refused to speak to him for days afterward. And it just about killed him every time she behaved that way.

A poignant thought Devan had, though, was what if he became a drunk, just like the poor lost soul in Biloxi who'd attempted to rob Siddharth? He thought about what that might mean to his wife and his children. And after he considered all that, the most disturbing thought he had was about his unborn child and the world into which it would be born. So, he crushed the foam cup in his hand, allowing vodka and 7-UP to spill onto his pants. And then he threw the cup under the desk, stomped on it, and tossed the vodka bottle into the trash.

CHAPTER EIGHTEEN

T he following day, Fardeen got up early to relieve his father from taking over the night shift. He'd been shocked when he went upstairs and saw that his mother and sisters had slept through the entire ordeal. Then again, Sridevi and Anaya slept in the same bed every night, wearing hi-fi headphones connected to cassette players he gave them during Diwali the year before. And his mother, Savitri, slept so deeply ever since she became pregnant.

Fardeen and Devan hadn't had a chance to discuss anything, and while he dreaded it, Fardeen just wanted to put it behind himself. He hadn't slept much because he kept going over what he would say in his head. Fardeen didn't like lying, let alone to his parents. He'd never lied to them his whole life. So he'd just be honest with his father about everything that happened. He'd explain about the two boys in the office. Then he'd tell him he dozed off and woke up to police cars tearing into the parking lot. Yes, he was guilty of napping. But he couldn't imagine how the situation might have unfolded any other way that he could have prevented.

However, the lingering issue he didn't know how to reckon for was Michelle. Apart from his mother's emotional outburst over the matter, there'd never been any ground rules for his interaction with girls. That subject was taboo between Fardeen and his mother, to begin with, but Fardeen and Devan never talked about it before either.

When he entered the office, Devan initiated the discussion.

And Fardeen was taken aback by how it started and then what all he told him.

"I'm not going to say anything to your mother about the girl, Fardeen," Devan said, sitting behind the desk as Fardeen walked in, drying his hair with a towel.

Okay, that was good news. It was surprising but still very good news. Then Fardeen braced himself for the line of questioning he expected about what happened the night before. But his father surprised him again. He didn't grill Fardeen or corner him through a stepwise progression of logic as he usually did. Instead, Devan told him about something he experienced in Tomahawk earlier in the year.

"While you were in Biloxi, Fardeen, I fell asleep behind the front desk one night. I'd drunk very heavily, and I couldn't keep my eyes open any longer," Devan said to an astonished Fardeen.

Devan took on an aura of shame and regret. Fardeen hadn't ever seen him that way, and he found it unsettling as he stopped drying his hair and stared at Devan.

"And a man came into the office and stole from the register. I was on the couch, asleep the whole time because I'd drunk so much alcohol," he continued.

Fardeen's astonishment grew to disbelief.

"I woke up to a police officer tapping me on the head with his baton. He had the man in custody in the backseat of his police car and made me go outside to ensure he wasn't my employee like the man said he was."

Devan's story was so bizarre to Fardeen. It painted a fallible side of his father he never imagined existed. All he could do was stand and listen.

"After I told him the man was not my employee, he had me say to the man that he was under arrest and that I didn't want him to ever return to my property. It was so strange, Fardeen. I didn't understand why I had to talk to the man at all. In one way,

I was thankful the police were watching the property, looking out for us while I was asleep and drunk. And I was grateful for that, Fardeen. Very grateful."

"Of course, Papa. I understand," Fardeen said, unsure where his father would take the discussion next.

"But then, in another way, it was like the policeman was warning me. He acted annoyed. And he behaved like he was telling me to do a better job. He was right, Fardeen. The American policeman was right. However, it was also as though the police told me that we were on our own in this wasteland. Like we didn't have their protection or support if we couldn't do any better than I had done. And if that's what he was doing, then again, I have no defense for what took place. But I still don't fully understand, and I worry about what might happen next time, even when we've done everything we could to protect the property."

Then Devan rose and came from behind the counter. He walked up to Fardeen, placed his hand on his shoulder, and smiled.

"I didn't tell anyone about that night, Fardeen, not your mother and certainly not Siddharth. I didn't want anyone to know. But when I woke up to sirens and gunshots last night, all that came to my mind was my only son. I cursed myself as I walked down the stairs, thinking what a fool I'd been to use you the way I have. I was afraid of what I'd see when I came into this office. And when I didn't see you and found the door locked, I feared the worst."

Then, in another moment so unlikely to Fardeen, he watched as his father teared up.

"Fardeen, this is a difficult business I've chosen. It's not like the shoe store in Ahmedabad or the plantation where your grandparents raised me. It's very different. I struggle every day, considering if I've made the right decision to bring my family here. These Americans aren't like any other people in the world,

Fardeen. They're extraordinarily dangerous people, and the ones you think are your friends are the most dangerous."

Devan looked down and stopped speaking despite seeming to have so much more to say. But Fardeen could tell he was too afraid of becoming even more emotional, so he spoke up.

"I know, Papa," Fardeen said, becoming emotional himself, "I know."

After several seconds, Devan looked up and said, "Once I saw your face and that you were alright, I realized what had happened. I knew you'd fallen asleep, Fardeen. I knew that because I knew you'd never willingly let anything happen on the property that you could have prevented. And then I felt ashamed that I'd left my son behind the front desk of an American motel overnight. And as I sat here, I got angry, Fardeen. I was angry at myself. I was angry at the police. And I was angry at Siddharth. Because no matter what he tells us about calling the police, it is not your job to go into the parking lot to break up a brawl, son. But I still worry about what might happen next time we call the police. Will they take their time because we've angered them? Or will they just not come at all?"

They didn't get a chance to talk any further before the door to the office jingled, and a stocky man wearing a short-sleeved dress shirt with a clip-on tie walked in. His belly hung so far over that it obscured the badge on his belt, and he carried a small, flip-over notepad like the ones they put in golf carts to keep score. He had a pencil tucked behind his right ear. And he presented like he just didn't give a damn about anything. Devan quickly wiped his eyes on his sleeve and cleared his throat.

"Are one of you fella's Paddle?" the man asked in a crisp Midwestern accent, looking between them and whatever was on his notepad.

A moment passed before Devan spoke, saying, "Yes, sir, I'm Patel."

"Oh, Pah-tel, ok, I'm sorry, Mr. Pah-tel," the man said.

Fully anticipating this, Devan began, "Please, sir, what can I help you with? Can I get you a cup of coffee?"

Looking up, the man relaxed his shoulders and said, "Well, sure. I'd love a cup of coffee, Mr. Paddle, uh, I mean Pah-tel. Cream and sugar, please."

Devan looked over at Fardeen, directing him to fetch the man a cup of coffee from behind the front desk. Then he moved toward the chubby man, whose expression changed from carefree to afraid as Devan moved closer. That was because Devan had a look of disgust on his face.

"Uh, Mr. Pah-tel," the man started before Devan came within arm's reach, "I'm Detective Greely with the Tomahawk Police Department, and I just have a few questions about last night, sir. That's all."

Devan was tired and perhaps bolder than he'd typically be. But he was fed up. He was fed up with a police department that he'd grown to mistrust. He was sick of Siddharth and his insufferable, fat, pregnant, and disrespectful sister. He was weary from doing laundry like some hotel matron in Mumbai. He was tired of staying up all night and slaving for the peanuts Siddharth paid him and the false hope of owning The Seagull one day. But more than anything else, Devan was tired of being in Tomahawk damned Florida and all the bullshit that came with it. He'd done nothing wrong, and his boy certainly hadn't done anything wrong either. So he was just before snapping as he approached the detective. And even he didn't know what he'd do once he reached him.

Seeing the expression on his father's face, Fardeen thrust a cup of coffee between his father and Detective Greely.

"Here's your coffee, sir," Fardeen said.

Detective Greely raised his hand and took the cup, thanking Fardeen.

"Mr. Patel," he said, "I'm only here to get information, sir. I don't want to upset you anymore than you already are."

Then, as though things couldn't have been any more awkward, the bells above the office door jingled again, and Thomas Cole walked in, followed by Michelle. Fardeen sighed and stared toward the floor. When he looked back up, he met eyes with her for a moment, and it appeared that she realized she and her father shouldn't be there.

"Come on, Dad," she said, tugging at Thomas's arm while staring back at Fardeen.

But Thomas disregarded Michelle and said, "Oh. Oh, dear. Are you a police officer, sir? Does this have anything to do with last night? Because if it does, let me just tell you that it's all my fault, sir."

Detective Greely, feeling relieved, turned around and said, "Yes, I am a police officer, and I'm here investigating an assault."

Thomas lowered his head, made the sign of the cross, then looked back up and said, "If I can help you in any way, please let me know. I was in charge of the kids last night. They were in my prayer group, and the fight the two boys got into started there. I made them leave. But instead of making sure they went back to their rooms, I continued in worship with the other kids. It's my fault, officer."

Then, like a shark sensing blood in the water, Detective Greely turned toward Thomas Cole and opened his little notepad. Pulling the pencil from behind his ear, he licked his thumb and flipped to a fresh page.

"You say you were in charge of the kids? Tell me, sir. Are you the parent or guardian for either of the boys? We have the one boy's mother in custody. Is that your wife?"

"Oh, my no," Thomas said through a chuckle.

Detective Greely laughed and said, "No, I didn't suppose she was."

"My wife died three years ago. Now it's just Michelle and me," Thomas continued, reaching his arm around Michelle.

Detective Greely stopped laughing immediately and said, "Oh, oh. I'm very sorry to hear that, mister uhh?"

"Cole, officer. My name is Thomas Cole," Thomas said, walking over with his hand held out.

Detective Greely looked up from scribbling on his pad and shook Thomas' hand, "I'm Detective Greely, Mr. Cole. It's nice to meet you."

"Absolutely! Praise the Lord," Thomas said.

Greely paused before saying, "Uh, Mr. Cole, would you mind coming out to my vehicle for a second so I can get some information from you?"

"I certainly will, detective. Michelle, could you wait here, honey?" Thomas said.

"Oh, that won't be necessary, Mr. Cole. She can come along. I just need to get some particulars from you. Do you have a driver's license?" Greely asked.

Without answering, Thomas pulled out his wallet and presented his license to Detective Greely. Greely took it, then he and the Coles walked out of the office toward the detective's Ford Fairmont that was still running. Michelle looked back at Fardeen as she walked out of the office behind her father, and the detective held the door open. Fardeen made eye contact for a split second before looking away, worried his father might notice.

Once they were gone, Devan said, "I'm going back to bed, son. Will you be alright? Sridevi and Anaya will pull the rooms today. But I'd like you to do the laundry. Okay? Your mother is sick this morning."

It was as though nothing had happened the night before and that he and his father had never spoken about the turmoil. And that was just fine with Fardeen. He wanted to forget about all of it anyway.

"Yes. Yessir. Of course," Fardeen said as his father grabbed the sides of his face and kissed him on the forehead before turning and going upstairs to sleep.

It didn't take long before all the riffraff they'd rented so many rooms started moving around the property again that day. It was the first time Fardeen had gotten a good look at them en masse, and they were not an impressive group. The boys outnumbered the girls three to one, and there was only a handful of adults. They all wore horribly mismatched clothes like those Fardeen saw for sale as souvenirs at the amusement park in Biloxi. Their shirts either had phrases or movie themes, like scenes from Star Wars or Jaws, and none of the people looked like they'd bathed for some time.

Looking on, Fardeen shook his head. He felt like he needed to return to his roots, the decent and familiar aspects of being Hindu. He went behind the desk and took out the Hindu book of prayers Savitri gave him when he went to Biloxi. Then, he lit one of her agarbattis and prepared for a restful afternoon. He had to get Michelle out of his mind. But he knew that would be difficult.

Just as he began to relax, the office door swung open. Two fat American girls walked in, and they seemed aggravated. Fardeen looked down at his book and waited for them to speak. He wouldn't allow them to detract him from what he was doing unless they were polite and addressed him respectfully without using some slur.

"Hey!" one of the girls barked.

Fardeen didn't look up, so she continued.

"Hey! Hey, boy!" she said.

Fardeen raised his head slowly and looked at the girl. She

wore a pink t-shirt that was two sizes too small to accommodate her huge breasts and belly. And emblazoned on the front was an iron-on depiction of a waitress holding a platter. The middle-aged red-haired woman on the shirt had an unpleasant expression, and a speech bubble from her mouth read, "Mel! Kiss My Grits!"

Fardeen struggled with his conscience for a moment to be polite before he answered.

"Ma'am?"

"Your Coke machine took my money," the fat girl growled, "I put a corter in it, and nothing came out when I pressed the Meller Yeller button!"

Fardeen closed his book and said, "Ah, yes, ma'am. I'm sorry about that. The machine is probably empty because of so many guests. It's not supposed to take your money when it's empty, but sometimes it does anyway. Coca-Cola won't be here to refill it until Monday. though."

"Huh?" the fat girl asked.

"I said the Coca-Cola man will not be here to refill it until Monday," Fardeen said, exercising exquisite restraint.

"Well, that's fuckin' bullshit!" the girl said.

To Fardeen, she looked like a bull scratching its hoof on the ground before charging a matador. And in relative terms, she was every bit as large and fearsome.

"Ma'am, I will be glad to refund your money," Fardeen said.

"I don't want no money! I want a fuckin' Meller Yeller!" she hollered back at him.

Fardeen breathed deeply and closed his eyes before opening them and responding.

"Ma'am, there is a 7-11 grocery store nearby. Please bring me your receipt, and I'll gladly reimburse you for your Mello Yello beverage," he said, praying that would resolve the matter.

No such luck.

"I ain't walkin' nowheres! I'm sick of this shit!" the chubby girl screamed, "This is the worst damn motel I ever been to! You fuckin' forners piss me off! You need to go back to I-ran where you come from! Tommy pays y'all all this money, and you ain't even got a ice machine! Then you called the cops on us!"

Fardeen had enough. He'd had enough of these people, whoever they were. And he'd had enough of being talked down to by them. So he slowly rose from his seat to redress the matter.

But just then, he heard someone shout, "April! Leave him alone! You don't need another Mello Yello!"

When Fardeen looked to see who was shouting, he saw Michelle standing in the office doorway. Then she continued.

"Go! Go on back to your room, April! The law's gonna' kick us out of here if something else happens!"

April snorted, then looked back at Fardeen and said, "Gimmie my corter!"

Refusing to expend the energy to open the drawer, Fardeen reached into his pocket, pulled out a quarter, and gave it to the fat girl.

She grabbed the quarter then she and the other fat girl moved out of the door as Michelle stood in front of it, holding it open. But just before she left, April whipped around and yelled at Fardeen, "You stupid faggot! Mattie was right! You ain't nothing but a sissy! Just like Jamie, you faggot!"

Then she turned to Michelle and said, "Y'all ain't nothin' but a bunch of faggots!!"

Michelle raised her hand like she'd slap her, then April raced out of the door.

Once April was gone, Michelle closed the door, turned around with her back to it, and then smiled at Fardeen. Her crooked little smile and everything else about her were irresistible to him. He couldn't help but smile back.

"I'm so sorry, Dean," Michelle said as she walked toward the front desk, "these people are such bad people. It's like they never had a mother or something."

Those words gave Fardeen pause for thought. Who was Michelle to talk about someone not having a mother? If Michelle had a mother, she wouldn't be standing in a Tomahawk Motel, entreating a boy like him with her eyes. Then, suddenly, Fardeen was glad Michelle didn't have a mother. No, Fardeen was ecstatic that Michelle didn't have a mother.

But then he nerded-out just like he always did before he knew what was going on and said, "Would you like to watch television, Michelle?"

Fardeen's mind winced as it played his words back to him. *Would you like to watch television?* What kind of a line was that? It certainly wasn't cool. *Would you like to watch television?* He may as well have asked, *Have you noticed the weather lately?* Or *Do you like American potato salad? Because, golly, I sure do!*

So he was delightfully shocked when Michelle said, "I'd love to watch television, Dean."

The ball was in Fardeen's court then. Except he couldn't remember what he'd asked Michelle. So he just stood behind the desk, nodding like an imbecile. That went on for several moments before she asked, "What do you want to watch, Dean?"

That jarred Fardeen back into reality, and he raced from behind the front desk and ushered Michelle to the faux leather sofa.

"Oh, I don't care," he said, "let's see what's on."

Then he remembered that the channel selection at The Seagull couldn't hold a candle to the one at The Sunkist. He wasn't even sure what the antenna he'd helped his father install on the second-floor roof would show on that screen. So he held his breath when he turned on the television. And after a moment of snow, his worst fears were realized. A pastor materialized on the screen, pounding a podium and pointing toward the camera. But the reception was so poor that it didn't even pick up sound.

Michelle snickered, watching Fardeen fumble with the television. And when he turned around and saw her laughing, he started laughing too. Then she patted the space on the sofa next to her, luring him to sit down. Fardeen didn't need her to ask him twice. He hurried over and plopped down next to Michelle.

Within moments, the two kids tangled up on the sofa, kissing and groping each other, Michelle aggressively reaching for Fardeen's groin while judiciously protecting her own. And Fardeen just did whatever Michelle steered him to do. The whole affair took only moments before Fardeen lay back on the sofa, thinking about what kind of car he'd buy Michelle one day. But Michelle was a little more casual, kissing Fardeen on the forehead and adjusting her white tennis shorts before standing up and saying, "I've got to go now."

"What?" Fardeen asked.

"I have to go, baby," Michelle said, leaning over and kissing his cheek.

"Oh," Fardeen said, "oh, okay. Yeah, sure."

Michelle hung her head to the side as she twisted her hair back into the ponytail it was in before they'd gotten started. Then she looked at Fardeen and smiled. And within a moment, Michelle was gone as quickly as she'd come to his rescue in the office, leaving behind a cloud of her perfume, which drove Fardeen wild.

Fardeen laid back, exhausted from a day of washing and folding laundry. Then, realizing he might fall asleep, he jumped up and went behind the front desk. His father would be around to relieve him any minute now. He spent the rest of his shift fantasizing about Michelle and their life together.

CHAPTER NINETEEN

October 14th, 1981

"We're sorry, the number you have reached has been disconnected or is no longer in service. Please hang up and try your call again."

Devan felt like he might pass out when he heard the words after dialing Mr. Carmichael's number a third time. He was slowly beginning to realize the man from Horizon Christian Ministries was a fake, an imposter. Still, he put his nickel in the payphone and tried again. But he got the same result.

Minutes earlier, as he filled out his check to Florida Power and then stuffed it in an envelope, he glanced up at the pegboard in the post office. Then he walked over and dropped his bill into the "Out of Town" slot. But just as he started to walk back to the parking lot, he stopped cold. He raced back to the table where he'd drawn his cheek and looked at the pegboard again. Staring back at him from an FBI bulletin was the man who'd identified himself as Chester Carmichael over the summer. Devan was almost sure of it.

But the man's real name was Ralph Mayhew. And his crimes included Sexual Exploitation of Children, Selling and Buying of Children, and Activities Relating to Material Involving the Sexual Exploitation of Minors. The man's face he looked at fit the description, too. It was devoid of the pleasantness and cheerfulness he'd displayed as he visited with Devan at the front desk while paying his bill and renewing his reservations each week. The man Devan looked at was a hardened man, an evil man. And Devan thought he would throw up as he looked into the man's eyes.

He ran outside to the payphone at the parking lot entrance. He wanted to confront Carmichael first because the implications were so horrifying and grave. He needed to make sure.

He fumbled through his wallet until he found Carmichael's business card and began trying to reach him. He dreaded what he had to do after that. But he saw no way around it. Picking up the receiver a final time, he dialed the number at the bottom of the bulletin for the local FBI office in Panama City.

It might have been because of nerves, or it may have been that he didn't precisely know how to describe what happened up to that point. He probably should have gotten an idea when the agent told him over the phone to stay where he was. But in any case, Devan Patel was unprepared for what was about to happen.

Back at The Seagull, things were lively again. Radios and tape players blared music from the doors of open rooms, even as their air conditioners blew. Teenagers ran around the lot next door, throwing frisbees and footballs. A couple of them played Jokari at the back of the parking lot. It may not have been Biloxi, and it certainly wasn't the caliber of clientele he hoped for, but Fardeen felt as though things were finally where they should be in Tomahawk. Permanently on the day shift now, he sat in the office folding linens while his mother and baby sister, Anaya, came downstairs intermittently and filled the washing machines and dryers. And Sridevi, poor Sridevi, was left pulling the rooms until Devan could get back and help her start cleaning.

Already somewhat of a loner, an intellectual that liked studying Western philosophy, Sridevi was put off whenever she had to perform any duties at the motel. She couldn't abide Americans, and she thought they were unlearned savages for the most part. So, cleaning up after them was insufferable for her. But she was biding her time until she heard back from one of the universities in the region she'd applied. The Universities of Florida, Georgia, and Alabama were among them. She'd wind up as a philosophy major at Auburn University, less than four hours away. Ironically, it was there she'd meet an American boy from Saraland, Alabama, whose family was prominent and wealthy from the timber industry. That's who she'd marry and where she'd move, seldom returning home for the rest of her life.

"Ding ding!" Fardeen heard a familiar voice say as he looked up from folding pillowcases. He saw Michelle standing at the door to the front office, having opened it slowly so he wouldn't hear her. He was so happy to see her. He laid the pillowcases he held on the stack and raced around the front desk to meet her. They hugged a moment before pushing away from one another. He didn't realize what it was, but she smelled like a combination of Clairol Herbal Essences shampoo and strawberry bubble gum. It drove him wild. So much so that she had to fight him off for a second. Then she just gave in, pushing Fardeen backward toward the sofa after reaching behind herself and locking the office door.

Devan paced back and forth a few miles away next to the family's Le Sabre. Siddharth was going to kill him for this. Of all the caveats and guidelines he'd given Devan, the principal one was: *do not involve law enforcement unless it's absolutely necessary.*

When Siddharth told him that, it seemed so foolish to Devan. Law enforcement was who kept people safe in America. They prevented places like Biloxi and Pensacola from becoming slums. Americans didn't tolerate crime in their communities, and the police enforced their will.

Devan was right for the most part. Americans couldn't stand

crime, especially in towns like Tomahawk. But what Devan had grown to understand was that criminal activity was an inescapable part of the motel business in America. So you had to pick and choose your battles when you enlisted the police to deal with it. If you picked up the phone every time somebody raised their voice or spat on the sidewalk, you set yourself up for a lot of grief. Like it or not, the police didn't want to be viewed as lackeys, rushing to a businessman's aid on cue. It didn't even matter if they sat on their asses most of the time as they did in Tomahawk. You'd best just go about your business, bothering them only when things were about to move beyond anything you could do about them.

And while the states, counties, and municipalities of The United States were happy to collect lodging taxes, they balked at the responsibilities accompanying that business. Introducing people from all over the place brought all their sins and baggage with them. Moreover, rather than accepting that responsibility, those institutions often blamed the shortfall in law enforcement on the people who conducted that business when things went awry. Even with a modest annualized occupancy, a typical small motel the size of The Seagull could house thousands of people per year. It had forty-five rooms, which translated into anywhere from 6,000 to 10,000 additional people annually—more than twice the population of Tomahawk.

And the smaller the community was, the more apt they were to angrily and sanctimoniously shift blame.

"Everything was wonderful here until they put that motel up."

"Them foreigners brought in all kinds of drugs and stuff when they got here. It's a wonder we was able to build our new school!"

They were the typification of biting the hand that fed them.

And now, Devan hadn't only called law enforcement. He contacted the highest echelon of law enforcement in The United States—perhaps in the world.

As Devan stood outside of the phone booth, he was, at first, relieved when he heard the sirens in the distance. But when he saw how the Tomahawk Police turned toward where he stood and the pace at which they moved, he grew concerned. By the time they raced up within a few feet of him, slamming on their brakes and flinging their doors open, Devan was terrified.

"Get your hands in the air!!" were the first words he heard from one of the squad cars blocking off both sides of the street next to the phone booth.

Devan complied, thrusting his hands upward and falling to his knees without being asked. But that was just another of his missteps that day.

"Get up off the damned ground! And if you do anything else I don't tell you to, I'm going to kill you!" the young officer closest to him yelled.

The six policemen approached him with weapons drawn, two moving directly toward him while the other four splayed out to either side, then came up from behind. Before it was over, Devan stood, surrounded by police officers, as he held the FBI bulletin in his trembling right hand.

An officer he recognized tore the bulletin away from Devan and looked at it before looking back at him. Then he said, "Strike three," before flipping him around like a child about to be taken to the woodshed.

He slammed Devan onto the hood of his car while two other officers came up and frisked, then cuffed him. Afterward, the officer in charge grabbed the handcuffs as another opened the back of the squad car. And he hurled Devan into the back seat where he landed face down.

As Fardeen rolled on top of Michelle, he thought he heard someone fumbling with the doorknob to the office. He looked over before Michelle grabbed his chin and redirected his attention to her.

"It's just somebody wanting change, baby," she said, "ignore them."

Once again, Fardeen did as Michelle told him and kissed her passionately as he ran his fingers through that gorgeous white hair that smelled like heaven.

But then he suddenly felt like someone was watching him. He had the distinct feeling that someone saw everything he and Michelle were doing on the sofa. He looked over his right shoulder and saw a Tomahawk police officer looking down at him with his face pressed to the office window, cupping his eyes with his hands before motioning with the pointed finger of his right hand.

A second later, Fardeen heard a crashing sound as a Tomahawk police officer kicked the office door in, and three others raced in with their guns drawn.

"Hands up! Hands up!" the lead officer said as he came barreling across the office with his pistol aimed at Fardeen and Michelle.

Fardeen screamed and rolled off Michelle onto the floor onto his back with his hands extended upward. What were these police up to now?

One of them stepped onto the center of his chest, staring down as he pointed a .357 magnum at his head. Fardeen was convinced he was going to die. Then he heard another one of them shout, "Get up! Hands in the air! Let me see 'em! Hands up! Hands up!"

He realized they must be talking to Michelle now.

But then he heard a man's voice. He couldn't tell where in the room the man was, but he would've sworn the voice came from within just a few feet of the sofa. His mind struggled with the possibilities of who it was or how that could be. Then it came to him.

Thomas Cole somehow slipped into the office after he and Michelle got started. Thomas Cole watched the whole thing and probably alerted the police. Fardeen concluded then that he was going to jail. But why were they talking to Mr. Cole like that?

"You're under arrest!" he heard an officer snap.

"What the hell for?" Mr. Cole said as Fardeen continued to stare at the officer planting him on the floor and aiming his gun at his face.

"For unlawful carnal knowledge of a minor, you sick, son-of-a-bitch!" the officer said.

But then Fardeen heard a brawl, and he could see two officers' legs rush toward the sofa.

"Watch him, Deke!" one of them shouted, "He's got a gun in them pants! I can see it!"

The struggle intensified, and Fardeen could hear Thomas Cole grunting and snorting as he wrestled with the officers.

"That ain't a damned gun!" another officer shouted.

But ultimately, just as always happens with an assailant against a superior number of police officers, they got Thomas Cole under control. However, what was not so predictable was the ass-whipping Fardeen heard them put on Mr. Cole after that. He listened to the clacking sounds as they struck their clubs against Cole's head while he screamed. He could see black patent leather shoes rising from the floor before stomping and repeatedly kicking him. That went on for about thirty seconds until Fardeen couldn't even imagine the condition Thomas Cole must be in by this time—if he was still alive. The officer detaining him shifted his gun nervously between Fardeen and whatever was going on the entire time as though he considered shooting Thomas Cole.

But the officer ultimately relaxed as Fardeen heard Mr. Cole yell, "Fuck! Fuck you, motherfuckers! I'll have all your badges tomorrow!"

Fardeen felt so sorry for Mr. Cole and Michelle. He was sure she must be in shock, watching her father get beaten mercilessly. And it was all his fault. If he hadn't taken up with Michelle and allowed the girl to engage him on the sofa, none of this would be happening. He's the one that deserved the beating that Mr. Cole was on the receiving end of. He was the one that instigated all of this. It was his fault, all of it.

But Fardeen's estimation of things changed as the struggle climaxed, and the officer holding him down yanked him from the floor by his front belt loops. That's when Fardeen realized that Thomas Cole was nowhere near the office. It's when he saw his beloved Michelle panting and gasping like some captured wild, rabid animal with multiple contusions to her forehead and face as they cuffed her. Her lips ballooned, both her eyes were swollen shut, and her seersucker shorts were down at her ankles with blood splattered on them.

That was also when Fardeen realized Michelle, his beautiful muse, with her silky, aromatic hair, her gentle caress, and her tender whispering of forget-me-nots into his ear, was a fully-grown man.

The officers accidentally ripped off Michelle's seer-sucker pants while detaining her, except they discovered she wasn't armed. No, Michelle didn't have a firearm. But now, she stood in the office, unabashedly flaunting an enormous, floppy penis that was still partially erect.

Fardeen gagged. Then he screamed. He fell to his knees and wept as two officers braced him to ensure he didn't go crazy or do anything else stupid. Then as the other officers wrangled with Michelle, dragging her toward the office door, she spoke again. Except this time, she spoke in the dulcet tone he'd always heard her speak in. And as they whisked her past him in handcuffs, she managed to say, "I love you, Dean!"

The horrible revelation would linger with Fardeen for the rest of his life, and he'd never truly get over it. It was so horrific that, many times, he contemplated suicide. And were it not for his Hindu upbringing, he may have taken his own life in solitude during the absolute torture of his soul that he experienced for years afterward.

But to kill oneself was the equivalent of murder according to Hindu scriptures. And doing so would banish yourself to a banal if not hellish existence in the next life. Salvation meant that one became part of the soul of all living creatures, thus ending the cycle of rebirth. If someone took their own life, they'd forfeit that pathway to eternity. And these were tenets Fardeen drew upon during his most desperate moments.

He'd done nothing wrong. He wasn't guilty of anything. He wasn't anything but a victim. But these shouldn't have been the considerations of a child. They were the contemplations of much older and wiser men than he was at the time. Yet he still faced them, and he did so bravely, and he did it alone without counsel from Siddharth, Devan, or anyone else. He also faced trying to keep his family safe and well-fed. A fourteen-year-old Fardeen grappled with budgets, revenue projections, marketing, and cost controls. He hired, fired, worked, and endured all the things his ancestors had for centuries before him.

And all that was left after that was a hardened businessman, only a teenager, aged well beyond his years.

He'd find out later that Michelle Cole's real name was Michael Ortiz, and Michael was a nineteen-year-old scofflaw facing felony warrants in multiple jurisdictions across the Southeast. Several counts for prostitution, illegal possession of a controlled substance, trafficking, and assault littered his rap sheet, which featured an additional couple of dozen misdemeanors. His newest charge would be just what the officer described because of his conduct with Fardeen—among others—who was still a child at law.

The entire operation was a sham perpetrated by Thomas Cole, Mr. Carmichael, and a few other men that law enforcement would never find. All the children were orphans or runaways that they'd vacuumed up like detritus from the streets of places like Dallas, Houston, and New Orleans—except for Jamie. Jamie at least had a mother. But he was now in the protective custody of the State of Florida while his mother, Eloise Bennet, sat in the Tomahawk jail awaiting a court date. Her charges were about to ramp up appreciably, though.

Instead of prayer meetings, Thomas, Michelle, and the others filmed pornography in room 24 the entire time—child pornography. But that wasn't the worst thing they did, as horrific and vile as that was.

Thomas Cole, whose real name was Elvin Reichardt, was a maestro, but it wasn't because he was a master carpenter. He was renowned in the porn industry, and a single one of his epic productions fetched about a hundred times what an ordinary kiddie-flick brought. He took his "artwork" seriously, as though he were a legitimate director or producer. He referred to his subjects as "the talent." Eloise, his production assistant, used a clapperboard between takes, and he even had a folding chair with "Reichardt" stenciled on it, which he sat in during shoots as he shouted things like "Action!" and "Cut!"

In addition to his ordinary feature films, his "epics," sometimes lasting as long as four hours, commanded a staggering price. But it wasn't because of the broad demand for them. Those films catered to a precise clientele whose tastes were as extravagantly evil as their bank accounts were large. In addition to his dozen or so other releases each year, Elvin Reichardt blended the two most deplorable subgenres within the industry, churning out one film per year that even the most seasoned and stoic FBI agents weren't able to sit through. The few that did were left emotionally ravaged, sobbing in some cases.

Because Thomas Cole, aka Elvin Reichardt, was the originator of the kiddie "snuff" film. Child pornography was horrible enough. And "snuff" films were the absolute basement of wicked as they featured one or more of those filmed getting murdered at their climax. Elvin brought those horrifying themes together into a juggernaut of sickening depravity.

Those details were thankfully never disclosed to anyone in the Patel family. The police only told them that most of the children were kidnapped and enslaved, even though Devan knew better. Although they didn't apprise him of everything, he'd seen enough at the post office to know some of what had happened. He only hoped his son wasn't too ill-affected because of his emotional ties with the girl.

Still, he was curious when the police forced him to take room 24 down for three weeks. And he was upset when they stretched crime-scene tape across the door and instructed no one to go into that room until further notice, or they'd charge them with interfering with a criminal investigation. The parade of men in suits going into and out of room 24 was a cause for concern. And Devan was livid when he finally re-entered the room to find it stripped of virtually everything—including the curtains, which they replaced with a sheet of plywood drilled into the wall. Devan already knew about that one, but he presumed it had something to do with allowing sunlight into the room. He never imagined they'd leave it that way.

Neither the Tomahawk Police nor the FBI disclosed to Devan that Michelle Cole was a man. The Chief of police, Mickie Montgomery, made sure of that, and his rationale was noble. Because he knew everything. He knew about it all. And the way he figured it, he'd only do more harm to this family who'd already suffered through so much—particularly the boy—if he revealed it all.

He put himself in the boy's shoes at that age, wondering how he might feel if he discovered his first love was what Michelle

Cole was. He thought about the strain that might have put on his relationship with his father, realizing things would never be the same between them, at least from his vantage.

He'd wind up communicating with Fardeen face-to-face the day it all unwound under the guise of taking a statement from him. However, he'd tell Fardeen not to worry and to refrain from saying anything about Michelle to his father or anyone else. He felt it was for the boy's own good, even if he didn't realize it. And while it was awfully presumptuous and illegal, the Chief did the right thing. He was sure of it.

The Chief made another momentous decision before that, though.

Fardeen would never have to testify against Michelle or Thomas Cole, nor would his father or anyone else in the family. Instead, the Chief involved a few of his best men, the ones he trusted unequivocally, and he made them fully aware of the depth and breadth of Michelle and Thomas Cole's transgressions. Afterward, he put the wheels of justice in motion on a trajectory he thought was appropriate. And that trajectory didn't have a damned thing to do with due process.

They arrested Thomas Cole at the 7-11 ten minutes after taking Michelle into custody. It was dumb luck, too, because they noticed him gassing up as they drove past the store. Instead of putting him in a separate vehicle, they put him in the car with Michelle and awaited further instruction. Then, once the order came down from the Chief, the car carrying them continued straight instead of turning onto Oak Street, where the police station was.

The squad car continued another fourteen miles before turning onto a dirt road in what increasingly became the middle of nowhere to the protests, kicking, squealing, and screaming of Thomas and Michelle Cole in the backseat. They knew what was coming.

It didn't do them any good, though. Upon arriving at the deer camp, the officers got out and dragged them from the car as the two continued to screech and plead for mercy.

None came.

What did come were six slugs of about twelve thousand pounds of force each into the backs of their heads. And the flames' glow from the pile in which their bodies burned that night lit up the entire cleared section of the deer camp's acreage, and one could see it for miles.

The officers involved sat around, drank beer, and told stories like any other hunting weekend. They only broke from their camaraderie occasionally to throw a few more gassed rags into the flames and stoke the fire. But beyond that, it was business-as-usual for the good old boys, who some might argue deserved a medal for their felonious brand of law enforcement.

Yet another fortunate twist that day was that Devan Patel was on his way to that same destination before someone got a call from dispatch to redirect his path back to the station. On a hunch, the Chief wanted to confront Devan first. And, thank God, someone from The Bureau had the same suspicion and called, urging him to proceed with caution as things related to Devan Patel.

Michelle Cole or Michael Ortiz spent the last moments of his life insisting the Patels hadn't known what took place in their motel rooms. It was anyone's best guess why he did so. But he was vehement to the bitter end, even as an officer twisted his hair in the same circle Fardeen did only an hour before. But instead of being a prelude to a romantic encounter, the officer, Roddy Miller, blew Ortiz's brains through the front of his face before lighting him on fire and hoisting his body into the burn pile with a galvanized flat shovel.

Ortiz realized he was a dead man before the shots came, so maybe he wanted to wipe the slate clean before meeting his maker. Perhaps he realized the injustice of leaving a family like the Patels behind with so much to answer for on account of his sins. Or maybe it was because he'd indeed fallen in love with Fardeen, just like he said. And he wanted to protect him.

The Chief didn't know what motivated a person like Michael Ortiz. He couldn't even imagine it, even though he thought he'd seen everything up to that point of his career. All he knew was that Michael Ortiz and Elvin Reichardt needed to go. They needed to go immediately. And if the Chief didn't act, he'd be partially responsible for Horizon's filth extending beyond Tomahawk and oozing into the darkest quarters across the country before propagating itself abroad.

By the time the FBI arrived in Tomahawk two days later, fully expecting to collar these men who were so evil, the Chief told them they'd escaped. It was an "Aw-Shucks" tactic the Tomahawk Police Department used to deflect any further inquiries into the matter beyond the protracted lies they told them.

Special Agent Avery Smith was quite sure that what they'd told him was bullshit. But Special Agent Avery Smith didn't give a damn. Because Special Agent Avery Smith was one of the Federal Agents who'd endured the entire 238 minutes of Elvin Reichardt's final epic production, entitled "Michelle's Kiss." Smith sat with four other agents all night as they winced, heaved, shuddered, and wept. But Smith didn't. He sat stoically, allowing the movie's horrific screenplay and action scenes to burn an indelible blight on his soul.

Following the movie's horrific crescendo, there was one less thirteen-year-old boy in the world. And one less patron of The Seagull Motel of Tomahawk, Florida.

CHAPTER TWENTY

February 14, 1982, Pensacola, Florida

"He looks funny to me, Papa. Is he alright?"

Fardeen asked a simple question.

He was concerned for his newborn baby brother. To him, the baby's head was funny-shaped like a cone. His complexion looked splotchy, too. His hands and feet were white, while his arms were brown. And his lips looked blue.

Nevertheless, Fardeen's layman-evaluation of things earned him a slap from his older sister, Sridevi. It stung and left him dizzy for a moment.

"If you wanted to see funny-looking," Sridevi growled, "you should have seen you, Fardeen! You were the funniest-looking baby ever! And you're still funny-looking!"

"At least," Fardeen started.

Devan stepped between his children as he had when they were little ones. They'd fought over everything since Fardeen was able to talk. Lincoln Logs, Pick-Up Sticks, it didn't matter. They were forever at odds with each other, and it seemed it would be that way for the rest of their lives. Devan never experienced anything like it either. These two were like a couple of stray cats, fighting to the finish should their paths cross. But he'd had enough today.

"Sridevi! Go! Go sit down! Fardeen! Be quiet, boy! Keep your mouth shut! Do you understand me?"

Prefaced by countless others, the sibling's current qualm was over their little brother, Sanjay, who they stared at through the glass of the Sacred Heart Hospital nursery.

Fardeen was wrong on this one, though. Notwithstanding his funny-shaped head and peculiar skin tone, Sanjay Patel was one of the prettiest babies that any of the nurses at Sacred Heart had ever seen. Several of them took Polaroids of the little guy who was born with a full head of coal-black hair and what they all swore were long, curly eyelashes poking out from his tightly shut eyelids. The nurses' and everyone else's reactions were such a foretelling of how he'd impact women for the rest of his life.

A woman would always rush to Sanjay's defense. They'd champion him and make excuses for him. Whoever tried to hurt Sanjay Patel would have to get past an ambush of Bengal tigresses first. And from the outset, there were no bolder advocates of Sanjay Patel than his mother, Savitri, or sister Sridevi. But they were just the first of hundreds of women whose favor he would garner over the years.

The ride home with Fardeen and Sridevi wasn't much better than their hospital encounter. Fardeen shouted directions the entire time Sridevi drove their fabulous, new "Superior Blue" Cadillac Fleetwood toward Tomahawk. He rose from his seat several times, pointing at oncoming traffic that Sridevi didn't seem to notice. He gave directions, starting at the hospital, and they didn't end until they pulled onto the Tomahawk exit. Sridevi was mad, partly because her brother hollered at her, then she was also upset because she knew he was right. Sridevi couldn't drive a nail, let alone an automobile.

In consideration of how horrible Horizon Christian Ministries had been, Devan decided to charge the credit card of Chester Carmichael, wherever he was, for $17,900. That was Devan's approximation of what their room nights would've cost for the remaining time frame Carmichael reserved had they been legitimate guests. Devan felt like that was a fair thing to do, given the predicament they'd left him and his family in.

There was no follow-up from authorities or the credit card company because the law didn't much care. Once Devan explained things, the card company shuddered at the prospect of acknowledging that one of their cardholders was a child predator who financed most of his production costs with their card. And they dared Carmichael to initiate a chargeback.

Devan used half of the money for a down payment on the Cadillac. Then he lobbied Siddharth for the balance, who begrudgingly obliged. The truth was that Siddharth was tired of his sister constantly riding him about their living conditions. He also couldn't stand coming out of pocket for repairs to their LeSabre, whose odometer rolled past 100,000 miles months after purchasing it. He just wanted to shut Savitri the hell up.

Fardeen was right on one point, though. And that was that his sister couldn't drive. And he legitimately feared for his and his family's safety on the way home. When she pulled out of the ingress lane at the hospital, Fardeen raised his legs from the seat as he screamed. He yelled at her again when she rode out the onramp to I-10 on the shoulder because she was too frightened to merge. The grand finale was when she passed the Tomahawk exit because she was too afraid to cross into the far-right lane.

Devan was in a terrific mood following the birth of his son, though. He was also a lot happier recently because he believed the Patels were on the cusp of better days simply because they couldn't get any worse. As Siddharth had in Biloxi, Devan established an understanding with the Tomahawk police. They realized the Patels were there to make money, but only legitimately. And as Fardeen continued to improve the property, fixing running toilets and clogged air conditioners, word got around to all the contractors that they didn't have to pay top dollar in Pensacola and could rent quiet, clean, and safe rooms in Tomahawk.

Then, what Devan formerly viewed as harassment by the Tomahawk police became a selling point. They came through the parking lot each night, ensuring it was clear of indigents and drifters. They also called in tag numbers to verify The Seagull's patrons were a wholesome lot. Consequently, The Seagull was full nearly every night. The cash flowed so freely that Devan questioned his sanity for having ever worried about coming to Tomahawk.

Indeed, Devan thought, things were good. He sat in the back of a big American luxury car, holding his baby boy in his hands while Savitri stroked his hair and his little girl, Anaya, fawned over the child. He was proud as the Cadillac glided toward his property with the giant new sign you could see from the interstate. It was blue on white and depicted two seagulls swooping downward before rising toward its opposite side.

Then, he was even prouder as Sridevi wheeled the Cadillac into the entrance to the parking lot where Fardeen had planted azalea bushes on either side. They were arranged in alternating colors of pink and white and served as a beautiful welcome for anyone who pulled off the interstate. Everything was coming together now. The strife and anguish they'd experienced were finally all worth it.

Devan intended to surprise the family when they had dinner that night with the news that he'd bought a lot in a subdivision where they'd break ground on their new home within the next few years. They could live there while he remained at the motel all day before his night person relieved him. Even though Fardeen missed the window for registering for school that year again, Devan decided to use him only sparingly until they built their house and life became more structured.

However, Fardeen haunted the front desk anyway. He believed The Seagull was as much his as Devan's because of all the time and suffering he'd invested.

Then, as they pulled into the parking lot, the Patels' world changed as though a tornado had set down in Tomahawk. They just weren't aware of it yet.

Fardeen yelled, "308 GTB!"

No one in the car knew what in the hell he was saying. But they could assume with some accuracy once Sridevi pulled up behind the red Italian sports car parked in front of the office.

A man with darker skin, holding a beautifully wrapped present, leaned his back against the car, and when Sridevi pulled up, he immediately stood at attention and began smiling as he stared back at them through the windshield.

The man looked like a celebrity, and Sridevi noticed he had the prettiest blue eyes. He dressed in head-to-toe black and wore a shining gold bracelet on his left wrist. The man stood, nodding for a moment as Sridevi brought the land barge to a halt behind his Ferrari.

Devan didn't like this. He didn't like this at all. He handed Sanjay to his wife and instructed everyone to stay in the car while he got out.

"Yes, sir, how may I help you?" Devan began, just as he always did when someone unknown came on the property.

He held his hand up to silence Evon, the part-time front desk girl who'd covered three and a half shifts since getting the call two evenings before. She'd raced out to greet the family and was delighted to see them. But she was also glad someone would finally relieve her.

The young, handsome man flung his arms out to either side, holding the present in his right hand, and hollered, "Abhinandana! What a happy day, cousin!"

Devan ignored the man's blessing and continued, "Sir, I'm sorry. I believe you are in the wrong place. I'm sure you're confused."

But the young man's response startled him.

"Oh, no, cousin. I'm not confused. You might be confused, and I fear you are. But I'm not confused!"

Then, as he finished speaking, Savitri handed Sanjay to Anaya, leaped from the car, and raced toward the man, hollering, "Armand! Armand!"

And as she called out her cousin's name, Devan became both worried and disgusted.

The man standing in the parking lot was the esteemed, revered, and simultaneously reviled Armand Popat, one of the youngest Indian millionaire hoteliers in the country. He conducted himself as Indian when it suited him. But the rest of the time, he behaved like a white man, demanding attention at every turn. And as handsome, captivating, and alluring as his wife and daughters found the man, he was just as repulsive to Devan. That was especially true as Devan watched the young man embrace his wife and raise her from the ground, smiling and laughing over her shoulder. The man's stock plummeted further when Fardeen jumped out of the Cadillac and charged up to the Ferrari, planting his face on the window and looking inside.

Devan hardly had a chance to complain before Armand lowered Savitri to the ground, turned, and threw Fardeen the keys. Then he shouted, "Come on, cousin! Let's go! Let's take her for a ride!"

Devan barked, "Fardeen! Give this man his keys back! You don't even have a learner's permit! You could kill both of you!"

"I have a license!" the seventeen-year-old Evon yelled before Devan hushed her.

Embarrassed, Fardeen looked at Armand before shouting back at his father, "But you give car keys to Sridevi, who almost killed us ten times on the way home? What kind of logic is that?"

That was it. Devan had had it. He moved toward Fardeen with his fists clenched, fully intending to beat some sense into his son. But Savitri stopped him, clutching his arm and tugging him backward. Fardeen wisely rushed to the other side of the Ferrari and stood staring back at his parents.

"Please, please, Papa! Not today," Savitri pled, "today is a happy day!"

Then Armand shouted, "Yes, cousin! Yes! Today is a happy day!"

After that, Armand handed Savitri the present he'd held the whole time and said, "For you, cousin! And for my little cousin, Sanjay!"

Devan was the only one who found it strange this man knew his son's name. His boy had been in the world less than twenty-four hours, and they'd not even called Siddharth yet with the news. So how was it that Armand knew Sanjay's name?

Savitri tore the paper from the box, opened it, and found a ribboned, cellophane bag of dried dates and nuts with a card that read, "For Momma!" in Gujarati. Then, a small stuffed elephant wearing a shirt with the name "Patel" stitched into it rested in the corner of the package. She became emotional, holding the box toward Devan for him to look at it. But he was still so mad, staring at Fardeen, who was too frightened to come within slapping distance of his father.

"Look! Look!" Savitri begged her husband.

"Yes. That's very nice," Devan said coolly, scowling at Fardeen.

Then he looked over at Armand, who still stood smiling in a way Devan believed was insincere, almost taunting.

He knew of Armand. He knew all about him. He also realized Armand's presence had nothing to do with his familial relationship with his wife or any possible interest in his newborn son. He knew what Armand's motivations were.

Armand was nothing more than a pirate, a bandit. He made

a practice of swooping in and hijacking undervalued properties to add to his collection. It sickened Devan to consider that. He'd worked so hard, putting up with Siddharth's bullshit and everything else. He wasn't about to give up everything he'd slaved for to this cobra standing in front of him. But he knew his brother-in-law. He'd sell his wife and children into bondage if the price were right. So what would stop him from doing so in Tomahawk?

Much like Devan, Armand took over a small property in Duluth, Georgia, almost a decade earlier. However, unlike Devan, he was only nineteen years old at the time, but the circumstances were very similar.

Armand purchased the property from his uncle, Madhu Popat, having worked for him for the first couple of years. His relationship with his uncle was on a much sturdier ground than Devan's was with Siddharth, though. Madhu nurtured the young man, teaching him as much as possible before turning him loose and watching him go. Armand responded by revamping the business and changing the complexion of the property and the stature of its patronage.

Hear told, the boy was a wizard in the business. He had unqualified backing from several members of the Gujarati sect of hotel owners because he made them all money. He pulled their underperforming properties back from the brink of disaster. Then, he leveraged himself with his sweat equity for their purchase. Armand Popat was considered a genius in many circles, then a pariah in others.

His uncle handed him the reins of a tiny property to learn the ins and outs of the business. He had no idea of the megalomania he gave rise to, but Armand was the epitome of a one-man show when he did. Armand worked the property's front desk, performed all maintenance orders, cleaned rooms, and took care of the grounds, all by himself. Although he'd never cranked a lawnmower, set a nail, turned a screw, or anything else mechanical in his life, he learned it all from the skeletal staff in place when he took over. He got away with it, too, because the property was so small, and it was unbranded.

After standing back and looking at all the boy had achieved, his uncle, Madhu Popat, had no choice but to give Armand the opportunity of a lifetime. So he sold the property to Armand, making provision for collecting the sales price through the motel's collections. But the difference between their arrangement and that of Devan and Siddharth's was that the amortization period lasted for only five years instead of the fifteen-year period to which Devan agreed. So yes, his payments were more than Devan's, but so was the amount of equity Armand earned in each sequential year.

Another stark difference was that Armand vigilantly networked the entire time, establishing inroads, allies, and private capital sourcing. In contrast, Devan sat back and struggled with Siddharth, law enforcement, and his crazy, intrusive wife, who also happened to be the boy's cousin.

Moreover, Devan had a family to take care of the entire time while this young half-breed answered to no one. It wasn't fair. None of it was fair.

Armand's portfolio consisted of twenty-eight hotels and motels in seven states. About a third of his properties carried flags, meaning major franchisors branded them. But almost without exception, they overperformed. His Indian contemporaries used several adjectives when discussing young Armand. Ambitious. Innovative. Discerning. They also referred to him as "The Parrot" because of his flamboyance and high profile. But Armand's favorite characterization was "Notorious."

A fellow hotel owner once introduced him as "The Notorious Armand Popat" at an Atlanta meeting, and Armand ate it up. Yes, Armand was, indeed, notorious. That was the most appropriate description for him.

ॐ

Just as Devan suspected, Armand's visit wasn't all family-related matters. He was in Tomahawk on business—serious business. Devan's accomplishments had created a stir in the collective of nosy Indian hotel owners, and just as he always did, Armand was in Tomahawk to see what all the fuss was about, poking around to see where he could plant his beak next.

It didn't take him long to realize the sparse number of cars on a Sunday afternoon in The Seagull's parking lot must translate into a full house for the remainder of the week. That meant all the business he'd heard it did was primarily legitimate instead of a bunch of drunkards and druggies. That was always a good thing, although sometimes difficult to achieve. But legitimate business meant less harassment by law enforcement and, consequently, less pressure from the community.

Armand knew the parking lot would fill with work trucks and equipment to the point one could barely walk around within hours. But he wanted to see it for himself.

So when Savitri invited him to stay for dinner, he enthusiastically accepted her offer, taking her hands into his and saying, "I'd love to, cousin! Tell me, have you always been this beautiful? I was just a little boy the last time I saw you."

Savitri giggled and blushed while Devan fumed a few feet away.

CHAPTER
TWENTY-ONE

"Who does your maintenance?" Armand asked as he scooped another heaping mound of *Gujurati masala bhaat* onto his plate before ceremoniously tearing into it as though it was too delicious to be true.

As he stared at him, Devan could tell Armand would stop at the nearest McDonald's or Burger King once he left Tomahawk. He wasn't fooling anyone.

"I do," Fardeen said, reaching for the rice and helping himself to another healthy serving.

"That's good, that's good," Armand said, "you've learned that these people will rip you off whenever they can."

Devan leaned forward with his elbows on the table, glaring at Armand, and said, "These people? Which people do you mean, cousin? Which people are you referring to?"

It was just a ploy, though. It was a chance for Devan to feign a morally higher ground and make Armand look prejudiced in front of his family. But it backfired miserably.

Armand stared back at Devan as he stopped chewing and left his mouth open, craftily waiting for virtually anyone else at the table to come to his rescue as though he were falling victim to Devan's impudence. It didn't take long for that to happen, either.

"Papa!" the American-leery Sridevi interjected. "You know these people tried to take advantage of you ever since we came here! Don't you remember the air conditioner-man? Or what about the plumber?"

Devan clenched his teeth without responding, then looked down at his plate and played with his food. But Armand wasn't letting him off the hook that easily.

"Plumber? Air conditioner-man?" Armand asked in the most saccharinely innocent tone.

Devan raised his head back up, staring at the ceiling as he crazily smiled before Savitri interrupted, preventing him from going off.

"Hush!" she said to Sridevi, "That's no one's business!"

Devan had his jugular fully exposed at that point. And Armand had the opportunity to rip it out and maraud around the room with it had he so chosen. But he refrained. Still, he sat dramatically for a moment, with his fork held just above his plate, acting naive, as though he were trying to absorb it all. Armand used his expression to convey to everyone at the table his confoundment at someone possibly getting duped by some tradesman. Only a simpleton or a nincompoop could let that happen. That's what Armand's expression told everyone before he finally lowered his fork and began eating again. Devan wanted to take that fork and jab it into Armand's eye.

After dinner, as the women cleared the table and Devan stared at Armand as though he were a mortal enemy, Fardeen opened the discussion again.

"I service all the air conditioners and do all the maintenance here," he boasted to Armand, "I learned it all from my uncle."

"Oh, right," Armand said, "Siddharth. Yes, he's a good man. A little old-fashioned, perhaps a little short-sighted, but my cousin is a good man."

Armand looked at Devan the whole time. His mannerisms outraged Devan. How stupid did this fool think he was? He was a damned child. How dare he condescend to his brother-in-law that way? Then Devan caught himself. He realized that if he were to the point of defending his idiot brother-in-law, then surely he was blinded by anger. He crumpled his napkin, threw it on the table, then lashed out, passive-aggressively at his son.

"Fardeen, I'll need you to cover the front desk tonight," he said as he rose from the table. He acted childishly, and he knew it, but he felt like he'd lost his voice in his own home ever since this fop arrived earlier. And he aimed to reestablish himself as captain of the ship.

"But, I haven't slept!" Fardeen griped as Sridevi and Savitri stopped doing the dishes and turned toward the table.

Then, in a reaffirming show of immaturity and resentment, Devan said, "Well, that certainly never stopped you before, did it?"

But Armand interrupted.

"Oh, hey! Listen, cousin! That's okay! I'd love to work front desk with you! If you get tired, I'll cover you. I know Evon is ready to go home, so let's do this together!" Armand chirped like he had the answer to everything.

Who did he think he was, calling Evon's name and involving himself in Devan's business? Devan looked over at Savitri, who stared back cautiously as she wiped a dish dry. This boy had ruined everything today. Devan no longer wanted to surprise his family with the news about their house because he felt Armand might either belittle him or top him somehow. Hell, maybe they didn't even deserve a new house after all. Realizing all that was left for him to gain was more rage, Devan didn't say anything else. He walked over to the basket where his son slept, carefully picked Sanjay up, and went into the bedroom with him.

"Goodnight, cousin!" Armand called after him, which Devan didn't even acknowledge.

Fardeen was excited to start his shift since he'd have Armand's company. He stood up just as Sridevi placed two parfaits on the table for him and Armand. Fardeen grabbed them both and said, "Come on, cousin! Let's go send Evon home! I'm sure she's tired like you said!"

Then he darted out of the room and down the stairs, stopping midway and looking back to see if Armand followed him. Armand chuckled and rose from the table, walked across the room, and hugged Savitri, Sridevi, and Anaya as they continued to do the dishes.

"I haven't eaten like this since I was in Ahmedabad, cousin. It's going to be difficult to leave here if you keep feeding me this way!" he told Savitri as he hugged her again for the fifth time since arriving.

Savitri ate it up, hugging him back before taking his face in her hands and kissing his cheeks several times.

Armand knew what he was doing, and everything he did and said was part of the masterful finesse job he attempted to pull off.

Armand got more than he'd bargained for by offering to sit with Fardeen. He was stunned by the number of contractors who flooded the office to check in to their rooms. Not only that, but it was mostly just the foremen checking in their crews. He couldn't imagine what it would have been like if everyone coming to the motel had checked in individually. But by ten o'clock, they were done, the motel was full, and it was remarkably quiet. Armand was impressed with what Devan and Fardeen achieved in such a short time. Still, he saw room for improvement.

First of all, the foremen asked for extra towels and soaps, which Fardeen honored upon each request. Then Armand was outraged when one of the men brought in a large garbage bag of greasy towels.

"Sorry about these, Dean. Some of the fellas got to washing the trucks Friday and didn't have time to bring'em back to Miss

P before they headed out," he said, hoisting the bag onto the counter.

Armand was appalled as he watched Fardeen pull out the mounds of oil-stained towels and set them aside for the laundry. There was no way anyone could put those greasy things back into service. Armand's temper flared, and he moved to the front desk and addressed the man.

"Ah, sir, that will be an additional twelve dollars," he said to the foreman as Fardeen's eyes widened and he watched Armand in action.

"How's that?" the man said in a thick, East Texas drawl as he turned around.

Fardeen was terrified.

"For the towels, sir. They're unusable now. Just look at this, sir," Armand said, holding one especially blackened hand towel up for the man to see.

"We have already discounted your rooms considerably, sir. We just ask that you respect that and respect our property in return," Armand continued.

Fardeen began to speak, but Armand looked back and quickly shook his head to keep him quiet.

The Texan squinted his eyes and turned his head sideways while rolling his tongue around the front of his mouth. He studied Armand intently. Fardeen was so frightened now. He was sure the man would beat Armand before loading up his men and going to another motel.

"I don't guess we've met, have we, fella'?" the intrigued cowboy said, still staring at Armand.

"No, sir, we have not," Armand said, as he extended his hand with a brilliant smile, "My name is Armand. Armand *Patel*. And I am purchasing this property next month."

As he shook Armand's hand, the Texan's face went pale, then

he reached into his pocket and pulled out his wallet, handing him a twenty.

"Is that a fact?" he asked Armand, who skillfully pulled the cash drawer open and gave the man eight dollars back. You could tell the man didn't believe anything the boy was saying. A kid? Buying a motel? Bullshit.

"Yes, sir. And I'm very happy to have your business, sir. But I won't be in business very long if I give towels away—even to hardworking Texans like yourself, who pay me most of what I earn," Armand replied.

Instantly, the man, Scottie McElroy, was impressed. He cracked a tobacco-stained smile and chuckled, saying, "Well, naw, I don't reckon you would now, would ye'?"

Then the handsome man winked at Fardeen, turned around, and went about his business.

Fardeen was dumbfounded. Within seconds, Armand showed him how to alleviate the weekly tension the Patels experienced when tallying the cost of permanently soiled towels. It was the source of many a family quarrel, but Armand effortlessly and gracefully brought it to an end. He couldn't believe how smooth Armand had been, confronting the frightening man Fardeen heard shout at his crew in the mornings. Fardeen had so many questions for Armand, but he could only come up with one because he was so excited.

"How did you know he was from Texas?" he asked.

"Did you see the oil rig on his cap, Dean?" Armand said, "That's the symbol on the helmet of the Houston Oilers football team. You wouldn't know that because I'm sure you don't watch American football. But you should learn to be in tune with your customers, Dean. I'll bet a lot of them are football fans. It will pay you dividends the whole time you're in business."

Fardeen didn't know what a "dividend" was, but he was so impressed that he just nodded and smiled as though he did. He also appreciated that Armand addressed him as "Dean" instead of Fardeen. He'd apparently paid careful attention to things since he arrived and realized how much he wanted to be called Dean. That meant so much to him.

"And you told him your name was Patel. Why did you do that?" Fardeen asked.

"Dean, Americans think we're all named Patel. It's what they're used to. And while they might not love us, they trust us more than people from many other places. Besides, at least I'm Indian. You've got everything from Arabs to Pakistanis calling themselves Patels if they're in this business. That guy would've probably thought I was Iranian or something if I said my name was Popat."

Fardeen wouldn't ever forget that discussion. And it would come barreling back to him like a freight train in years to come.

"Well," Armand said, thumbing through the register on the counter, "it looks like that's it. Full house. Great job, Dean! Great job! I can't believe what you've done here in Tomahawk! It's not even on the maps because I looked when I was trying to get here. But you, you have a full motel, Dean. You should be proud!"

Fardeen glowed from his cousin's praise. Devan never acknowledged any of the things he worked so hard to achieve. But Armand recognized them immediately, and Fardeen felt he could learn so much more from him.

Armand pulled out a timepiece from his pocket and looked at it. It was a beautiful gold piece of jewelry with a platinum bezel and an attached sterling chain. It looked like something a wealthy older man might have hanging from his vest or dangling from a pocket on his trousers. The watch's face was a scintillating color depiction of Saraswati, the Hindu goddess of music and knowledge, resting a veena in her lap with one of her arms raised while another two held the Indian guitar and the fourth hung by her side.

"That is beautiful!" Fardeen said, "My uncle would pay a lot for that! You know Saraswati is my aunt's namesake!"

Armand laughed and shook his head, "Siddharth. Yes. I know. But you'd be surprised how cheap the old man is, Dean. I bought this watch at a Sotheby's auction for $3,000 four years ago. When he and your aunt saw it in Atlanta, she wept and told Sid she wanted it so badly. Do you want to know what he offered me for it? $200. Not only that, but after every meeting, he approached me, upping his offer by $10 each time!"

Armand burst out laughing, and despite how disrespectful it seemed at first, Fardeen couldn't help but laugh too. He could just picture his uncle getting all frantic as he did when he thought he was missing out on something.

"By the time the conference was over, he'd topped his offer out at $274.50!" Armand continued through hysterical laughter.

Fardeen exploded, holding his stomach and shaking his head while motioning toward Armand, begging his funny cousin to stop.

"No! No! Please!" Fardeen coughed.

Armand looked down at the beautiful woman on the watch and said, "You'd think he'd pay more! She has such nice tits!"

Fardeen raced to the couch and laid down, staring at the ceiling in pain from laughing so hard. But the notorious and mischievous Armand followed him, dropping to a knee and saying, "I'm talking about your aunt! Not this stupid watch!!" before falling back onto the floor, cackling.

Fardeen screamed, placing his hand over his eyes and laughing until it hurt even worse. That went on for another few minutes. Each time Fardeen thought he'd gain control, Armand dangled the watch over his face while Fardeen swatted it away.

In those moments, Armand wasn't a ruthless businessman. He acted like what he was, instead. He was a kid who'd missed the better portion of his childhood, either getting beaten by his father or slaving in the motel business. It was a fleeting moment in which all the animosity about his upbringing was overtaken by what remained of his youth. He was even more entertained than his young cousin was.

They both rolled over and shot upright, though, when Sridevi asked, "What is so funny?"

She stood in the doorway that led up to the apartment, holding fresh bedding for Armand to use on the couch. Then she warily eyed the two "boys" as she laid the linens on the counter.

"Nothing, nothing, Sridevi," Fardeen said hurriedly, "go back upstairs."

"No! Wait!" Armand said. Then he shielded his mouth with his hands so that Sridevi couldn't hear him and whispered, "She has nice tits too!"

Fardeen rolled off the couch onto his knees, again falling into a bout of irrepressible laughter. Armand followed suit until Sridevi stormed back up the stairs. She was incensed.

They spent the rest of the night with Fardeen on the couch and Armand on the floor. Armand took advantage of that time to plant seeds in his young cousin's head. He steered him toward the prospect of severing ties with his Uncle Sid. He was an old man with old ideas, Armand told him. His intentions were good, but the business had passed him by, and soon it would pass by his father, Devan, too.

"Is that why you told the man you were purchasing The Seagull, cousin? Are you? Is that why you're here?" Fardeen asked.

Instead of giving a direct answer, Armand introduced other things for Fardeen to think about because the matter was too complex to address at that moment.

"You have a baby brother now, Dean," he said, "and it's up to you to make sure he doesn't wind up as an engineer or a shoe salesman in a shopping mall."

That last comment could not have been more pointed, even though Fardeen didn't realize it. It came across to him as prophetic rather than insulting. But then again, he didn't know what lay on the floor a few feet away from him. He wasn't aware that Armand had learned every possible thing he could about his father's past before his visit. Armand met Devan in Ahmedabad years before, but only briefly. He knew his cousin, Savitri, reasonably well. But they'd lost contact over the years, so he dug around, gaining any intelligence he could about the family. He had amassed quite an arsenal by the time he pulled into The Seagull's parking lot.

Fardeen also didn't understand that Armand played hardball or that he was a cold-hearted killer in the business world. Armand stopped at nothing until he got what he wanted—even if it resulted in him losing money at first.

Because Armand believed he could turn any property around, no matter how small the footprint or tight its market was. Armand's ego was what fueled his ambition, but he also had a colossal bone to pick with Gujarati men that were Siddharth's age. He wanted to bring them all to their knees, just like his father, Chandu, brought him and his mother to theirs on the floor of their Ahmedabad home.

Albeit he was a good man, Armand was a grieving man. He hurt profoundly over the things he'd experienced in his short lifetime, leaving him bereft of compassion or sympathy. But even as intelligent and talented as he was, Armand didn't realize what he was up against incident to his lifelong pledge.

And as tragically as his childhood had unfolded, the remainder of his life was just as bleak.

CHAPTER TWENTY-TWO

A rmand ended up staying at The Seagull for three weeks, annoying the hell out of Devan the whole time. Armand and Fardeen were inseparable during his stay, making it nearly insufferable. They did everything together, balancing each other while tending the front desk or fielding maintenance orders in the rooms. Every time Devan turned around, he saw Armand and Fardeen, Fardeen and Armand, as they bounced around the property or sat in the office watching movies on a VCR Armand bought from Texas Bob's Superstore. They developed a strong bond while all Devan could do was sit back and watch his son drift farther and farther away from him. It was maddening.

What Devan didn't realize was that Armand educated Fardeen the whole time. Fardeen was listening to and learning from a man several years younger than Devan, but one whose experience in the business far outweighed his. Armand was doing what he'd done for several years, indoctrinating Fardeen into the motel business, just as he had the dozens of other Indian immigrants that managed his properties. Except in Fardeen's case, he offered him every bit of knowledge he had, teaching him all the nuances of owning a successful property.

It wasn't all one-sided, though. Fardeen bragged about tricks of the trade he'd learned from his Uncle Siddharth that even Armand didn't know. Armand may have been a prodigious young hotel owner. But spending time with Fardeen taught him that he wasn't all-knowing.

Fardeen was like a sponge that absorbed everything he learned along the way, and he had several offerings that proved invaluable to Armand. Most of them related to cost savings because he was a disciple of Siddharth Shakur, and Sid was the cheapest man alive. Nonetheless, some of them were takeaways that Armand planned on implementing after he left Tomahawk. He was just astounded that he learned them from a teenage boy.

All The Seagull's toilet tanks, Fardeen told him, had bricks stacked inside them, which Siddharth swore lowered the monthly water bill by a third. The light bulbs in the lamps and overhead fixtures were forty watts instead of sixty watts, and all the shower heads were low-flow apparatuses imported from Taiwan. It moved on to the earnings side from there, though.

The Seagull charged a premium for parking. Any more than a single space per room was an additional charge. Then every guest's bill was riddled with surcharges and fees for everything from phone use to the continental breakfast, and all obscured by jargon on the pre-printed forms and checkboxes that served as their receipts. A given folio had line items checked off for things the customer hadn't anticipated. But they were glad to pay, simply because of The Seagull's base rate, which was far beneath their competitors'. Inch by inch and dollar by dollar, The Seagull moved from red to black in such an insidious fashion that none of their guests paid a second mind or complained it came at their expense. You had your occasional nit-picky cheapskate, but guys like that would try and chisel the price down anyway.

Work crews happily spent an extra ten bucks a night to stay at The Seagull for their trucks, dozers, backhoes, trenchers, and front-end loaders to sit visibly and safely in its parking lot. Realtors, lawyers, local "celebrities," and businessmen coughed up the extra change they spent on phone calls because they had to call their mistresses to see when they'd arrive for their next fling. Who gave a damn? Certainly not the boys who phoned corporate and said they booked a room for a pittance in a market that often fetched nearly twice as much.

Many times, guys like that received bonuses for lowering project costs, and Fardeen was all too ready to make that a reality for them, often receiving a kickback in the process. It was remarkable for a kid his age to be that cunning, and Devan would've had a fit if he knew about Fardeen's under-the-table dealings. But Fardeen figured what he didn't know couldn't hurt him. He was just like Siddharth in so many ways.

So they got charged twenty-five cents per call to use the lobby phone. There were two dollars more on their invoices because their crew sat in the lobby, devouring toast, grits, and fresh fruit in the mornings. Who cared about change for phone calls or two bucks? It was a lot less than they spent, sitting in the line at McDonald's twenty miles away, taking a chunk out of a workday. It was much healthier, too, as Sridevi and Savitri spent hours each weekend, hopping from grocery to grocery, poring over the fruits until they found the prettiest oranges, apples, grapes, and pineapples.

Armand laughed as he listened to Fardeen and thought about his older cousin, Siddharth, who was more seasoned in the business than he was. Sid was assuredly a force, and he'd thought of avenues for earnings that Armand would never have imagined before. Siddharth was someone to be reckoned with, and he'd deal with him, by and by.

It bothered Armand, too, though.

Armand wanted Fardeen to be *his* apprentice, absent any outside influence from those Indian sons-of-bitches. He wanted his cousin to be his and his alone to inspire. Fardeen was a blank page, uninfluenced by the American fold of Gujjus, and he was also someone Armand could mold into his likeness. Fardeen was like the little brother Armand never had but always wanted.

Armand was impressed by Siddharth's craftiness, as related by Fardeen. But, out of pride, he went on to tell Fardeen about all the opportunities for revenue and cost savings he missed. He pointed out that The Seagull kept their sign on all night, which he felt was unnecessary.

"If you're full, just turn it off. Besides, no one coming to your property in the middle of the night cares about those two goonie birds you have hovering over that rate you flash, Dean," Armand said, "Turn that thing off at night but leave the rate up. That'll save you at least a hundred bucks every month. Those big electric birds you've got cost a fortune. It's not the 1950s, and you're not on the beach. Nobody gives a shit what your sign looks like. And I know we've gone over this before, but those damned towels and the laundry are your profit margins, cousin. For every towel they soil beyond service, you're losing around three cents on the dollar. It doesn't sound like much, but I assure you it adds up to plenty of money that should've gone into your pocket. These rednecks are running you out of business, a few pennies at a time, but you aren't doing anything to stop them."

Just as he'd done with Siddharth's complaints about his father's mismanagement, Fardeen listened. He hung on every word and always made notes in the "Hotel Folder" he kept.

That three-ring Trapper Keeper was his Bible. He kept notes about everything, including pictures he cut out of magazines, contacts at regional construction companies and other prospective guests, and pricelists for appurtenances and linens. As his industry experience grew, he made lists of things he'd do differently had he been involved in the construction and design of The Seagull. While most kids his age wasted time watching MTV and HBO, Fardeen planned his future in the hospitality business. He studied it as diligently as an A-student with aspirations for college and professional school pursued their studies.

Fardeen and Armand's association was more like a brotherhood than mere friendship. They worked front-desk shifts together, during which Fardeen gleaned everything he could from Armand about customer relations. Armand was savvy and always seemed to remedy whatever problem arose. People gravitated toward him because he could talk his way out of anything.

When they fielded maintenance orders, Fardeen was amazed at how much his cousin knew about everything from air conditioners and television sets to plumbing and electrical repairs. Armand used a wrench like a tradesman with his long, bony fingers, which were covered with callouses and scars from years of doing so.

Fardeen enjoyed working with Armand and visiting with him when they weren't working. Armand taught him to use a stick shift in the parking lot of Cordova Mall, and he let him drive his Ferrari nearly the entire way home. Of course, they stopped the next exit up from Tomahawk and switched seats because Devan would've had a fit if Fardeen pulled into the parking lot driving the exotic sports car.

In the simplest terms, Armand became somewhat of a hero to Fardeen. He was a role model. And Armand was equally taken with his young, impressionable cousin.

It drove Devan bananas.

As much as Fardeen revered Armand, Devan detested him in equal measure. Devan couldn't stand the sight of his son following the little dandy around the property like a lap dog. Devan spoke little whenever the two showed up for dinner, and he ate even less. He didn't like being around Armand. And he couldn't stomach watching his son make a fool of himself for such a con man. He brought the issue up to Savitri once, but she told him it was his imagination and he was too protective.

Things grew so intense that Devan had to speak to someone about it because he couldn't take it anymore. So, in one of the few instances he ever would in life, he willfully sought counsel from his idiot brother-in-law, Siddharth. But he was surprised when he spoke to him, and Sid seemed to know everything already when he called him.

"I understand you have a visitor on the property, brother. Is that right? Vitri told Saraswati that our young cousin had arrived a few days ago. I hope he finds Tomahawk and The Seagull to his liking," Sid said, and Devan could almost see him gritting his teeth as he spoke.

"Uh, yes. We have a guest with us, but I'm not sure why," Devan said.

"Why didn't you tell me about this, brother? Were you saving this information as a surprise for me? Is there anything we need to talk about, Devan?"

Devan could tell Siddharth was peeved and believed he had every right to be. Armand's diplomacy was pitifully transparent, as were his ploys to ingratiate himself to the other members of Devan's family.

"Siddharth, I just didn't think of it. I wasn't trying to hide anything from you, though. We've been very busy in Tomahawk. Busier than usual. We're doing very well," Devan choked out as he waited for his brother-in-law's response.

"Devan, you know me. You know how I am. I'm a peaceful man who puts his family first. Wouldn't you agree? I put my sister and her children ahead of myself to bring them here so my nephew and nieces wouldn't have to grow up in an Ahmedabad slum with your shoe sales. You understand that, don't you? What I'm saying makes sense to you, doesn't it? You're such a learned man."

This was the Siddharth that Devan despised the most. It was the calculating, subjugating, selfish, condescending, and very likely drunk Siddharth who dared call into question Devan's intelligence or ability to understand things. He wished he never made the call once Siddharth laid into him as he did. Ironically, though, Siddharth was his only ally against Armand. The rest of his family, including his son, were so enamored of Armand that Devan felt he was aboard a ship under mutiny. But after

Siddharth insulted him, all he felt was alone as he nestled his baby boy in his lap and held the pacifier in his mouth while he endured the abuse.

"So tell me, brother. Why are you calling? Is there something we should discuss about business? Maybe something that little bastard said to you has you upset. Has he approached you, Devan? Has he said anything to you that you feel I might need to hear?"

It was the pivotal moment he'd waited for. Devan found himself at another of those junctures at which he could face up to matters and deal with Siddharth head-on. Or, he could do as he usually did, which was to stand down without causing any fuss or turmoil. After a pronounced lull, he responded. But within seconds, he was sorry for how passive he became with Siddharth.

"Uh, no, Siddharth. I've not spoken to the boy about business matters. I'm only calling to see if you, Saraswati, and the kids might like to join us for Dhulandi this month. I have to get a permit from Escambia County to build a bonfire on their beach, so that's why I called you. But I know Savitri would like to see her friend and her nephew and niece. Why? Is there something you'd like me to discuss with Armand about business?"

Siddharth disregarded Devan's invitation as well as his question. But he continued after another long pause.

"Good. You need to remember where you came from and your fortunes before I brought you to this country. Do you understand me?" Siddharth asked.

He'd never been so cold or disrespectful to Devan before.

"Siddharth, why." Devan began.

"I said, do you understand me?" Siddharth interrupted.

He talked to Devan like a child, lording over him as he always did. Devan gulped and answered Siddharth.

"I do, but," Devan said, then Siddharth abruptly hung up the phone.

Devan put the receiver down, wondering how Siddharth might have interpreted his call. He behaved as though Devan was so obvious that he knew why he called him. Devan prayed he was wrong. But he sensed more trouble awaited him and his family, incident to Armand's visit. A thing he was sure of, though, was that he wouldn't contact Siddharth again for the remainder of Armand's stay.

Just then, little Sanjay started crying, and Devan realized his pacifier had fallen out of his mouth.

"Oh! What do we have here, my little raja? Did Papa ignore you? Here you are, sire!" he said as he poked the pacifier back into Sanjay's mouth.

Then he cradled Sanjay in his lap and began cooing and talking to him the way Savitri always spoke to the children when they were babies.

"You're going to be so important one day, little raja! Yes, you're going to be a doctor or a scientist! You won't spend any time on this terrible business! No, raja! You won't! You won't have any time for it at all!"

"Let me have him, Papa," Sridevi interrupted, startling Devan as she reached down and scooped Sanjay out of his lap, "it's time for him to eat, and Mama is awake now."

Devan yielded to his daughter, allowing her to carry the baby away. At first, he thought he was alone. But then he noticed Anaya sitting on the floor a few feet away, playing with her Oscar the Grouch doll that Devan created a trash can for using an old bucket from the laundry. He went so far as to fill it with empty soda cans and old cleaning rags. When she noticed him staring at her, she put Oscar back in his can and smiled at Devan. She was so beautiful. She looked just like his mother, Manorma.

"How about some Baskin Robbins?" Devan asked his little girl, whose face brightened before he even finished asking.

"Yes, Papa!" Anaya squealed as she jumped to her feet and took his hand.

When they reached the door, Devan heard Sridevi holler, "Mama wants a pint of Jamoca Almond Fudge! And I'd like a double-dip of grape and orange sherbet! Have them put it in a cup! But bring me a cone!"

Devan groaned, shook his head, then walked out of the apartment toward the office, holding Anaya's hand.

Even though he said he wouldn't, Devan shifted Evon to days and relegated Fardeen to nights after Armand had been there for a week. He figured that with two of them there, Fardeen was plenty safe. While he hated admitting it, he knew Armand was a pro at handling the front desk, probably way better than he was. He'd be ready to deal with whatever came along, and Devan wouldn't have to worry about one of them falling asleep. Hell, they had too much fun together to sleep. But a small, deplorable part of Devan still wanted to stick it to Fardeen for being so disrespectful and cozying up to that precocious lothario.

Fardeen and Armand continued growing closer. They ordered Pizza Hut, played Colecovision games, and, of all things, watched collegiate basketball on the office television. Armand was a bit of a gambler and kept close contact with someone he referred to as his "bookie" the entire time he stayed in Tomahawk.

Devan knew Fardeen could never get drawn into such a pastime. He liked to think it was because he was so smart. But when he was honest with himself, he knew how money-hungry and what a control freak his son was. There was no way Fardeen could be convinced to bet on people's performance over which he had no control. While the rest of Fardeen's behavior during Armand's visit surprised him, he was sure on that point.

At night, the two boys talked, sharing secrets and baring

their souls to one another as they lay in the office before falling asleep.

"Do you ever miss Ahmedabad? India?" Fardeen asked Armand one night.

"No. Hell, no," Armand replied, "what the hell is there to miss about Ahmedabad when you're in The States? I can't stand Ahmedabad or Gujarat or India—any of it."

"What are you talking about, cousin? We had a beautiful home in Ahmedabad. It was much nicer than how we live here," Fardeen said defensively.

After a few seconds, Armand said, "Yes, well, you have your father's family, the Patels, to thank for all that. My experiences in Ahmedabad were a lot different from yours, Dean."

"How, Armand? How were they so different?"

Armand lay quietly on the office floor, recalling all his father, Chandu Popat, put him and his mother through. The excessive discipline, the control, the beatings. His was an insufferable existence in India. He didn't want to relive it or tell his cousin about it. So instead, he hedged by changing the subject.

"You're getting to an age where this should matter to you more. So let me tell you. I'd much rather be here if, for no other reason, than the women."

Fardeen didn't immediately understand what Armand referred to.

"Oh," Fardeen began innocently, "I see. But you would rather have an American wife than an Indian? Why?"

"Who in the hell said anything about marrying one of them? They're loose, Dean. They drink and smoke cigarettes like men. They go out on the town and dance with strangers. Then they go home with them at night. These aren't the kind of women you marry, Dean. But that doesn't mean they don't serve a purpose," Armand laughed.

"Oh. Okay," Fardeen said.

Notwithstanding his dalliance with Michelle, he didn't have all the particulars about sex yet. But Fardeen wasn't so young and naive that he didn't understand what Armand meant.

"But not all American women are that way," Fardeen said.

"I didn't say that, did I? I just meant that the younger and more beautiful they are in America, the more likely they will look for a good time. They aren't worried about things like cooking or sewing. Most of them have jobs and make their own money. But instead of getting married, they stay single and play the field. Can you picture Sridevi acting like that? Going out, drinking, dancing?" Armand asked.

"No! Papa would beat her to death if Mama didn't first!" Fardeen said.

"That's right, and that's good. That's how people should raise their daughters. But they don't do that here in America. I don't know. I guess if I ever do get married, I'll marry an Indian woman. But marriage is for old men and much younger women, Dean. I'm not ready for that, so I'd rather have a good time with American women than commit myself to one Indian woman. At least, for the time being," Armand said.

They lay quietly for a while before Fardeen started the discussion again.

"I could see myself marrying an American woman, the right kind of American woman. They seem a lot more fun than women like Sridevi."

"Oh, they're more fun, alright. But it's not the kind of fun you'll be having for a long time," Armand snickered.

"What do you mean?" Fardeen asked.

But Armand didn't say anything. They both just lay there for a while.

Fardeen finally spoke up. He told Armand about the daughter

of one of their most frequent guests, Mr. Lassiter. She was eighteen, her name was Jenny, and she had the most beautiful crop of lustrous blonde hair that hung down to the center of her back. She also liked to sew, as his mother did. He knew that because he'd seen her stitching a button onto her Papa's shirt, then again when he watched her hem some of his work pants while Fardeen pulled their linens. She kept her Papa's room so clean that housekeeping never had to spend more than a few minutes in it. Then, when Mr. Lassiter returned home each day, Jenny waited for him at the door with a bag of McDonald's or Wendy's she'd fetched from Pensacola.

"You see? That's the type of American woman I could go for, Armand. She's sweet, caring, and knows her place. That's a good woman," Fardeen explained.

But he wasn't prepared for his worldly cousin's response.

"Are you kidding me, Dean?" Armand asked.

Fardeen looked down at the floor where his cousin lay beneath his old Empire Strikes Back sleeping bag.

"No. I'm not kidding. What are you saying? Just because she's American doesn't mean she's loose, cousin. She's kind and thoughtful and takes care of her Papa."

Armand rolled over, looked up at his naïve young cousin, and said, "Dean, that's not his daughter."

"What?" Fardeen asked, "What are you talking about?"

Armand realized he better tread lightly because he wasn't sure what all Fardeen knew or didn't know.

"Dean, do you know what a rubber is?" he asked.

"Of course I do!" Fardeen said.

Devan explained what prophylactics were within a week of their coming to Tomahawk. Fardeen hadn't known what they were before that, but he sure knew what they were now. Devan made him put on lawn gloves from the cart whenever they happened across one in the rooms.

Armand stared at his cousin briefly, making sure Fardeen told him the truth before he went on.

"I honestly don't know if it's his daughter or not, but even if she is, she's having fun with him, the kind of fun I was telling you about," he said cautiously.

"What??" Fardeen asked, shocked by what Armand implied.

Armand laughed. He didn't want to, but he couldn't help it. Nevertheless, he gave Fardeen all the details.

"I took the trash out for that room today, and a Big Mac box fell out of the bag. There were, like, a dozen used rubbers in it, Fardeen. You want to tell me she's having fun with someone else while her Dad's at work? No way, man. That girl's a whore, Dean. It wouldn't surprise me if she slept with everyone in that crew of men. It's probably the reason she's even here."

Fardeen was heartbroken. He didn't want to look any stupider than he already did if what Armand said was true. But it just seemed so unbelievable. How could that girl, one of the prettiest Americans he'd ever seen, be what Armand suggested she was? Like one of the women that Siddharth ran off from The Sunkist?

Then the images of Michelle Cole, or whatever his name was, and his giant penis started returning to him. She, too, was beautiful and a wounded dove. How could he be so stupid? Wouldn't he ever learn? He asked Armand if they should call the police and have them haul Jenny Lassiter and her father away.

But all his doubts and misgivings gave way when his streetwise cousin continued.

"No, Dean. You said she was eighteen, right? Technically, they're not breaking any laws, even if he is her father."

"Yuck!" Fardeen blurted, causing Armand to laugh again before going on.

"You need to forget about anybody that stays here, okay? Just consider them off-limits. Nothing will ever come out of fooling around with a guest but grief, cousin. You don't know who these people are. You don't know where they're from. And I guarantee you that anybody living hand-to-mouth in a Tomahawk motel room isn't anyone you want to be involved with, and she's too old for you, anyway. I can't believe Sid didn't go over this with you. No. Wait. Yes, I can. Sid would sleep with anything that moved and then charge them for his services!"

Yet again, Armand transformed a tacky situation into a humorous one. And Fardeen started laughing.

Armand was so funny. So kind and forthcoming with his experiences and knowledge. He made Fardeen feel betrayed by "Gujjus" like his father and Uncle Siddharth. That was lingo he picked up from Armand over the past few weeks.

For some reason, it seemed like Armand held a very dim view of Gujjus. He didn't respect Siddharth, and Fardeen sensed the tension between Armand and Devan, although he didn't understand.

Maybe he acted that way for a reason, though. Perhaps there was some code or credo by which Gujjus lived that Armand considered a personal affront. Fardeen didn't know. All Fardeen knew was that this weird, half-Indian with blue eyes was more honest with him than even his uncle had been. He appreciated and admired Armand and wanted to continue learning from him. He'd never met another Indian like him, from Gujarat or anywhere else. Fardeen wanted to be just like his cousin. He worshipped Armand.

TO BE CONTINUED

[CS1]

CHAPTER TWENTY-THREE

"These," Armand announced to the table full of his cousins as he held up the box of Krispy Kreme doughnuts, "are unbelievable!"

He'd snuck away early that morning before Fardeen woke up, and he went into Pensacola to buy the family breakfast. He knew the Patels seldom, if ever, went out to eat. So he threw fresh doughnuts into his seductive scheme. He was pretty sure he'd won over his cousin and her two oldest children, but now he wanted to seal the deal by going after the little one. The doughnuts were just an additional inducement.

He dropped two glazed doughnuts on each plate as he walked around the table. Afterward, he stopped and said, "Dean, would you please get me that other box from the counter?"

Fardeen hurried and returned with another Krispy Kreme box, holding it out for him. Armand flipped the top up, revealing one half-dozen jelly doughnuts, which he also doled out to everyone as Fardeen followed him, carrying the box. When Armand got behind Sridevi, he stopped, put his muscular hands on her shoulders, and began to massage her neck.

"Thank you, cousin, for bringing me fresh sheets last night. It was so sweet of you! Please enjoy these doughnuts even though they're not even half as sweet."

Sridevi melted under him, giggling and rolling her eyes upward in response to his firm hands that squeezed her neck and shoulders.

"Sridevi!" Savitri snapped at her daughter, who behaved decidedly un-lady-like.

"What??" Sridevi barked back at her mother just before Devan swatted the table so hard that he frightened everyone, including Armand. Devan didn't say another word, though. He didn't have to. He'd carried his point. Then, after a moment of silence, Armand continued.

"Cousin, I also brought chocolate doughnuts because I know chocolate is your favorite!" Armand said to Savitri after the uncomfortable moment passed.

She, too, succumbed to Armand's irresistible charm as she laughed and said, "Well, thank you, my beautiful cousin!"

Devan sighed and tore into one of the doughnuts as he glowered across the table at his ridiculous wife and daughter.

Anaya, who stayed tuned in to her father, sat next to him, staring up into his eyes to see how he felt. She pouted, crossed her arms, and refused to touch the doughnut on her plate, which glistened so brightly. She wanted it more than just about anything.

"I don't like doughnuts," she said, sneering at Armand.

But Armand countered and said, "I don't like them either, but I bought them for the family because I knew they do."

Then he walked over and knelt between Devan and the prized love of his life, Anaya.

"I like cookies, though! Do you like cookies?" he asked Anaya, knowing he had the little girl cornered and there was no way she could escape his spell.

Still frowning, she cut her eyes up at Devan, who smiled back at her and winked as he sipped his coffee. Then she slowly nodded her head and continued staring at Devan.

"Well, good!" Armand said.

He jumped up and grabbed a brown paper bag from the counter along with the half-dozen chocolate doughnuts he promised.

He set the donuts on the table in front of Savitri and opened them before rounding back to the little cross girl whose adoration he was determined to earn. He reached in the bag and pulled out a box containing a googly-eyed Cookie Monster doll. Then he rifled through it and produced a sleeve of Pecan Sandies, which he knew to be Anaya's favorite, and placed them on the table in front of her.

The squeal she let out was another, and perhaps the harshest steely spike driven into Devan's heart as the last and strongest bastion of female adoration in his family crumbled right in front of him. Anaya hugged the box containing the Cookie Monster, then she reached out and hugged Armand with her free arm as he stared over her shoulder at Devan with a look of triumph that Devan would never forget.

But Armand was just getting started. And before it was over, he hoped to win Devan over just as decisively as he had everyone else in his family. After all, Armand wasn't mad at Devan. Armand didn't view Devan much differently than he viewed himself. In his mind, Devan was just another man overpowered by the whims of a very hateful and greedy man. He didn't want to harm Devan. And he certainly didn't want to break his heart even though he realized that was probably inevitable.

But Devan was in the way. And anything that didn't get out of Armand's way got crushed as he moved forward. So he genuinely hoped Devan would step to one side as he charged ahead. He felt like the envelope he had might influence him to the point that he would.

"Oh, I just couldn't eat another bite!" Savitri moaned as she stretched back in her chair with chocolate in the corners of her mouth.

"The workers of Krispy Kreme everywhere, thank you," Devan said as Savitri leaned back forward and glared at him.

It was such a hateful thing to say to a woman already so insecure about her appearance and pregnancy weight. It wasn't like Devan either. And he instantly regretted it and wanted to take it back. But he was too late.

Savitri rose and walked out of the room, signaling Sridevi to follow her with a glance. They stormed off and slammed the door to the bedroom where the baby was asleep.

A moment afterward, the door creaked back open, and Sridevi snapped, "Anaya! Come!"

The little girl looked up at her father, who motioned his head for her to do as her sister instructed. Anaya grabbed the Cookie Monster box and her Pecan Sandies, then walked slowly toward the bedroom, looking over her shoulder at her Papa one last time before Sridevi yanked her into the room and slammed the door again.

They sure knew how to hurt Devan when they wanted to.

"Eh, it's just as well, cousin," Armand said, moving to the chair next to Devan, "we have some business to discuss."

Armand caught Devan off-guard.

"Business? What business do we have to discuss?" he asked.

Devan thought back to his conversation with Siddharth and became afraid. He struggled to imagine what business this half-breed referred to without Siddharth being there. But he was even more shocked once things got underway.

Armand handed Devan a manilla envelope that felt heavier than expected before he took it in hand. Just as he started opening it, Armand reached over and put his hand on Devan's, stopping him and looking at him with a severe expression.

"Please," Armand started, "consider everything, Devan.

Consider your beautiful wife and daughters. Consider your strong, loyal son before you decide anything. And consider yourself, cousin. Consider what you've been through, the path you travel, and what that all means. I beg you to consider everything."

As Devan stared back at Armand, the boy seemed to have aged fifteen years from only moments earlier. Devan suddenly didn't view Armand as a boy anymore. He'd seen the exact expression and look in Siddharth's eyes. That look scared the hell out of him.

Devan pinched the golden tines of the envelope together, then unfolded its flap before reaching inside. Realizing there was more than he could grasp in one pass, he raised the envelope, turned it upside down, and dumped its contents onto the table. Then Devan Patel became light-headed.

A tightly bound but extremely thick sleeve of one-hundred-dollar bills plopped onto the table, followed by a checkbook and several pieces of paper, which he had to shake free. Instinctively he reached for the money, but his hand was stopped again by Armand's, who grabbed his wrist.

"It's $10,000, Devan," Armand said in a low tone, devoid of emotion.

That's because Armand was in kill mode. He'd chummed the water, cast his line, and was now reeling in his catch. Gone was the happy-go-lucky boy that drove a $50,000 automobile onto Devan's property and made peppy, uplifting, but disingenuous comments to the women in his life. No more was the cheerful, carefree soul that lured his son in, suggesting that life was just a big dance instead of the grueling, daily grind that it truly was. No, the only thing left sitting across from him now was something that had designs on his property, no matter what it took to make that happen. Devan just wished Fardeen could be the one staring back into the dead eyes that met his as they queried his soul.

Armand wasn't a hotelier. He wasn't even a businessman, Devan realized. Armand was the American Devil of its lore. And as far as you might run, and as hard as you might struggle, you could never get away from the Devil. That was a certainty in Devan's mind as he waited for Armand to continue speaking.

"Please," Armand said, sliding the papers across the table in front of Devan, never flinching, never blinking, "that $10,000 is for you, no matter what. But please read."

Devan pulled his glasses from his shirt pocket while looking back at Armand and peered down at the pages' content. What he read, though, didn't even include him. Instead, Siddharth Shakur's name was all over the pages. But as Devan read on, what it amounted to was an option for Armand to purchase The Seagull from Siddharth for $400,000 with a non-refundable cash payment of $10,000. Not only that, it called for an additional $10,000 retention payment to "Manager" at closing. There were several contingencies in the legalese Devan read, but that was its gist.

Looking up from the contract, Devan asked, "Why? Why do you come to me with this? I can't sign this. Nothing I even say could bind Siddharth. So why are you presenting this to me now in this way?"

Armand didn't hesitate.

"Because he might listen to you, cousin! He might understand that he doesn't call all the shots and that some might dissent his absurd decisions! That's why, Devan. That's why this document is in front of you now. You're a reasonable man, while Siddharth is a silly one. You are thoughtful while he's foolhardy! And I'll pay you twice what he's paying you! Hell, I'll pay three times! Do you honestly think he's going to let this property go to you? Do you really believe you're purchasing it? Because you're not! He'll double-cross you, cousin! He does it to everyone!"

Based on Devan's initial expression, though, Armand knew

he'd missed the mark. Devan all but rolled his eyes as he exhaled and tossed his glasses on the table along with the pages and the money. So Armand down-shifted.

"But if you can't see this, then maybe I've miscalculated. Perhaps you aren't the man I thought you were. And if that's the case, I'll leave now, and you might never hear from me again. But then again, you might."

Devan snapped, slamming the door on any further opportunity for Armand to schmooze or present his case.

"You're trying to strongarm me! You're trying to force your will on me! But it won't work! I don't care how much money you have, boy! It won't work!"

Armand slowly closed his eyes and lowered his head before looking back at Devan.

"Cousin. I understand your apprehension. I realize how overwhelming this all might be for you. But be warned, Gujju. The last man that called me 'boy' lost his front teeth and spent a week in the hospital. So, please, please. Approach me with the same respect you do with your master, Siddharth. Because one way or another, I'll stand in his shoes tomorrow. It's all I ask because that's a guarantee."

As Fardeen watched and listened, he couldn't believe it. He couldn't believe the words Armand spoke. And he especially couldn't believe his father's resilience in the face of them. Because Armand scared Fardeen to death that morning, and as he did, all his respect and reverence for Armand vanished.

Devan stood up and moved toward the kitchen.

"I'll call Siddharth now. Maybe you can explain all of this to your cousin like you've explained it to me," Devan said defiantly.

Armand pushed back from the table, grabbed the papers and checkbook, and said, "Don't bother. You know what, Devan? I thought you were different. I thought you understood things better than you do. I'll call Siddharth my Goddamned self.

You don't even need to worry yourself anymore. But what you should worry about is where your future lies in my company. That's what you should ponder over the next month or so before I come back here with the deed to The Seagull."

Then Armand shot up from the table and stormed out toward the stairs.

Fardeen and Devan were left in the room looking at one another, Fardeen eternally shamed and his father eternally grateful. Devan looked down before looking back at his boy with a slight smile. Then he turned toward the bedroom where he'd grovel to all the women in the house over the next several hours.

Fardeen charged down the stairs to confront Armand. But he got as far as the back entrance to the office before seeing the red Ferrari's rear-end fishtail and tear out of the parking lot, hopefully forever in Fardeen's mind.

He was so ashamed. How could he have forsaken his father for a stranger? How could he have put his faith in someone so reprehensible as Armand just because he drove a nice car and flashed cash? Fardeen felt like he betrayed his father, who'd stood by him steadfastly throughout his life.

"What happened?" he heard Evon ask as the Ferrari raced down the road toward the interstate before moving on toward Biloxi.

"Mr. Dean?" she continued as Fardeen stood silently.

Finally, he said, "Nothing, Evon. Nothing. Thank you."

"Well, sure, Mr. Dean," she said, "just let me know if there's anything I can do."

"Ahhh, I'll have a Whopper, a medium French fry, and a large Coke!" Armand said through the speaker at the Burger King on Highway 90 in Pascagoula.

He detoured from I-10 to Highway 90 because he was

starving. He hadn't eaten a single doughnut, and his cousin's disgusting food had made him sick over the past weeks. How could someone eat rice and fruit for every damned meal?

"Ok, that'll be three-forty-two," the girl said back in a Southern drawl.

Then Armand heard a chug and felt his steering wheel shimmy. Damnit. He was running out of gas. He saw an Exxon station less than a block away, so he decided to park and worry about gas later. He was just too hungry after eating dogshit all month back in Tomahawk. So he told the woman through the speaker that he'd come inside for his order, then he wheeled into a parking space.

Inside, he strolled past the counter, telling them he was the one with the Whopper order and that he was going to the men's room.

"Ok, sug!" the girl replied cheerily, having noticed him park his Ferrari.

As Armand stood at the urinal, two large men walked into the restroom and went directly to the sink.

"After you," he heard the large black man say to the even larger white one. Both of them wore suits. But they looked like every street-tough Armand had ever seen before.

Then he heard the water pouring into the sink. And he felt an urgent need not to be there in the bathroom of the Burger King in Pascagoula. He finished pissing and turned toward the door as he heard the black man say, "Whoa! Whoa, there! Aren't you going to wash your hands?"

When he turned to answer, though, a giant white fist was the last thing he saw before yellow light flashed in his eyes, and his nose exploded in pain.

"Easy there, fella'," Armand heard the white man say as he struggled to focus and meet eyes with him.

Then he felt a piercing pain in his right temple as he found himself staring up at the black man while falling to his knees.

"Upsa-daisy!" he heard the white man say while Armand looked at him from the far corner of his left eye and his right arm began to shake involuntarily.

The black man slid the ice pick out from the side of Armand's head just before the white man began thrusting a large Bowie knife into Armand's chest repeatedly. The pain Armand felt was matched only by his hopelessness, knowing that this was how things would end for him. He fell on his back and stared up as the men stomped on his chest and face.

It all took less than sixty seconds before Armand Popat surrendered himself to the afterlife on the floor of a Mississippi Burger King men's room with his face pressed onto the urine and water-speckled tile floor.

A few hours later, while he watched from the balcony of The Sunkist as the sun dropped into the Mississippi Sound, Siddharth Shakur took a sip of his Chivas and Sprite while his wife affectionately rubbed his temples.

"Oh, Siddharth! I love you so much! Thank you! Thank you! Thank you!" she gushed before kissing his head and sitting beside him in a lawn chair. She removed his shoes so she could move on to rubbing his feet.

Sid looked across the street at the amusement park, thinking about his nephew, Fardeen, as he watched a young couple, its lone patrons, pound into one another on the "bumpy cars." Then he looked down at his beautiful wife, who was still emotional as she raised the watch depicting her namesake holding a veena in the foreground of a beautiful blue sky. It dangled and sparkled in the waning sunlight a moment before she put it back in the pocket of her sari. Then she returned to rubbing Siddharth's feet.